POISONED LEGACY

OF GOLD & BLOOD
BOOK ONE

Jenny Wheeler

Published by Happy Families Ltd

ISBN: 978-1-99-117250-1 (large print)
ISBN: 978-0-473-43003-0 (paperback)
ISBN: 978-0-473-43004-7 (Kindle)
ISBN: 978-0-473-43003-0 (epub)
ISBN: 978-0-473-43006-1 (iBook)

By Jenny Wheeler

Poisoned Legacy #1

Brother Betrayed #2

Double Jeopardy #3

Tangled Destiny–A Christmas Novella and Prequel #4

Unbridled Vengeance #5

Hope Redeemed–A Spanish Novella #6

Book Bundle Of Gold & Blood Series One, Books #1–3

Book Bundle Of Gold & Blood #2

Poisoned Legacy #1 and & Tangled Destiny #4 (A prequel)

Tainted Fortune #7

Captive Heart–A Hawaiian Christmas Novella #8

Ancient Deception #9

Book Bundle Of Gold & Blood, Three Holiday Novellas (Books #4, 6 & 8)

Dangerous Desires #10

Sadie's Vow Book #1 in Home At Last Series

If you enjoy Poisoned Legacy, get a FREE PREVIEW of the first four chapters of Brother Betrayed, Book #2 in the Of Gold & Blood series, and read on.

Hong Kong born John Russell prides himself on building a business empire from nothing. But when family rivalries threaten to blow his world apart and destroy the life of his closest friend, opera singer Pania Hayes, they must work together in undreamed-of-ways to beat the destroyer and live.

You can find preview details for Brother Betrayed at the end of Poisoned Legacy

"For here the men danced as they did everything else, with all their might."—J. Borthwick, *Three Years in California, (1851–1854)*.

"Even while you sleep among the campfires, the wings of my dove are sheathed with silver, its feathers with shining gold."
—*Psalm 68:13.*

One

Saturday, June 27, 1868
San Francisco

Hector de Vile leered at Graysie Travers Castellanos over his wineglass with the confidence of a man who owned half of San Francisco's Montgomery Street, and let his eyes rest on her cleavage a few seconds longer than good manners permitted.

Graysie—she'd inherited the family name from her long-dead mother, Elanora Grayson Travers Castellanos— was glad the turquoise gown she'd worn for tonight's show was, like all her stage costumes, modestly cut, but she tensed at the devilishly handsome financier's blatant appraisal.

"Your 'Uncle' Eustace has set you up for a big fall if you swallow his stories. The Ophir is no great shakes. He just didn't want to admit it."

He swirled the red wine in the glass, spinning the crimson liquid right up to the rim without spilling a drop, then bent, sniffed the bouquet, and sipped. He ran his tongue slowly along his upper lip after he swallowed.

As an acting display, it ranked up there with Edwin Booth, she thought, and it provoked the desired result. She was a mouse being toyed with by a feral cat as he eyed her, tapping his glass with long manicured fingers.

"You may be young and beautiful, but I don't think you're a fool."

They were seated in her performer's

sitting room at Maguire's Opera House on Washington Street. Her glass of soda sat at her elbow beside the riotous oranges and pinks of the 'last night' bouquet on a low coffee table. The final curtain had fallen on a great run of full houses; she the popular chanteuse, sharing the spotlight with a French magician who pulled rabbits from hats.

She'd plopped into a backstage armchair with a grateful sigh when the stage manager announced de Vile's uninvited arrival.

His cheek astounded her; she'd never met him before, but he was a well-known benefactor of the arts and she knew she owed it to theater owner Tom Maguire to play the welcoming hostess.

She took a slow sip of her soda. "So, you knew Eustace?" She made it sound like a casual inquiry, but she could barely suppress a groan at the needling stab of uncertainty that twisted inside her at the mention of her 'uncle's' name.

Bachelor Eustace Mountfort was no blood relation but an old family friend of her mother's. She couldn't honestly recall if she'd ever met him.

Life had turned to chaos after her mother died when she was nearly five years old, and she'd never seen or thought of the man until three months ago, when a Sacramento solicitor advised her Eustace had bequeathed her some shares in an old partly worked out gold mine in the Sierra Nevada mountains.

The solicitor had explained that the mine had closed a year ago. She'd no idea whether the shares were worth anything, and she didn't know anyone she could trust to advise her, so she'd done precisely nothing but lock them away in a safe deposit box. Nor did she have a clue why Eustace had got it into his head to leave her anything, particularly a shutdown mine.

"Eustace?" He settled back in his chair. "I handled some cargoes for him when I was still at sea. He partnered up with Sir John Russell, as you probably know, but he didn't have the killer instinct for deals. It was the romance of it all that got him fired up."

"Really? I don't know about the romance, but the lawyer indicated Eustace had high hopes for the Ophir."

"My point exactly. The Ophir closed down a year ago because it wasn't paying its way and he couldn't afford to keep working it. Does that sound like a great proposition?"

He cleared his throat and frowned. "It's

of passing interest to someone like me, who already has machinery and men to work it. But to anyone else…? Too much expense with a low chance of a good pay-out."

Graysie felt like a fragment of rock being flushed downhill under a hydraulic flux. She was calculating whether she could resist the momentum or if she should go with the flow when she heard a child's wail outside the dressing room door.

She was on her feet in alarm as the nanny burst in without knocking, Graysie's four-year-old adopted daughter on her hip.

When she saw de Vile, the middle-aged woman hesitated nervously, then she plunged on into the room regardless, carrying the red-faced, screaming child like a hot coal she couldn't wait to drop.

Graysie turned to de Vile and, with as much authority as she could muster, shouted over the noise, "Mr. de Vile, a domestic emergency, I'm afraid. We will have to continue this conversation later."

De Vile pursed his mouth in irritation; he plainly hadn't expected to be cut short. "Later? Well, sure. It's not convenient now, I get it." He paused, the interruption temporarily robbing him of momentum.

Then, as if remembering his status as a respected businessman, he pulled his shoulders back. "I must advise you, Miss Castellanos, my offer isn't open-ended… I need a response within a week. It affects my plans for how many men to keep on…"

He shouted to make himself heard over the child's cries. Graysie gazed at the tousle-headed toddler who was slowing slipping out of the nanny's grasp. Her nose and eyes were running; her cheeks flushed in an angry heat rash.

"I apologize..." Graysie began, then stopped herself. He wasn't here by her invitation. He'd have to accept he'd come at an inopportune time.

De Vile hesitated as if he was going to say something else, but thought better of it. Taking up his hat, he strode out.

The air quivered in the vacuum he left behind him, and then the nanny said defiantly: "I'm quitting, ma'am. I can't take another minute of this baby girl's tears. And I want somewhere proper to live. Not another hotel."

Her heart dropped. Not again! She was the third nanny to come and then go in the four months she'd been Minette's guardian. She took the wriggling bundle into her arms, and the child's cries faded almost immediately.

Graysie draped the feverish little body over her shoulder, nestling Minette's damp curls against her neck and making comforting shushing noises as she stroked her back. "There, there, baby girl, you'll be fine. It's only a nasty dream. A horrible dream… It will go away soon…"

She looked inquiringly at the nanny, who nodded. "She woke up and wanted to know when her mother was coming back. I didn't know what to say…"

When Minette began having bad dreams, three months after her mother had died in a gambling hall blaze, the doctor had warned Graysie that four-year-olds didn't understand that death was irreversible.

Minette might expect her mother was coming back, or think it was her fault she'd gone away.

Once, she'd wandered off looking for Francine, convinced she was nearby. All she could do, the doctor said, was keep Minette's routines as regular as possible. *Surround her in a secure circle of familiarity*, he'd said.

And what had she done? Well, been forced to do? They'd been touring with the show, staying in different hotels, in different towns, all over the state, with Minette in the care of different nannies when she was on stage—always at night when the child needed to be settled to sleep.

She must recognize it. Life on the road wasn't working for either of them.

She sank back down into the armchair she'd recently vacated, Minette's cries dying away to quiet little snuffling sounds. She was still stroking her back and the top of her head and crooning softly, "There, there little one, you can sleep now."

The room fell quiet except for Minette's intermittent, breathy little sobs. As the child fell into a light sleep, Graysie sipped the now flat soda and sank into a familiar daydream. Imagine it. Her own little house on a hillside, with flowers and fruit trees in the garden and enough grass for a pony.

She could stay there forever with Minette; they'd never have to worry about another curtain call or fend off another pushy man. Goodness knew if the old mine was worth a dime, but she would not accept de Vile's assessment without question.

Maybe, if she was exceptionally lucky, it could be the doorway to the life she craved—one of peace and loving stability for Minette. She'd promised Francine she'd give Minette a good life, and she didn't intend to renege on the promise.

Maybe she could sell the shares at their true value—she bet it was twice what de Vile was offering—or even find investors to help re-open it.

She shuddered as she recalled de Vile's phrase: "You're young and beautiful, but I don't think you're a fool." Errgh! Was she supposed to be flattered?

Well, she'd finished this run. She'd purposefully put off making any new commitments, and she'd stockpiled a small savings fund, so they could live for a few months without her having to sing for their supper.

Now was the time to take a break from the stage and call de Vile's bluff. He'd claimed he was doing her a favor by offering to buy the shares, but nothing he said rang true.

She needed to find out whether the mine was going to be a blessing or a curse. To discover if it could provide the stable home she so desperately needed. And if she was playing by de Vile's rules, she'd got one week to do it.

*****

Australian adventurer Nathan Riley Russell stole a look around the popular Cliff House dining room and smiled in disbelief. For the first time since the death of his father in Hong Kong eighteen years ago, he and his two older half-brothers were in the same room. And not only in the same room, but eating at the same long table.

At its head sat the eldest of the clan, China Pacific trader Sir John Russell, one of California's most prominent merchants. Next to him, in the right-hand place of honor, sat real estate magnate and mine owner Hector de Vile, who Nathan had heard had a keen eye for a good deal.

Beside him, two empty seats awaited late-arriving guests. He wondered fleetingly whether they'd beat de Vile in social standing.

Three sons from his twice-widowed empire-builder father's three wives, one English, one American and the last—his mother—Australian. He'd been closest to Seb, the American, who was bumping elbows next to him.

Nathan wasn't even born when John had left at age eight to attend an English boarding school, but after his eldest brother had returned to join the family business at fourteen, the three half-brothers had shared five momentous years in a rambling Queen's Road house with Nathan's mother Arabella presiding at head of table when Sir Robert was away on frequent business.

They'd hiked islands and mountains, rallied the neighborhood kids into impromptu athletics and football—John the win-at-all-costs born leader, Sebastian the cheerful loner, and him.

All he'd wanted was to win the older ones' approval. They were lucky they had their first cousin, Ollie, the son of Sir Robert's comprador, as mediator. But the curtains had come down on that world when their father died.

Chung Ting Hon — the high-ranking Chinese merchant who'd been Sir Robert's entrée to China—governed the Hong Kong business like the Mandarin he was, while the Russell boys had dispersed to two continents.

As the youngest, aged ten, Nathan had

returned to Australia with his mother because, without his Taipan father, there wasn't any reason for Arabella to stay in Asia.

At nineteen, John was being groomed to set up Russell & Chung Trading in California. His father's death had sped up that plan, and he'd moved to San Francisco around the same time as Nathan had gone to Sydney.

Sebastian, the engineer and middle brother, had been twelve when their father died, a boy who'd only ever known Hong Kong until he'd gone to live with an uncle in Boston, and then come west after the Civil War.

It was hard to believe Seb was now thirty, a Union veteran of Gettysburg. And still a loner. At thirty-seven, 'Sir' John—he'd inherited his father's title gained for heroism during the first Opium

War—had lost none of his drive to win and ran an enterprise that included mines, real estate, and railroad investments, as well as his China interests.

Cousin Ollie—their Aunt Amelia's son from her liaison with the charismatic Ting Hon, now headed the Chinese side of the business, though his father was always on hand for advice if needed.

As for himself? Once a carefree adventurer, at twenty-eight Nathan was struggling to recover from the deaths of his wife and baby son and desperate to save his stepfather's bankrupt estate from dissolution.

A sharp dig in his ribs cut short his reverie. With a lurch, he hauled his thoughts back to the present, where Seb was saying, "I was telling Ollie about your mining adventures."

"An alchemist," Nathan chimed in. A hollowness clutched at his insides. He hoped his desperation didn't show in his smile as he turned to them. "That's really what I'm looking for. Don't tell anyone. Or maybe we could incorporate my Sydney export house into Russell and Chung and turn it into a Pacific-Asian force," he joked.

On any normal Sunday, Cliff House, perched on a Pacific Coast headland a fast carriage ride from town, would overflow with the city's fashionable set—the silver barons, railway millionaires and real estate kings who frequented the place for lively lunches that lasted till sunset.

Today it hummed with the Russell family and John's invited guests, mainly business associates—the merchants, politicians, mine owners, and developers hoping to get wind of a share tip or real estate deal that would make them their next fortune.

Typical of John to turn a family reunion into a business opportunity filled with people like me, Nathan mused. People who are desperate for their next big deal. His stomach cramped. Life would be so much easier if his mother and two teenage stepsisters were secure; if they weren't threatened with losing their home unless he paid up the loan within the next year.

As the waiting staff served platters of tasty hors d'oeuvre, he turned back to Seb. "Old John certainly knows how to put on a show."

Sebastian gave him a slow smile that lit up his tanned, round face. "Yeah. So he should—he's an old man. He should have married long ago." His eyes glinted with mischief, and they both laughed.

It had been a standing joke. They'd always had to defer to John because he was older.

"But he always knew how to impress." Seb's admiration was grudging.

Wait staff plied them with tasters of tiny, savory meatballs, creamy French cheese, Hickory-cured ham, and celery and dill pickles, but they were getting restless for the next course when the lively conversation suddenly hushed.

Nathan's fellow diners had turned to stare at the door, where a handsome woman in a red-and-black feathered hat was making a dramatic entrance. Behind her strode a tallish man, obscured from view by the lady and her remarkable plumage.

Sir John stood and made his way towards them, hand outstretched in greeting. "Ah, Mrs. Hayes. And Martens, old chap. Welcome."

Following his brother's lead, Nathan had also stood as a mark of courtesy, but at the mention of the man's name, his heart plummeted. He'd known a Willoughby Martens in Sydney. His stepfather had dismissed that Martens for fraud, and his activities had played a big part in the family's subsequent financial collapse.

He watched and saw the shocked instant when Martens recognized him. His face was still sun-bronzed, his upper body strong and well-muscled, but there was a wariness about his glance, a darting slipperiness that hadn't been there when Nathan had seen him last. As their eyes locked, Martens froze mid-stride, and the woman at his side hesitated.

"Are you alright, Mr. Martens?" Her voice was a pleasing blend of flowing Californian phrasing and clipped Antipodean vowels. Another Australian? Martens looked past her to Nathan, an uneasy rictus smile frozen across his face.

"Well, well, you're a long way from home." He seemed to exaggerate his Australian drawl as they sized each other up like circling dogs.

John cut in. "Of course, I should have thought, Willoughby—you know my brother Nathan, then? I guess Sydney's a small town when it comes to business. I gather you've already met? That's good."

He turned to Nathan. "I'm working on something with Willoughby that might bring us both a very nice profit."

Nathan saw his brother's eyes narrow

at the word profit. They'd be hoping to make a killing if he knew Martens. And they'd probably not be too fussy about the business ethics, either.

John turned to the room and clapped his hands for attention. "Everyone, please welcome an Australian business friend, Willoughby Martens, and the New Zealand opera star Mrs. Pania Hayes— I'm sure Mrs. Hayes won't need any introduction for those of you who patronize the theater."

He drew the newcomers to the two empty places near him, and Nathan saw Martens greet de Vile like they were old friends.

The rest of the Cliff House lunch passed in a blur. Nathan had set all his hopes on this trip providing him with an opportunity to get on top of the family's mountain of debt. He didn't know how he would face his mother and half-sisters if he failed them.

But Martens being there? And already in a cozy, trusted business relationship not only with Hector de Vile but with Nathan's brother as well—two of California's most influential businessmen?

He suspected unless old John had changed a lot in the last seventeen years, if it came to choosing between family loyalty or a winning deal, he'd take the win every time.

Two

Wednesday, July 1, 1868
Ophir Mine, Sierra Nevada Mountains

Graysie wriggled her toes appreciatively in her strong leather riding boots and drummed her fingers on the water bottle in her lap. He was late. She'd been waiting in the borrowed wagon at the rendezvous she'd agreed upon with mines engineer Vance Pedersen for longer than she expected, and it was getting hotter with every passing minute.

With her mule she waited in the spotty shade from a scraggly tree close to the road, but it was taking all her self-control not to dig out the watch she carried in her riding habit pocket for the umpteenth time. She resisted. She didn't want Minette to sense her rising anxiety.

They'd agreed to meet at the junction of the main out-of-town road with the Ophir Ridge Track, and that's where she was. She was sure it was the right place.

She reached over to Minette, seated beside her on the wagon's front bench seat, and patted her bonneted head. The little girl beamed a dimpled smile. That was one thing to be grateful for: she was a different child since they'd come to the mountains. She'd been nightmare-free since they'd arrived.

And Graysie's mood was improving with every day, too. The tightness in her chest that had been there ever since Francine's death was easing. That was the plus.

The minus was she'd quickly

discovered it was going to be harder than she thought to research the Ophir's prospects by herself. Willie Watson, the prospector who'd done the report for Eustace a couple of years ago, was out of town on a job, and his sister didn't know when he'd be returning.

Instead, she'd struck it lucky tracking down Vance Pedersen, an engineer people said knew more than anyone about local mines, but he'd warned that the Cornish miners—Cousin Jacks, as they were known—who made up a big part of the town's workforce considered a woman's presence anywhere near a mine bad luck.

The Tommyknockers—leprechaun-like ghosts who haunted the diggings—would curse them with death and destruction if a woman went anywhere near, they said.

She'd got the message fast; she

couldn't drive to the Ophir with Pedersen without provoking suspicion. If the miners got wind of what she planned, they'd likely resort to violence to stop her, or else refuse to return to work.

The last thing she wanted was to cause trouble, but Pedersen was a tough-minded Norwegian who dismissed the Cousin Jacks' tales as silly superstitions. He'd suggested they leave separately and meet up on the track once they'd cleared town.

But where was he? From where she sat, she could see clearly back down to Grass Valley, population 6000, the bustling mining hub she hoped to make home; a town that had survived and even thrived after the first rush of gold had petered out.

Panning the rivers, hydro-blasting the gully walls, these old mining techniques weren't providing enough ore to live on any more, but Grass Valley's deep quartz was still producing riches.

From her ridge lookout, Graysie could see some of the mines that were bringing the town wealth, their bulky roofs clearly distinguishable from workers' houses.

The North Star, the Golden Center, and the Empire—these and half a dozen like them were producing hundreds of thousands of dollars' worth of gold every year. But the ore-bearing rock was only accessible if you had money to pay experienced workers and install heavy crushers.

Even at this distance, she could hear the thump of the stamps that worked day and night. She could make out the Main Street boardwalk that saved citizens from sinking knee deep in mud in winter, and for a moment she imagined the Wells Fargo coach drawing up outside the two-storied brick Exchange Hotel where she and Minette were staying.

She sensed movement, and the sharp tang of trampled sage brush filled her nose. Up the slope ahead, the track disappeared into a scrabble of mountain grass and rocks.

The dark shape she'd at first taken for a rock formation was actually a man on horseback, coming towards her fast, a large hound bounding alongside. She pulled her rifle up from under her feet and laid it across her lap. Hopefully, this was the engineer, but she wasn't taking any chances.

As the rider approached, she brought the rifle up to eye level and sighted along the barrel, as if lining up a shot.

The rider wasn't Vance Pedersen, who she knew from their previous meeting was in his fifties with grizzled gray hair.

This man was much closer to her age, a confident fellow with a jaw-hugging light blond beard and a direct, fearless gaze. He rode with effortless grace, but his carefree air deserted him when he spotted her rifle.

"Whoa! Hold it." He held up his hand in a checking gesture and reined in his horse. "No need for the gun, lady." He tilted the brim of his hat forward, casting a shadow over eyes that crinkled in the glare. "What's this? Alone out here with a child?"

He didn't need to say another word. His censure was clearly written in the cocky way he lifted one eyebrow and stared from her to Minette and then back. Graysie had long hardened herself to ignoring other people's opinions, but her skin burned. Her face was turning red. She knew it.

He was sassy, she could see that, and the tilt of his head carried a charming impudence. But he wasn't threatening, and she sensed immediately that he intended no harm.

"We're doing fine." She lowered the gun and gave him a playful grin. "Thanks for asking. But you can never be too careful."

"So, what are you doing out here alone?" he persisted. "It's really not the best place for a woman and child to be without protection."

"I can take care of myself," she said with more confidence than she felt. "We're exploring." She tried to inject finality into her words to discourage further questions, but the newcomer ignored her lead.

"Exploring what?"

Her pulse quickened, and she tugged at her cuffs irritably. She was uncertain whether she was annoyed at herself for getting into this situation or with him for being so nosy.

Of course, she knew it was not 'done' for a young woman to meet an older man alone out in the middle of nowhere, but she'd been successfully ignoring 'normal' social expectations ever since she'd run away from her stepmother at fifteen.

She was oddly unwilling to meet the newcomer's gaze. She waved her hand lazily in front of her face, as if warding off a fly. Why should she care what he thought? She could tell him straight out she was meeting the engineer.

But why should she have to explain

herself? What business was it of his anyhow? It galled her to admit she cared what he thought.

"I don't believe we know each other," she said in an imperious tone. "And I don't see why I should explain myself to someone I don't even know."

"Oh, forgive me, Madam." He shot her another incorrigible grin and tipped his hat in fake deference. "Happy to oblige. Nathan Russell, it is. Farmer and businessman. Most recently of Sydney, Australia."

He brought his horse parallel with the wagon and extended his hand for her to shake it. An electric spark coursed up her arm when their fingers touched, and she drew a sharp breath.

Her haughty irritation melted, replaced by excited little bubbles that ran up the back of her spine. She edged her fingers awkwardly under her collar, as if suddenly in need of air. What was wrong with her? She drew a deep, slow breath and replied in the same jocular vein.

"Graysie Castellanos. Singer and newly minted mine owner. Recently of parts various. And my 'adopted' daughter, Minette, my best friend's child."

His eyes rested on Minette for a few moments and he extended his hand to shake hers, too. "Hello Miss Minette." He grasped her tiny hand with two fingers, and his voice was low and warm.

He gestured towards a white and brown hound, who had bounded behind his horse and was now flopped on the ground, dozing in the sun. "And this is Vulcan."

Minette smiled broadly. "Hi, Mister. We're on an adventure," she said, as if confiding a secret.

Nathan Russell's face creased in amusement and he turned back to Graysie, looking deep into her eyes. "Oh, I see. An adventure. I understand. That explains everything." When he smiled again, his blue-grey eyes had a naughty twinkle.

A new, deep energy charged between them, and she found she couldn't break eye contact or think of a thing to say in response.

The drumming of hooves shattered the strange tongue-tied spell. Graysie picked up the rifle which still lay across her lap, and squinted up the mountainside, her eyes screwed up against the harsh light.

Bearing down on them was a man bent low over his saddle, his horse stretched in full stride. From his drunken pitch, she could see there was something wrong. He lurched awkwardly with each stretch of his mount's legs and was in danger of sliding off altogether.

Russell wheeled around and pulled out a rifle stowed alongside him. "Get the child down," he yelled. "And then, if you can use that thing"—he brandished his own rifle—"be ready."

Horse and rider thundered on, and it was unclear if the man hadn't seen them or didn't have enough control to bring his horse to a halt. "I'm going after him," Nathan called.

He jammed the rifle back down the side of his saddle and raced across the ground that separated them. As he drew level, he nudged his mount alongside the runaway horse. It slowed. With fluid grace, he leaned over and grabbed the runaway's reins with one hand while controlling his own steed with mesmerizing legwork.

Graysie watched, dry-mouthed. Calmly, he brought both horses to a slow walk, then to a stop. The rescued rider's last strength gave out. He groaned and pitched over the side of his saddle, raising a little cloud of dust as he thudded to the dirt.

She gathered up her riding skirts in both hands and ran to the prone form, sprawled face down in the dust. She knelt beside him and felt for the pulse point under his ear. His heart was still beating, but weakly.

"We need to get him on his back," she said.

Nathan slid from the saddle and ran and tethered both horses to the back of the wagon. When he returned, he stood on the other side of the man's still body and braced to turn him face up.

"One, two, three... and roll," he called.

As soon as Graysie saw the gray frizzled beard, she understood why Vance Pedersen was late for their appointment. He lay on his back with a bullet wound to his shoulder and another in his chest.

His glazed eyes flickered open briefly, but no spark of recognition filtered through the veil. He whispered something so quietly she wasn't sure she heard correctly. A woman's name. She couldn't say what.

Then he gave a long, fading sigh. She waited expectantly, but his chest did not rise or fall again.

They crouched over him in silence. She should honor the man's unmoving form—talk to him, pray for him—do something, anything to avoid acknowledging that he'd never hear, nor have need of, prayer again.

Finally, Nathan spoke. "I'm afraid the only thing we can do for him now is get him back to town and report to the deputies." He shrugged. "Sorry. I guess that's stating the obvious. Do you know him?"

"Yes, yes, I do," she stuttered. Her mouth tasted of dust, and she struggled to swallow. Nathan was looking at her, waiting for her to answer. She cleared her throat. "It's the mining engineer, Vance…" Her voice wavered.

"Vance Pedersen. I was waiting for him. We were supposed to meet up here more than half an hour—maybe an hour ago."

"Really?" The censure was back in Nathan Russell's voice. "And why was that?" There was a sharp edge to the inquiry.

"He was going to advise me on a mine.

He knows—knew—more than pretty well anyone about this area."

Nathan paced a few strides in one direction, turned, and paced back. He gave her a hard look. "You realize that might have led to this attack?"

She stared at him, too shocked to speak. What was he talking about? This had nothing to do with her. Vance must have been involved in some trouble she knew nothing about. She shuddered.

"I can't see how... no... no, I don't see that at all. Why would you think that?"

"Did anyone in town know you were planning to meet up with him?"

"I don't know. I don't think so. Why?"

"If the Cornishmen got the idea a woman was going down a mine... Someone could have stirred things up. Maybe things got out of hand..."

Graysie was silent. It was a remote

chance, but she supposed it was a possibility.

Nathan rubbed his forehead, as if warding off a headache, and sighed. "We need to get him back to town anyhow… report what's happened."

He lowered his voice. "And what about Minette? Is she going to be alright?"

The implied criticism stung. She was supposed to be the responsible one, and this stranger she'd only known for five minutes was showing her up. She clamped her lips together to stop her bottom lip trembling.

Here she'd been imagining she'd freewheel along with Minette in tow, as she did when she was solo, but life was already getting much more complicated than she'd expected.

Thank God Minette was safe. She was suddenly grateful that someone like

Nathan was there. What would she have done if she'd been alone when Vance turned up? She wiped across her teary eyes with the back of her hand.

Nathan had been right to warn her. This wasn't a good place for a woman and child to be alone. She seemed to be failing all round. With Minette, with Vance… even with Nathan. Her cheeks burned.

His mouth twisted into a grim line, and his eyes cut straight through her. "We need to get moving. I'll load Vance into the wagon and you drive. I'll take Minette up front with me and keep her entertained. It's sad a child has to see something like this at all."

Three

The deputy's office was directly across the street from the Exchange Hotel, and when Nathan pulled up ahead of Graysie's wagon with Vance Pedersen's lifeless body slung in the back, a sullen knot of men was waiting.

Word had spread fast that one of the town's most respected miners had been gunned down, and the men regarded them with hostile suspicion. Nathan knew many of them would jump straight to the conclusion that Graysie bore responsibility for his death somehow or other.

Pedersen, a steady family man, was held in high regard; she was an unknown outsider. They'd already be rehearsing wild scenarios for what might have happened.

"She went out there alone and got into trouble, and now a good man is dead." That would be the consensus. He wasn't sure he didn't agree, but right now, protecting the innocent had to be foremost in his mind.

He stood shoulder to shoulder with his brother Sebastian, recently sworn in as a temporary deputy, in a protective cordon as Graysie hauled the mule to a stop and lightly jumped down to the street. He passed Minette, who he'd hoisted on his shoulder, smoothly into her arms.

"There she is," a gruff voice snarled. "What's she done to Vance?"

The crowd surged forward as men craned to get a view of the body, crushing Nathan against Graysie and pressing her slim form hard up between his taut body and the ungiving wagon side. An unwelcome heat flooded his senses.

In the two years since his wife's death, he'd been frozen numb, but something about this capricious woman melted that ice. Another kind of heat—fury at his own stupidity, followed his desire.

His hands braced on the wagon rail on either side of her; he protected her—a slip of a girl and a child, swamped in a sea of unfriendly, sweaty men in heavy boots—and prayed for the turbulence to cease.

Her red-gold hair straggled in a muggy mess around her bewildered face, highlighting her vulnerability. He saw she was on the verge of tears.

Sebastian, who'd been sworn in the week before to stand in for one of the town's permanent law men who'd been called away on urgent family business, took command.

"Take the lady across the way to the Ladies' Lounge," he said with a nod in the hotel's direction. "We don't need her here. There are plenty of others to help get Vance inside. I'll come across and talk to her later."

They crossed the street in silence, and Nathan was holding open the separate entry from the street to the Ladies' Lounge when a rotund red-headed woman appeared down the hall, hands on hips, jaw set in a hard mean line.

Along her top lip ran a fuzz of dark facial hair. He knew from bar hopping a few nights prior that this was the innkeeper the hotel patrons covertly called Madam Moustache, and she was on the warpath.

"You're not coming in here. Not in our Ladies' Lounge. We don't tolerate no scandals here. It's bad for business."

As they'd reached the doorway, Graysie had put Minette down to stand on her own feet. At the sound of the woman's harsh voice, the little girl shrank against Nathan's leg and grasped his trouser with a grimy hand. He turned to the innkeeper with a placating smile.

"We've had a distressing time of it, Madam Ring, and that's the truth of it. Miss Castellanos is badly in need of rest and a glass of water. Perhaps we could leave the talk till later?"

His deep, calm voice had a soothing effect; the hotel manager hesitated for a couple of seconds, and then moved aside to allow them in.

Graysie put one leg forward and her knee buckled under her. Nathan made a quick grab for her elbow to hold her up, and after a few seconds, she regained her footing.

Once again, something inside him rose to welcome the pressure of her slim, firm body resting against his thigh. He didn't want to let her go.

"Sorry," she said, her cheeks pinking as their eyes met. "I'm a little woozy."

Madam Ring followed them down the corridor. Once Graysie settled in a leather armchair with a glass of water, the innkeeper resumed her belligerent stance.

"Like I said, you can't stay here… everyone knows Vance, and they liked him. The miners could riot tonight if they think you're staying here. I'm not taking the risk."

Her voice was hoarse and rasping, with a hint of a Continental accent—German or Dutch, maybe? Nathan was about to respond when there was a knock at the interior door from the hotel lobby, and his brother John entered, his handsome brow set in deep frown lines.

"What's going on here, Madam Ring? Nathan? Is there a problem? Seb tells me you're the one who brought Vance in."

His black eyes flicked from Madam Ring to Nathan, and then to Graysie, who stared back blankly.

Nathan took charge. "John, I don't think you've met Miss Graysie Castellanos? My brother, Sir John Russell, Miss Castellanos. We ran into each other today out on my ride, John,— and then, unfortunately, Vance Pedersen ran into us."

John dipped his head in her direction. "Graysie Castellanos? Really...? I was a close associate of Eustace Mountfort's for many years… If I can be of any help…"

Graysie flinched and blinked rapidly. She opened her mouth as if intending to speak, then closed it again. When she opened it again, her words tumbled out in a rush.

"Eustace? You knew Eustace? Oh, my goodness, I'm so surprised to meet you. Shocked even. I'm here because of Eustace, and it's all turned into a terrible mess."

Madam Ring cleared her throat impatiently. "Sir John, I was telling the lady there's no room for her here. She'll have to go to the common boarding house on Federal Street, or to the nuns."

Her fat lips puffed out in contempt. "I can't afford to have guests who get mixed up in killings."

Nathan interrupted. "To be fair, Madam

Ring, Miss Castellanos did not get 'mixed up' in it. We were both simply there when Pedersen appeared.

"He'd already been badly wounded. We could do nothing for him, and we did not see who attacked him. All Miss Castellanos and I could do is to bring his body back to town."

Graysie's eyes flicked to Sir John. "I asked Mr. Pedersen for advice about a mine Eustace left me shares in. That's all I know. I can't imagine that had anything to do with what's happened."

Madam Ring's feet remained planted in a wide, determined stance, her arms folded across her chest. "That may be, but he's dead. And you were meeting him, weren't you? That's scandalous enough."

The room fell silent. Graysie reached out and gathered Minette into a reassuring cuddle. "Everything will be fine soon, sweetie, you'll see."

Nathan spoke. "Seb will want to talk to you, Miss Castellanos, but I can vouch that you had nothing to do with Vance's death. It's all very unfortunate."

And it wouldn't have happened if you weren't a reckless and rash female, he added privately. He flicked a look at John, but he wasn't registering anything. He was lost in thought. Nathan continued on gamely.

"But now…"

He paused and locked eyes with the Castellanos woman.

"Perhaps it would be best if you stay at the convent for a night or two while you make other arrangements?"

Graysie Castellanos snapped to attention, like a woman doused with cold water. Her head jerked back and the glassy vagueness in her eyes lit into high alert. "Other arrangements? What are you talking about?"

Nathan hesitated and shoved his hands in his pockets, suddenly uncertain about the wisdom of continuing his line of thought.

"I mean setting a fresh course. Finding something else to do with yourself. Be a governess in San Francisco or something, I'm sure you could find somewhere that would take Minette as well…"

He faltered at her frigid stare, but she didn't speak, so he took a deep breath and stumbled on.

"As Madam Ring has said, you can't stay here. None of the other hotels will be keen to have you either, at least until after the shock of Vance's death has blown over.

"And what's left for you here, anyway? Some vague idea about a mine you've inherited? I don't want to interfere with your plans, but…"

Graysie stood up with such a rush, Minette slipped sideways. She reached out one arm to guard the girl from falling without taking her blazing eyes off Nathan.

"You sound remarkably sure you know what's best for me, Mr. Russell." Her face glowed with a magnetic energy.

"You don't know a thing about me. I don't know how Mr. Pedersen came to be attacked, but it's nothing to do with me. Of course, I regret his death. But I'm not about to give up my dreams because of one momentary setback."

She drew a long breath. "I will remove myself to the convent—if they can take us—as soon as the deputy has finished with his questions. Perhaps you could ask him if we could do that soon?"

She thrust out her jaw, and he didn't need an interpreter to get the drift: *Back off. Leave me alone. Get lost*. She communicated it all wordlessly. Then she took another deep breath.

"The sooner this is over, the better," she said stiffly. "Can you find out please if the deputy can come now?"

There was a long silence as she glared at Nathan and he gazed back. Even when she was furious with him, the attraction still gripped him. His throat was so dry he could barely swallow, but he feigned disinterest, shrugged lightly, and turned to fetch Seb.

John held up a hand to stop him. "Nathan, it occurs to me. We've got plenty of room at Gold House. It seems appropriate to invite Miss Castellanos to stay for as long as she needs. Eustace was very helpful to me over the years; it's really the least I can do." He turned to Graysie.

"What do you think, Miss Castellanos? It would give you a chance to catch your breath while you decide what's next."

Graysie stared, momentarily blown away. "I'm overwhelmed, Sir John," she said with a wan smile. "If you're sure, I'd be delighted to accept your kind offer."

She dipped her head in Nathan's direction as if to confirm that the last thing she'd want would be to spend any more time with him.

"I'll try not to get in your way." He didn't miss the flicker of a grateful smile that tipped up the corners of her mouth as she turned her back on him.

As Nathan left to get Sebastian, he

shook his head in disbelief. He wasn't sure if he was more unsettled by his brother's sudden eagerness to entertain this new guest or her unwillingness to see common sense.

John never played a straight hand. There was almost always some deeper motive at work, so what was it this time? Not that he cared, he simply didn't want any extra distraction. He'd his own business to see to.

As he strode across the street to find Sebastian, he shook his head in frustration. How stiff-necked could you be? She may well have stirred up the trouble that led to Vance's death. Who knew? She was like someone who'd get the bees angry but still be determined to steal their honey.

As he shouldered his way through the grumbling mob of men who hung around outside the deputy's office door, he told himself her leave-me-alone message was one he whole-heartedly shared. She was going to be trouble. It was the kid he was sorry for.

Four

Thursday, July 2

When Graysie opened her eyes in her charming room at Gold House, the first thing that caught her eye was a lemon and white orchid in a blue and white traditional Chinese pot on the bedside table. A hint of an exotic vanilla fragrance lingered. Did orchids have a scent? She wasn't sure.

She let out a deep, contented sigh and allowed herself to sink deeper into the feather mattress. Despite the anxiety over Vance's death and the hostility of the miners, she'd slept right through with no bad dreams.

The filtered light from the window screens played across the white bedcover appliqued with turquoise peacocks. Her relaxation was so deep she wanted to pinch herself to prove she wasn't dreaming. After yesterday's disaster, Sir John's kindness gave her a few days' grace before she made some hard decisions.

It had been dark by the time she and Minette had arrived at Gold House, which was lavishly set in several acres of gardens a mile and a half out of town.

She'd probably been in delayed shock because she'd barely registered anything of her surroundings, although she'd been told about the greenhouses for Sir John's orchids as well as for grapes and salad vegetables for the house.

It was hard to make out much detail in the twilight, but the silence had immediately struck her, broken only by the cry of a night bird. No rumbling of the quartz mills here.

Sir John's servants had been unobtrusive and efficient, settling her into a balcony room on the second floor with Minette in the nursery down the hall.

A woman in a Chinese robe, who appeared to speak no English, brought her fragrant hot green tea which had eased her tense shoulders and turned her liquid and silvery inside. She suspected she'd fallen asleep before she'd finished the cup.

Her mind flicked back to the scene outside the sheriff's office the night before, and she remembered all over again the heat of desire that had caught her by surprise as Nathan Russell's arms had protectively encircled her.

He'd infused her with a calm strength which, like his musky masculine smell, still seemed to linger. At the thought of him, the sensation of butterflies in her stomach returned. She lay there, dumbfounded by the strength of the emotion, then abruptly levered herself up on her elbows and swung her legs over the bed edge.

Time to get up and clear your head of this nonsense, she told herself sternly. *He's made his views plain—he doesn't approve.*

Last night, Nathan Russell had been the model of gentlemanly patience, collecting their belongings from the hotel room and transferring them up to Gold House. But he'd kept his distance, and she'd been relieved not to have to talk.

When Minette had tried to cling to her at bedtime, however, he'd stepped in and settled her to sleep in no time with a bedtime story about kangaroos. It was surprising how the child had taken to him in such a short time.

She hated to admit it, but he would have been almost impossible to resist if he wasn't such a know-it-all. Luckily, she'd had plenty of practice at resistance. She shuddered at the memory of her stepmother's iron rule.

She'd learned the hard way that the only person you can ever count on is yourself, and she'd do herself a favor to remember it. A tiny nagging voice reminded her she'd spent the night in this deep comfortable bed courtesy of someone's kindness, but she ignored that fact.

The faintest sound of servants speaking in a Chinese tongue—she didn't know if it was Mandarin or Cantonese—

wafted up from the floor below. Maybe this room was above the kitchen. She stretched appreciatively. Now she'd had a good rest, she needed to get moving. She couldn't afford to loll around, delicious as it was.

First, where could she go for advice, now that Vance was dead? How could she assess whether she should take Hector de Vile's offer and run?

She thought about Vance's last words… It had sounded like a woman's name. Was it Ruth? Or Ruby? She wondered if either of those meant anything.

Probably a woman who is important to him—his wife or mother or sister?

She dressed quickly and made her way to the kitchen where Minette watched, fascinated, as the ruddy-faced cook spooned muffin mix onto a griddle. The kitchen smelt of sugar and cinnamon.

The cook scraped the last of the muffin mix out of the bowl.

"Sir John says he will see you for coffee and muffins on the terrace in one hour, if you're ready for it," the other woman said, a gentle concern underlying her business-like manner.

A quick nip of hunger reminded Graysie she'd had nothing to eat since yesterday morning, and breakfast couldn't come quickly enough.

*****

Nathan could hear the weeping funeral guitars before he reached the front door of the Spanish mission-style house Vance Pedersen had built for his Mexican wife and five children. As he stepped through the front door into a crowded room, the music stopped, the sad melody replaced by the scraping of feet on hard wooden floors and a soft expectant hush.

In the middle of the room, the engineer's open coffin was set in a green bier, the body covered with a white sheet pulled up to his chin, his face tranquil and empty in death.

The memory of earlier deaths rushed at him, and for half a minute Nathan closed his eyes and held his breath tight, hardly daring to look or breathe, bracing himself to remain standing. When he opened them again and looked along Vance's cold length, the revelation he'd found it hardest to grasp last time around, when he viewed his father-in-law's body, struck him once more.

There's no one there.

Our bodies really are only a mortal casing, holding an eternal soul and spirit. The shell is still present, but the essential center is already gone.

Amid the circling greenery, Pedersen's

bier was lit at regular intervals by creamy, wax-dripping candles which filled the air with a calming scent that seeped over him like an embrace.

A single line from Psalms came to him.

Like precious oil poured on his head… running down on the collar of his robe.

Over in a corner, two older men sat playing chess. The band members who minutes before were playing a lament stood around watching, their shoulders draped in bright hand-woven shawls, and their instruments—guitars, a violin, and percussion items in their hands or resting at their sides.

When the time comes, they'll send him off in fine style.

A reverent yet oddly relaxed atmosphere filled the house, the indistinct murmur of talk broken by occasional soft laughter, but everyone deferred to a handsome olive-skinned woman with deep brown eyes who sat at Vance's head.

A fine white and gold silk shawl partially obscured her face, but despite the raw grief etched there, she radiated a deep peace.

Vance's sister-in-law Anna Santa Maria might be in shock, but she was in command of herself and her surroundings. She drew comforting arms around the small children who nestled against her on either side.

As he'd learned at the undertaker's the night before, when Vance's wife, Anna's sister, had died suddenly several months ago, Anna had stepped in as a second mother to his five children. Already widowed with one son, Vance's death had left her with responsibility for the sole care of six children.

The room was a good size but crowded, and its thick adobe walls hugged the heat in. The sultry air carried an earthy dog odor mixed with the candle wax and a fresh flower-filled sweetness from the informal altar set up beyond the bier.

Nathan's face was sticky as he stepped forward to pay his respects. People parted to allow him through, and Anna rose to meet him.

A serious-faced boy, the tallest in the group sitting with her, stood up when she did. Nathan took both her hands in his and bowed his head over them in deference.

"I'm Nathan Russell," he said as he raised himself again. "I stopped Vance's horse. I'm sorry I couldn't do more."

He handed her a canvas bag containing enough of John's gold to feed her and her children for several months.

"From my brother, with our sincerest condolences," he said.

She dipped her tear-stained face in gratitude, and taking his elbow, drew him aside. "Do you mind if we sit over here? There are some things I'd like to ask you."

He nodded. "And me you."

Two much younger, dark-headed children trailed after her, a rat-like, short-haired dog with a question-mark tail tagging at their heels, and as they tripped along, dancing on the balls of their feet, they vied to pet it.

Anna Maria turned to the older boy still at her side. "Antonio, can you take the little ones and give them some water?" She stroked his head gently.

Antonio shot his mother a frustrated glare, then scooped the dog up under one arm and drew the children to his side with the other.

"Come and play, chiquitos."

Anna sank into a cane chair in a quiet corner and poured two glasses of water from a pitcher on the table beside her.

"You've probably heard already. Vance was my sister's husband. He was a good man." She gave a deep sigh.

"Tell me." She fixed her dark eyes on Nathan. "Do you believe this was an accident? How can it not be? Vance hurt no one."

"I'm afraid we don't know who or why…" He paused as the band started up again with another soulful Latin chant, the guitars adding liveliness to the wailing cry of violin.

"You might be able to help me," Nathan ventured. "You say he hurt no one? So as far as you know, he didn't have any enemies? There was no reason for anyone to target him?"

Anna shook her head. "None that I know of. Vance didn't talk about his work. He was upright, a righteous man, who'd never agree to falsifying prospecting reports like some would. I've no reason to believe he'd got off side with anyone. He didn't mention any problems."

She hesitated and then took a long drink of water. "Nothing much got past him. If anything was going on around here, there's a good chance he'd know about it. But he didn't seek trouble. I suppose..." She paused and her eyes widened suddenly, as if remembering a past remark.

"You suppose what?" asked Nathan.

"Well, the only time he got riled up was when he saw the powerful cheating the powerless. Especially if he saw cruel treatment of women left to bring up children alone. He was very protective of family, of seeing that children got a good chance at life. Ironic, really. He did his utmost for his family."

Nathan sipped at his water and considered. "Did he mention anything along those lines? Where he suspected someone was being badly treated?"

She held the glass cupped in her hands, relishing its coolness, as she considered the question. Her eyes searched his face, as if remembering something.

"He was sorry for Lisette Guilliame—losing her husband like she did and being left with a struggling mine. I think he talked to Willie Watson about it. But from what I know, that's as far as it went... feeling sympathy for her."

The temperature in the room was

rising, and as their conversation lapsed, the children tumbled back to surround Anna's chair, accompanied this time by a mountain dog big enough for the smallest of them to ride.

Antonio was holding the smallest urchin, a cherry-cheeked girl, in place for a 'pretend ride.' As they halted by Anna's side, he lifted the child down and she hugged his knee.

"Can I ask a question?" Antonio's thin little face creased in an anxious frown.

"Sure, you can." Nathan smiled at the circle of fretful, innocent faces. "That's a big dog you've got there. What's his name?"

The dark-headed sprite hanging off Antonio's leg regarded Nathan with soulful eyes. "This is Neptune. He's our guard dog," she said. She was about four years old, Nathan judged.

"Really? Aren't you lucky?" Nathan fixed Antonio, who looked closer to nine or ten, with a steady gaze. "I'm happy to answer your question if I can, Antonio. What did you want to ask?"

Worried eyes darted towards Anna. "If Uncle Vance found out something about someone, will they come after us, now he's not here anymore?"

In the silence that followed, the boy rubbed the back of his neck nervously. Nathan could see from a stiffening in Anna's posture that she was as surprised by the question as he was. Did the boy know something they didn't?

Nathan took a deep breath, and was considering how to answer, when Neptune turned towards the door with a low growl. Two newcomers had arrived, carrying a large basket of food between them. Anna put a hand on the dog's back to calm him and rose. "If you'll excuse me," she said.

Nathan turned back to the boy. Antonio was regarding him gravely. "I guess it depends on what sort of thing you're thinking of, Antonio," Nathan said. "Is there something that's worrying you?"

The boy held his gaze for a second longer. In the dim light, Nathan thought his face darkened in color. He dropped his eyes to the floor.

"No, nothing. I was wondering, that's all."

"I'm very sorry about your uncle. I know you will miss him. But we'll do our best to see that you're all well cared for."

He wished he sounded more convincing. At the door, Anna was greeting the visitors and ushering them into the room. Nathan glanced across and saw Willoughby Martens was hanging on Anna's every word.

Alongside him stood another man Nathan didn't recognize, but he could see Neptune was regarding the pair with suspicion, straining towards them against Anna's hand, hackles raised all along his backbone.

You've got good instincts, dog, he thought.

As Nathan stood and approached Martens, the other man recognized him. Nathan saw him mumble something to Anna, and then stride across the room to meet him.

"Well, well, if it isn't Nathan Russell. Seems I can't go anywhere these days without you turning up like a foul smell." He regarded Nathan with blatant dislike and then sneered. "Don't you have enough meddling to keep you busy at home, or wherever it is you hang out these days?"

Antonio had trailed behind Nathan, and he turned to the boy and gently squeezed his shoulder.

"I think your mother might need a hand there, son."

He gestured to the door, where another knot of mourners had flooded in. "Can you help show them where to go?"

The pinched, serious little face gazed at him for a minute and then he made for his mother's side.

Nathan turned back to his fellow countryman. "It's nice to see you too, Martens," he said in a dry tone which suggested quite the opposite.

"Why are you sniffing around here? I never picked you as one to have any concerns for widows and orphans— unless you could make money off them, of course."

Willoughby Martens' froggy eyes

bulged with unabashed loathing. "You don't know a thing about me, you ratting black-leg," he ground out through clenched teeth. He threw a furtive glance in Anna's direction, as if checking to see if she was watching, sucking in a breath as he did.

"As it happens, someone I'm working with had close ties with Pedersen. He's concerned to see the family is cared for, and he's got the means to do it. I suspect that's more than can be said for you."

His lips curled in an angry accusation. "You couldn't even keep your own family safe."

Nathan tried to ignore the crippling agony that jabbed deep in his chest. It was time for him to go. He tossed his last word over his shoulder as he moved to the door.

"I'll leave you to pay your respects, Martens."

At the entryway, Antonio was ushering in more visitors, his young brow crinkled in concentration. Neptune paced beside him. Nathan paused and leaned down.

"That's it, Antonio. If Neptune's happy, all's good."

The boy's face broke into a sunny smile, the first Nathan had seen during his visit. It lit up the boyish lines of his face and made Nathan realize how seriously he took the role of protecting his family now Vance was gone.

He wondered again whether the boy knew something he wasn't ready to disclose. If Martens was sniffing around, he certainly hoped not. The man contaminated everything he touched. He hoped Anna's little family would escape the contagion.

Five

"But, of course, Eustace was always dramatic," — John Russell paused on the word and raised one eyebrow in mute criticism—"in the way he conducted his business. He always needed someone to keep him tethered to reality."

He poured steaming black coffee into a porcelain teacup so delicate it was almost translucent.

They were sitting on a secluded terrace at the back of the house, overlooking a blooming rose garden. Bees were burrowing into the deep red flowers, filling the fragrant air with a low, steady hum. Across the valley, Graysie could see the pine-covered slopes of the lower

Sierra Nevada mountains, where she'd been the calamitous day before.

John's servants had met her every need with invisible precision, bringing cinnamon muffins, cornbread, and molasses hotcakes in a flowing feast. The china tea service, linen serviettes, and delicious fare made it hard to remember they were in a mining town populated mainly by rough-skinned men who'd likely be breakfasting on days-old salted bully beef.

Minette's tinkling laughter floated up from the garden below. Under the watchful eye of the groom, she was playing with a little Capuchin monkey in a blue satin jacket and black cap.

It was tiny—*barely weaned from its mother*, Graysie thought—but it seemed as delighted by the child's presence as she was with his, scampering up her arm and over her mass of dark curls to perch on the top of her head before tripping down again.

Graysie pushed back from the table contentedly. She'd been explaining her shock at the lawyer's letter she'd received a few months prior. When she asked Sir John what Eustace had been like, he'd surprised her with his answer, which seemed more measured than the enthusiasm he'd expressed the day before.

"Did you like him?" She looked across the table directly into his eyes. She saw them widen in surprise, and then the mask came down.

"Eustace?" He considered her question, returning her gaze. "He was very impulsive, and that sometimes got him into trouble. A good-hearted fellow, but his enthusiasms often ran away with him. He could be persuasive though, so he often carried others along on his mad schemes."

He fixed his gaze on the silver tea service, and the tension that chased across his face told her there was more to this story. She switched tack.

"This town is so small you've probably already heard it from somewhere else—but I want to investigate re-opening the Ophir."

This morning Sir John was in a black velvet shooting jacket and slim matching trousers with shiny black boots. She tilted her chin to emphasize her determination. "The preliminary assay reports I got from Eustace's lawyer show there's a good chance there is still quality gold there. Vance considered it promising."

She paused as she thought of Vance.

Sir John had reported that Nathan had gone out earlier that morning to pay his respects to his family.

Russell regarded her silently for a few seconds and then gave a dismissive laugh. "You don't understand what you are suggesting, my dear," he said. "You need capital to run mines these days. And Eustace always was a dreamer.

"I wouldn't put too much faith in any assay report he commissioned. Likely the prospector who wrote it told him what he wanted to hear."

She took a deep breath. There was no doubt Sir John had a lot more mining experience than she did, but his response seemed altogether too glib.

"I accept you know a lot more about mining than I do," she said carefully. "I wondered if you'd act as my adviser? As my godfather by proxy—wasn't that how you described yourself last night? I'd be grateful for your expertise."

She gave him an ironic little smile. She figured it couldn't hurt to lay claim to the relationship that he himself suggested on the first day she ever recalled meeting him.

"Of course, I will help in any way I can," Russell said expansively. "But really, it's a damn fool idea for a young woman to be thinking she can operate a mine. I agree with Nathan. Mining is a dangerous business. It's the domain of engineers.

"And then there's the problem with the superstitious Cornishmen. You'd be better advised to marry a mine owner than try to run one yourself."

Heat rose up her neck. Graysie plowed on, regardless. "I understand it's unusual, but I don't accept it's impossible, not if I find the right business partners. Continuing on the stage with a young child to care for is not the life I want for Minette. I promised her mother I'd look after her like my own child, and I'm not letting her down."

She was angry that the last part of her statement sounded more like a plea than a declaration. The last thing she wanted was to appear as if she was begging.

He considered her. "You could sell the mine to someone better equipped to work it. I might even be interested myself.

"And of course, you've no need to be concerned about your present care. You are welcome to be my guest here at Gold House for as long as you need. You and the child," he added as an afterthought.

She wondered at his motives. Did he want to get his hands on the mine? Or—

heaven forbid—on her? The temperatures were already rising, but she shivered. She guessed he was only tolerating Minette because he knew she would not agree to any other arrangement.

Minette. It was a few minutes since she'd seen or heard her. She half rose from her chair to survey the garden below. She couldn't see Minette or the groom.

"Minette. Where is she?" She jerked her head towards Sir John, her breath suddenly short, her chest tight.

John lifted one dark brow. "I suggested to Nelson, the groom, that he take her to the stables to see the ponies," he said casually. "No cause for alarm."

"The stables?"

He pointed farther down into the woodland that edged the Gold House orchard. "Down through the trees. There's a path that takes you to the stables. I keep several ponies there.

"I'm sure Nelson can look after one four-year-old on a pony. But why don't we take a look?"

As they sauntered along the path in the hot late morning sun, he took her elbow and ushered her down a gentle grassy slope to the orchard and stables. She momentarily stiffened, unused to being so closely handled by any man, and especially one she'd not known twenty-four hours prior.

She debated whether she found his paternal gesture intrusive or reassuring. She didn't really know how fathers operated.

Much as she'd loved her own, she'd always given him more care than he'd given her. Was he simply reassuring her she was safe, or was he making a more subtle claim?

As they neared the stables, she could hear childish squeals of delight, and they rounded the corner to see a shaggy-haired white pony snuffling at Minette's outstretched hand, ingesting apple pieces as fast as the little girl produced them. The pony's rubbery dark lips muzzled her flattened palm, and she could barely stand still for giggling.

"It tickles," she said, bending over with laughter and drawing away her empty hand. Minette's head popped up, and she saw them walking into the yard at the same moment as the groom placed his hands on either side of her waist, ready to lift her into the saddle.

"Sissy!" Minette called, her voice high pitched with excitement. "This is Starlight, and Nelson says I can go for a ride."

Her face was as bright as sunshine until her gaze fell on John Russell. The smile faded. The little hands which had eagerly reached out to Starlight tightened involuntarily into fists at her side.

"Is it alright if she sits on the pony, Miss Castellanos?" The groom had picked up on the tension sparked by their arrival and stepped back.

Sir John leaned down and made as if to lift Minette onto the pony, but as soon as his hands touched the child's sides, she cringed away from him.

"Minette, don't be silly, darling. Sir John wants to show you the pony."

Minette stared at the ground, not speaking.

"Didn't your mother teach you any manners?" Russell chided.

Minette raised her eyes, took one swift

look into his stony face and burst into tears.

Great. The perfect houseguests.

Graysie sighed. "I think she must be upset by the accident yesterday. She's not her usual self," she excused, scooping Minette up and turning to go back to the house. "She probably needs a nap."

As they meandered back to the house, Graysie reflected on how unpredictable children could be.

Minette adored Nathan Russell after one meeting. But even with the sweeteners of pet monkeys and shaggy-haired ponies, it was taking her a lot longer to warm to his older brother.

Six

The mastiff reared up in the dark doorway, teeth bared, in a barking frenzy. Martens raised the revolver and felled it with two shots. The beast's momentum carried it forward a few more feet. It collapsed in a shuddering heap, its gaping jaw resting on the toes of his boots. In the silence that followed the gun blast, he smelt blood and sensed its warmth leaking onto his sock.

Behind him, Weavers giggled nervously and Martens tensed, anticipating that the commotion might have aroused a neighbor, but a deep quiet cloaked them as the dog lay bleeding on the bare wooden floor.

Everyone in the street was at Vance Pedersen's Requiem Mass at St Mary's, and the platform where his body had lain a few hours ago was empty, though the room was still fragrant with the mingled scent of flowers, candle wax, and the strange sweet smell of death.

It was late afternoon, and although it was still light outside, it was dim in the cave-like room with its thick walls and small windows. Martens stepped over the dog's remains, lit the candle in the pierced tin lantern he carried, and beckoned Weavers to follow the flickering light.

They couldn't risk being there any longer than the time needed to do a thorough search; the family would be back to continue their grieving within the hour.

"You take the bedrooms. Look under

the beds, in any trunks stowed under them. Check anywhere he might have stored papers." He grabbed Weavers by his lapel with one hand and drew his face into the tight little radius of light that spilled from the lantern. "Don't muck this up."

He pushed the lantern into Weavers' hand and lit a candle left behind on the bier, then by its light moved to the sideboard set up as an informal altar. The house was large enough to house Vance's family but furnished simply; he'd checked for likely hiding places when he'd visited earlier in the day and noted there seemed to be no desk or storage chests and few cupboards apart from the modestly fitted kitchen shelving.

If a man with a sprawling family like this one had a document he wanted to keep private, where would he put it?

Martens rifled through the two drawers and cupboards in the sideboard and found only the usual cups, plates, cutlery, and table linen. No papers. He moved on to the kitchen with the same result. Pots and pans, cooking utensils, and a chopping board. Nothing resembling documents of any sort. Weavers stumbled back into the main room, shaking his head. "Nothing in there except kids' toys and clothes."

"Let's get the hell out of here, then. Check if anyone's about and we'll get rid of the dog. No point in shouting to the world that we've been here."

Weavers ducked out the front door and returned soon after. "Nah, they're still all at the church. Let's move."

He bent down and picked up the dog's back haunches while Martens took the front, and they swung it up between them like a butchered pig.

"Let's ditch it behind the outhouse and leave them to wonder," Martens said as he pulled the front door closed behind him. "If they take a few days to find it, all the better."

*****

Hector De Vile reclined in a luxuriously cushioned armchair, his feet resting on an ottoman, arm extended, as a pretty Chinese girl tended his nails. Willoughby Martens watched in fascination as the girl massaged each finger with a warm, sweet smelling oil—almond oil, he guessed—and then dried it off again with a soft towel.

De Vile was the only man he knew who was rich and eccentric enough to have regular manicures and not care what people thought of it.

One day, Martens vowed, *I'll have the*

power to please myself like him.

"I don't want to hear about the dog. Dogs have no place inside, anyway. Please, tell me you found what we were looking for."

De Vile took a satisfied gulp of whiskey from a tumbler he clasped in his free hand and set it down with a clunk.

Martens squirmed on the hard-backed wooden seat de Vile had motioned him to when he'd arrived. How to break the bad news?

"We made a thorough search and found nothing. How sure are you there's something to find?"

De Vile picked up the whiskey and nursed it against his chest as he contemplated the question. "I can't say for certain, but I don't have a good feeling about this one—and my intuition usually serves me well. Didn't you say

Weavers heard whispers that Pedersen was onto our interest in the Ruby?"

Martens gave him a hard look and then flicked his right hand dismissively. "I don't think we need to worry about Pedersen. He won't be talking to anyone." He grinned.

"We only need a couple more weeks and we'll have got ourselves a nice little bonus. No one need ever know." A long silence fell as de Vile considered. Martens tapped out a tense rhythm on the flat of his thigh with his fingers.

De Vile dismissed the girl, blew across his nails as if drying them, and settled back in his chair, his posture rigid.

"Knowing when to say no is as important in business as knowing when to say yes," he said, fixing Martens with an assessing glint. "I hope greed isn't leading you to confuse the two."

Martens shook himself to toss off a prickling irritation that raised the hairs on his arms at de Vile's condescension. He'd won the magnate's confidence with a couple of small real estate deals he'd proposed, and they'd come to an arrangement which gave Martens a finder's fee and a generous cut of the profits for any further deals de Vile accepted.

He was a freelance middle man for a merchant baron and on his way to big things. But he was becoming frustrated with de Vile's cautious approach to his more ambitious schemes. Proposals that were more high-reaching, and dirtier.

It had been Martens' suggestion that they work the Ruby Mine on the sly behind the bereaved Lisette Guilliame's back, after he'd gleaned the French widow's situation during a drinking session with Octavius Weavers. It was his idea, too, to encroach next door into the Ophir tunnels.

De Vile had seen no harm in it. Anyone in his situation would have done the same, he'd justified. Until Vance Pedersen's violent death. When Pedersen died violently, de Vile got cold feet.

Martens knocked back his whiskey and slammed the glass down for a refill. De Vile had become obsessed with some blasted report Pedersen was supposed to have put together for Eustace Mountfort, apparently noting illegal incursions into the Ophir claim.

Had it had been completed and delivered before Mountfort died? He wanted to know. If it had, de Vile reasoned, it wouldn't be long before that Castellanos chit—or her protector John Russell—would be onto them.

Martens couldn't see why he needed to worry. So what? Even if they noticed the raid, they couldn't pin anything on them.

He watched as de Vile drew a cigar out of his pocket and lit it with a flourish. The man was clearly buying time, making a point that he wouldn't be pushed around. Belatedly, he thrust a second Havana across the table to Martens. "Try one. They're good."

Martens held the smoke in his mouth, savoring the mellow tingle.

One day…

De Vile leaned towards him. He rested his elbows on his thighs and fixed him with a commanding glare. The smoke from his cigar grazed Martens' right ear.

"You've got a week, Martens. I want that Pedersen report on the Ophir in my beautiful hands,"—he grinned and waved the cigar provocatively in Martens' face—

"by this time next week. It's dangerous to have it lying about out there for anyone else to find. I see no reason to buy trouble. Understand? No more trouble."

Later, she could never remember whether it was the dream or the desperate cries of the servant that had woken her. She lay in the deep feather bed in her elegant room and even the heat trapped under the rafters from the afternoon sun couldn't thaw the chill that gripped her.

Moonlight spilled over the peacock bedspread, and she could see the hands of the mother-of-pearl clock on the bedside table. It read 3 A.M.

She'd dreamed she was floating amongst the trees in a pine forest, hovering halfway up their towering trunks. Beneath her, she saw a black yawning hole, like a cave opening in a canyon wall. As she watched, a white wolf emerged, paused at the cave entrance, raised his head to the stars, and howled.

She'd the weirdest sense he was calling her, and that she was supposed to answer, but her throat was stiff and dry, and she couldn't have opened her mouth even if she'd wanted to. She was as inconsequential as mist and as frozen as the snow-covered landscape below her.

Suddenly, a man stepped out from a vantage point above the cave and lined up a rifle on the big alpha male. Her throat was raw as she tried to yell, to warn the wolf he was in danger, but the only sound was the thunderous report of the gunshot.

That's when she woke to the sound of panicked banging on her bedroom door. She reared up like she herself was in danger of being shot. The door swung open and the servant detailed to watch over Minette stood there, wailing in Chinese. Seeing the bewildered look on Graysie's face, she abruptly stopped crying and keened, "Bebe gone... bebe gone..."

Seven

Friday, July 3

Madam Moustache's rubbery lips curled in indignation. "I've gone to a lot of trouble to make sure things happened as you wanted," she whined. "It costs to have other people do your dirty work."

Hector de Vile contemplated the stag's head on the wall above them and imagined the Madam's in its place as she droned on.

"They were supposed to sedate her, and yet I've been up half the night with her crying. I had to dose her with laudanum, I did. It's a wonder she didn't wake the whole hotel." Her lizard tongue flicked in and out, reminding de Vile of a venomous reptile.

They sat in one of the Exchange Hotel's small private rooms, designed for exactly the sort of confidential meeting they were conducting. He didn't want it known that he and the Madam did business together, and she'd locked the door from the inside to be sure no one disturbed them.

"I'm doing my best, but I'd hate for word to get out. Wouldn't look good for either of us." She gave him a sly sideways glance.

Hector de Vile was the silent majority shareholder in the Exchange, and though few knew of his business dealings with the Madam, he was regretting he'd ever laid eyes on her. She was a former dance hall girl who'd seduced a silver baron she'd later married when his first wife died.

The Madam had fallen on hard times when her husband died, leaving his estate to a son who had no interest in the hotel. De Vile had bought it for a song, the son was so keen to be rid of the place and the unwanted step mother.

The miners had nicknamed her Madam not because she ran a brothel—though she turned a blind eye to what went on when it suited her—and not out of affection for her eccentricities like the snappy little lap dogs that accompanied her everywhere. Nor because of the tooled leather double holstered gun belt slung on her hips.

She was Madam out of the fear she aroused with her ruthless instinct for wheedling out secrets from loose lips.

Many a man had awoken with a crippling hangover to find he'd gambled or sold his latest promising claim in a drunken stupor the night before, with no memory of who to or why, but with the uneasy suspicion the Madam and her free-flowing booze had fueled the exchange.

There was no doubt about it. The Madam knew how to run a profitable business, keeping the liquor supplies filled and staff in check, intimidating drunken miners with her readiness to draw.

She'd been grateful for her twenty percent share and a job, and she'd repaid de Vile handsomely by maintaining the Exchange as the town's premier meeting place, tarting it up with velvet curtains and fancy artwork, and overseeing the installation of gilded mirrors in the foyer and a chandelier above the stairs.

Today, however, she'd committed the

cardinal sin in business—attempting to renegotiate a deal after they'd agreed on terms.

She'd got cocky because she knew he couldn't afford to call her bluff and risk exposing how the child came to be in the hotel. De Vile tapped his fingers impatiently on the edge of the table.

Unfortunately, she was in a powerful position. She knew about the skeletons in his closet, and she was shameless. He knew for sure this wasn't the first young child she'd seized and sold for personal gain.

He shuddered involuntarily as he considered what it would cost him personally if even a hint of those dealings ever became public, and then forced himself back to the present.

"The deal was that you would take the child, hide her, and then make her disappear when I said so," de Vile reminded her. "I wasn't talking about harming her. Plenty of homesteaders need an extra pair of hands.

"I'm just reminding the Castellanos woman how perilous life can be out here in the mountains without a protector."

The Madam fondled the rat-faced pooch nestled against her rounded belly. Her dogs were the only thing he'd ever seen her show any affection to, and despite himself, he thought with a pang of pity for the child in the basement.

"I need more than you're paying. It's difficult passing on a kid these days. What am I supposed to do with her?"

He shook his head, his face stony. "You knew the score. You've been there before."

She blushed at the coldness in his voice. The Madam had always been accommodating with her 'extra services'. She employed enforcers to ensure things fell her way, and heaven help a man if he stood up to her.

Some of de Vile's best gold finds had come through whiskey-fueled boasts at the Exchange. Like taking candy from a baby, she always joked. Until today.

Now Moustache was saying the price they'd agreed on for her to take the child and make her disappear wasn't enough— she needed to double it. The child was "all wrong" she said; too old for adoption and too young for indentured labor.

"It's your job to take care of it. I don't want to hear anything more about it." De Vile picked up the hat that sat on the table beside him, as if to conclude the discussion. He reached out to stroke the piece of fluff the Madam cuddled in her lap.

The ratty little mongrel bared its

needle-like teeth and snapped, narrowly missing his fingertips. He pulled his hand back with a jerk. He'd seen enough of the mistress and her dogs for one day.

He watched as she took a large iron key that hung from a chain at her waist and unlocked the door. She was old and expendable; her breathing labored, her fleshy jowls too bright under her heavy rouge.

As he strode up Main Street, he mused. Should he get tough and threaten to turn her over to the law—accuse her of child trafficking?

It wouldn't matter how much she protested they had an arrangement—no one would accept her word against his. Or should he shut up and pay up to get rid of a problem? And what would that mean for their future business arrangements?

By the time he reached his waiting coach, he'd decided. He gave a satisfied sigh as he settled himself on the leather seat and lit another cigar.

Moustache might be good at her job, but she needed to learn nobody was indispensable.

*****

The Castellanos woman was breathtakingly beautiful, even if she looked wan and distracted this morning, Hector de Vile thought as he strode into John Russell's dining room, where the remnants of breakfast lay spread on the table—dry toast in the toast rack, cold scrambled eggs and uneaten bacon in the silver serving dishes.

Come to think of it, he preferred her as was today—docile and defenseless—over the confident performer of a week ago.

He read the room. The opera star Pania

Hayes and Sir John sat on either side of Graysie at the table. Melancholy suffocated the mood so heavily you'd think there'd been a death in the house.

Satisfaction warmed de Vile as he realized the disappearance of the child was biting deep, not only with the Castellanos woman but also, it seemed, with her host and his friend. John Russell stroked Graysie's hand and made comforting noises as de Vile gave a perfunctory knock.

"I know it may not be the best time, Miss Castellanos, but I need an answer to my proposition. Your week is up."

He swiveled to meet Sir John eye-to-eye and saw Mrs. Hayes half rise from her chair, darting a hard look at Sir John as she did.

"It certainly is not the best time," she said emphatically. "In fact, there couldn't be a worse one." She shot another look in John's direction, this time one of appeal. "I really think…"

John let go of Graysie Castellanos's hand and stood. "Miss Castellanos does not wish to see anyone today, Hector. You can understand that."

De Vile spread his hands wide, palms up. "So, the gossip down in the village is true. I thought it was all wild talk… Someone's nabbed the orphan."

Graysie jerked to her feet and swung to face him, emerald eyes blazing. "Of all the insufferable…" She stopped and let out a long breath, swallowed hard, and began again.

"Mr. de Vile, the last time I saw you, we had a domestic emergency. Today we have another. Kindly see yourself out. And for your information, Minette is not 'the orphan'. She is a much-loved child."

Her voice faltered, but she stood erect and unflinching.

"My apologies," he said with a slight bow, knowing he did not look in the least bit sorry. "But I gave you a week to decide, and that week is up. You seem to attract a succession of 'domestic emergencies,' but that's hardly my concern."

She glared, as if she couldn't believe anyone would be so rude and uncaring, and he blatantly returned her gaze.

After a long silence, he said. "One week I said. It's up tomorrow, and I need an answer."

Graysie stared back at him, her brows raised in disbelief. "I haven't decided what I'm doing about my shares, but I can tell you most definitely I won't be accepting your offer. I may end up selling them, Mr. de Vile, but it will not be to you."

She flashed him a bitter smile that said more clearly than words, *Not if you were the last man on earth.* He stood his ground in the doorway. A tense silence replaced the earlier melancholy. Sir John's expression darkened, and de Vile wasn't sure if it was because of his behavior or hers, and he didn't care.

Russell cleared his throat. "Probably not a good time, old boy. You've got a son, haven't you? Surely you can understand?"

At the mention of Alexander, de Vile's stomach clenched, a reminder of the many nights he'd lain awake worrying that some hand would reach out from his son's past and reclaim him; disappear him like he'd arranged for this child to vanish. He gave his shoulders a light shake, as if to dislodge the thought.

"Yes, yes, I have a son. He's doing

very well, learning the business. I tell him that, despite what the Good Book says, more often than not, the race *does* go to the swift and the battle to the strong."

He flashed Russell a challenging smile and then settled his gaze on Graysie.

"I hope you don't live to regret your hasty decision, Miss Castellanos. You may not get an offer that will better mine—not after I've finished spreading the word, anyway. But you have other things on your mind, I'm sure. Good luck with finding the child."

He raised his hand in a light mock salute and turned and strode out into the warm sunlight, pleased with his morning's work.

Let her stew.

He doubted she'd be around town for much longer.

Eight

When Nathan thundered into the Gold House dining room a few minutes after de Vile's departure, his older brother and his guests were sitting in stunned silence.

"What's going on? Apart from the obvious, I mean," he said as he took a seat opposite Graysie. "It's awfully quiet in here."

She shrugged. "We've had a most unwelcome visitor. But never mind that. How's the hunt going?"

He could read in the violet shadows under her eyes that she was close to exhaustion. The fine-boned hollow in her throat pulsed with urgency, and despite the unflinching set of her shoulders, she had the fragility of a crushed dove. He wanted to hold her in his arms and tell her everything was going to be alright.

"The search is well underway in this area. If she's wandered off, we're certain to find her. It's all a matter of time…" The certainty in his tone faded to something more tentative. "While John's men focus near the house, I thought I might trace the side roads back towards town."

Graysie had a blank expression, as if she wasn't taking in what he was saying. "She's so little. A bear might attack her. Or she could step on a snake. Or be stung by a scorpion…" Her eyes had a faraway look as she mused on her fears.

"She'll be hungry… And terrified, out there alone. And she's still missing her mother. It's all too much…"

Her voice trailed off, and she put her head in her hands and rubbed her eyes, as if trying to wake herself from a bad dream.

Nathan could sense she was steeling herself, willing herself to hold on.

Graysie looked up from her hands. "I don't know what could have possessed her to leave the house. She's done nothing like this before. And she knows where my room is if she's frightened."

Her green eyes were beseeching. "I can't sit here doing nothing. She might hide because she's frightened. If she senses I'm near, she might come out."

Nathan nodded. "Why don't you get a wrap and we can take a drive around the area? You might have the best suggestions for places she'd be likely to go."

The thing he didn't say yawned open

before them. In his heart of hearts, he didn't believe the child had wandered off in the middle of the night, either. He feared something a lot more sinister was afoot.

*****

Graysie and Nathan had spent a discouraging couple of hours driving to the end of every mining track wide enough for a pony trap near Gold House, looking for any telltale signs of Minette, calling her name. They'd found nothing.

Her heart ached, but it was such a beautiful summer's day that if they hadn't had this chilling search underway, it would have been a day for celebration. They were there in Grass Valley, and the way was open for her to push on with her plans for the Ophir.

Her irritation at Nathan's take-charge attitude had transformed into deep gratitude at his unquestioning willingness to back her search one hundred percent. After she'd been so prickly the first time they met, she wouldn't have blamed him if he'd got on with his own business and left the search for John's men.

She shivered despite the warm day and wondered whatever had possessed her to think she could provide and care for a four-year-old on her own. After they'd traced the fifth narrow mountain road to a dead end with no result, Nathan suggested they continue on into town and have a cool drink at the tea shop near the Exchange.

"You're worn out." He took her hand in his and squeezed it gently. "You need a break."

The moment their hands touched, the same tingly spark ran up her spine as the first time he'd shaken hands with her in the Sierra wilderness; the familiar sense of never wanting to let go. She gave her head a slight shake of dissent and willed herself to disengage. When she did, a hollowness opened up inside.

Although she knew he heartily disapproved of her plans, he hadn't pestered her with talk as they'd searched. Now, as they entered the teahouse, she thought of Minette's mother, Francine, and wondered what she would make of everything if she were alive.

She'd only had the child for a couple of months and she'd already put the girl's life at risk more than once. It still bewildered her how and why any of it had happened.

Breaking the companionable silence, Graysie turned to Nathan. "I keep going over it all in my head. I don't understand how she got out. The outside doors were all bolted.

"The handles are too high for her to reach, the bolts too heavy for her little fingers to unlatch. Someone must have let her out deliberately. And that makes no sense."

She'd gone round and round trying to uncover something that would tempt Minette from her room in the middle of the night. Yes, she'd loved seeing the monkey, but Graysie didn't believe she'd get up in the middle of the night and go looking for it.

"Maybe something frightened her," Nathan suggested.

"But if that happened, she'd run to my room, not outside," she protested. "I'm sure of it."

They were sitting in a Chinese teahouse in a shaded leafy courtyard off

Main Street, sipping iced green tea, when a pretty waitress approached their table. She hesitated, checking that no one was watching, then bent down to clear their glasses and whisper to Nathan.

Her tone was panicky, and her eyes frequently darted to the doorway. Maybe she was worried about her boss catching her talking to a customer? As she continued speaking, Nathan's eyes turned cold and hard.

She couldn't understand a word of what they were saying, because they were speaking in Chinese. After several minutes of conversation, the girl slipped nervously away.

"What's going on?" she asked, perplexed.

"Oh, that was White Pearl—she works at the hotel and there's something going on there that concerns her." Nathan was trying to sound nonchalant. He took a last gulp from his tea glass and stood. "I'd better take you home," he said. "You're looking dead on your feet."

She shook her head. "No. No, I prefer to sit and wait for you. If I go back there empty-handed, it's like we've failed. You see to whatever it is you need to do. I'll wait." She gave him a wan smile. "I didn't know you spoke the lingo," she said, tilting her head in the departing waitress' direction.

"I grew up in Hong Kong. I was fluent when I lived there, and I picked a lot up again on the Australian goldfields. There are a lot of Chinese miners there too."

Graysie nodded. "Look, you go. I'm fine here. I want to sit and think a while longer."

"If you're sure…" Nathan stood and set

off across the square to the Exchange with long urgent strides. He really wanted to get somewhere in a hurry. She ordered more tea and sank into a reverie. She was so tired, she could barely keep her eyes open.

Afterward, she wondered if she'd nodded off and for how long. Because one minute it seemed she was fighting exhaustion and the next she was bolt awake. Across the square, an angry crowd spilled out from the crowded Exchange bar into the courtyard.

Amid the melee, Nathan was clearly visible, standing half a head taller than most of the surrounding men. She saw there was something else that marked him out, too. And that was the small child he held aloft in his arms. In a heartbeat, she was on her feet and running across the planked yard, the noise of chanting growing louder as she ran.

"Kill her! Kill her!"

And then one voice louder than the rest: "The hag deserves to die!"

✶✶✶✶✶

Hector de Vile heard the catcalls and chanting from his private sitting room on the floor above the Exchange Hotel bar. It sounded like a dangerous scene was brewing, and he hurried downstairs to find out what was going on.

A boiling throng of miners filled the courtyard that linked the public bar to the street. In their midst stood a man half a head taller than most of those around him.

De Vile stiffened in shock. Sir John's Aussie brother was holding a small curly-headed girl protectively against one shoulder, his other hand shading her from the angry faces crowding around them.

"How do you explain this, Madam Ring?" Nathan Russell's voice was compelling, and the men surrounding him murmured in support. They milled around the hotel manager in an angry mob, like a swarm of bees driving out a foreign invader.

"Yes, tell us, Madam."

"What's the child doing there? What's going on?"

Nathan Russell held up his free hand for calm and addressed the crowd. "Irish Pete and I found Minette in the hotel cellars. What I want to know is, how did she get there?"

The big Irishman, as well known to the locals as Vance Pedersen and with a similar reputation for staunch honor, stood at Nathan's shoulder, glaring at the Madam. but saying nothing.

All turned their attention on the hotelier, who scowled back, feet set in a defiant, wide-hipped stance. She wore a brilliant green velvet jacket topped with a boxy green felt feathered hat. Crimson lipstick rimmed her pouchy lips. The pistols hung below her coat hem, and the sharp-toothed dogs cowed at her feet.

For a frozen minute she stood like that, eyes bulging in brazen insolence, and then the air changed. The men parted like wheat before a whispering wind, giving clear passage to the Castellanos woman. She burst through and stopped before the Australian, taking a deep gulp of air as she reached him.

De Vile saw her silently mouth, *Is she okay?* Her rescuer nodded. She stroked the child's head. The unfolding tableau mesmerized the crowd; the open space was so silent, de Vile could hear her whisper from the other side of the courtyard.

"Sissy's here now, sweetheart. Shall we get your favorite drink?"

Her voice was melodic, soothing, every decibel that of a star performer.

Gently, Nathan Russell set the child down on the ground and she buried her head in Graysie's skirts. Graysie caressed the child's head and mouthed "Thank you" to her liberator. Then she gathered the child up in her arms and carried her away.

"I'll see you in the teahouse," Nathan called after them. "I've got a few loose ends to tidy up here first."

A few loose ends indeed. De Vile cursed as he pushed his way through the throng.

Nathan returned to confronting Madam

Ring. "She didn't wander in here alone," he challenged.

"Two of your hard men are going to have difficulty walking for the next few days because they got in Irish Pete's way. They weren't keen to let her go. So, I ask again. How did she get here?"

Like a cornered rat, the hotelier's darting eyes settled on de Vile. She grinned nervously. "I have my hands full running the hotel. Mr. de Vile will confirm it. I don't know who snatched her—if that's what happened. We've only got your word for it." Hands on hips, she wasn't backing down.

"Not only his word." Irish Pete, built like a wrestler and sporting a bushy red beard, planted himself in front of Nathan. Hector de Vile knew him to be a bullet of a man, with the tenacity of a bulldog for righting wrongs, the manager of one of the richest operations in the district.

Miners respected him as a no-nonsense boss who kept his word, and the crowd surrounding them knew it.

Irish Pete glared at the Madam. "The Aussie didn't make this up. You ask the singsong girls who work in your house. They heard the child wailing. The walls whisper their secrets; the girls know what's going on."

No one moved. Irish Pete's words hung in the air, and de Vile sensed the crowd was with him.

A man wearing a red bandana shouted, "That's turrible. We've few enough children in this town without the ones we have coming to harm. I reckon we string her up."

"Mr. de Vile!" Madam Ring's voice had a shrill edge, her shoulders slumped forward and her bluster evaporated. "Tell

them there's been a silly mistake," she
pleaded. "I know nothing! If she was in
my cellars, she was there without my
knowledge."

The crowd murmured in disbelief, and
de Vile saw his opportunity. "Woman, it's
a miracle the child didn't die down there.
How did she get there? We're all waiting
for an explanation."

The crowd erupted into more chanting
and catcalls. The red bandana man
yelled, "Hang the crow."

"Hanging's too quick. Let's tar and
feather her and run her out of town,"
yelled another, a beetle-browed fellow
with an exuberant black beard.

What had until now been a disgruntled
mob was turning dark and deadly. De
Vile smelt it. He guessed Nathan Russell
could, too.

The black bearded man grabbed

Madam Ring and pinned her arms behind her back, while his red bandana pal whipped out some rope and secured her wrists. Others joined them and hustled her from the courtyard to the street, where a barrel full of pine tar used for keeping ropes flexible stood outside the lumber merchant's store.

Like water running downhill, the men pooled around the bound woman. Within seconds, they stripped Madam to her waist, her green jacket and hat trampled underfoot. Tied to the hitching rail, exposed in her wrinkled nakedness, she might have been pitiable, if not for the raging fury that burned from her.

"A pox on you all," she screamed. "You'll learn."

A haggard old crone, brush loaded with dripping pine tar, stepped up. With a slashing blow, she slapped it diagonally across the hotelier's right cheek, then back across her left.

"Take that! And that! There's justice after all," she howled.

Madam Moustache's head whipped back.

"That's payback," the old woman cried. "You discarded me like old rags. You can go rot in hell."

Others were joining in now, dipping brushes into the golden pine tar which had melted to the consistency of honey in the rising temperature of the day. It dripped through the hotelier's hair, down her shoulders, and over her sagging breasts.

The old hag who'd started the assault produced a feather pillow and, with one knife thrust, opened it over the woman's head. The feathers stuck to her hair, a fluffy shower that might have been benign if not for the sticky tar.

Every place they landed, they adhered to her skin. Rough hands picked up those that fell to the ground and slapped them onto her again, so that her skin showed red and sore under the sticky film.

"See how you like that! Kidnapper! Whore monger!"

De Vile watched, almost light-headed. At least they hadn't tried to hang her. They'd taught her a lesson, and she'd know she was lucky to escape with her life.

They'd leave her to stew in the blistering sun for a few more hours before they finally ran her out of town. She'd be sore for days from the combination of sunburn and the solvents she'd need to get rid of the persistent tar. She wasn't dead, but they'd finished with her in Grass Valley.

As de Vile turned away with a grim smile, he saw Nathan Russell regarding him thoughtfully. He paused to congratulate him.

"That was smart work, finding the child like that. What put you onto it?"

"What put me onto it? I heard it on the grapevine." He shrugged. "I've talked with the girls since I've been here. They're amused by a white man who speaks their lingo; it's amazing what you pick up."

John came up and joined his brother. "How the blazes...?" He was at a loss for words. "I'm delighted the child's safe, but I've still got questions."

Nathan shrugged. "Me too, John. But right now, I'd better find Graysie and get her and Minette back home. If she wants to return, that is..."

His brother dipped his head in surprise.

"Not sure I follow. Why wouldn't she want to return?"

Nathan lifted a single eyebrow and gazed at him. "Why? I'd have thought that would be pretty obvious, brother. They've spirited her away from Gold House once. She didn't get into the Exchange Hotel cellars by herself. Graysie might wonder if it's safe to come back."

John laughed. "Lightning doesn't strike twice in the same place, old man. Besides, thanks to you, we've got at least part of the answer in that sorry sight over there." He gestured towards Madam Ring, her head flopped on her chest, surrounded by a jeering crowd.

"Mmmm." Nathan seemed to address his next remarks straight at de Vile, he thought—or is this what guilt feels like? He wasn't sure, it happened so rarely.

He concentrated on what the Australian said next.

"We know where she ended up." Nathan scratched his head, deep in thought. "But I'm not at all sure we know how she got there. And I'm talking about the woman as much as the child."

Nine

Saturday, July 4

"You can't be serious!"

When Graysie Castellanos got excited, her eyes sparked fire. And that was a glorious sight, one that left Nathan with a warm glow in his chest like nothing he'd ever experienced before. Funny how even inciting her outrage was pleasurable.

He'd been regaling her with stories of the pranks Australian miners played on each other, exaggerating the facts for effect. It was the day after Minette's rescue, and following a good night's sleep, the curly headed poppet bounced and chattered at breakfast as if the world was exactly as it should be.

Graysie's heart burst with gratitude at her resilience.

She's an amazing wee trooper.

She displayed no signs of shock or trauma, but they'd agreed a fun day out at the county fair was the best remedy for any lingering fears she might be harboring.

Sir John had left early for a business meeting, and they'd spent the morning wandering the county fair exhibits, cheering the Spanish cowboys—the vaqueros—as they ran down and lassoed wild cattle. They applauded the flamenco dancers and devoured pit barbecued beef and tortillas.

Minette had deemed the magician, who made blue birds fly out of his handkerchief, the best thing ever, and then she'd dozed off on Nathan's shoulder, overwhelmed with the heat and excitement.

They'd settled on a pine bench in the amphitheater with two glasses of iced lemonade, waiting for the big show—the bull and bear baiting—to begin.

Graysie sat opposite him, one hand lightly clasping her cold glass, the other propping up her chin as, elbow on the table, she basked in the early afternoon sun. When she relaxed and was open like this, she was irresistible. The bubbly fizz he'd recognized the day before sizzled again, as she let out a long, contented sigh and gave him a smile that lit up her emerald eyes.

How had he missed till now that they shone with tiny violet flecks?

"Thanks for this. It's been a lifesaver for both of us." She eyed Minette, flopped against his shoulder, the child's slow warm breath feathering his neck.

"Really. It has."

They locked eyes in a moment that stretched on and on. He'd known her for three days and he already knew he wanted her in his life forever.

"How is it you're not married already?" The question was out before he could censor it. His cheeks flushed pink, he knew, but he held her gaze.

How gauche was that, buster?

"Um… Gosh. What can I say? The right man hasn't asked me yet?" She let out a spontaneous peal of laughter, and her eyes widened with candor.

"I guess you've already seen. I'm not the most biddable of women. I don't like being told what to do. I guess it takes a particular sort of man to appreciate that."

He took a deep breath and delivered another conversational bombshell.

While I'm at it, why not? I am an uncouth Aussie.

"And it must have occurred to you it would be much easier to care for Minette if you had a husband?"

Graysie raised an eyebrow speculatively. "It hadn't crossed my mind," she said dryly and fell silent, though she couldn't suppress a twitch of her lips.

I'm already neck-deep in muck. I may as well finish the job.

"What happened to Minette's mother? We haven't mentioned her."

She raised a speculative eyebrow and jabbed; "You want my entire life story?"

And then her lips twitched again, and she relented.

"Francine was a wonderful mother and

a darling friend. She died in a gambling hall fire. When her husband left her destitute, she returned to her job as a dealer to feed herself and Francine. So when the tent walls went up in smoke, the fire trapped her inside.”

She paused and added, “Having a husband didn’t help her much.”

Nathan could only nod. “Touché.”

He fiddled with his glass and re-settled Minette, who’d slipped down his chest, into a more comfortable position. She didn’t stir.

“And Minette. What do you want for her?” Nathan suddenly wanted to know more about this infuriating woman with violet-flecked green eyes and impossible dreams.

“I want her to know she has a place on this earth that’s hers. Somewhere she’s loved and accepted, come what may.

Where she can discover and delight in her strengths and talents. Something I never had."

She gave a quick smile, but Nathan glimpsed a longing that was at odds with the self-reliant, pugnacious woman who appeared whenever Graysie sensed she was under attack.

"Oh? Where did you grow up?"

She shrugged, as if it wasn't significant, and the slight movement released a fresh fragrance of lemon and sunshine. "Here in California. I was born back East, but my parents came out here to escape family, I think.

"They'd eloped, and Mother's family never got over it. A New York heiress and Spanish photographer weren't quite a match in their eyes. Even an exceedingly talented portrait photographer... He didn't fit their expectations. Anyway, she died when I was young, and Father never really coped after that."

Graysie pressed her lips into a tight line.

"I've never heard the story—how did you come to have a stage career?"

She gave her head a soft shake and took a deep breath. "A pushy stepmother. I didn't really have any choice.

"She was greedy to get money any way she could, and by then my father had lost his will to work—or to stand up to her."

Their eyes locked, and for a moment, she seemed to relax. She was seeking something from him—understanding, was that it? With a jolt, he realized circumstances had forced the fiercely independent Miss Castellanos to adopt

her free-wheeling posture out of
necessity.

He glimpsed what might be if she
dropped the shield, and if he allowed
himself to trust his intuition. The void of
learning to love again yawned open, then
slammed shut.

She stood suddenly, as if shaking off a
fantasy, and he wondered if she too
sensed the promise that hung in the air
between them.

Her voice hardened. "Look, this is all
ancient history. I'm focused on the now."

A trumpet blast sounded, and they
both turned. Two Mexican riders clad in
blue velvet riding coats and breeches
had ridden into the ring, followed by a
phalanx of roughly attired mountain men
dragging a bleeding and enraged roped
bear.

Fur matted and bloody, it raised its

head and roared, pink-tinged drool dripped from the yellow fangs in its cavernous mouth.

The captors released it, and the bear whirled around and reared up to face the horse-mounted vaqueros. But before it could reach them, the arena gates opened again and a big-horned Spanish bull, bleeding from sword strikes along its sides, charged in, head down. Nathan watched as the bear caught the smell of the bull and swung away from the vaqueros.

Graysie turned to him, wide-eyed. "I've never seen this before. Where did they get the bear?"

"They would have staked a carcass out in the forest and then waited to trap and rope it when it took the bait," Nathan replied.

"The bull will be some half-wild thing

they've found roaming on the grass flats by the river and run down. They wound it before the fight to get it riled up."

Bull and bear spotted each other at the same moment. The bull launched forward, its treacherous horns aimed straight at the bear's abdomen. It covered the few feet separating them in seconds.

There was a heavy crunching noise as the bull's horns tore open a wound low on the bear's side, then the bear closed its mouth over the bull's muzzle with an unnerving growl.

The pair danced in a deadly circle; the bear holding fast, the bull powerless to escape, as with one great paw, the bear clawed its sides, opening fresh ribbons of flesh with every stroke.

The bear was screaming; the bull bellowed intermittently through breathless pants of terror. Then the bear seemed to lose strength. It released the bull, which turned in a circle as if chasing its own tail before once again turning to face its enemy. Head down, horns glistening in the afternoon sunlight, it charged again.

This time the bear visibly faltered on the crunching impact and, for a few seconds, seemed to sink to its haunches before again rearing up and advancing. The bull's panting increased, and its tongue lolled out. In a second, the bear had fastened onto it and ripped it out. The crowd which had flooded into the arena stood as one and roared approval.

As the bull sank to the dust in exhaustion, Nathan saw Graysie had turned very pale. Beads of sweat stood out on her forehead. Another roar from the crowd distracted him. As they watched, they saw it had been a contest to the death. The bull lay dying in the dust, the bear sinking in a pool of blood beside it, also on its last legs.

Graysie turned away sharply. "How cruel," she gasped. "I'm so glad Minette isn't awake to see this."

Nathan regarded her thoughtfully. "That's frontier life," he said. "Wild and cruel—and no place for a single woman with a child."

He knew he was pushing it, and her reaction was instantaneous. Any sense of connection between them evaporated.

"Can you take us home?" she snapped, turning away from the arena. "I've had enough. I'm undyingly grateful to you for rescuing Minette. I really am. I know what I'm trying to do is hard—jolly hard, believe me. You don't need to tell me.

She turned and marched purposefully

toward the exit. A sharp pain shot up the side of his face and he realized he was gritting his teeth.

Endeavoring not to wake Minette, he hurried to catch up. "Graysie, stop. Stop, please."

She halted and turned, hands on hips. "What?"

"I apologize. I was out of line. But that changes nothing important. I'm concerned for your safety—yours and that of this little darling on my shoulder. I'd never forgive myself if anything happened to her."

His stomach turned over as he stared at her. Unwanted, the image of Joshua, not yet one-year-old but already tottering around on two feet like a drunken sailor, rose in his mind's eye. He'd failed him when the boy had needed him most. He shook his head to banish his son's presence.

"Look what's happened already. First, they killed Vance. Then Minette lost—almost certainly abducted. How do you know it won't happen again?"

"It won't," she snapped. "Sir John will make sure of it."

"John? I'm not sure any of us have much idea who or what we're up against, my brother included. That puts us at a distinct disadvantage."

The set look on Graysie's face told him it was pointless to go on. If he was going to protect Minette, he needed to dig a lot deeper to understand who was behind the disappearance and if it had any link to Vance's death.

The heaviness that sat in the pit of his stomach told him without a doubt he couldn't walk away and leave this woman to work out her own folly. It had nothing to do with the woman or his irrational reaction to her. He couldn't fail another child.

"Don't you understand you could put Minette at risk?" he said in an urgent whisper. "You may compromise your own safety, but I'm darned if I'm going to step aside and let you take risks with the child."

"Chivalrous of you, Mr. Russell, but why the need to appoint yourself our guardian? The things that have happened? Simply coincidence. Unusual, I agree, but I can't see the link between Vance's death and Minette going missing.

"How could they be related—we barely even knew the man? No. We'll be extra cautious, but I'm not willing to give up."

He sighed and fell into step beside her as they turned to walk to the pony trap.

"Promise me one thing," he said. "Trust no one—not even my brother—until we have a better idea of what's going on."

Ten

Gold House was bustling with activity when Nathan and Graysie returned from the fair. Nathan had bought a newly wakened Minette a stick of candy floss as a last treat, and as they traipsed through the front door, Graysie noticed the child's rosebud mouth was ringed with a sticky brown smudge from its sugary remnants.

She supposed they both resembled a couple of hillbillies after a morning in the open air, and she was turning to make a brief farewell to Nathan and escape upstairs to tidy up when she caught sight of Pania Hayes in full sail on Sir John's arm, heading for the garden.

The Maori singer was impossible to overlook in a pale gold shot silk day dress which shimmered subtly as she moved, the gold complimenting her perfect olive complexion. On her head she wore a turban style wrap in the same gold fabric trimmed with black feathers.

She carried herself with regal grace, head tilted as if to catch every word Sir John uttered, and as Graysie watched, she paused with queenly assurance to gaze at him, fascinated by his latest remark. One glimpse and you knew this was a woman with a presence few could rival.

The housekeeper, who had been hovering in the hall, heard their footsteps and gave a welcoming cry. "Oh Miss Castellanos, you've returned!"

Pania halted and turned, beaming.

"Miss Castellanos, I'm thrilled Minette's home!" She gave Graysie a light embrace and bent down to tweak Minette's arm.

"And how is this little treasure? I might have a wee surprise for you!" She delved into the bag that hung from her wrist and extracted a lollipop.

Minette's sugary mouth dimpled. "Thank you," she whispered.

Sir John cleared his throat. "We're going to sit in the garden. Why don't you and Nathan"—he nodded to his brother who'd come into the room behind them —"join us for afternoon tea?"

Graysie wanted to protest that she was dusty and travel-worn and needed to change, but instantly thought better of it. All the concert hall chatter indicated that, underneath the grand dame manner, Pania was a grounded, pragmatic woman.

As they settled into seats in the garden arbor, the older woman reached out and took Graysie gently by the hand. "Your happy resolution is such good news!"

She whispered, so Minette, who was stroking a plump tabby on the steps leading into the arbor, didn't hear.

Graysie grimaced. "It was horrible. Terrifying, in fact. But thanks to Nathan… Mr. Russell…" She flushed with awkwardness. What was she supposed to call him? It wasn't as if they were really friends. She cleared her throat and focused on Mrs. Hayes's sympathetic deep brown eyes. "As you say, thank God for a happy ending."

Sir John interrupted with noisy coughing. "I believe Mrs. Hayes knew your Uncle Eustace many years ago, Miss Castellanos. Were you aware of that?"

Graysie peered at Pania in surprise. "Really? No, I hadn't realized. When was that?"

The housekeeper brought in a tray set with blue and white teacups and a pile of steaming hot scones. As she left, she picked the cat up under her arm. She took Minette by the hand and headed for the door.

"Come, my dear, let's take you to the kitchen to give Whiskers some milk and get something for you to eat."

"Don't let her out of your sight," Graysie said, suddenly anxious. "Promise me." Her eyes flicked to Nathan, who was sitting in the corner, his mouth already half-ull of strawberry jam-topped scone. He caught her eye and frowned.

"So, you knew Eustace?" Graysie prompted, after the housekeeper had gone. With the ease of someone who was mistress in her domain, Pania Hayes took up the teapot. "Yes—only briefly—we all did. But first let me do the honors. Milk or lemon, my dear?"

When she saw everyone had been served, Pania sat back, satisfied. "Eustace was utterly charming. Quite artistic, loved to dance, but he was also an astute businessman. I believe he worked for the family firm in the West Indies for a few years before he came out here. He much preferred the excitement of the frontier to the society salons his family favored."

"His family?" Graysie had to admit she hadn't considered Eustace's family. She'd assumed if he was leaving her a mine he didn't have anyone close.

"Like who?"

Pania hesitated. "Honestly, Miss Castellanos, I don't know. He mentioned a sister. I got the impression he was glad to escape his family."

Like me and my stepmother, Graysie thought.

"He was very fond of your mother—they knew each other back in New York. I guess that's why he's left those mine shares to you?"

"I suppose…"

"So, are you still planning to do something with them? You're not selling them?"

Graysie shook her head. "Right now, people think it's washed up. I'd get a poor price and then someone else might make a fortune if it comes good. I want to know its true value. Then I guess I might consider selling.

"That's why I'm here in Grass Valley. To find out more about it and decide what to do. If I can get it to the stage where it's considered a worthwhile investment, I'd have a better place to start from."

Hoping for a supportive comment, she turned to Sir John and caught an impatient scowl crossing his face.

"You work the mine?" said Sir John. "Graysie, anyone who knows anything about the substrate in Grass Valley knows the Ophir wasn't ever much cop, and it's now exhausted. Run out. It's a fool's errand to think it's worth re-opening.

"Eustace was always one for chasing dragons. I hope he hasn't filled your head with unrealistic dreams of getting rich from gold."

She blushed at his bland assumption that she could be easily duped. She took a deep breath, told herself to stay calm, and said, "I've had a look at the prospector's reports the lawyer gave me, and there's good evidence for another rich seam running along the western wall. The question is how difficult it might be to reach."

Sir John gave a grudging nod. "I'm happy to look at the reports for you and give you an opinion, if you wish. But I think Eustace had completely unrealistic ideas about that mine, and I'm sorry you're influenced by them.

"Regardless, it's hardly likely investors would back a young woman—charming as you are, my dear—for such an operation. You'd be much better off considering marriage. That's the only way a woman of station is going to secure her future." He leaned in and topped up Mrs. Hayes' wine glass.

"Wouldn't you agree, Mrs. Hayes?"

Pania took a sip of her wine. "Do you

know, John, as a woman who has made her own fortune—a modest but good fortune—for the last fifteen years, I'd have to disagree. Much as I valued my late husband, knowing I don't have to rely on anyone else does something for a woman's soul."

Graysie saw his face darken with annoyance and warmed with gratitude to the woman bold enough to stand up to him. Maybe she'd found her first ally.

She flashed a smile at Pania and studiously observed the leaves in her teacup in the uncomfortable silence that followed. Maybe despite the Russell brothers' disapproval, her dreams weren't so nonsensical after all.

Eleven

Sunday, July 5

Graysie sat at an oak dining table in a large private room in the Exchange Hotel, sandwiched between Mrs. Marjorie Keegan, a mousy older widow whose conversation was limited to household matters, and the logging magnate Sherwood Sylvester, who was as silent as his trees.

She yearned for her days as a saloon singer, when she was free to choose to chat to whosoever she pleased, though it wasn't at fine dinners like this one.

Candlelight from two six-armed candelabra sparkled on the silver cutlery.

Crystal vases of red and yellow roses from Sir John's garden stood between them, the candles' warmth stirring a subtle fragrance from the cut blooms.

A comforting aroma of roast meat hung in the air, and as the guests tucked into buffalo steaks, a contented murmur filled the room. Sir John certainly knew how to host a dinner party.

Mrs. Hayes filled the role of hostess admirably, greeting the guests at John's side as they arrived, and then taking her place at the opposite end of the table from him, deftly volleying conversation, a shining star in a crimson gown with winged shoulders and a scooped neckline which displayed her sensuous ripe beauty to perfection.

Harvey Miller, the fabulous impresario who could make or break careers with one stroke of his purple-inked pen—and

John's biggest social triumph of the night—sat at Pania's right. Anyone who knew anything about entertainment knew he'd introduced both the 'Swedish Nightingale' Jenny Lind, and Lola Montez, controversial countess and Spanish dancer, to the West.

A flamboyant bear of a man with a well-trimmed beard and spiky sandy hair that stood out from his head, his broad shoulders strained the seams of an immaculately tailored deerskin jacket.

He bubbled with joie de vivre, lifting his glass at regular intervals to offer random good-natured toasts.

Graysie, however, was a faint reflection of her normally resilient self. She'd been tempted to plead a headache and dodge dinner altogether. The events of the past couple of days had taken their toll; her natural buoyancy had deserted her.

She wondered whether she'd ever fit into this kind of life, playing the respectable townswoman, observing convention. Years of being out on her own had left her out of practice as a charming, biddable companion.

The desserts were being served when she realized her fellow guests might hold the answer she was looking for. Many were wealthy, and it sounded like most of them—except for the flamboyant impresario—had a wide range of business interests, from mines to railroads, real estate to ranching. They were the shakers and movers of the Mother Lode region—and she needed to interest one of them in her project.

She stole a look to where Nathan Russell sat, a long way down the table, out of her conversational reach. It occurred to her he'd cheekily asked her why she wasn't married, but she'd not got around to asking him the same thing. And he was a few years older than her, she guessed. That made it even more surprising if there was no wife back home in Sydney.

A pretty doe-eyed brunette was patting his arm, drinking in his every word. He seemed more interested in the businessman seated on his other side, darting quick looks at him and listening in to the man's remarks whenever Miss Doe Eyes fell silent.

She could overhear snatches of their conversation. From what she could pick up, the fellow had made a lot of money in San Francisco real estate. For the first time that night, the tight band across her forehead eased.

Mrs. Keegan had launched into a long complaint about the shortage of fresh vegetables when Sir John's powerful baritone cut her short.

"Miss Castellanos here"—he gestured vaguely in her direction—"has inherited shares in the Ophir mine, but I've been telling her there's no future there. They took out all the ore years ago."

She briefly calculated whether it was worth disagreeing so publicly, and then saw a golden opportunity. She jumped in before she wimped out.

"I fully respect your opinion, Sir John. Of course I do, but the prospector's report paints a brighter picture than you're allowing. Vance Pedersen suggested this mine could hold promise, given the right management."

Sherwood's brother Stephen Sylvester, a prematurely white-haired, beefy man who sat opposite her, stirred in his chair. "Vance Pedersen, ay? Such a shame. He was pretty astute at reading rocks."

She smiled in acknowledgement: Sir John's foray had silenced other talk, and all the dinner guests now sat watching the debate play out.

"I'm hoping to spark interest from investors to get the mine working again," she said with a rush of enthusiasm. "I don't accept that it's washed out. Before I give up, I want to push it further."

Graysie was aware of Hector de Vile's look of cool calculation. As if sensing their host's resistance, Sylvester nodded and said nothing more.

Sir John interjected, switching the subject. "Time for our surprise entertainment before the gentlemen retire for port and cigars."

On cue, Pania Hayes rose and made her way to the corner of the room where

Graysie saw a music stand stood on a small podium. Mrs. Hayes looked around at the seated guests.

"Sir John and I have been friends for a very long time," she said with a brief smile. "I'm delighted to bring you this modest interlude."

Pania's dark eyes rested on Harvey Miller, and her allure again struck Graysie. She wondered for a minute about the relationship between her and John Russell. They were obviously close friends, enjoying one another's company. and Pania appeared happy to act as his hostess.

Had they ever been more than 'just friends' she wondered?

Then, swept along by Pania's stage presence, she had no more time for nosey musings. Assuming a confident singer's stance, her hands clasped above her waist, the star performer launched into a set of popular ballads.

Her voice had a heart-touching resonance, and the guests clapped enthusiastically. She followed up with a tragic aria, the jilted lover lamenting her loss before dying, demonstrating her dramatic range.

She'd impressed Harvey Miller, Graysie could see. At the end of the aria, he gave her a standing ovation before stepping forward to escort her back to her seat. But before he reached her, Sir John interrupted. He clapped his hands for silence, and then inquired, "Miss Castellanos, I know you sing too. Indeed, I understand you're a star in our own right. Won't you grace us with a song?"

The guests around the table stirred, and all eyes focused on her. The attention left her self-conscious, though she knew she looked the part in her elegant, black and white gown set off with an ermine shoulder cape. A gold-coated fir cone around her throat, the only thing left from her mother, was her sole embellishment.

She'd sung on stage hundreds, probably thousands, of times, but the raucous semi-drunk miners and gamblers who usually made up her audience were far less demanding than this wealthy coterie and a famous impresario.

She took a deep breath, stood, and pushed back from the table. "Perhaps Mrs. Hayes would be kind enough to sing a couple of popular ballads with me? There is no way I could match, let alone rival, her superlative performance."

As Graysie walked towards her, she caught Pania's eye and was relieved to see she was regarding her with a welcoming warmth. The opera star leaned forward and kissed her lightly on the cheek, leaving a delicate orange blossom and cologne scent after her.

Back at the table, Mrs. Keegan clapped her hands and cried, "So charming!"

"Delighted, I'm sure," Pania said, laughing as she turned to Graysie and whispered, "Monsieur Miller will love you. It's like the old saying, we're destined to make 'the gay rich and the rich gay', isn't that right?"

Graysie let out a long, calming breath and thanked her lucky stars for a wise female friend.

"Let's do this favorite old folk song— I'm sure you know it." She waved a sheet of music under Graysie's nose.

She'd barely had time to take in what the music was before they launched forth, Pania's rich depth underlying Graysie's pure soprano, instinctively reading each other's body language to exchange parts, Pania taking the verse and then sharing the chorus, and then Graysie taking over the solo on later verses.

"And only say that you'll be mine, and in no other's arms entwined, down beside where the waters flow, down by the banks of the Ohio."

It was as Graysie's angelic top notes overlaid if Pania's earthy, life-imbued accents. Experience and innocence, interweaving and interchanging, first one dominating and then the other.

As they worked through the second song, Graysie's spirits lifted higher than she'd experienced in weeks, even months. Singing with Pania seemed ordained. Their harmonies soared, the ebb and flow of the sound blossoming and then fading away with an inherent sense of rightness.

As the last note died away, they turned and smiled at one another, and then each did a spontaneous bow, first to one another and then the audience, acknowledging the deep satisfaction in their shared song and their excited reception from the table guests.

Harvey Miller, who had been standing off to one side, stepped forward and embraced them, Pania under one arm and Graysie the other.

"What a team!" He beamed and turned towards Sir John, rising from his seat. "Where have you been hiding these gorgeous women? That was truly wonderful. Rivalled anything I've heard since Jenny Lind.

"I think you should develop a duet

program and then do a Sacramento season. That's for starters. What a novelty! Two outstanding talents together on stage, not just one, however admirable. Audiences will love you!"

Before she could respond, John Russell stepped forward.

"I'm so glad you enjoyed hearing my house guests sing, Harvey," he said deliberately. "They've entertained us royally, I agree. But I think you're jumping the gun to assume the ladies can take up your kind offer." He adjusted the silk cravat at his neck, as if he was rearranging protective armor.

"Mrs. Hayes already has a tour booked, I understand. And I believe Miss Castellanos has other plans and responsibilities that prevent her being able to take up your generous invitation."

As Graysie stood, hollowed out and dumbstruck by the magnate's presumption, he edged Harvey aside and placed his hand on the back of her neck. It was warm against her skin. Despite herself, she couldn't help drawing comfort from his strength.

The impulse to let him take over was so strong. He'd stamped a territorial claim on her. That seemed clear. She darted a nervous glance toward Pania. Did she mind?

Was she going to fall quietly into line? Her cheeks flushed hot with shame for even thinking that way.

Russell bent down and whispered, "It's time for the gentlemen to retire for port and for you to entertain the ladies. I'd be most grateful if you could charm Mrs. Sherwood Sylvester. I need her husband to be amenable to my proposals, and it

would help to get onside with his wife."
He raised an eyebrow in a private
gesture of collusion.

Graysie was stunned to discover his
attention flattered, even aroused her, a
blatant declaration of interest registering
in his glittering black eyes. Her eyes
roamed back to where Nathan sat and
she saw he was watching their exchange.

His face bore an unreadable
expression, and for reasons she couldn't
fathom, she blushed again.

*****

Graysie lay back on her primrose yellow
pillows, still in her evening dress, and
tried to make sense of the evening.

After the impromptu recital, she'd
joined the ladies in the drawing room for
tea while the gentlemen continued with
port and cigars in Sir John's bachelor
den. She'd deflected the shower of

effusive compliments towards Pania and prayed Russell's attention hadn't soured their nascent friendship.

"She's the one who held it all together. All I did was add a trill here and there," she told Mrs. Sherwood Sylvester, who fluttered to her side. "Mrs. Hayes is unsurpassed. It's no surprise she has such a flourishing career."

But while she smiled and passed around the tiny madeleine supper cakes, the gaiety of the night passed her by. The success of the music recital had created a cheerful camaraderie. After all, she and Pania had impressed the famous impresario, and John's guests had witnessed his approval.

But as she enjoyed the afterglow of their shared triumph, part of her was somewhere else, trying to make sense of Sir John's actions. Surely, he couldn't have serious intentions towards her? He'd been a bachelor his whole life, and he was much older... She tried to think what age he would be.

He and Eustace had been in business together for many years, and Eustace was forty when he died. That would probably make Sir John around the same age, maybe even older. But it wasn't only because of his age.

He was remote, unreadable. Capable of being charming if he wished, but there was always the sense of some calculated purpose behind his actions. Was he ever spontaneous? Could she trust him?

Until the previous night, she'd got the impression that he regarded her like a distracted uncle might see a distant niece. Now she was clueless. John had some business to attend to after dinner and had returned late, so they'd not seen each other again. Surely, he wouldn't suggest she become his mistress?

Her insides clenched at the thought. But if he helped her... She hardly trusted herself to imagine how the world would open up with the support of someone like Sir John.

With his experience, resources, and business contacts, they could reopen the mine within weeks. But would he? So far. he'd dismissed the idea as outright folly. And he seemed barely to tolerate Minette.

At the thought of Minette, she chilled. She could not imagine the girl being welcomed into this house. And there was still the pall surrounding her disappearance.

She swung off the bed and began undressing. She knew next to nothing about the powerful, enigmatic man giving her shelter, and she would not surrender her determination to live life on her own terms now—she hoped never.

If Harvey Miller was serious about the Sacramento concerts, she would grab the opportunity with both hands, even if it meant risking Sir John's displeasure. It wasn't the life she wanted for Minette in the long term, but she must make her way as best she could in the meantime.

Twelve

Monday, July 6

It did not surprise Nathan Russell to find the Sixways Saloon tables already crowded when he rode up to the notorious gambling house at Town Talk on the Grass Valley-Nevada City road early the following afternoon.

Named Sixways because it sat at the junction of six roads leading to mountain diggings like bustling Gold Flat, the rugged canvas-walled roadhouse was a popular haunt for weary miners who couldn't be bothered making the trip to town.

Some didn't have enough money to

warrant the journey, others lacked a clean jacket or the tidy trousers which were the stipulated dress code in Grass Valley's gambling halls.

Here they could turn up at the end of a working day in their mining gear. As long as their boots weren't dripping with mud and they'd washed their hands, One-Eyed Jack turned his blind eye to tatty trousers. And there were always the undesirables banned from other halls who found their way to the Sixways tables.

It was the sort of dive where a man could end up dumped in an old shaft if he got into an argument; the ideal hangout for a tarred and feathered outcast to lie low and regain her dignity. Nathan was intent on understanding what had really happened with Minette's disappearance, and he was confident

Madam Ring knew a lot more than she'd let on.

It hadn't been difficult to get the Exchange Hotel's cellar man to cough up that she was most likely hiding out at Sixways, after Nathan had threatened to bring Sir John's wrath down on him if he refused to cooperate.

The afternoon was sultry, and thunderstorms threatened. Men looking for an excuse to finish work early were already casting bets at the faro tables. He tied his horse up on a hitching post outside and called over a small boy who was standing in the middle of the crossroad, kicking stones with the toe of his boot.

"Watch the horse for me. Anyone makes a move on it, come and get me straight away." He pressed a gold coin into the astonished boy's hand.

As he entered the saloon, some of the chatter died away and men turned to look him up and down. He knew he looked more like a reverend than a miner in his charcoal coat and well-turned-out trousers and reproached himself for not thinking about how he'd fit in.

Damage done now, he thought, and continued to the back of the bar where a rough-looking man with a patch over one eye perched on a stool surveying the patrons.

"Waddya want? You're not going to cause trouble, are ya?" the man said in a surly tone, while his good eye wandered everywhere but to Nathan.

"Not at all. I'm simply wanting to look up an old acquaintance. Madam Ring."

The man glared and finally gave him his undivided attention. "Who wants to know?"

"Nathan Russell. Sir John's brother." He wasn't sure if name dropping would be an advantage or not, but he plowed on. "I had dealings with the Madam when she was running the Exchange. I helped advise her on certain aspects of her business."

He didn't mention he'd tried to ensure that the girls in the Madam's establishment—many of whom were Chinese with little English and no one to defend them—were being treated and paid fairly.

The man tugged on his right earlobe, as if straining to hear inaudible voices. "So. One-Eyed Jack is asking himself what you want with her now—not that I'm saying she's here, mind. But if she was here, I don't think she'd be wanting visitors from Grass Valley."

"Yes, well, it's in connection with

dealings in Grass Valley that I'm wanting to talk to her. I thought she might be interested in getting her revenge on folks who maybe didn't treat her fairly." Nathan dipped his hand into his silk-lined coat pocket.

"A pint would go down well while you're at it. I'm happy to recompense you for any inconvenience in getting a message to her. One for you and one for her."

He settled on a stool at the bar and watched as One-Eyed Jack poured him an ale and then shuffled to the rear doorway and hailed a bald-headed bruiser of a man. They talked for a few minutes and then disappeared together out the back.

Nathan sipped the beer and waited while the noise of the saloon swelled around him. He'd almost finished his drink when the muscle-bound heavy reappeared alone.

"You the fellow who wanted to see a lady?"

Nathan thought the description debatable, but he didn't argue. He got up and followed Muscle Man through burlap drapes covering a door in the back wall to a second canvas-walled shack. Daylight streamed from greased paper windows into a small room comfortably set up with a bed, table, and two chairs.

Bloated and red-faced, the Madam lay slumped in a chair beside a rumpled bed. One side of her face drooped, and she dribbled from the side of her mouth. But it was her eyes that captured Nathan's attention. They burned with hatred, and she did not disguise it.

He crossed the room and attempted to

shake her right hand, but she stiffened and glared at him. He retreated to a chair placed on the other side of a low table on which sat a tray with a water jug, a glass, and various medicines.

"I'm sorry to see you're unwell, Madam." Nathan broke off as she snarled something incomprehensible. "If you don't mind, I'd like to ask you about the other day. I don't believe you got a fair deal." He might as well have been delivering a divinity lecture to a rabid dog.

"Worried about your girlfriend, are ya?" she retorted. The words came out distorted, but still comprehensible. "You've got good reason to be." She let out a cackling laugh. "He won't let anyone pinch that mine out from under his nose."

Her bitter mirth unsettled Nathan. Who

was she talking about? Not his brother, surely? Had the beating she'd received affected the woman in the head?

"Pinch the mine? I don't understand. What mine? And who are we talking about?"

Before the Madam could answer, Nathan heard a flurry of movement outside and saw a man's shadow on the canvas walls. Madam Ring's eyes widened in terror.

"I knew he'd send them," she whispered. "I knew it."

A shotgun blast reverberated, and Nathan heard a guttural cry as a big man toppled across the threshold, partially blocking the entry, half his head blown away.

The section of scalp that remained intact gleamed with an oiled sheen. The muscle man who'd shown him in here must have been hovering in the entry, eavesdropping.

Nathan reached for the revolver he carried in his boot. It went against his grain to carry a gun, but John had been adamant; it was plain dumb not to be armed in Gold Country, even if it was for protection from snakes or bears.

The Madam sat petrified in her chair, and Nathan realized the seizure had affected more than her face. She could not move; frozen and angry, she sat staring up at the intruder.

"You!" she screamed. "He sent you?"

A big black-bearded man loomed in the entryway, holding a double-barrelled shotgun aimed squarely at Madam Ring.

He pulled the trigger and as the blast reverberated, Nathan dove behind the wide-armed leather chair he'd been sitting in a second before. Madame M's attacker reloaded the shotgun in a brisk snapping move.

The pause gave Nathan his opportunity. He jerked upright, using the chair back for partial cover, and shot straight at the man's chest.

Blood bloomed like an evil flower, and the man staggered. Nathan ducked as the assailant's gun waved wildly and another shot crashed overhead. The noise in the confined space made his ears ring, but the charge flew high and harmless, peppering the canvas with holes. His attacker crashed like an enormous tree and did not move again.

Nathan remained crouched behind the chair for another minute, waiting for someone to come running, but no one did. Three people dead or dying in as many seconds. One of them at his hand. And no one cared.

Nausea overcame him. He bent over and retched several times. Sweat trickled down his neck and back, but his hands were icy.

He couldn't believe how close he'd come to dying. One thing was obvious. Madam M had known her killer, and Nathan was pretty sure he'd been on the man's hit list too.

As the minutes ticked by and his breathing calmed, he reflected on the past few minutes. Had his visit precipitated this attack, or would it have occurred, anyway?

Manic energy washed through him, followed seconds later by a breathless desperation. He'd no choice but to decipher what was going on here, or he was sure more people would die.

Saving his family's fortunes had taken a big back step. He'd worry about that

when he'd stopped the killing. He hoped
his brother Sebastian had a better idea
than he did about where to start.

Thirteen

Nathan pulled up outside the Excelsior Livery Stables in Grass Valley's main street and dropped from his saddle. As he hit the ground, he braced his legs for the impact. When it came, his knees barely held him up. He'd ridden hard to get back to report Madam Ring's execution, and his horse stood, head down, nostrils flaring, and sweaty sides heaving.

He needed someone to walk and water the animal to cool it down safely while he visited the sheriff's office.

A rooster and chickens scratched in the dust. The sun was scorching on his back, but in the shaded stalls he could see horses resting contentedly. He was about to call for attention when a wiry, dark-headed boy he recognized slid out from behind some hay bales.

"Antonio."

Sympathy and guilt spiked within him. It had been a few days since Vance Pedersen's funeral and, despite his assurances, he hadn't been back to check on how the family was making out.

"You're working here now?"

The boy nodded and stepped forward to take hold of Nathan's reins. "I can cool him down for you. How long do you want to leave him for?"

"Not long. I've got some business next door. How are things at home? Neptune still keeping you all in order?"

It was a jocular remark, aimed at establishing common ground, but as soon as the words were out, Nathan realized he'd made a mistake. A huge one.

The boy's head jerked up, and he stared into the yard with devastated eyes. After a long silence, he shook his head and said in a flat voice, "Neptune's dead."

The boy took up the reins and started to walk the horse away.

"Hey, hey, wait a minute. Hold on there."

Antonio paused mid-stride, but kept his eyes averted.

"What do you mean, Neptune's dead? When did that happen?"

Antonio shrugged, as if the world was unfathomable. "He vanished while we were at Uncle V's mass."

His voice was barely a whisper, and Nathan had to lean closer to catch his words.

"We didn't know what happened to him. Where he'd gone. We thought he'd run away, but he never did that. Then yesterday, we found him behind the outhouse, shot dead."

"No." Nathan didn't know what shocked him more, the news of the dog's death, or Antonio's shattered state.

"No," he said again stupidly. "Shot? For goodness' sakes, who'd shoot him? Did the neighbors hate him?"

Antonio shook his head. "They all loved him. No, it must have been the same men who killed Uncle Vance." He tugged at the reins with a grim hopelessness, like a man going to his death. "I'll water your horse."

"Wait. Wait. Why do you say it must have been the men who killed your uncle? We don't have any evidence that anyone deliberately set out to harm him.

It might have been an accident."

Antonio gave him a hard, disbelieving look and spat out three words. "You think so?"

*****

Smells of tomato and pork lard filled Anna Santa Maria's kitchen; a fragrant soup that bubbled on the wood-fired hob gave the house a welcoming air, but the cook herself stood stone-faced, hands on hips, implacable.

After giving his brother Seb the barest account of the deaths at Sixways, Nathan had collected Antonio from the stables and brought him home. Antonio's mother was not pleased to see him.

"I don't want to take this any further, Mr. Russell. We will not waste time looking back. We need to keep going forward. Do you understand?" She stared at Nathan, partly defiant, part imploring. "I can't get involved. I've six children to care for..."

Nathan sighed. "I understand, Anna. Really, I do. Please. Please, let's sit down and take a breath."

He gestured to the table and pulled out a chair and slumped into it. She hesitated and sat down opposite him with a reluctant "humph."

"The children will need to eat shortly. I don't have a lot of time to sit and talk."

"Please, go over with me what happened with Neptune. Antonio says someone shot him?"

She glared at him in a way that said, 'You try raising six children alone,' and his temples flushed hot. It was shameful to be putting this vulnerable woman under extra pressure.

"They shot him inside the house while we were at the funeral. We found blood in the hall when we came home, but we didn't know where it came from. And then almost immediately we realized Neptune wasn't there to greet us. They'd dumped him outside, around the back. I suppose that was to delay us from finding him."

"Was anything missing from the house? Anything stolen?"

She shrugged angrily.

"We've nothing worth stealing. But it's terribly upsetting for the kids. Neptune gave them a sense of safety."

Nathan nodded in agreement. "It's really knocked Antonio, I can see. On top of Vance's death... He's concluded the world is against him. He seems without hope."

Maria sighed. "They were very close. The others are too young to understand much, but he's not. He's convinced it's all part of a bigger plot involving his uncle's enemies. Though who those enemies might be is beyond me. I certainly don't know of any."

Nathan's stomach churned with a bitter queasiness. He thought back to the boy's question on the day of the vigil; if Vance had found out something about someone, would they come after them now?

"Think again, Anna," he said. "Is there anyone Vance disagreed with?"

She shook her head vehemently. "He wouldn't have told me if he did. He believed in protecting his family from worry as much as he could. His whole reason for living was keeping his family safe."

Anna's voice choked, and she got up and attended to the stove. Steam rose as she lifted the lid on a simmering soup and stirred it.

"I told you before. He fought for justice. There's nothing else."

She picked at a fingernail reflectively, as if considering any hint Vance might have given of conflict, and shook her head again, this time more slowly.

"I need to get dinner. There is nothing to be gained from poking around in Vance's affairs. It's likely to bring us more trouble. Stop asking questions, Mr. Russell. And please..." She smoothed her skirt against her thigh nervously. "Please, leave us alone. It's not good for us to be seen talking to you."

With that, she turned her back on him and began ladling soup into the bowls arrayed before her. As he made his way to the door, he spotted Antonio hanging around outside the kitchen, shoulders hunched and his face dark and sulky. He averted his eyes as Nathan walked by.

Fourteen

"Slow down, Nat. Slow down." Sebastian Russell let out an irritated sigh and massaged the bridge of his nose like he was fighting to understand something. His usually cheerful face—hazel eyes, reddish brown hair, lightly freckled, even features—was grim.

Too keyed-up to sit, he stood, one foot resting on a chair, elbow leaning on his thigh, listening to Nathan's account of the killings at Sixways. They were in the modest Sheriff's office next to Seb's rented accommodation.

It was too late to ride out to Sixways tonight and start his investigation, and that made his brother edgy.

Removing his foot from the chair, he paced to the door and back. He was the same kid he'd been when the family split after their father died.

Even as a six-year-old, he'd kept his own counsel, and now that he'd matured, Nathan recognized he possessed a 'still waters run deep' quality about him.

Maybe that was because Sebastian's mother, Honor, daughter of wealthy Boston merchants, had died giving birth to him. For the first year of his life, wet nurses and an amah raised him.

When Nathan's mother Arabella had married Sir Robert Russell, Seb had been a robust, resolute one-year-old who rode rough-shod over adversity, barely acknowledging its existence. At two, he'd already developed a sense of being his own man. He'd stolen Arabella's heart.

Nathan took a deep breath and re-started his tale. "When I got there, everything seemed normal. Everything happened so fast. I got no warning."

He reached down and pulled out the gun he'd used and placed it on the table in front of them.

"He definitely shot at the woman first. That was my good luck. If he'd been gunning for me as his number one target, I'd never have had time to fire."

Nathan slumped into a chair at the table. "I've never killed a man before. It's strange. I'm light-headed or something. I feel weird. Does that seem odd to you?"

Seb shook his head. "Not at all. You never want it not to affect you."

For a few seconds, neither of them spoke. During their long separation, Seb had studied engineering and fought on the Union side in the Civil War. He'd seen more death than Nathan could contemplate, but they hadn't talked about his wartime experiences.

As boys, they'd been inseparable. Like John, Seb hadn't married. Strange about that, Nathan thought fleetingly. Of the three of them, he was the only one who'd married, and he was the youngest.

"So. We've got three people killed. Two by an unknown assailant or assailants, and one by you." Seb recounted the facts as they knew them.

"Right. I don't know how many of them there were. As I say, it happened so fast. But that's not the only death. Someone killed Vance Pedersen's watchdog the night of his funeral.

"Looks like someone broke into the house and butchered the dog so they could look around. That seems proof that Vance's death was no accident, if we needed it."

"When did you hear this?" Seb narrowed his eyes in irritation. "Anna Maria said nothing to me."

"Antonio told me tonight when I left my horse at the stables. They didn't discover the carcass until yesterday. Whoever it was, they dumped Neptune in a ditch out the back. When he wasn't at home, they concluded either someone stole him or he'd had run away."

Seb nodded in agreement. "That certainly reinforces the idea that Vance's death was no accident."

There was a rattle behind them, and John stepped into the office. "Evening, boys. Is what I'm hearing right? Someone's murdered Madam Ring?"

"'Fraid so," said Sebastian. "And

Nathan only narrowly missed joining her."

"Heaven's above!" The older Russell looked from one brother to the other. "Tell me."

They spent the next ten minutes filling him in on the day's events over some good, strong coffee brought in to them by the cleaner.

"I needed that," said Nathan, taking a last appreciative sip and putting his cup back on the serving tray. "Okay, so, Seb, let's get down to business. You've been sniffing around ever since they killed Vance six days ago. What are your conclusions? Let's assume these deaths are related. Who's got the most to gain?"

John cleared his throat and joined in. "If you were making a suspect's list, who'd head it?"

Seb cast a fleeting smile his brother's way. "A rogue version of you, John. Someone with money to burn who's got no scruples and is determined to get their hands on that mine."

Seb got up from his chair, hauled a large piece of slate out of a corner and scrabbled for a piece of white chalk from a nearby shelf.

He wrote numbers across the top and made notations underneath in a bold clear hand: V killed, M abducted, Dog killed, and V house burgled, MM guard and MM killed.

"We've already got quite a list," said Nathan, eyeing his brothers. "You'd have to think whoever it is knows something about that underground real estate—I'm referring to Graysie's mine—that the rest of us are missing. Otherwise, it seems to be an enormous risk for doubtful rewards."

Seb tapped the slate with his chalk to get their attention. "So how many rogue Sir Johns have we got out there?" He regarded his oldest brother with a twinkle in his eye.

John perched on the edge of his chair, tapping his toe in an anxious cadence. He cleared his throat. "First, I assure you again, I've got nothing to do with this mess. I like to win, and I've done plenty of things I'm not proud of, but I draw the line at extortion and murder."

He pulled his mouth down in a sour grimace. "I hope that would be obvious to you two without me having to spell it out, but just in case…"

Seb nodded. "I don't think either of us thought for a minute you'd be involved. But the fact is that the longer this goes on, the more likely it is to be someone like you, pulling the strings," said Seb.

"And they're almost certainly not the ones also pulling the triggers. They're paying someone else to do their dirty work."

Nathan chimed in. "That's exactly what I meant the other night in the hotel when we found Minette. That was all too neat. I suspect someone did the dirty on Madam M and then killed her because they're afraid she'd squeal. The kidnap wasn't her idea, but for whatever reason, she was stupid enough to go along with it."

"Yeah. Think you're right there," said Seb. "And now she's paid the price."

He turned to John. "So, Jonno old boy, you know the territory. Who around here has got plenty of dollars and no scruples?"

Russell grimaced. "As far as money goes—well, quite a few. But having money doesn't make them guilty, surely. I'd be reluctant to comment on their morals."

"You can let us be the judge of that," Nathan said. "Like who? Name names. How about Hector de Vile, for starters? He was very aggressive that morning Minette went missing. Brutal in fact."

John shifted uneasily. "De Vile? I hear he's trying to get to Washington, and he's not stupid. I can't see him risking a national political career as a Senator for a crummy bit of worked-over mine."

"What about Willoughby Martens?"

"What about him? He seems a decent enough chap."

"He's not." Nathan gave John a hard look. "He's an out-and-out crook."

John returned his gaze with a dubious stare. "Since when?"

"Since he swindled twenty thousand

pounds from James Barclay, at Barclay's Investment House. He was Arabella's husband, in case you've forgotten. My stepfather. Jimmy only ever recovered a few hundred of what Martens took. The stress destroyed him."

As Nathan was speaking, John had put a hand up to his eyes, as if to ward off the information being delivered. There was a stunned silence when he'd finished, and then the older man shook his head.

"I had no idea. You're certain of this? You're not being influenced by personal animosity? Martens is your brother-in-law after all,"—his eyebrows curled up as if seeking confirmation of their relationship—"and I gather he's still angry about his sister's death?"

Ice gripped Nathan deep in his gut. His diaphragm locked down so tightly he struggled to breathe. "He said that?"

John nodded. "In passing. He didn't make a big thing of it."

Nathan shook his head in disbelief. "It *is* a big thing. Believe me. None of us have got over it. And he's got completely the wrong story."

John regarded him with a grim twist to his mouth. "It's been tough, I understand that. But I wonder if you're the best judge."

"Obviously you think not." Nathan's throat burned with indignation. He flexed his shoulders to loosen up his rigid posture. He wasn't going to take this conversation any further, or they'd both regret it. Instead, he changed tack.

"Apart from de Vile and Martens. Who else?" He barked the question, unintentionally sounding angry.

John linked and flexed his fingers, the

joints giving a succession of clicking sounds as he manipulated them. "There's any number who would be capable, I suppose. The problem is we don't have a shred of evidence against any of them. Is that right, Sebastian?"

Seb nodded, and Nathan couldn't shake the conviction they were further behind now than when they'd begun.

Fifteen

Tuesday, July 7

Hector de Vile took a slow draw on his finest Cuban and blew a stream of blue smoke in the other man's face. Martens tamped down the boiling anger that rose within him at the Belgian's arrogance. He couldn't allow flushed cheeks to betray his true feelings.

They sat at a table in a quiet corner of the Wolf Creek Hotel at the bottom of Mill Street. It was early, and there was no one else in the bar. The barman had served them a quart each and then disappeared out the back.

A soothing yeasty smell hung in the

air, and the tension in Martens' shoulders momentarily eased, then strained again as de Vile took a long gulp and, stony faced, banged his beer pot down.

"I thought I'd made it clear, Willoughby. I wanted no fuss. No mess. And certainly, no more violent deaths to draw attention. So how is it we've now got the deputy investigating three suspicious deaths—and a near miss on his own brother?"

De Vile cleared his throat angrily and glared at Martens over his half-raised beer mug.

"You've had a full week to get the widow's shares signed up and to find that Pedersen report. Still, we've got no result, and now you've messed up with Russell's annoying brother. If you're not careful, you'll have the deputy on your back sooner than you can draw breath.

"No more bodies, Martens. You hear me? You've got three days to get the business done—the share deal finalised and to find the report. Three days, or our agreement is off. And don't underestimate Nathan Russell."

At the mention of Nathan Russell's name, acid rose in Martens' throat. Memories of the confrontation in the Sydney waterfront office, the humiliation of being walked off the premises, stripped of his keys and his reputation, all because he'd taken a 'temporary loan' from the investment accounts.

He'd fully intended to pay it back. It was all Nathan Russell's fault. He was the one who picked up the discrepancy in the accounts and reported it to his stepfather. If the spoilt boy hadn't ratted on him, his stupid old man wouldn't have been any the wiser.

And Russell wasn't even willing to keep quiet for a cut. What a loser. The guy had no killer instinct.

He cleared his throat and took another sip of beer. "Forget Nathan Russell. He couldn't defend his own grandmother." Or his wife, Martens thought bitterly.

"He accounted for your Sydney Duck, no problem." De Vile pulled on his cigar. "Maybe you should have left that sidekick in the San Francisco stews where he belongs." De Vile leaned back in his chair and picked up his beer again.

Martens relaxed his gritted teeth as pain shot down the side of his face. "Nobody's going to miss those losers up at Sixways. And nothing is going to link their deaths back to us."

"I certainly hope not—not to me, anyway. I'm telling you again. Not to me, they aren't." De Vile raised one eyebrow. "Best you use Weavers for backup from now on. And cover your trail at the mines by lying low, not making headlines."

Martens stood up, propelled by a sudden need to escape. A poison ivy twitch itched in his thighs, and he momentarily wondered if he was breaking out in an aggravated rash.

He would not step back from the Ruby, whatever this domineering foreigner said. It was the best opportunity for easy pickings he'd come across since... well, since Sydney. He'd have to make sure he didn't get caught, that's all.

He hated Nathan Russell more every minute. What kind of bad luck to have him turn up here, on his California patch? Him with his righteous ways and a rich brother to protect him.

He swallowed the burn that flared in his gut at the thought of arrogant mongrels like de Vile who imagined they controlled him, then finished his beer in one long gulp and stood up.

"I'll get Weavers onto it. You'll have what you want by Friday."

*****

A sturdy, companionable housekeeper who identified herself as Mrs. Danville answered Lisette Guilliame's door at Nathan's knock.

They explained briefly who they were and why they were visiting, and she ushered him, along with Graysie and Minette, into a comfortable living room, where a tense, pale young woman met them, a small child hanging from her skirt. She'd dressed all in black, and her forehead wrinkled as she stood to greet them.

Lisette Guilliame was a petite brunette, a young woman who he guessed would once have been described as dainty, but who was now rapidly approaching gaunt. Her shoulder blades poked out from the draped back of her dress as she turned to sit down.

A portrait of a strong-featured man with a decisive jaw, its oval shape framed by a bay leaf wreath, hung above the fireplace, and black fringing draped the arms of the sofa and chairs.

The blooming woman he spotted in a wedding portrait on the other wall had vanished. Too many tearful nights had left tight, tired lines around her eyes. The child, a teddy bear dangling from one hand, regarded Nathan warily.

They quickly exchanged handshakes, and Graysie handed the young widow a bunch of white roses she'd cut from the

Gold House garden.

"With our sincerest condolences for your loss," she murmured. "I'm so sorry to intrude at a time like this, but I believe we have urgent mutual interests."

Lisette hesitated in surprise and then bent down to the little girl at her side. "Seraphine—this is Minette," she said in a half whisper. "Why don't you take her to play with your dolls in your room?"

The two little girls considered each other for a few seconds, and then Seraphine smiled, took Minette's hand and led her out of the sitting room.

Graysie turned as if to follow them and then checked herself. "They won't go outside, will they? I want them close, within hearing."

Lisette shook her head. "They'll stay in the room next door." She sighed.

"Andre's death's been such a dreadful shock. We hardly leave the house. We have no family here…" As she gestured for them to sit, as her voice, lightly accented with her original French, trailed off.

"We won't impose, Mrs. Guilliame. We're grateful you're willing to see us," said Nathan.

Lisette Guilliame gulped in a breath and gave him a brave smile. "Thank you, Mr. Russell. Andre's death has turned our lives upside down, but I must carry on for the sake of my daughter. That's what Andre would have wanted. However, I'm sure you're not here to talk about that."

Nathan nodded in sympathetic agreement. "If you're able, we'd like to talk to you about the Ruby Mine. I understand your husband was managing the operation. Miss Castellanos has inherited the Ophir next door, and we're wondering what's been happening with the Ruby over the last six months."

Mrs. Guilliame sighed. "That mine! Sometimes I wish Andre had never laid eyes on it. He did well out of it at first. I appreciate that. If only he wasn't in the mine the day the timbers caved in…"

"Oh, I'm sorry. I didn't know…"

Nathan wished he'd taken the time to make himself better informed, but Lisette Guilliame took no offense.

"Oh, he didn't die down there, but he got a bad leg fracture that became infected. He died from complications several months later."

Graysie cleared her throat. "Things hadn't been going so well at the mine, is that right?" she said with a sympathetic smile

Lisette Guilliame nodded. "Not for a year or more. The ore Andre was getting was of poor quality. It wasn't paying enough to cover the costs of extracting it. Then his manager left, and he couldn't afford to replace him, so he filled in himself.

"He couldn't afford to do the maintenance that was needed. In the end, the tunnel supports gave way. Andre was standing underneath when they did. His injury confined him to bed for weeks. We couldn't pay the workers, so we had no choice but to close the mine."

Nathan nodded in understanding. "What will you do? Would you consider selling up?"

Lisette fingered the black fringe on the sofa arm nervously. "To tell you the truth, Mr. Russell, I've already had an approach from the man who used to manage the mine for us. Andre owned a majority share, but there is one other shareholder—the manager I spoke of who left us more than a year ago. Octavius Weavers.”

Mrs Danvers, who arrived with a tray of steaming coffee and biscuits, momentarily interrupted Lisette’s account. “I thought you’d appreciate refreshments for your guests, Mrs G,” she said, and hesitated as she set it down. “Would you like me to pour?”

“That would be marvellous. Thanks Mrs Danvers.” She lifted her eyes to Graysie and said, “Forgive me. I’ve been forgetting my manners. We’ve not had any visitors in weeks.”

They settled in with their coffee, and Nathan brought the conversation back on track.

"You were explaining about Mr Weavers getting shares?"

Lisette's face clouded over, and then her expression sharpened.

"Of course," she said, her voice brighter than before. "He accepted mine shares instead of wages for a time. We couldn't afford to pay him, so Andre kept giving him more shares. By the time he left, he owned thirty-three percent of the Ruby.

"Now I'm worried he is going to sell his share and leave me exposed. I can't do anything with the mine myself. I want to sell up here and go home to France, where Seraphine can be with her grandparents and cousins."

Her breath quickened, and Russell noticed a fine sheen of perspiration on her cheeks and forehead.

"Lately, this Weavers fellow has been

badgering me. He tells me the mine is worthless. That my shares are good-for-nothing. I could light fires with them, he jeers."

She wrung her hands together and threw an appealing gaze at Graysie and then Nathan.

"He says I'd be wise to sell them for what I can get. He also claims he's got someone interested in buying them, but he won't say who. And when I said I didn't think he was offering was enough, he got nasty. He hinted I should be grateful for the offer, or I might be sorry."

Nathan interrupted. "You have no notion who this mystery buyer is?"

Lisette shook her head.

"Weavers says the buyer insists on anonymity," She put her coffee cup down with a clatter, irritated by some memory which had come to mind.

"It is so difficult, no, to decide? Andre certainly believed the mine was worth a good deal more than what I've been offered."

Nathan nodded. "And to be clear—this secretive purchaser is also buying Weavers' shares, so whoever it is will own one hundred percent?"

"I understand so, yes," she said.

"Doesn't that compromise Weavers in negotiating a sale on your behalf? What's stopping from him getting a good price for himself and then pushing you to accept a lot less? You can see that an unscrupulous buyer might suggest to Weavers that if he got you to settle for a cheap price, he'd get a bonus?"

Her eyes widened in sudden comprehension. "You know I hadn't thought of it that way... but you are right, of course. I've had such an awful *sensibilité* about this whole thing."

Lisette placed her hand over her heart, as if even discussing the subject pained her.

"And then for him to hint something horrible might happen to us if we stayed here much longer... It's as if he's trying to frighten me into taking the money and disappearing."

Nathan's heart thumped so loudly it was knocking against his rib cage. "But no one in Grass Valley would intend you or Seraphine harm?"

Lisette Guilliame darted an uncertain glance at Graysie, and when she spoke next, it was much more quietly. "It is safe to mention this, yes?"

When Graysie nodded, she said in a whisper, "He said I should be careful, or the same thing might happen to

Seraphine that happened to your little girl… Except I wouldn't get Seraphine back."

"No!" Graysie half rose in shock and took a few steps towards the door, then pivoted and paced back. "I can't believe… Is it possible…?"

Nathan stood and led her back to the sofa where she'd sat before. She slowly sank back down.

"When was this?" he asked.

"This morning. He has called before, but he was furieux—furious—today. He said the buyer was losing patience."

Nathan had the sensation of things moving too fast to process. His pulse was racing like it did after a long sprint. The chatter of childish giggling sounded through the wall. At least the girls were having a good time.

Even as he listened to their childish

delight, Nathan's stomach cramped tight. There was nothing random about the hit on the hotelier and he'd asked himself if he'd unwittingly led the assassin to Madam Ring's hiding place?

Now it struck him like a thunderclap.

What if by coming here, I've led the killers to Lisette Guilliame's door?

He turned to the French widow. "Mrs Guilliame, could I ask you, did you commission anyone to do a report on the Ruby recently?"

Lisette Guilliame ran her hands through her hair with a distracted air. "Report? No. Nothing like that. Why?"

Nathan looked at Graysie and shook his head. "I was wondering, that's all. No real reason."

No point in making her more anxious. But he was certain he'd guessed the relevance of Vance Pedersen's last whispered words. Not Ruth, but Ruby. It wasn't a woman he was remembering; it was a mine.

Sixteen

"You what?" John Russell lowered the double-barrelled shotgun he'd raised to fire and stared at Nathan, who was standing outside the low fenced circle that marked the boundary of the shooting range. Vulcan was one of the two French hounds that circled them with excited yaps, eager for the chance to collect killed or wounded birds.

"I called on the French widow who owns sixty-seven percent of the Ruby mine this morning. She's under a lot of pressure from Octavius Weavers to sell cheap to a mystery buyer. He threatened to make her daughter 'disappear' like Minette."

"He what?" John's head jerked back and his entire frame stiffened. He gave a low whistle. "Unbelievable."

A thin, grubby boy of eleven or twelve crouched a few feet away with a rock pigeon cupped in his hands, ready to release it on command.

"Hold the bird, boy."

John leaned his gun up against the fence and stepped out of the shooting circle. The dogs followed excitedly, and Vulcan nudged Nathan's hand. He stroked the hound's silky head as he waited for his brother to respond.

John's reluctance last night to believe that Willoughby Martens was a fraudster was still a kick in the guts, but over the last few days Nathan had sensed a reawakening of the bonds formed during their Hong Kong years. Thanks to Arabella. She'd a motherly instinct that defused their petty rivalries and had drawn them all together, and Nathan knew John still thought highly of her.

John's brow contracted in a worried frown. "Is that right? He said what exactly?"

"That she'd better be careful or her girl would disappear 'like yours', but she wouldn't be so lucky. She wouldn't come back."

John stabbed at the ground in front of him with the toe of his riding boot. "If that's how it is, she needs protection. I'm still trying to process the implication that they kidnapped Minette. That there was no mistake, like someone accidentally leaving a door open."

Nathan nodded. "The other thing is, I think I know what Vance Pedersen's last words were. Graysie heard him whisper something that sounded like a woman's name—Ruth or Ruby, she thought.

"It should have occurred to me earlier than this, but I bet it was the Ruby mine he was thinking about. He said Ruby. And I'd wager his death has something to do with that mine as well."

"I respect your instincts, Nathan, I really do... but... I wonder if the upheavals you've suffered these last twelve months or so..." He put one foot up on the lower rung of the wooden fence and gazed over the field.

"Well, I hate to say it, old boy, but have they affected your judgment? This all seems so far-fetched."

A familiar anger burned in the pit of his stomach, but Nathan fought to keep his voice low and controlled.

"Upheavals? We're not back on this tack, are we, John? First, isn't it more about you not wanting to give up on your dealings with Martens, in case you lose a few precious dollars?"

John blanched. "Now steady on, old chap. That's not fair."

"Isn't it?" Nathan's blood was roaring in his ears, the rage dictating his words. "What's not fair is you hinting that I'm unstable. You're suggesting you can't trust my judgment? Jim dismissed Martens for embezzlement. Why would you want to do business with a man like that?"

He clenched his fists and turned sharply away so his brother wouldn't see his deep hurt. When he'd recovered his equilibrium, he swung back to stare John down.

"No, old boy, neither the deaths of my wife and son nor my stepfather's suicide unhinged my judgment." He spat the words out.

"The things I've gone through have

forced the carefree adventurer to grow up faster than he might otherwise have done. And maybe made me appreciate life more. Having a shotgun leveled at your chest does that for a man."

John shrugged and shoved his hands in his pockets. "I'm not trying to minimize what you've been through, Nathan, believe me. And I take your point about Martens. You're right."

Nathan let another half minute lapse and added, "When I think it could be a woman or child facing that gun... Well, it doesn't bear thinking about."

John flicked at a beetle that had landed on the sleeve of his coat. The day was fast heating, and grass flies buzzed around their faces. "Do you really think it could come to that? Because if you do, then yes, I agree. We must do something."

Nathan picked up a stick Vulcan had dropped at his feet and threw it down into the orchard. Both dogs took off in a rush to chase it.

John watched the animals, tails waving, for a minute or two, deep in thought. Then he turned and stepped over the fence, back into the ring. He took a stance with his gun pointed skyward and yelled, "Boy! Release!"

The boy leapt up, twirling on his toes as he lifted the bird into the air and released it. A plump blue-feathered pigeon flapped energetically, rising fast before momentarily pausing in flight to sense the direction of the sun.

Two shots in quick succession set off an alarmed clamor from the pheasants in the nearby field as the pigeon fell with a plop to the grass inside the circle.

"Release!"

In quick succession, the boy released four more birds from a lidded basket at his feet, and four more birds landed within the circle. As the fifth bird dropped, John lowered his gun with a satisfied grin. As if on cue, the dogs loped over to the dead and dying birds. Gathering them one at a time in their mouths, they returned them to the boy, who put them in the basket as John watched.

"Take them to the kitchen, Jeb," he instructed, as he turned back to Nathan. "Why don't you go visit Willie Watson? He knows more about the old mines around here than anyone, except maybe Vance.

"He might have a clue what's going on. But be careful, Nathan. Why don't you take Vulcan with you? He's taken a shine to you, and he might be useful. And make sure you're armed."

He wandered over to Nathan and punched him affectionately on the shoulder. "Look, I respect your judgment. The things that are going on—it's hard to understand why a clapped-out mine could be so desirable. But let's not allow that to stop us from reconnecting."

He turned towards the house and gestured for Nathan to precede him up the path. "We're only coming to know each other again after all these years. I'd hate to lose that after having so recently found it once more. Now let's have some pigeon pie for lunch."

Seventeen

Straight after lunch, Nathan loaded a jubilant Vulcan in the buggy and headed up the mountain road to Willie Watson's cabin, but the place was deserted. He'd have to try him again later. He decided he'd take a poke at Octavius Weavers, the middleman who'd been pressing Lisette Guilliame to sell cheap, instead.

Half an hour later, he arrived at Burnadetti and Co., the local assay house which combined selling mining supplies with analyzing and transporting gold. Weavers was a burly man with a pugnacious manner, and he wasn't happy when Nathan turned up at his workplace.

"I don't care who you are, I can't talk now," he snarled when Nathan told him he wanted to ask him about the Ruby. "I've got work to do. And the Ruby is none of your business."

Nathan skewered him with an intense stare. "It is if I want to buy shares. Or would you rather I spoke to the Widow Guilliame directly?"

Weavers narrowed his eyes and pivoted on his heel and left the room. Nathan could hear him yelling at someone in the back office. "I've got some business down the street, Xavier. Keep an eye out front, will you?" He grabbed up his hat, stepped around Nathan and shouldered his way through, throwing his voice back as he shouldered the door. "You coming or not?"

They entered a nearby billiards saloon and settled at the end of the bar farthest away from the felt-covered gaming tables and were immediately delivered with beer by the idle barman.

Weavers took his first sip, brought his head up and glared belligerently. "So, what about the Ruby? What's it to you? And who wants to know?"

"My name is Nathan Russell, brother of Sir John, visiting from Australia. I've mined in Aussie, so I've got a special interest.

"And I hear on the grapevine there could be Ruby Mine shares coming up for sale. First, is that correct?"

Weavers' pale eyes glittered, and he took his time to answer, as if calculating his best advantage. Then he shook his head

"No. You're too late. They're all spoken for."

"Oh, no? You're talking about yours,

right? What about the French widow's lot? Are they still available?"

Weavers stiffened. "That same gentleman who's buying mine has already spoken for hers, too. I don't even know who he is. Probably an out-of-towner. He's got an agent working on his behalf, he has."

Nathan nodded, seeming to go along with it all. "I see. And you're satisfied with the price? 'Cause the mine ran out of ore, the way I heard it. It hasn't been working for nearly a year. But you'd know that, because that's how you got the shares in the first place, isn't it? Guilliame couldn't afford to pay you."

"That's right. But there're things down there he didn't know about, ain't there? I had time to look into it good and proper. Reckon you could get a good deal more out of that property than the Frenchie was."

"Oh Yes? Sounds good."

Nathan made a show of taking notes in a small notebook he pulled from his coat pocket, along with a stubby pencil. Weavers frowned and bit his lip. "What are you doing?"

"Oh, making a few notes about the potential value for when I see the widow. If your shares aren't available, then I'll need to make her an offer instead, won't I?"

"No, you can't do that... I mean, she's in mourning and everything. She's asked me to deal with the sale for her. And as I say, the interested party wants hers as well, so there isn't anything left to buy."

Nathan ignored him and stared at a spot beyond the edge of the table they sat at, as if he was already figuring how much he would need to invest to get things going.

"How many men did you have working it when you were the mine manager? I'm trying to figure costs."

Weavers bristled. "I told you, it's not for sale. Someone has already made an excellent offer that we've—me and her—accepted."

Nathan stared at him with studied disbelief. "Oh, come now, Mr. Weavers, you're a smart man. You've been around in business. You know the deal isn't done till the money changes hands. What if I want the Ruby so much I'm willing to pay more than this cove you're talking to? You wouldn't turn down good money, would you?

"You certainly shouldn't be turning it down on the widow's behalf—Lord knows she'll be needing every penny she can get, being without her husband and with a child and all..."

He smiled, as if taking Weavers into his confidence. "Course I'd need to know who the other shareholder is. Can't go into business with an invisible man. And actually, between you and me, I prefer having the controlling interest. Means I can have the run of it without having to pay up the full hundred percent for it, doesn't it?"

Nathan faked looking pleased with himself and suppressed a grin when Weavers turned beet-faced. Beads of nervous sweat broke out on the other man's forehead.

"No, I've told you. You can't buy any part of the Ruby Mine. It's already sold. Haven't I made myself clear?" His vehement spittle sprayed onto the table. He stood and pushed his stool back so violently it crashed to the floor behind him.

Nathan acted amazed. "Mr. Weavers, I don't understand. What man would turn down a competitive offer on mine shares? What's going on? And I wonder what Mrs. Guilliame will think?"

Weavers was striding for the door. He stopped dead in his tracks and swung around. "Mrs. Guilliame? What do you mean Mrs. Guilliame? I told you, she can't be upset. She's in mourning. And she's quite happy with the arrangements."

Nathan assumed a man of the world stance and spread his arms wide. "She might be quite happy because you haven't told her the full story. I bet she won't be so happy when she hears you are refusing to accept a better offer. The question I'm asking myself is why?"

Eighteen

Graysie was silent as Nathan drove her wagon back up the winding mountain road to Gold House, Minette perched on the front bench seat between them. Vulcan rode shotgun in the back, scampering from one side to the other with his tongue lolling out as they ascended the crest of the ridge, his claws clicking and sliding on the floorboards as they climbed.

She smiled to herself. The dog brought a bright spot to their days, making them all laugh with his mischief. The day before, he'd narrowly failed to steal a leg of ham when Mrs Snively's back was turned.

He adored Nathan, and he'd extended his affection to Minette as well, playing happily with her and her new friend Seraphine in Lisette's garden that afternoon, under the watchful eye of the housekeeper.

They'd returned to the Guilliame home because the girls got on so well together and it was a real treat for both of them to have a playmate, but Nathan had also wanted to check on Lisette's safety.

The afternoon sun cast filtered golden stripes across the narrowing gravel path up to the house. It was a warm, settled afternoon, but after talking with Lisette, Graysie's nerves were on edge.

Lisette's description of Weavers' bullying, of how he now swaggered about, a different man from when he was her husband's manager, left Graysie uneasy.

Who's pulling his strings?

What did it say in Proverbs? 'Under three things the earth trembles, under four it cannot bear up; a servant who becomes king, an overbearing fool who prospers…'

Funny the things you remember.

Without wanting them to, her thoughts turned to Nathan. Even in a basic workman's jacket and pants, Nathan was easy on the eye. For a moment she allowed herself to contemplate his strong profile, his capable hands relaxed around the reins as he guided the mare up the little-used road.

Most of the vehicles that came this way were headed for Sir John Russell's estate, so there were only a few other vehicles to be concerned about.

Nathan appeared his usual calm self, his face giving no sign of disquiet, but

Graysie guessed he was good at hiding his anxiety. She'd sensed his indignation when he'd related to Lisette the conversation he'd had with Weavers.

Graysie was grateful he left off interrogating her on her plans like he'd done at their first meeting. When he didn't tell her what to do, he radiated an allure like nothing she'd ever experienced.

There was something irresistible about his soulful decency and the impish grin that refused to take himself—or anyone else—too seriously. And it touched her how much attention he paid to Lisette's situation. After his talk with John, the two men had insisted on organising a minder to protect Lisette and Seraphine from further harassment.

They had rounded a gentle bend half a mile from home when she jolted forward so violently she almost slid off her seat. The docile mare up front reared in alarm, shrieking in a high-pitched squeal that set Graysie's nerves jangling.

The horse tumbled forward, collapsing onto her knees. The wagon's forward momentum continued, the front board barrelling into the mare's hindquarters, causing her to cry again in terror and struggle to get up.

On instinct, Graysie braced Minette with her right arm to stop her from sliding off the seat while grasping the buggy side with her left to stop them both from pitching out onto the road.

They slid to a stop, the horse still thrashing under them. She could see the mare's right leg was red and bleeding, with a wound that had bared the bone right down the shin.

Nathan jumped down and ran forward,

grabbing the horse by the halter and stroking her neck to calm her. Coiled wire glinted in the dust. Nathan reached for the gun at his belt as a man's voice cut through the cloudy air.

"Hands up. Now."

A bulky, broad-shouldered man with a scarf tied across the lower half of his face stepped onto the road from the forested margin, holding a shotgun determinedly out in front of him.

Nathan turned to her, his eyes raking her face. "Run. Now." His words came in a low rush, but she couldn't move. She was stuck, draped against the back of the seat in a tipsy-looking sprawl, Minette whimpering beside her.

The scarf-clad man thrust the barrel hard into Nathan's back.

"I said get them up," he yelled.

As Graysie half lay dumb and petrified,

a second man emerged from the shadows and, in a couple of strides, was at her side. Dirty blonde hair hung over feral features in greasy hanks. The unwholesome stench of rotten meat and stale body odor hit the back of her throat as he grabbed her arm and twisted it up behind her back.

The thought that Vulcan might launch himself from the wagon galvanised her. "Go home, Vulcan. Go home." She was begging.

Her foul-smelling attacker pulled her close. As he lent over to hiss into her ear, she caught the whiff of wild pig and whiskey.

"Behave yerself and yer won't get hurt."

He prodded her with a revolver while snatching at Minette with his other hand.

"Yer coming with me," he snarled, and

dragged the girl wailing behind them.

Graysie was craning to see where Nathan was being taken, but her captor propelled her roughly away into the forest on the opposite side of the road. She stumbled over tree roots as they made their precarious way down the side of a steep gully.

Halfway down, the bandit let go of Minette, grabbed Graysie by the throat, and pushed her hard against a tree trunk. His body pressed into hers. With a nasty laugh, he hauled a coil of rope from his belt.

Within seconds, he'd looped it around her and the tree and lashed her there. A few seconds more, and he'd bound her wrists together in front of her.

"Try anything funny and the kid gets hurt… And then you do, too." He leered at her, and his mouth, with its few remaining nicotine-stained teeth, yawned open.

"I wouldn't mind that," he jeered. "But for now, we've got to silence that pretty little mouth." He whipped a gag out of his fringed pocket and tied it around Graysie's lower face so tightly she felt like she was suffocating.

"I'll be back—if the bears and wolves don't find you first, that is."

He grabbed Minette and tied her hands and feet, but he didn't gag her; instead he allowed her to drop to the ground at Graysie's feet. Then he left as abruptly as he'd appeared.

In the silence that followed, she thought she heard muffled curses. They were taking Nathan away, she supposed. Then all was silent, pregnantly so, as if the forest was holding its breath, awaiting the next catastrophe. The lengthening shadows loomed across the track, warning her not to cross them.

It was hard to breathe with the gag on, and she fought for air so she wouldn't faint. She wanted to stay alert to protect Minette, even though she knew in the state she was in, she was helpless.

She was about to drop into a light-headed swoon when she heard a noisy rustling in the trees on the ridge above. Not a bear, she prayed. Or wolves. Please God. She peered into the dusk in terror.

Then, bounding towards her, she saw Vulcan's joyous white and brown head, tongue lolling, jaws drooling. Normally she would baulk at a slobbering dog. Right now, it was one of the sweetest sights on earth.

Minette sat up with a start and cried softly, "Vulcan! You came back!"

Graysie gave a great gulp of relief through her gag as Vulcan stopped in delight and then, head raised, bounded over to Minette and danced around her, going down on his front legs before her as if inviting her to play.

Minette laughed in delight. Vulcan seemed to sense she could not pat him in the usual way. He rolled herself close into Minette's side and snuggled there, paws out in front, happily panting.

For no good reason, the dog's arrival awakened her hope.

They would get through this. They would not sit waiting for some wild animal to find them or for their attackers to return. She hummed one of Minette's favorite nursery songs, "Frere Jacques. Frere Jacques. Dormez vous? Are you sleeping, are you sleeping, Brother John? Brother John?"

How many times had she quietly sung this lullaby to the child as she was falling asleep? Long before she'd become her guardian, Graysie had helped Francine when she'd needed a babysitter. Now the song took on a new purpose.

Through her gag, she crooned the well-known tune. Minette picked up her challenge and began repeating the words in her dulcet, faintly lisping child's voice: "Sonnez les matines... Sonnez les matines... Ring the morning bells! Ring the morning bells! Ding, dang, dong. Ding, dang, dong."

She thanked God they hadn't gagged Minette. As she bent down to nuzzle the top of the little girl's head with her tied-up face, the last rays of sunlight lit on a jagged rock lying by Minette's feet.

She strained against the rope around her middle, working her body from side to side until it slacked off enough for her to slide down the tree bole, within grasping distance.

Leaning forward, Graysie picked it up with her still-bound hands and gestured for Minette to get into a position where she could work on the ropes that bound the child's feet. She perched on top of some fallen logs to get within Graysie's reach.

Graysie had to move with care to avoid scratching her delicate skin, and by the time the cords severed, the temperature in the forest had dropped with the sun, and Minette was shivering. But all the way through the exhausting exercise, Graysie hummed nursery tunes and Minette took up her lead and sang along quietly.

At last, she'd freed Minette's legs and hands, and the child set to work feverishly, pulling at the knotted rope that bound Graysie to the tree. Her fingers were tiny but nimble, and before long, she'd freed first the ropes and then the gag.

With her hands and feet still tied, Graysie clumsily hugged Minette to her and ran her mouth over her hairline, dotting little kisses at the point where her dark curls crowded over her perfect, plump little face. How precious this child was to her! And what a lot she'd already suffered!

Graysie laughed and whispered to her, "We're going to be fine, my darling. You know that, don't you? We're going to be wonderful." And kissed her again. Then she held her hands out in front of her and said, "Get that rock I used to cut your ropes, and I'll go to work here."

Minette eagerly retrieved the stone.

Graysie placed it at an angle jammed in a crevice so its most jagged edge was upright and facing out of the boulder. She began sawing her wrist bands against it and, within a short time, the rope frayed and gave way.

With her hands free, she cut the ties around her ankles. She stood and exulted in the pins and needles sensation as blood rushed through her cramped muscles. Then, with Minette on her hip and Vulcan loping alongside, she started back to the wagon.

It took only minutes, and they were there. Concealed in the trees, with her hand firmly on the dog's neck to stop him from darting out and revealing their position, she watched.

The horse, barely alive but still panicked, lay hitched in the wagon shafts, her big brown eyes rolling in distress. Graysie waited, searching the dark spaces between the trees opposite for any sign of her attackers, but saw nothing.

Finally, satisfied she was alone, she stepped out onto the road. As she worked to release the trapped horse from the wagon shafts, her eye caught Vulcan dancing back and forth in his familiar come and play dance. Between each little bob, he was tugging at Minette's skirt, nudging her down the track where Nathan had probably disappeared.

She ran over to restrain him and saw beneath her feet a trail of blood drops. The dog was working on a regular pattern—putting his nose to the ground to sniff and then dancing and tugging at Minette's skirt.

I'll be darned if the animal isn't telling

us where Nathan is. He wants to take us to him.

Darting back to the wagon, she retrieved the bag with her pearl-handled revolver. She settled Minette onto the wagon floor with the quilt and the music box she always carried for emergencies. "You stay here, darling, safe and sound. Vulcan is going to show me where Mr. Nathan is, and he'll come back to take us home."

She thought of the times when she was only a little older than Minette, and her father had comforted her when she was frightened. One memory shone in the darkness, the day when flood waters swept away their wagon at a river crossing late one afternoon and they'd barely escaped with their lives.

"Time for one quick bedtime story," she said. "My papa always said in tough times we need to look for the dove whose wings are sheathed in silver and its feathers in shining gold."

Minette smiled and echoed her with a giggle. "A dove with silver wings?"

"That's right. A dove with silver wings and gold feathers. Keep your eyes open. She'll be around here somewhere."

"Really?" said Minette, a surge of interest in her high-pitched little voice. "Somewhere near?"

"Yes, my darling girl. Even when we're sleeping around the campfire, lost in faraway dreams, God is up and fighting our battles for us. He's already preparing the victory for the morning. That's what it says in Psalm 68."

Minette peered up at her, her face shining. Graysie could see her eyes were heavy. She sat with her, stroking her head gently, whispering about the silver-winged dove, which was God's sign of protection, until she fell asleep.

She'd no idea if Nathan was still alive, but she owed it to him to find out. She gave Minette one last loving pat and tiptoed off down the forest trail, following Vulcan's waving tail.

Nineteen

He heard children's lilting, excited voices... Nathan struggled to open his eyes and see who was calling to him. Through a mist he saw them, a long way away in a sunlit clearing, a little girl and a smaller, much younger child, a boy, hand in hand, tripping close to the banks of a rippling stream. No... Don't go too close. It's dangerous!

He stretched out his arm to reach them, but they were too far away for him to save them. He struggled to rise, but his legs were unresponsive, like heavy logs. A corrosive, strangling cry came from deep in his throat; he was gasping... He could taste blood.

His eyes opened in a shocking rush. The stream of his imaginings was real, and bubbling close by, but the children— he knew in his bones they were Minette and his son, Joshua—were gone.

Sharp pain stabbed his side. Craning his head, he saw where his shirt hung off his body, red and shredded. One side of his face throbbed, his eye swollen shut. He struggled to rise, and that's when he remembered.

They'd splayed his feet and hands out at diagonal angles, stretched uncomfortably tight and tied to stakes driven into the valley dirt. He collapsed back, staring up into a canopy of branches.

Octavius Weavers had been straightforward about Nathan's intended fate, and business-like in its delivery. A beating to incapacitate him, and then left for the predators—bears or wolves—to find and feed on him. What they left wouldn't be recognizable.

"So no one comes looking for your killer, see," he'd sneered. "Boss wouldn't be happy if they came looking."

Nathan did not know how long he'd been unconscious, but the blood on his face was hard and congealed. From that and the slant of the daylight through the forest canopy, he guessed they'd pegged there him here at least a couple of hours ago.

He sagged into the soft dirt, recalling the hijack, the rough way the men had handled Graysie and Minette. Where were they now, and how were they faring?

He gritted his teeth as he silently berated himself for failing to keep them safe. That dream or vision or whatever he'd had of the children. Please God, don't let that mean they're both dead.

A sharp sting pierced his abdomen. It lingered, like a painful note, so enduring, he suppressed a cry. Ants. Black carnivorous ants. He'd seen the beasts in the wild, swarming over fresh meat. The predator vanguard had arrived. He squeezed his eyes tightly shut and tried to think of something pleasant.

Graysie Castellanos rose in his mind. What a waste. Would he ever see her again? Seductive, indomitable Graysie. He focused on remembering her finely chiseled face. The violet-shot green eyes, sun-kissed hair, the tilt of her lips. The sweetness of the image faded around the edges. He was slipping away.

He fought to stay conscious, but the mist was back, and the children with it. He took Graysie's arm, and with the children dancing alongside them, they began a slow walk towards sunlight. An overwhelming sense of warmth and rightness flooded out the pain.

He jerked awake, instantly fully conscious of the dim light and something wet licking his face. A tongue, a sloppy tongue. His heart stopped, and he screamed a sharp cry of alarm.

He forced his good eye open and then he saw Vulcan, a delighted, slobbering incarnation, elated to have found him.

He laughed, and once he'd started, he couldn't stop.

I must be hysterical.

His circumstances were still dire, but his relief at not looking into a brown bear's pointed snout was so great it needed release.

Every time his laughter died down, it bubbled up again. He was laughing for no particular reason, he decided, except that he was still alive and he could do it.

*****

Graysie peered through the dim late afternoon light, searching for the flag-waving tail she'd followed deep into the valley. If she lost sight of the hound, as sometimes happened on a tight corner, the dog doubled back to ensure she was still there, but this time Vulcan had been gone for longer than usual.

To free her movement, she'd tucked her multi-layered muslin skirt up into the ribbon tie at her waist, and as she ran she thanked her creator she wasn't wearing a more formal day dress. That would have made it near impossible to scamper along this forest trail behind a dog.

The faint chirps of birds settling for the night were the only sounds in the cooling air, heavy with the fragrance of damp earth and decaying leaves.

They had scrambled deeper and deeper into the forest, descending gradually at first and then more sharply into a steep-sided canyon.

Graysie heard water gurgling over rocks as they worked their way down, getting louder as they descended.

The half-light upset her sense of balance, but there was still enough illumination to see places where heavy boots had crushed grasses on the trail edge, the imprint clearly delineated, and she spotted animal scat—the pebbles of mountain sheep probably—as she moved onward. She didn't want to think of what other animals might lurk in the gloaming.

She'd surveyed her surroundings and wondered if she should go on without Vulcan's lead when she spotted his white and brown form bounding towards her.

She could have sworn he was smiling, and he gave a little yipping bark of welcome. He rushed on ahead of her, as if reassuring her they were on the right path. The trail was bottoming out, the chuckling of the stream growing louder by the minute.

Vulcan had come to another halt, and when she peered at him to see why, she gasped. A man lay spread-eagled, tethered to stakes, in the middle of the clearing. She rushed forward, aghast at what she would find. As she crashed to her knees at his side, he opened the one eye he could see out of and gave a laconic smile.

"What took you so long?"

"Nathan. Nathan, oh heavens above… Nathan. You're alive." She bent over him and gently kissed the top of his head.

"Thank God you're alive."

The intimacy of her gesture hung in the air between them. Then Vulcan sounded a deep throated low growl. He was standing guard, hackles raised, looking back up into the valley.

In a whirlwind of movement she pulled out the sharp-bladed knife she always tucked down her boot and, in seconds, she'd whipped around him in a circle, slashing free the cords that held him down.

With a low, urgent whisper, she leaned into his ear. "I'm going to have to move you, whether or not you like it. Brace yourself."

As he struggled to raise himself, she slipped behind him and circled her arms around him in a chest lock. Then she began dragging with frantic energy towards the stream bank, into a low depression overhung by mulberry bushes.

In panicked haste, she laid him down, scattering dead branches and deep leaf litter over him to camouflage him as best as she could.

"Stay still," she hissed. Then she skirted away from the clearing and, giving the forest trail a wide berth, she stole back up the hill. Twenty or thirty yards up, but still with the valley floor in sight, she found a boulder large enough to crouch behind.

She'd only been in position a few minutes when the man who had menaced Nathan with the shotgun, no longer wearing the scarf, came stumbling down the track with her weasel-faced attacker behind him.

Weasel Face was grumbling to his companion about something, but not loudly enough for Graysie to hear. The other man responded to his belly-aching in a peevish voice. The higher pitch of his whine carried to Graysie more clearly.

"He won't like it."

"You watch yerself or you'll be next."

Then: "Let's get on with it."

As they rounded the bend into the clearing where Nathan had lain staked out, the man in front stopped suddenly and the one following barrelled into him.

"Oi, watch it! What the blazes...?"

Mouths gaping, they stood staring at the empty ground; the stakes sticking up out of the dirt with the frayed ropes still attached.

As Graysie watched, hardly daring to breathe, they edged to the spot where they had left Nathan.

"I told you we should have put a bullet in him to finish him," Weasel Face moaned.

The bearded man shook his head in vigorous disagreement. "And leave bullets for the sheriff to see? When was the last time you saw a bear with a Colt 42? I told you, Martens wants it to look like misfortune.

"That's why if he wasn't already dead, I thought we'd dump him in the river. How the hell did he get away? And where is he? He can't have got far."

The bearded man turned in a slow circle, surveying the area. "Looks like someone pulled him this way."

Graysie's leg was cramping from being jammed in one rigid pose, but she held on, biting her lip to stay silent. The leading man breached and checked his shotgun and turned towards the river bank.

Graysie rose in alarm; she knew she was way out of range for her revolver and it was no match for a shotgun, but it was all she had. She pulled the gun out of her bag. Now, holding it at her side, she worked her way down to the next hefty boulder, crouching low.

I'm aiming to get close enough to get in a shot, even if it only distracts them, she thought wildly. If they find him first, it was only a few seconds' work to blast him at close range and then dump his body in the river.

She was hesitating on the edge of a scree incline when she spotted a small flock of mountain sheep settled for the night in a rocky hollow off to one side. She could make out the rounded shapes of woolly backs and the whorl of a ram's impressive horns in the darkening gloom.

And then it came to her. If she could divert Nathan's attackers long enough to skirt back around the back of the clearing... She picked up a fist-sized rock and threw it with all the force she could muster.

It landed right in the middle of the resting sheep, who a second before had been chewing lazily, eyes closed. Their reaction was immediate. With the ram leading the way, they leapt up and charged off down the slope, away from danger.

Head down in a menacing charge, the ram landed with a thump on a scree incline, which began moving under his weight. The ewes and lambs panicked and followed blindly, setting more rocks rolling down the hillside.

From a silence broken only by the call of an owl a few minutes before, the dell echoed with the sound of sliding rocks and scree and the panicked bleating and rattle of hooves on the cascading mass.

Once they began moving, the momentum of the moving scree carried the sheep on. They couldn't have stopped if they'd wanted to.

The man with the shotgun swung around at the noise and fired wildly, but the sheep continued inexorably on down the slope. Weasel Face was slower to react and closer to the advancing flock.

As he turned, screwed-up eyes straining to see what was causing the commotion, the horned ram hit him hard at crotch height, carrying him along for several yards before trampling right over him as the ram continued on.

The man collapsed with a scream, clutching his groin. Graysie could see blood was spurting from the top of his thigh like a fountain. The man with the gun swung and fired again, but the shot was wildly astray.

The rest of the sheep veered to the right in one woolly mass and followed the ram, disappearing into the trees.

Weasel Face lay sprawled on his back, screaming. The gash in his groin soaked his hard canvas trousers crimson red. His bearded companion put down the gun and bent over him.

What was he likely to do next? Before she'd time to decide, she caught the white flash of more movement below her. Not more sheep disturbed by the shot gun noise, surely?

With explosive force, Vulcan leapt from a head high jumble of rock debris, aiming right at the bearded man's throat. The conflict was over within a minute. Vulcan's muzzle was bloodied; the bearded man lay like a broken doll, bleeding to death over his accomplice's prone form.

The dog sniffed once, then loped back up onto the rocky ledge, raised his head and howled at the moon showing over the top of the trees.

Twenty

"You saved my life." His voice was a trembling whisper, but it was the best he could do. Heedless to the muddy puddles that soaked through her clothes, Graysie slid onto her knees at his side and carefully took hold of his wrist, gauging his pulse.

He smiled into her eyes. He couldn't remember a day when he was more than glad to be alive.

"You certainly are one out of the box, Graysie Castellanos. I don't know another woman who could do what you've just done."

The lines of exhaustion in her face softened. She shook her head in slow denial, watching him. He stroked her cheek with the back of his finger. "It should have been me protecting you."

His awareness of everything except Graysie fell away, spiraling into one image: this amazing woman, looking at him with rapt attention, as if nothing existed except them.

The caress of the cooling breeze on his face, the doggy smell of Vulcan snuffling in leaf mold, the iron tang of fresh blood, the heightened reality of their surroundings, all vanished.

They were in their own world, gazing at one another in wonder. His stomach somersaulted. Warmth curled up from deep within him.

She hesitated, and then he saw when she remembered where she was. She rolled back on her haunches. "Nathan, I've got to get help. Minette is alone up in the wagon."

She shook her head, as if she too had to drag herself back from the seduction of togetherness.

Nathan dropped his hand. "Of course." He placed his hands on either side of his thighs and tried to lever himself upright. "We've got to get out of here."

She gave a light laugh and placed her hand lightly on his shoulder. "There's no way you're walking out of here. You're staying put with Vulcan.

"I'm going to collect Minette from the wagon—where she's hopefully still fast asleep—and then I'll get some of John's men to carry you out. I imagine they've a search party looking for us by now."

She caressed the side of his face. "I'm so glad we survived this, Nathan. Life wouldn't be the same without you. And stranger still—whoever those men were—we didn't kill anyone. Nature—in its various guises—did it for us."

Nathan placed his hand on hers and held it in place for a few moments before pulling it away and gently kissing her palm. He held it longer than he needed, reluctant to lose the connection. He cleared his throat.

"One of them was Octavius Weavers. No doubt about that. And when they were arguing, I thought one of them mentioned Martens' name. My brother won't like that. Proving it though—that's going to be a whole lot harder."

*****

She'd left him in the glen, the faithful Vulcan standing guard while she climbed back up the path to Minette. Minette! How long had she been gone? Her legs were like lead, but she pushed on.

It was much harder going uphill in the

dark than it had been following Vulcan down, but the thought of Minette alone drove her on. It felt like she'd been away half the night, although it was probably only an hour and a half.

From the trajectory of the moon, she guessed it was around ten o'clock. She tiptoed to the wagon and gave a relieved sigh. The child was fast asleep under her quilt, breathing in a slow, regular pattern that betrayed no sign of anxiety or distress. She really was a remarkable little girl.

The hours that followed disappeared in a haze. She'd barely started out for Gold House before she met the search party John had assembled to look for them. She escorted the farm manager and stable hands with a stretcher back to where Nathan lay.

Sir John had been a silent commanding

presence as his Chinese servants bathed Nathan's wounds, applied herbal lotions, and gave him a draft of sleep-inducing tea.

Satisfied nothing more could to be done for Nathan that night, he drew Graysie aside in the hall outside his brother's room.

"Tell me everything. Sorry, I know you're exhausted. You need to sleep. But I must know what happened. "

She'd given him the briefest of accounts. Two men were dead, but not by their hand. Nathan had recognized Octavius Weavers. "Oh, and they mentioned Willoughby Martens when they were arguing, but he wasn't there."

John's face darkened ominously. "Really."

It wasn't a question.

∗∗∗∗∗

That night, as she pulled off her blood-stained dress and poured the warm water left by a servant into the porcelain washbowl, she mulled over the day's events and thanked God for the sheep.

They were getting closer every day to uncovering the truth, but how much time did they have left? As she patted her face dry, she asked herself the question that had been nagging her for days: could she save the lives of those closest to her by giving up on her quest?

She could admit defeat. Accept the poor offer.

Tonight it's Nathan who nearly died. Who will it be tomorrow?

An image of Lisette Guilliame's drawn face came to her mind. If they were going to acquiesce, Lisette would have to give in to the extortion as well. A burning indignation rose within her at the unfairness of it all.

One last image seared her brain as her eyes fell shut. She was scrabbling in the ditch where she'd left Nathan concealed, desperately searching for him.

But instead of Nathan, all she found was a scarlet red stain in the shape of a man's body. She woke with a churning stomach and lay wide awake until dawn broke.

Twenty One

Wednesday, July 8

"Look at me! Look at me!" Minette was holding on tightly to the front of the saddle, smiling from ear-to-ear as she sat abreast a docile pony being led around the garden arena by an easy-going Geraldine Ranch stable hand.

It was a gloriously warm, still afternoon, with enough breeze from the mountains and shade from the well-planted garden to keep the guests from getting too hot or sunburned.

As Graysie gazed out on the merry crowd assembled for the Cornish Choir concert and picnic, hosted annually by

Geraldine Ranch owners Sam and Rebecca Winthrop, she shook herself to recall that this time yesterday she'd been fighting for her life.

Minette's gay laughter pealed across the lawn, and Graysie gave a sigh of gratitude for the child's resilience. To her, it all seemed a big adventure, especially with Vulcan playing a leading role.

A crowd of about fifty of Grass Valley's merchants and business owners had gathered at the Winthrops' to hear the acclaimed Cornish Choir and enjoy a picnic lunch at tables that were set under trees in a garden with a long rose arbor.

Pania insisted Graysie and Minette accompany her to the festivities. Graysie had finished chatting with local dressmaker Cressida Washington about a new shipment of fabric she was getting in when she saw Nathan gradually making his way across the garden towards her.

Her heart lurched at the sight of him, and although he stopped every few feet to talk with different people, appearing to mix randomly with friends and neighbors, but she sensed he was making his way to her without being obvious about it.

A gauze dressing partially obscured his wavy blonde hair, but he'd dispensed with the previous night's full head bandage, and although he sported a black eye and a bruised face, he looked fit and focused.

Butterfly tremors flickered in her stomach, and she challenged herself. Where was she going with this? Shyness overcame her at the prospect of seeing Nathan again and she was putting on a splendid show of being oblivious to his approach when he came alongside her.

"And how are you today, Miss Graysie Castellanos?" He shot her one of his irrepressible grins. Everything seemed alright in his world, that was for sure.

"Fully recovered?" he continued. "I woke up this morning very glad to be alive—thanks to you."

She blushed crimson red and made to deflect his enthusiasm.

But before she got a word out, he leaned towards her and dropped his voice to a murmur, and said: "I'm planning to take Minette on a little expedition to the duck pond to feed the ducklings."

He straightened and waved a twist of paper in the air. "I got some bread from the housekeeper here. Would you like to accompany us?"

They moved across the lawn towards Minette, who was being helped off the pony. Nathan said in a low voice for Graysie's benefit only, "I'm devastated at having put you both at risk from that madman Weavers. I deliberately provoked him when I went and saw him. I had no inkling he'd turn outlaw on us…"

They paused at the pony stall, and Graysie bent down to hug Minette. "Would you like to see the ducklings now? Mr. Nathan has some food for them."

Minette skipped off down the gravel path ahead of them, enticed by the promise of a new diversion. As Graysie turned back to Nathan, all over again, the invisible power she'd sensed before linked them and held her in his thrall.

"*You* put *us* at risk?" She gave him a sideways glance. "I think it's the other way round entirely. After all, isn't it my interest in the mine that's sparked all this trouble and put both you and Minette at risk? Perhaps even got Vance killed?"

She cleared her throat.

"Think about it. Lisette and I, both with interests in neighboring mines, both the subject of peculiar threats. I'm wondering if we've all narrowly escaped harm because of my fixation with re-opening the Ophir. And no human life is worth that."

They'd reached the pond. Nathan busied himself passing bread to Minette to feed the five ducklings who circled behind their mother at the water's edge, little webbed feet paddling furiously.

Then he turned back to her.

"Someone—probably de Vile—is aiming to frighten you and Lisette into selling cheap, okay. We get that. But kill to do it? That's craziness, not business. And de Vile isn't crazy."

He searched her eyes, seeking a sign—but of what, she wasn't sure. She stepped back to put some distance between them, to reduce the magnetism that drew her in.

"You remember that first night we met, you wanted me to go back to San Francisco? I think you said something like 'you'll find a place that will take Minette.'"

His cheeks reddened, and she laughed.

"I was only teasing," he lied. She gazed at him, enjoying his discomfort, the slightly sheepish grin that tipped the corners of his lips upwards. She waved a hand, dismissing the joke.

"The thing is, Nathan, I'm thinking you were right. Maybe I should give in. Let them win. I don't want to put anyone else at risk. Otherwise, how far will it go?"

There was a long silence. She was vaguely aware of Minette's carefree chatter as she skipped up and down the path by the pond's edge, calling to the ducklings and scattering little pinches of the bread Nathan had provided for them to eat.

She was aware of his eyes on her, as if trying to read her mind. Then he sighed.

"And what about Lisette? Would you leave her dangling?"

"Ah. There's the rub." She flicked her gaze to where Minette played, checking she wasn't too close to the water. "I don't know what to do about Lisette. I've been worrying about her and Seraphine all night."

She shrugged. "I suppose the fact that

Weavers is dead is small comfort. It doesn't mean they're any safer."

A lock of red-gold hair fell across her face in the light breeze, and she smoothed it back behind her ear as she gazed directly into his eyes.

He sighed, and his eyes flicked to the meadow. "Graysie, why not leave it a few days? I know what I said when we first met, but I'm not so sure that it's correct any more.

"Maybe we've already stirred up the hornet's nest so thoroughly that backing down now won't help. Give Seb more time to flush something out. Let me help. You don't have to do this alone."

He took her elbow and turned towards Minette. A comforting warmth flowed into her. Maybe he was right. Perhaps she didn't have to do it all alone.

They'd been ambling slowly in

Minette's wake as she patrolled the water's edge where the ducklings swam. Now he took both her hands in his and drew her down to sit on a bench with a full view of the child playing. The sounds of the picnic faded in the stolen private moment.

"I know we've only known one another a week, Graysie, but you've both become important to me. And it's not only my well-known tendency to rescue damsels in distress." He gave her a self-deprecating grin. "It's more than that."

He dropped her hands and gazed out over the pond.

"There's a lot going on in my family. I've got responsibilities to my mother and half-sisters..." He watched Minette for a few more moments, then turned back to her.

"I can't only please myself, you

understand. But I want you to know, I wish I could. And that you are a gem. I've met no one like you."

He leaned in and kissed her lightly on the neck.

Her heart thumped so loudly in her chest she suspected he must be able to hear it. She contemplated his artless, open face, the unaffected directness of him, and wanted to lean in and kiss him back, right on his sculpted lips.

Instead, she smiled into his eyes, minutely closing the space that separated them. "Well, you know you've passed the first test, Mr Russell. Minette adores you. As for me…" She drew back, giving herself a fraction more room to admire him. "I've met no one like you, either."

Twenty Two

Cressida Washington's exclusive fundraising annual soiree had become one of Grass Valley's most sought-after gatherings, showcasing the latest in mountain scene fashion, music, and food while supporting deserving community causes.

The town's citizens called in favors to get their hands on an invitation, and there was subtle vying among the single women for a chance to model Cressida's creations. This year they were raising funds for the recently opened Sisters of Mercy Orphanage for Girls while sipping tea and scrutinizing the smartest fashions.

Nathan knew many people took little interest in fashion for 364 days of the year but fought for the chance to attend Cressida's event. The canny dressmaker had cleverly followed the example of the anti-slavery bazaars that had raised thousands of dollars to support emancipation in the previous two decades.

The young women selected as models swanned around in Cressida's smart dresses, serving tea and cake and staffing sales tables piled high with the fruits of a year's activity for Grass Valley's Ladies' Sewing Circle.

A rainbow jumble of ladies' cloaks, cuffs, bags, purses, and dozens of dolls in different national costumes tempted the town's gentlewomen to empty their purses and treat themselves for a good cause.

And, of course, Cressida was likely to find her order book full with requests for new season gowns by the end of the evening. A win for everyone, Nathan thought as he stood on the edge of the gathering, searching for Sebastian's lean six-foot-four frame.

Seb was the exception, a man who would have preferred not to attend Cressida's show unless forced to, but he'd been determined to come along to monitor local gossip. He'd confessed to his brothers that the investigation wasn't making much headway and he was ready to widen his approach.

Nathan surveyed the room, which was filling quickly. On a small podium to one side, Pania Hayes and Graysie Castellanos stood, completing a set of popular songs together.

Their voices complemented one

another beautifully, Pania's mature vibrancy underlying Graysie's lighter, sweeter cadences. The predominantly female audience responded with warm applause.

Even he, as a man untutored in the ways of fashion, could see Cressida had been clever in the contrasting way she'd dressed the two; Pania was in black and white with a white turban that highlighted her imperious majesty, while Graysie's natural freshness shone in a cream chiffon dress with a ruffled neckline that framed her face perfectly.

As soon as the last notes of the final encore died away, Willoughby Martens swooped from nowhere, offering Graysie his arm.

Nathan saw Graysie hesitate, then sharply pull back, clearly unwilling to accompany Martens anywhere. Martens was talking loudly at her, crowding her with his bulk.

In half a dozen big strides, Nathan was across the room at her side, dodging other guests as he went. He was vaguely aware of Sebastian following behind, and before he could speak, Sebastian planted himself in Martens' path.

"Mr. Martens. I've been wanting to catch you for a chat. You're a tough man to get hold of."

Martens was fractionally shorter than Sebastian, but substantially broader. He reared back, plainly unused to being challenged by someone so close to his own size. He took in the deputy's badge pinned on the shoulder of Sebastian's old dark blue army jacket.

"And you are…?" Martens eyed him arrogantly. "Not another Russell? God forbid."

Seb regarded him coldly. "Can we find somewhere private to talk, Mr. Martens? Might be best away from the crowd."

"Talk about what? I've done nothing wrong." Martens thrust out his chest aggressively and stared Sebastian down.

"I'm not suggesting you have, Mr. Martens. Just routine questions."

"To do with what? I'm a boring businessman. You can ask Sir John."

"I will do that. But for now..." Sebastian gestured to Martens to move across the floor towards the door.

"Hold on. Hold on. I wanted to talk to Miss Castellanos." He flashed an over-confident smile in Graysie's direction and made a move to step around Nathan to get closer to her.

Nathan put a protective arm around Graysie's waist and drew her more closely to him.

Martens glared at him for a couple of seconds, and then pointedly switched his attention to Graysie.

"I'm prepared to offer you a good price for your shares in that mine of yours, based on a prospector's report that's come into my hands." Martens drew a folded document from his inside jacket pocket with a dramatic flourish.

"It's prepared by an experienced man who's been working these mountains since forty-nine. Take it and look at it. He thinks the Ophir has modest prospects. Some possibilities, but no offer of riches galore. And his considered opinion is that to extract what little ore there is would take significant investment and expertise."

Martens screwed up his face to emphasize the difficulties. "It is well-nigh impossible for someone with no working capital or engineering expertise, Miss Castellanos. But I'm looking for a challenge, and I'd take it off your hands. I've got the contacts to make it work."

Nathan's stomach soured at the man's attempt to look guileless.

Here I am, the simple businessman, looking for an opportunity to make money, for sure, but willing to play fair.

"I'm thrilled to take your report and consider it, Mr. Martens," Graysie said, all business. "Who is the author, by the way?"

"Oh, no one you'd know," Martens said carelessly. "He's a fellow I've done other mining projects with in the past."

"And his name is?" Nathan asked.

"His name is Lightning Bill Whitlock," Martens answered after a reluctant pause. "He worked around Sonora most of his life, but knows this region as well."

"Worked?" asked Nathan, his emphasis on the past tense.

"Yes. Sadly, he died in a rock fall a month ago, not long after he finished this report, actually."

"What a coincidence." Nathan didn't bother to conceal the cynicism in his voice.

"Look, I don't know what you are hinting at, but drop it. Mining's a dangerous business, you know that. You can't help yourself, can you?

"Always meddling. The only time you didn't step up like some blessed saint with all the answers to the world's problems was when your own wife faced death. You didn't want to know too much about that, did you?"

Martens sneered and flashed Nathan a look of mean triumph.

Graysie's spine stiffened at Martens'

words. She pulled back from Nathan's protective arm, a reaction that didn't escape his fellow Australian.

"What, he didn't tell you the sad story?" Martens' mouth curled in a taunting smile. "Oh, yes. Saint Nathan was so busy sticking his nose where it didn't belong he was missing when his wife needed him most."

Graysie drew herself in tightly, her backbone ramrod straight. There was a long silence. She faced Nathan. "You didn't tell me…" Her voice fell away to an embarrassed whisper, and Nathan was uncomfortably aware of Martens' smug silence.

He'd almost forgotten Sebastian was present, but his brother now stepped up with an authority that brooked no resistance.

"I think you've delivered your

message, Mr. Martens. Now, can you come with me, please?"

Martens tossed a last contemptuous look at Nathan and walked out, leaving a shocked silence behind him.

Graysie cleared her throat. "When you asked me the day at the fair if I'd ever been married, why didn't you mention you'd been married yourself?"

Nathan's tongue stuck to the roof of his mouth. He couldn't get his mouth open, let alone get any words out. His eyes locked on hers and an eternity fell between them. She couldn't drag her eyes away.

Then he spoke with controlled desperation. "My wife's death will forever be a source of grief to me. If I could do anything to reverse the events of that night, I would. But it has nothing at all to do with the matters we're discussing here. And Martens has an especially embittered view of what happened."

He stared into her stricken face. "But that doesn't really answer your question, does it? Why haven't I mentioned it before? I guess it's partly because we've hardly had time for that kind of private conversation. We've been too busy staying alive."

He took a deep breath and tried to ignore the stabbing pain in his chest.

"But the real reason is, I'm not proud of how I handled it. I deserve to be punished... and I can't blame Willoughby for what happened.

"Catherine got caught in a natural disaster. There was nothing I could do about that. But she was in that situation because she was chasing after me. I was never at home, always away on business. So, she came after me. When she needed me most, I wasn't there."

The skin bunched around his eyes, and he gave her a painful stare. "I failed her. I can't deny it. And Willoughby Martens is my wife's brother, my brother-in-law. He thinks he's got a right to be aggrieved. And perhaps he has."

Her eyes were deep wells of sadness. His heart turned to stone. "Not good enough, is it? And it's impossible for me to go back and change it."

Twenty Three

Thursday, July 9

As soon as it was decent to get up without appearing tragic, Graysie slid out of bed, put on her practical serge riding skirt and boots, braced her shoulders for the day, and started for the kitchen.

She'd heard John and Nathan discussing an old prospector named Willie Watson, who knew rocks. They seemed to think he knew the Ophir well, and he lived on one of the dead-end forest roads near Gold House.

The thought had crept in overnight, and she couldn't shake it off. If she was going to decide on what to do about the

Ophir, maybe she needed to talk to someone like Willie.

Besides, she wanted an excuse to avoid bumping into Nathan over breakfast. Seeing him was the last thing she could handle at this moment. She took a deep breath and gasped; her chest was so bruised and sore. Was her heart broken? He'd seemed so open, and yet he'd kept such secrets from her.

She tiptoed to the pantry and quickly assembled an impromptu breakfast: bread rolls, jam, fruit, and cheese. Then she took the stairs two at a time to Minette's room and roused her.

She was back to trusting her own instincts, relying on herself. She'd go see Willie Watson and show him the prospector's report Martens had given her. But first she'd drop Minette off to play at Lisette's. She must get her life moving again, regardless of the distractions, and Nathan Russell was proving to be a distraction.

By mid-morning, Minette was happily dressing paper dolls with Seraphine, and Graysie had savored a coffee with Lisette and Irish Pete, who'd called with a brace of game birds for the pot.

The Herculean red-bearded miner had worked for Lisette's husband and was so incensed at finding Minette in the cellars that he'd taken to checking on Lisette and Seraphine when he was passing.

Graysie could sense Lisette growing more cheerful and confident under his kind attention, and she set off up a gravel road to Willie's cabin with a lightened heart.

She loved the Sierra mountains in July. The cloud of betrayal that had enveloped her since the night before gradually lifted like morning mist in the sun the farther from town she went. The mountains were especially lovely in the morning before the air got so dry it tickled your throat.

Willie Watson had a long, gray beard which belonged to a much older man. Though she guessed he was into his fifth decade, his step was nimble and he looked a lot younger.

After she explained who she was, he welcomed her into his modestly furnished bachelor's cabin and offered her tea. Willie's dog—a red and white spaniel with a fine curly coat—ambled over and slumped down on the floor beside her chair with an audible "humph."

"Meet Argus. Been out chasing squirrels," Willie said with a smile. "It's tiring work."

As he put a kettle on the hob and stoked the wood fire, Graysie basked in the calm order of the one-and-a-half-room living space. Through an open archway, she could see a tidily made-up bed covered in a plump feather eiderdown and flowery quilt.

A small hand hewn table and chairs and a couple of easy chairs provided simple furnishing for the main room. She sat down in one of the easy chairs. Freshly picked salad greens lay on the pine bench under the kitchen window—bounty from a garden plot she'd noticed on the way in. It was the picture of homely comfort.

The kettle whistled and Willie poured a steaming hot cup of tea for them both before settling with a satisfied sigh in one of the straight-backed chairs at the table.

"So, you're the young lady Mr. Eustace Mountfort left the mine to." He paused and took a slow sip. "I saw him not long before he died. He wanted to talk to me about the Ophir, chew the fat. You know."

Graysie was stunned by his casual announcement. "You saw Eustace? Spoke with him? Where? Where did you meet him?" Excited bubbles rose from the pit of her stomach.

"In Sacramento. I was there visiting a friend and bumped into him. When he was a young prospector, we shared a tent on the banks of various rivers. I always liked him. He was a proper gentleman. Not so suited to the outdoor life perhaps…"

He paused and smiled. "He was a good businessman, but he didn't have the killer instinct."

Graysie licked her lips reflectively. "Funny thing. Someone else said exactly the same thing a few days ago."

Willie gazed into his cup. "Mmmm… You could never say the same thing about Sir John!" He gave a laughing cough.

"Another funny thing was that those two did a lot of business together over the years, but Eustace didn't want Sir John to know I was investigating the Ophir for him. Made me promise I wouldn't mention it. Seemed a tad strange to me, but I thought it was none of my business."

Graysie leaned down and stroked the spaniel's soft, floppy ears. "Curious. I haven't seen Eustace since I was a child, and I'd never met Sir John until a few days ago—well, not that I remember. I don't know much about either of them."

"When they were younger, they were very good buddies. They went everywhere together. As they aged, not so much."

Graysie had the sense he was holding back, uncertain of how to continue. "Do you think they were still close when Eustace died?"

"Hard to say, but from a few things Eustace said, probably not. He was feeling his years, and he was in a soulful mood. He voiced regrets and admitted if life granted him his time over, he'd make different choices.

"He even joked about seeing a priest and making his confession. I don't think Sir John is a man for that kind of talk."

Graysie's hand slowed on the dog's silky back. "Did he say what kind of regrets? Any idea what he meant?"

Willie shook his head and finished his

tea. "None at all. I suppose one conclusion you might draw is that he'd never married or had a family. He was a caring sort of man, so that was surprising, really.

"He could be hilarious… And when he was younger, he played the fiddle… He used to storm heaven with his music at the Sunday dances. Had a fine singing voice, too."

Graysie's stomach clenched with a pang of loss at not knowing him. She still hoped the inheritance he'd left her might provide for her future. If it ever all worked out, she'd have him to thank.

"I'm very grateful to him for remembering me in his will—although a little bewildered by it. I understand he was very close to my mother when they were young.

"Maybe they even entertained ideas of

getting married, but his father sent him off to the West Indies to grow up. By the time he got back, Mother had already married my father. Anyway... enough of ancient history."

She stood and squared her shoulders. "I have to focus my attention on today. I was wondering what you could tell me about the Ophir. Do you know much about it?"

Willie got up and went to a small wooden chest that stood against one wall from which he drew some tattered rolls. He spread the biggest on the table, displaying a parchment sheet with well-worn edges, the surface smudged by dirty finger and pencil marks.

"These are the maps Eustace gave me." She came and stood beside him and he traced down a black line on the map with his stubby index finger.

"This is the shared ridge that runs between the Ophir and the Ruby. You'll see the Ophir is lower down—below the Ruby—here to the west of it, but still on the same fall line.

"The Ruby has these mighty greenstone dykes which bind the ore veins, and there's a good chance those dykes continue down into the Ophir. They say we can always rely on the rocks to surprise, but those greenstone towers are so strong it's unlikely they'll disappear. And where there are these greenstone buttresses, there's likely a nice ore shoot locked in as well."

He turned his kindly face towards her. "You'd better take these home with you. They're yours now, though of course you have to examine the rocks up close to know for sure. A map will only take you so far."

Graysie bent over to examine the tracery of lines. It was easy to see where the Wolf River ran down the valley and then split into two tributaries, one of which flowed towards Grass Valley, and the other toward the Ophir.

She knew that some of the most productive Grass Valley mines edged the Wolf River lower down. She turned to Willie with a frown.

"What about random reports from people I don't know—and may not trust?" She pulled out the report Willoughby Martens had given her. "This one, for example. Someone gave it to me last night."

Willie stroked his long beard as his eyes flicked over the pages. "I'd have to take more time to do it justice, but it looks like something manufactured for a particular purpose—either to elevate or reduce a property's supposed value. Who prepared it, do you know?"

"Someone called Lightning Bill Whitlock?"

Willie nodded. "Funny how both the Ophir and the Ruby are attracting attention. And yet poor old Andre Guilliame couldn't get any investors interested when he was desperate to sell. I suppose that's the way of things.

"If you're too keen, buyers back off. And yet only last week Vance Pedersen came to see me and asked me to store some papers of his for safekeeping. Said he'd been doing a bit of investigating along the Ophir-Ruby fault line—don't know who for. Might've even been you."

She shook her head. "No, not me." He raised his eyebrows.

"That's where he died, isn't it? Well, in that vicinity. Poor sod."

Graysie was having trouble swallowing. Her throat was dry. A tingling sensation swept up the back of her neck and into her face.

"He was up there at my request—heading for there, anyway. But I hadn't got as far as commissioning any report."

As she was speaking, Willie had returned to the wooden chest and drawn out a package wrapped in oilcloth. "Here's Vance's report. He said something about how he didn't want to leave it at home with all the children. Not sure if he thought the blighters might get their hands on it or what?"

"How strange." said Graysie. "Thanks. I'll read it when I get back." She turned towards the door, the friendly little spaniel tagging along at her heels. "I've kept you for long enough, Willie. Would it be alright if I left this new report for you to look at?

Perhaps I could call by again in another few days? I'd value your opinion."

Willie nodded, and his brown eyes shone. "Happy to oblige. I'm not expecting much from it."

As she turned to leave, another thought suddenly struck her. "Willie, investors who seem interested in shares of these mines have approached both Lisette Guilliame and me, but naturally, they want to play down their value. I guess that's part of the game. There's Hector de Vile. for one. Willoughby Martens for another.

"That man Weavers says he representing a mystery buyer who doesn't want to be identified. Have you got any idea of their worth? What we should sell for? Or any clue who Weavers might have been working for?"

Willie stood on the doorstep, running

his fingers through his beard, considering. "My dear, if I were honest, I'd have to say anyone with money. John Russell, Hector de Vile, they compete over everything, even if they pretend to be disinterested.

"They're all scared the other will get their hands on something good and they'll miss out. It's the age-old problem, isn't it? Greed. You're holding onto something they want. I'm not sure what lengths any of them would go to get it."

He held the report she'd given him in one hand. He tucked it into the waistband of his workingman's trousers and pulled on his hat.

"I've got to water my lettuces and Argus, and then I'll sit in the sun and read it. Come back tomorrow about this time and I should be able to give you some answers."

Twenty Four

Willoughby Martens slipped around the back of the outhouse, pulled a black kerchief out of his pocket and tied it around the lower half of his face. If circumstances required, he'd play the outlaw.

Thanks to Russell's determination to drive him out of the finance business, he didn't have any other choice, but his luck was about to change. That's why he was standing on this flat, weed-covered patch at the back of the widow Anna Santa Maria's house.

The delicious gut heat that glowed when he was grinding Nathan Russell's reputation into the dirt last night warmed him. His fingers tingled with the pleasure of reliving the moment. Seeing Graysie Castellanos's slack jaw at the revelation of Russell's marriage. That was priceless.

I'd like to get my hands on that hot little number! Those cascading curls, the tempting rise of her breasts, the long legs…

He squeezed his eyes shut and shook the image away. There'd be time for that soon enough. Weavers had frightened the French woman good and proper—he was pretty certain she'd sell at the required price, even with Weavers dead.

But Martens needed that benighted report on the Ophir operation from Pedersen. By tomorrow. De Vile was adamant it existed, and Martens hadn't expected it would be this hard to track down.

It had to be here at the engineer's

home, or if it wasn't, his strumpet must know where he'd put it. If she wasn't his wife, so what? She was raising his kids, wasn't she?

His insides pinched as he thought of the dumb Mexican and snivelling tribe of children who stood between him and his chance to be somebody. There was no way they'd stop him, even without backup from bumbling old Weavers.

He tapped the pouch at his waist, checking for the newly sharpened steel blade. Good. All shipshape and ready. Casting a last look around to ensure he wasn't being observed, he doubled into a silent run and was at Anna's back door, pounding with his clenched fist.

He heard a strong female voice respond, "Who is it?"

He pulled the scarf down and yelled, "Open up! One of the children is hurt. It looks serious."

He flattened himself against the wall on the door's opening side, readjusted the scarf over his lower jaw, whipped out the knife, and waited. He heard a heavy bolt rattle in its casing, and the door flew open.

Anna Santa Maria stepped into the doorway, eyes fixed expectantly on the spot where he'd been standing a few seconds before. Her face screwed up in worry, she took a step forward and ran her hand through her long hair. "Who's there?"

As she turned in his direction, he grabbed her with a lock hold across her throat and dragged her backwards into her house, slamming the door behind him.

She was wheezing and coughing and struggling to breathe because of the brutal pressure he was applying, but he didn't care. She needed to be frightened. Very frightened.

She must get the message that she and all her children were expendable. He pulled her even tighter as he stretched back and pushed the door bolt smoothly back in place, locking them in.

He positioned the flat knife blade under her chin and ear at a diagonal angle across her jugular vein. It was so sharp he only had to place it against her skin and it opened bloody scratches, some deep.

Without him needing to apply any extra pressure, blood trickled over her collarbone and down her front. She stifled a sob but remained stiff and motionless except for a sudden release from her bladder. A gush of warm urine splashed onto his boots, the acrid smell overpowering a ripe tomato fragrance in the kitchen.

"Start talking, bitch. Where did your useless brother-in-law keep his papers?"

She froze, then said, dragging out her words; "Papers? I know of no papers."

He applied more pressure, and the blood flowed more freely. "Wrong answer. Try again. If you're wrong this time, I'll start on your kids."

Sharp children's voices erupted from the room next door, and then two small children appeared in the entryway to the kitchen. They stopped abruptly and stared at the woman with huge, frightened dark eyes.

"Mamma! Mamma!" Little mouths turned down at the corners, and they began whimpering.

Anna Santa Maria took a deep breath. "It's a silly game, darlings. Only a silly game. Go and play."

"His papers!" Martens hissed. "I haven't got all day. Where are his papers?"

Anna held herself even more rigid. He guessed she was steeling herself for death. Then she said slowly and deliberately, "I do not know of these papers. He was an engineer. We have no papers." A desperate gagging noise sounded deep in her chest. "I swear! I know nothing of any papers."

He was hot and panting, and a pleasurable tide of excitement rose in him as he heard the fear in her voice. Her neck against his arm was slick with sweat and blood.

He was about to press the knife against her throat one last time, but a gibberish wave of high-pitched wailing in childish Spanish interrupted the movement. The two small children had returned, joined by a thin, dark-headed boy of about nine or ten.

Martens hauled Anna around to face the boy who had come running at the sound of the younger ones' crying. The kid stopped short, his arms hanging loosely at his sides.

He stared at his mother with narrowed eyes, and Martens had the disconcerting sense he was recording every detail of the scene before him; the knife at her throat, the blood.

Martens could pick the moment when the full extent of the danger registered on his stark white face. He backed away like a small ghost, gathering the two smaller children in behind him, one on each side of his slim hips.

Before the boy reached the door, Martens yelled, "Stop! Stop! Not one step further or your mother dies."

The boy's quietly exaggerated backward steps froze in mid-air, and he released his sisters with a gentle whisper. "Play, little ones. Go and play." He gently turned them around and pushed them back the way they had come.

Then he stepped back into the kitchen, staring blankly at his mother as he moved.

He spoke urgently to her in Spanish, while she quietly sobbed. Martens couldn't pick up anything more than a few words: "Padre... perro... asesinato." Father... dog... murder...

The kid's sharp, he thought. Smarter than his mother.

"Come here." Martens barked the command at the boy, who didn't move. "I said, come here." His voice rose to a scream like a wind howling to gale force. The noise seemed to unlock something in the child, and he scurried to his mother's side.

"You can let her go. She knows nothing."

The child's hands shook violently. His eyes widened in terror, but his voice was surprisingly calm.

Martens had a strange sensation of the world tilting on its axis, jolting him onto unfamiliar ground. A kid was telling him what to do?

He grabbed the boy roughly by the shoulder with his free hand and snarled, "Stay still or the knife ends it."

The boy swayed and went momentarily limp under his hand, like he might be about to pass out, but he steadied himself and stood erect. When he spoke, his voice was louder, more determined.

"She knows nothing. Let her go."

The woman broke into a violent wave of wailing, and Martens loosened his hold on her throat, easing the knife back from her skin.

"Antonio, no, no. He is a devil. A devil. Vance had no papers. There is nothing here. Nothing!"

She broke into harsh sobs, her chest heaving, cheeks wet with tears. Now she'd started crying, she was fast approaching hysteria.

"There is nothing here! Only a widow with six children and barely enough food to feed them. What do we know of fancy papers? You are a fool! A fool!"

She howled, and the children who had disappeared earlier re-appeared. They rushed to her side, also wailing.

"Enough!" Martens roared over the racket. "Shut up!" He squeezed the boy's shoulder hard and his rakish body tensed with the pain.

"You know about those papers!" he yelled. "Where are they? I'm not waiting any longer."

The boy turned slowly and glowered. "She knows nothing. Let her go, and I will help. Otherwise, nada. Nothing."

There was a charged, drawn-out silence. The woman had stopped crying. Martens watched in disbelief as the stony-faced boy spread his hands wide.

"Well, cowboy. What's it to be?"

This kid should be a lion tamer.

He'd never seen such self-possession. Such courage. Or was it straight out gall? And did he even know anything?

"You're showing me where they are. And you"—he swung to the woman—"If there is so much as a peep out of you to anyone, you won't see the kid alive again. Is that clear?"

Martens released the woman. She pulled the boy against her hip, his head resting on her skirts, and cried until he thought her heart would break. He thrust the knife back into his waist pouch and waited, tapping his foot impatiently. When he'd had enough, he grabbed the boy by the ear and dragged him away from the keening woman.

"You'd better know where we're going, boy, because you're taking us there right now."

Twenty Five

The only bed was overturned, the mattress and quilt slashed open. Spilled feather down floated in the still air like snowflakes that refused to come to rest. Chairs lay up-ended, one with its legs broken. The table was toppled over, an edge resting against an armchair.

Willie Watson's homely forest haven was a mess. Willoughby Martens repeatedly thumped his clenched fist on the kitchen bench—up and down—in a rhythmic tantrum, howling in rage. He stopped to take a breath and glared venomously at the boy, who cowered behind an armchair.

"Where the hell is it, you little son of a bitch?"

In three steps, he towered over him. He lifted him off his feet by the back of his collar and flung him headlong towards the door. Antonio's shoulder hit the doorjamb with a heavy thump, and he slid to the floor and lay motionless at Billy B's feet.

Martens had recruited Billy, a notorious Aussie gang member, from San Francisco's Barbary Coast, and he was as ruthless as any man Martens had ever come across. He'd sunk many an ale with the ex-convict on both sides of the Pacific Ocean. When you needed good backup, there was nothing like being able to trust your own.

Martens strode over to the crumpled heap and hoisted the kid to eye level by his shirt front.

"If your uncle brought it here, where is it now?"

The boy barely registered the words. A cut had opened up on his right eyebrow, and blood trickled down his face. He shook his head wordlessly and touched his forehead, then looked down at his blood-covered fingers. He wiped his hand on his pants and his head crumpled to his chest. When Martens let go, he crashed to the floor.

Truth was, there were very few hiding places in the simply furnished cottage, and Martens was pretty damned sure they'd searched them all. Antonio had barely said a word since they'd hustled him out of his home. His only garbled admission that was that Vance was a good friend of Watson's and they often got together to talk.

"If there was a report... He might have

shown Willie…"

Getting anything else out of him was proving impossible. He'd lapsed into terrified silence and had not said a word since. When they arrived, the house was empty, and it had been the work of a few minutes to overturn the main room and find absolutely nothing.

Martens was not in a mood to be reasonable.

Holy Moses, I have to find that report by tomorrow. It can't be that complicated. And if the kid can't be more use than this, he'll have to pay.

His rage focused on one thing: to get the kid who'd led him on this wild goose chase. He saw the boy understood his danger.

He'd risen slowly to his feet and slipped out of reach of Billy's outreached hand when a clamor of high-pitched barking sounded from outside. Billy opened the door a crack to peer out. Gunfire peppered the wood, and he slammed it shut again.

"What the blazes…" He stared wildly at Martens as if expecting instruction.

"Grab the kid."

Billy lunged for Antonio, who scuttled sideways to avoid him, but the table blocked his way. Martens grabbed him by the hair.

"Stop shooting or the kid gets hurt!" Martens yelled so loud his throat hurt. "Hear me? Stop shooting."

He nodded to Billy, who slowly opened the door. Martens grasped Antonio's shirt firmly and pushed the boy slowly out through the narrow doorway in front of him, using him as a shield.

"If you shoot, he dies," Martens bellowed again. "Hold your fire."

There was a moment's silence. Nothing moved in the trees in line of sight of the door. Martens couldn't see Fat Jack, a gunslinger he'd left on watch outside.

His stomach roiled like it had on the festering barque from Sydney to California. He was hot and cold at the same time—how was that possible? The moment hung in a timeless bubble, and then frantic high-pitched barking shattered the silence.

A red-haired dog rushed at them from the cabin's left corner, teeth bared. After a moment's shock at the noise, Martens put back his head and laughed.

It was a contemptible sight, this lap-warmer going frantic, defending his patch. Billy raised his revolver and fired. The dog screamed in a chorus of squeals which faded to whimpering and then silence, rusty canine blood mixing with the red of its coat as it fell at Antonio's feet.

Martens stamped on the front porch and waved his rifle at shadows to swamp the nervous tingling at the back of his neck. What to do next? Where was Fat Jack? There were two—maybe three—of them against how many? The only advantage was, they had the kid.

Martens thrust the boy back to Billy and sidled along the front of the cabin, back to the wall. He peered around the corner where the dog had sprung from. A few feet away, Fat Jack lay sprawled on his back, bleeding from a chest wound.

He couldn't tell if the man was dead or alive. He stepped past Jack's body and continued his circuit of the cabin, back pressed to the log wall, rifle vertical. As he reached the next corner and caught his breath, cold steel pressed hard against the side of his neck.

A quiet voice said, "Drop the gun."

He hesitated, and the barrel pressed in harder. He let the rifle fall.

A bearded man stepped away from the back wall of the cabin and leveled the rifle straight at his heart.

"Turn around." The gun was in the middle of his back. "Now walk."

Step by careful step, they continued on a circuit of the cabin. They would come up behind Billy on his right-hand side. As they stepped out of the shadows, Billy whirled to face them, and then a contemptuous smirk lifted one side of his mouth.

He held the boy wrestled against his crotch, his arm across his throat, a pistol to the boy's temple.

"Uh-huh. No closer or the boy's brains are spaghetti. Drop the gun and let Fart Face go."

His captor halted, the gun in Martens' back pressed even harder against his spine.

"Let the boy go first."

Billy gurgled menacingly. "And throw away the ace? I don't think so, cowboy."

"Let the boy go." The voice was raised a notch but still steady; Martens could pick up on the man's determination, vibrating down the rifle barrel.

"And what? You'll invite us in for a drink?" Billy sneered.

"Let him go, and I'll let you go. No questions asked."

"Oh yeah. I'm sure." Billy tightened his grip on the boy's throat and frog marched him a couple of feet closer towards Martens and his captor. The kid's face drained of all color, his glazed eyes stared into the trees behind them as if he'd already flown to some place far away.

The gap between them had closed to a few feet. Billy's eyes skittered from Martens to the man holding him, and then to the broader area in front of the cabin. A sour, unwashed smell hit Martens as they all faced off, and he saw doubt shadow Billy's squinted-up eyes.

Then he was being propelled forward, slamming into Billy's belly; the gun that had been at his back suddenly leveled at Billy's throat. They both sprawled on the ground in front of the cabin. In the melee, Antonio broke free and scuttled into the yard.

"Get out of here, Antonio. Go for it. Quick, fast."

Antonio whirled one way, then the other. He came to an abrupt stop and gaped at his rescuer. "Mr. Watson! I didn't mean... I didn't mean..." He broke into intense sobbing. Watson's attention momentarily flicked to the boy, and Martens saw his chance.

From a grovelling position on the ground, he launched himself at Watson's legs. The man was tall and strong but toppled like a sack of potatoes when caught off guard. Billy was there with a gun at Watson's temples before Martens could get to his feet.

The boy stood for a moment, staring.

Willie Watson gave a defiant roar. "Go, Antonio. Go!"

Antonio whirled and sprinted out of the clearing and into the forest.

Then Billy fired.

Twenty Six

"Look, Sissy! I can ride by myself!" Minette's face was glowing with pride as she sat atop the pony's sturdy back, little hands relaxed at the front of her saddle as she grasped the reins. Graysie was riding abreast of her at an easy pace.

She'd started by walking alongside her with a trainer lead, but as the trail widened to a flat and easy path where they could ride two abreast, she'd relinquished the lead and let the child assume control.

Normally she would not go riding in the afternoon, when the sun was its hottest, but today she'd made an exception.

She'd been restless and jumpy ever since she'd picked up Minette from Lisette's and come back home to Gold House.

She needed to get out of the house and get some air while she turned over in her mind everything that had happened in the last few days. Minette was delighted with the suggestion that they take a quick ride.

As their horses paced quietly along, the brown lizards Minette loved to try and catch were out basking; the only noise in the still afternoon was their soft scuttling from rock to brown grass, set off by the horses.

A sense of uneasiness supplanted thoughts of Nathan Russell and yesterday's lingering pleasure at holding Vance's report.

She'd not yet looked at it, but she

couldn't shake the guilty sense she'd inherited someone's diary. Was it even right for her to have it?

Her body was as taut as a stretched wire, but her midnight-till-dawn heart-searching had led her to two conclusions. She couldn't desert Lisette, who needed a good pay-out from her mine shares even more than Graysie did. And she needed to put Nathan Russell well out of her mind.

Whatever he'd been hinting at when he'd talked to her at the pond, he was clearly still grieving for his wife and in no position to form any new relationship. She'd be better off quietly finding out as much as she could about Weavers and his co-conspirator without his help. Lost in thought, she maintained an easy pace alongside Minette's pony.

Without being able to control them, her

thoughts veered to Nathan's wife. She was
curious. Was she pretty? Were they happy
together? Her heart leapt at the thought of
Nathan's loss. It must be awful to suffer
such a close death, especially as they
probably hadn't been married long.

She'd seen his kindness to the Chinese
hotel workers, so she found it hard to
believe he would be unsympathetic to his
wife. The more she turned it over in her
mind, the more she doubted that
Martens' slant on the thing was likely to
be credible. But Nathan had been so
passive. He'd made no attempt to
explain or defend himself.

They were nearing the bottom of the
big meadow, where the ground fell away
into a forested gully, and Minette's head
was bobbing heavily with the pony's
stride.

"Poppet, why don't we turn around

now and go back to the house for a cool drink? Then we could take a visit to town and go to the Good Fortune Bakery for moon cakes?"

They were nearing the stables when she saw Nelson and Nathan hitching up Sir John's wagon in great haste, Vulcan looping them in big circles excitedly.

"What's happening? Is something wrong?" Graysie jumped down and moved to help Minette off her pony. "You look as if there's an emergency."

Nathan paused briefly. "More than an emergency. A disaster. Willie Watson's place is on fire. We've no idea if he's safe or not, but we're on our way up there right now."

"Willie's place? No! It can't be true."

"'Fraid so. The fire brigade boys called in to ask us to come. They're ahead of us on the road."

"Please. Let me see if Mrs. Snively can look after Minette for a couple of hours. I want to come with you."

*****

"Willie can't die! He can't!" Graysie held her head in both hands and shook it hard, as if trying to jolt herself out of a bad dream. The fire had gutted Willie's homely cabin, the smoke rising in a sinuous column from a blackened center.

The old miner lay stretched out on the Grass Valley Fire Brigade stretcher, his face deathly white, unconscious and bleeding from the top of his head. His breathing was whisper thin, barely audible.

Around the cabin, young men in blue firefighter shirts and curved safety helmets directed a modest trickle of water onto blackened debris. The hand-operated pump they'd pulled up behind a two-horse team connected into an underground aquifer that surfaced on the edge of the forest, but it was producing little more than a dribble.

Graysie crouched down on the ground beside Willie's stretcher and gently took his hand. "Willie," she whispered, "you've got to come through. You've got to. We're counting on you."

The disappointed firemen had the air of rescuers who've arrived too late to do their job and instead are left with the clean-up. And yet... Graysie snapped her head up. An electric shock, a sixth sense, propelled her out of her dazed musing.

She saw Nathan and another man standing in the middle of the smoking charred remains, gazing at a bundle on the floor—the remnant of an overturned armchair, perhaps? Then Nathan raised his arm in alarm and called to the other firemen, "Body down! There's someone else here."

*****

A half hour later, they'd pulled the body of a man from the rubble. Sebastian Russell stood in a huddle of men talking in low tones as the doctor pronounced the man dead and arranged for him to be transported back to town. He was so badly burned it was going to be hard—probably impossible—to identify him or the cause of his death.

They'd found Willie unconscious behind one of the two raised salad beds he'd built, huddled with his knees tucked to his chest as if he was trying to make himself as small as possible. Track marks in the grass nearby showed he'd most likely crawled there, probably semi-concussed from his messy head wound.

"I don't know who killed that man or

how, but I don't think Willie was in any state to do anything except escape," Sebastian said. "I think we're looking for at least one other man, maybe more."

He gazed around him at the devastation, his face streaked with sweat and ash.

"What puzzles me is what Willie could have had here that was of sufficient value to justify all this…" He gestured around the site. "This destruction."

A cry from one of the firemen Sebastian had asked to check the perimeter of the house distracted their attention.

"Sorry, sir…" He spread his arms in apology. "But I think you'll want to come and look at this."

The body of a red-and-white-haired dog lay stretched in a bloody sprawl, flies buzzing around its half-closed eyes.

"Oh, no! Not Argus, too!" The men who had gathered around the dog's body froze as Graysie Castellanos rushed forward with an anguished cry.

She half bent over the dog, sobbing, and Sebastian placed a comforting hand on her back as she slowly stood up. "Is there something else?" he asked. "Apart from seeing a poor, wounded dog, I mean."

"Oh, no, no sorry. I got a shock. I saw him earlier today, and he was so lively…"

Sebastian stared. "You saw him earlier today? And that was because…?

Graysie's face flushed red hot. She hesitated before replying.

"I asked Willie for his opinion on a mine report I got from Willoughby Martens last night. I had a cup of tea with him here at about ten thirty this morning."

"And you left when, exactly?" Sebastian pinned her down with his eyes, and she felt face darkening an even deeper shade of beetroot.

"We talked for maybe half an hour. I left around eleven? I couldn't say exactly."

"And you noticed nothing unusual? No outlaws? No men with guns?"

She ignored the sarcasm. "Nothing unusual at all. If there had been, I would have told someone like Nathan, of course." The words sounded garbled.

Does Sebastian know how close his brother and I have become these last few days?

"He helped me when Vance Pedersen was killed…" Her voice trailed off lamely.

"Vance Pedersen? Oh, of course. You were there too, weren't you? Curious thing, Miss Castellanos. Death seems to follow you around."

He turned his attention back to the dog. "Shot in the side at close range, the poor thing. He might have stood between his master and a bullet. Maybe he helped save Willie from ending up in that fire, too." He bent over and stroked down the sleek back. His hand froze on the dog's rib cage.

"Woah! He's not dead yet. Load him up with Willie and we'll see what we can do."

*****

Death seems to follow you around.

Bile surged in her throat. Her stomach heaved. She scuttled to the edge of the clearing and retched in the bushes.

Breathe in… slowly. Breathe out…

After a few minutes, the fluttering in her gut settled.

The deputy's right, though, isn't he?

Death is following me.

And they didn't know about the report Willie had given her yet, the report she hadn't looked at. She put her head in her hands and massaged her temples with her thumbs.

Think... Think...

She'd seen no one while visiting Willie earlier that day. The road was empty, both going to and leaving his house, she was sure of it. She could think of nothing unusual to could tell the sheriff.

And anyway, no one but her knew Willie had given her that report. How could she have led these killers to Willie's house?

It isn't possible. It's just another coincidence.

But she knew she must make sure it never happened again, whatever it took.

*****

The firemen had done all they could to dampen the embers. They had carted the unidentified body back to town for burial. Willie's still-unconscious form was stretchered onto the Gold House wagon for the trip to the Sisters of Mercy annex, the closest thing Grass Valley had to a small hospital, where nuns would provide around-the-clock nursing care. Argus lay on a dry sack at his feet.

Nelson, Sir John's groom, drove while Nathan squatted in the back with Graysie, helping to brace the stretcher and ensure Willie stayed in place as they rumbled down the rough track.

She'd insisted on accompanying him to the religious house. He watched as she dabbed Willie's face with a damp handkerchief streaked black from charcoal flakes.

She appeared barely conscious of her

surroundings, unaware of the black streaks on her own hands and face. Her pale complexion had a clammy sheen. Her breathing was much faster than usual, and her pulse fluttered through the delicate skin at the base of her throat.

She's showing all the classic signs of being in shock, he thought. The wagon slowed, and the wheels growled as they passed from the packed earth track to the town boardwalk and rolled to the convent gates.

The wagon had barely stopped when Nelson and Nathan were out and had each taken one end of the stretcher and carried Willie into the infirmary, Graysie trailing behind.

The clinic nurse, a stout, middle-aged woman with a stern but kindly face, received Willie with an air of calm authority. She patted the sheets around his shoulders and turned to face them. "Thank you for bringing him in. There is nothing more you can do for him right now. Get some rest. We'll take care of him from here."

"The nurse is right," Nathan said. He turned to Nelson. "Can you go on home ahead of us? I think Miss Castellanos needs a cool drink and a moment to catch her breath." The groom nodded and left.

"Come on," he said to Graysie. "I think you're in mild shock." She protested, but he made a silencing gesture, took her hand in his, and drew her across the street to the teahouse.

"Go to the ladies' room and freshen up," he said. "You're covered in soot. I'll get some iced tea for us."

"Thank you." She stood staring at him,

as if momentarily still unsure what she was supposed to do, and then she turned for the ladies' room.

Ten minutes later, they settled in a pleasantly cool corner with iced tea in front of them. Graysie took several gulps of her beverage and her face creased in distress.

"It's all my fault. Like Sebastian said, death follows me around."

Nathan shook his head slowly. "Nonsense, Graysie. You're upset. You're not to blame."

"No, you don't understand. There's something I didn't tell Sebastian. I couldn't, not in front of all those other men."

"Something you didn't tell Sebastian?" Nathan was aware he was echoing her statement with a hint of disbelief. "Like what?"

"When I was there this morning, Willie gave me a mining report. He told me Vance left it with him for safe-keeping last week."

She put her hands back up to her face and massaged her temples and forehead, as if easing away a headache.

"Don't you see? That could be what they were looking for today. It might be why they broke into Vance's place. It might be why Vance died." As she spoke, Graysie's voice lowered to a desperate whisper. "I'm scared. What am I going to do?"

As she stared across the table at him, tears slid down her cheeks, but she was so frightened she didn't seem to notice.

"Where is it?" Nathan said, more sharply than he intended. "Where's the report?"

She wiped the back of her hand across

her eyes. "The report? At Gold House. Under my mattress. I put it there when I got home. I haven't looked at it yet. Why?"

"Finish your drink and let's go. We need to show it to John or Sebastian. One of them will know what to do."

Twenty Seven

Minette was in the yard, sprinkling grain for the Gold House hens under Graysie's loving eye, when Sebastian and Nathan arrived back from checking out the mines. They dismounted and led their horses towards the stables.

"What happened? Did you find anything?"

Graysie's voice trembled, and Nathan suspected from the way she shakily picked her way towards them she was close to collapse. Even her willingness to remain at home while he and Sebastian had ridden out to inspect the Ophir and the Ruby showed she was not her usual buoyant self.

Seb picked up on her anxious scrutiny. "Sorry, Graysie, nothing to report. We couldn't get in. Everything's chained and padlocked. You didn't lock it up, did you?"

She blinked rapidly, and her arms hung loosely at her sides. "No. I haven't gone near it."

"Well, someone is keen to prevent anyone from getting in." Seb had a deep, kindly baritone.

"I don't understand. Who'd do that?" Her voice was high-pitched, another sign of her stressed state. Minette sidled to Graysie's side, reaching out her plump little fingers for her skirt like a safety line.

A few hours earlier, when they'd got back from the teahouse, Graysie had retrieved Vance's report from under her mattress and they'd spread it out and gone through it together.

Much of what it outlined was what Nathan might have expected. The bombshell came right at the end, after Vance had found what he considered being excellent prospects for future earnings.

However, he reported, a recent inspection had found evidence of rogue mining in the northern chamber which butted onto the Ruby, and unofficial work in the Ruby as well, although he knew of none of the town's laborers being employed there. So that was it. Illegal operations on one side of the boundary and rogue dealings on the other.

Nathan turned to Sebastian. "Graysie's overwhelmed. I think she needs a rest." He leaned down to Minette. Her free hand held a small wicker basket in which nestled two newly laid brown eggs.

"Sweetheart, why don't you take those eggs in to Mrs. Snively and ask her if we could have some iced water out in the pergola? If you're lucky, she might give you a biscuit, too. Take it slowly, now..."

Minette smiled up at him and began a purposeful walk back to the house. With a light touch on her lower back, Nathan guided Graysie to the pergola. As she sank onto the bench seat, she wiped her forehead with the back of her hand and gave a tentative laugh.

"I'm not sure I can handle any more excitement, Nathan. It's all a bit much."

"You're still in shock from this morning." Nathan cast his mind back to the gruesome blackened corpse, the mutilated dog, Willie's death-white senseless form, and he gritted his teeth. Coming on top of Weavers' attack, it was no wonder Graysie felt overwhelmed. He closed his eyes briefly, willing himself to refocus.

He'd been desperately hoping he'd get the chance to talk to her more about Charlotte's death, to clear the air. He wanted to explain the contradictions that warred within him. The guilt he carried that his love wasn't strong enough to make everything right. Shame that he'd agreed to a marriage he'd had doubts about from the start.

But one look at Graysie's lost, forlorn face and he realized she was in no state for deep talks. She was at the end of her tether.

"I've got this weird impulse. I want to go home." She stared down at her hands, and then up with a bewildered smile. "Except I don't have a home... I haven't had one for a very long time." She let out a long sigh and shuddered.

"If Willie dies…" He saw her lips were trembling. "If he dies, I'll never forgive myself."

Twenty Eight

"Nearly as good as the dim sum and steamed pork buns our old Amah Rose used to make." Nathan pushed his plate aside with a satisfied smile and patted his stomach. Seb and John murmured agreement.

"For sure. Who'd have thought we'd be eating great Chinese food together nearly twenty years later and seven thousand miles away from home?" John grinned at his younger brothers. "Although I grant you, it's a long time since any of us called Hong Kong home."

"No argument," said Nathan. "But no matter how long you're away, the tastes and smells of Queen's Road are always there, tickling your memory, aren't they?"

Nathan looked at his brothers over the remains of their dinner. They'd feasted on rice balls and steamed fish, an array of fresh Chinese vegetables usually eschewed by non-Chinese, with salted watermelon seeds, candied ginger, and pickled fruit to finish.

They were meeting at Seb's request in the deputy sheriff's office on the main street. Seb had wanted to brainstorm with his brothers on the murder inquiry, which had hit yet another dead end with their ride out to the Ophir that afternoon.

Vance's report spelled out the skulduggery that was afoot. They agreed on that. The locked entry was an admission of guilt by whoever was behind all this. They now saw why two supposedly worthless mines might be attractive to the wrong people. But that was as far as it went.

The chains and padlocks gave them no clue to who'd put them there, apart from confirming the hunch they'd been working on all along. The attacks—the deaths of the prospectors, the extortion and threats towards the female mine owners—were all tied into the real value of the underground ore.

Seb leaned back in his chair, hands locked behind his head. "We could go back tomorrow with bolt cutters and get inside for a proper look," he said.

"We could," John agreed. "But meantime Nathan, isn't it worth confirming with Lisette that she knew nothing about the mining going on in the Ruby? I'm pretty sure she's not seen a dime from it and she still owns around seventy percent, doesn't she?"

Nathan nodded. "As far as I know, yes. With Weavers dead, we don't know who owns the rest. Maybe he'd already sold it before he died."

Seb grimaced. "She's being fleeced, anyway. Despicable when you consider her circumstances." He yawned and stretched his long legs out in front of him.

"Thing is," said John. "How can we find out who's behind it? Apart from the obvious, setting a guard on it. But I'll wager they'll probably lie low for some time, maybe give up altogether. They'll realize we're onto them if we cut the bolts."

Seb made a growl deep in his throat.

"I suppose that will stop the illegal activity, but it brings us no closer to finding the killers." He ran his fingers over his temples and drew them down on either side of his face. "I need some sleep."

"Let's cut to the heart of the matter," John said. "Who are we expecting to find down there? Can we name names?" He challenged them with his dark eyes, as he'd done when they'd been children, Nathan recalled, and they were working out the rules for some game.

"If we set a trap, who would we expect to see turn up in it?"

Sebastian and Nathan exchanged looks. Neither seemed keen to name names. Then Nathan cleared his throat. "As we've noted before, John, de Vile has been rabid about getting his hands on Graysie's shares.

"You've seen the way he's gone after her. That display when he turned up at the house when Minette was missing was contemptible. But we won't ever catch him down there digging."

Sebastian nodded his agreement. "You're right. If he's behind it, we'll have no chance of pinning it on him. He'll have a chorus line doing his dirty work for him."

Nathan fidgeted in his chair. "You know what I think, John, but I'm not sure if you're ready to hear it. Willoughby Martens would be my pick. He'd rather play dirty for easy pickings than play clean and work for it, any day.

"But there's nothing much in the way of evidence. I accept that."

He put up his hand in an arresting gesture, expecting John's dissent.

"All of it's circumstantial. A mention of him by Weavers and his accomplice that night they nearly killed me. That someone employed a Sydney Duck for the hit of Madam Ring."

John regarded him with steady black

eyes. "I've dropped the business I had with him, Nathan. I've told him I'm not pursuing it."

Nathan's stomach tightened. "Really, John? You won't regret it. Was that hard to do?"

The older Russell shook his head. "Not really. When I considered his proposition a second time, it wasn't that attractive. But mostly it was because of your 'character reference'.

"You know him, after all. Though, of course, I didn't tell him that. I decided I didn't want to be involved with someone who's caused our family grief. Your word is good enough for me."

Nathan grinned and, for the first time that evening, a weight lifted from his shoulders.

"You'll live to be very glad you did. I'd bet on it."

"What happened between you, Nat?" John asked. "Why is he so bitter?"

Nathan shrugged. "Fact is when his father died suddenly a couple of years ago, they weren't even speaking. They hadn't been for close for at least a year. Willoughby disappeared up north on some rapscallion escapade after the old man cut him off because of his crazy drinking and violent fights. He was always getting into fights."

Nathan pushed at some hair that was falling over his face.

"When he got word his dad had died, he rushed back to Sydney and played on Charlotte's soft heart. He was always my wife's adored older brother... And with her father gone... She craved a substitute. Her mother died when she was only small, and her dad was everything to her, and she to him."

He picked at a fingernail. "I guess I failed her on that score. I didn't understand how much she still relied on her father, and when he died, she saw her brother as the replacement. She'd always viewed him through rose-colored spectacles. She so desperately wanted to believe that 'Will'—as she called him—was ready to turn over a new leaf." He shrugged.

"She convinced my stepfather to take him on at the investment house. To give him another chance. He'd matured, she said. He recognized he'd been irresponsible."

He spread his hands wide, palms up, and gave another slight grin. "Charlotte could be very persuasive. So, he got his second chance. He was smart, he was charming when he wanted to be, and he did well at persuading people—

particularly women of means with no men in their lives—to invest with us."

Nathan got up from the table and walked to a sideboard where a china tea pot sat with a set of classic smooth-sided cups beside it. He paused as he poured out three steaming, fragrant green teas and delivered them back to his brothers.

"He thought being family protected him. In his version of reality, Charlotte was his 'get off scot-free ticket'. He expected if we picked up on what he was doing we'd turn a blind eye to save her, and the firm, from the public shame. But he miscalculated on both counts. He got too greedy for Jim to ignore it.

"I picked up discrepancies in the banking ledger which he couldn't explain, and I told Jim. We never publicly shamed him. We quietly reimbursed the clients' funds and got rid of him.

"But for months afterward, Jim kept finding more losses. He'd even mortgaged Jim's house fraudulently. It was far worse than we'd ever realized initially. Finally, it destroyed Jim's health and the business."

He got up and went back for a second cup of green tea. He glanced up at his brothers mid-pour.

"Sad thing was, Charlotte refused to believe her brother had done anything wrong. Martens got in her ear and convinced her I'd made a dreadful mistake. I was away in Newcastle, north of Sydney, chasing up on export orders when it all blew up.

"She insisted she come up and explain to me why he was innocent. She and Joshua got on the overnight steamer and sailed straight into the most almighty storm we'd seen on that part of the New

South Wales coast for many a year.

"They hit a sandbar and didn't make the final hundred yards to shore. Punishing waves swamped any lifeboats as fast as the crew launched them. Sixty-six people on board, and only one man made it to shore alive. Bodies washed up for days afterwards."

Nathan slumped in his chair, head thrown back, waiting for the piercing pain to fade away. Seb's chair legs screeched against the stone floor as he thrust back with an edgy rocking motion.

John sipped his tea in silence, cupping the warm vessel in both hands. Nathan noticed for the first time that his brother's dark brown hair was showing silver streaks at the temples. John lifted his eyes and regarded Nathan steadily.

"So that's why he's got it in for you? Surely any sane man can see it wasn't your fault?"

Nathan flashed him a humorless smile. "He could blame himself or blame me. I guess it's not surprising he chose to blame me." He spread his hands open in a helpless gesture.

"But I can't help thinking about the 'if only's.' If only I wasn't away so much. Jim had me out of town a lot. If only I'd understood how much Charlotte was missing her own father.

"She was so desperately alone. I guess she couldn't face losing Will so soon after her father died. That's what I concluded, anyway. I never had the chance to ask her. In the end, I failed her when she needed me most."

Seb stood up suddenly, raised his arms over his head and stretched his long frame, then frowned.

"Willoughby Martens is obviously a

complete rotter and a fraud. No argument there. However, if he's also our rogue miner, I hate to tell you there's not a lot the law can do about it. When something like this arises, it's treated as a business dispute rather than a crime. The parties in disagreement have to go to court.

"We can go down there and check out what's happening on behalf of the rightful owners, but if we confirm there's a rogue operation, Graysie and Lisette have to seek a remedy in court. That will be long-winded and expensive."

John stood and stretched before sitting down again and turning to Nathan. "Seb's right. As a deputy, he's charged with finding the killers, but he can't get involved in a mining squabble, even if the right and wrong of it seems clear."

Nathan nodded. "One thing occurs to

me. Do you think, now the rogue operation is out in the open, the attacks will stop? Or rather, if we advertised we'd discovered it by cutting the bolts and chains, would it stop it all in its tracks?"

"Why do you think it would do that?" Seb asked.

"Well, maybe they've been trying to get as much free gold as they can before they're discovered."

John chimed in. "I see what you're driving at. Are you suggesting we go up there tomorrow and make a big deal of it?"

"Maybe," said Nathan. "Why not?"

Seb tapped his fingers on the back of a chair.

"I've got a better idea. Why don't we slip in there quietly and wait to see who turns up?" He glanced from John to

Nathan, his eyebrows raised. "Question is, which would work best to catch a killer?"

*****

Graysie awoke in a cold sweat, struggling to breathe. Moonlight flooded the room, but all around her the house lay silent and peaceful. She rested on her back, staring at the carved ceiling rose overhead, momentarily stunned by the rush of wakefulness.

She was panting, as if she'd been in a high odds race it was essential she win. And then the horror of the image she'd seen in her sleep floated back before her eyes.

A blackened corpse, curved like a pretzel, buried in the ashes. When the firemen had pulled him clear, he was protecting his head in futile denial, his arms two charred sticks. A glaring row of bared teeth offered the only clue she was staring at a human being.

She covered her face with her hands, racked by dry sobbing, as she remembered what came next in her dream. The gruesome spectre had straightened, looked directly at her, and begun beckoning to her. The lips moved around the macabre teeth in a terrifying smile.

She rocked back and forth gently in bed, crooning to herself. No more death. No more.

An overwhelming certainty that the charred man was Nathan gripped her. She trembled as she remembered what the dream seemed to tell her; if he continued to search for the men who had killed three times already, he would be the next one to die. Whoever the murderers were, they'd already tried and missed twice. She couldn't afford to risk a third time.

Death seems to follow you around.

Sebastian Russell's words echoed in her mind.

Her teeth chattered in the balmy night, and she curled into a tight ball, her hands pressed together, sobbing until her rib cage ached, willing the fear to melt away. When the sobs finally died, she lay rigid, eyes wide open, until the first bird calls signaled a new dawn.

She knew what she must do, and she planned to waste no time in getting on with it.

Twenty Nine

"The Sisters offer homes for orphaned children, Miss Castellanos. We're not here to provide accommodation for solo women and children who are passing through."

Tall, big-boned Sister Mor peered across her desk to Graysie, who sat with Minette snuggled in her lap, the top of the child's curly mop tucked under Graysie's chin.

The sister's voice had a cold, disapproving edge; Minette tensed against her chest as the nun spoke. Even if she didn't understand fully what the woman was saying, the child detected they were not welcome.

The religious woman's face puckered with distaste as she gazed at Graysie, silent judgment written plain on tight lips and narrowed, hard eyes. She could read her thoughts.

Respectable single women don't travel around singing with a stray child in tow... This one won't fit here.

Sister Mor's forehead wrinkled and her eyes bulged under the shadow of her wimple. She sat slightly hunched, as if she'd spent a lifetime concealing her unusual height; her arms seemed too long for her body and hung awkwardly at her sides.

'Mor'—meaning 'long' in Gaelic—was right for her, thought Graysie. Long in body and punitive judgement. The only thing she was short on was compassion.

Graysie had arrived at the Sisters of Mercy school and orphanage full of optimism that she might find safe lodgings for herself and Minette for a few weeks while she got her life sorted.

She'd be close to Willie, and she'd do anything she could to help his recovery. She'd lie low within the protecting convent and reduce the chance of being attacked again.

And she'd distance herself from Nathan to ensure he wasn't in the firing line any longer, either. It had seemed like the wisest escape plan when she'd lain awake in the dawn light. But the longer she sat in Sister Mor's presence, the more she realized the church didn't accept people like her.

The imposing, newly opened stone school building nicely complemented the impressive St Mary's Chapel built ten years before. Townsfolk had enthusiastically welcomed and supported the Catholic brothers in their work, bringing, as it did, opportunities for schooling, which encouraged more families to settle in Grass Valley. The townsfolk were always keen to leaven the numbers of wild single men looking for adventure when they weren't hard at work in the mines.

The priest who was in charge of the entire mission could not have been more different from the woman who sat in front of her.

Graysie had met Father John O'Brien at Cressida Washington's fundraising fashion show a few days earlier, and she'd noted the powerful sense of peace and love he carried. If there was anyone who brought Jesus alive in dark places, it was Father O'Brien.

His round, sun-tanned face was almost cherubic, but you'd be foolish to dismiss him as a jolly but inconsequential priest. Physically strong and weather-beaten from many years in the saddle, he carried with him an innate sense of vigor and purpose.

His determination and drive was the main reason Grass Valley had this impressive church complex in the middle of town.

Graysie knew he traveled many miles on his staunch mule in all weathers to minister to sick miners. Some of the roughest mountain men held him in warm affection because of his willingness to risk his own safety in times of dire need.

He'd identified likely candidates for the priesthood from the tough adventurers he ministered to, with two of them currently entered into Holy Orders, preparing to return to the diocese as assistant priests.

Father O'Brien was known for his open-hearted acceptance of people, and she realized she'd been hoping—anticipating even—that she might have been able to see him with her request for shelter. It was not her lucky day.

When she'd entered the cold, silent waiting area on arrival, it had been Sister Mor who'd emerged to meet her. And right from the start, they seemed to get off on the wrong foot.

When Sister Mor asked Graysie where she was currently staying, and she'd said with Sir John Russell, the nun's mouth tightened with disapproval. She'd explained he was her 'godfather', and the nun's eyes were chips of granite.

A rising sense of panic seized Graysie

as she realized it was likely she would not find refuge with the Sisters of Mercy. Sister Mor did not approve of her or her quest to care for Minette as a single woman. As if reading her mind, Sister Mor's voice broke through her reverie.

"We're willing to take the child if she's a genuine orphan. That is what our mission is called to do. But we're unable to accommodate both of you. And if either of the child's parents is still alive… Well, we would need consent or approval from them."

Graysie's thoughts flicked to Francine's husband, a feckless French adventurer who'd been in all kinds of escapades which made for fascinating story-telling during their short courtship. The confines of married life had shown a much less attractive side of Phillipe Coubert, who'd grown surly and bored with domesticity.

Francine had soon discovered he liked the idea of quick riches far more than settling down to domestic life. When she'd fallen pregnant with Minette, he'd been truculent and callous. He'd no plans to become some woman's pet, he'd announced, sitting in a shop or office every day.

He'd deserted Francine soon after Minette's birth, leaving town with another woman on the latest wild venture. His defection forced Francine to return to her work as a dealer to keep them fed. Her friend had no idea where he was or even if he was still alive, but if he was, he wasn't interested in his daughter.

But would that disinterest continue if he heard Minette stood to inherit a mine?

Graysie's insides turned icy at the sudden thought.

No, there was no way she would re-introduce him to Minette's life, even if she knew where to find him.

In the silence, as the nun glared coldly at her, another wild thought struck her Maybe she and Minette should disappear somewhere, just like Phillipe had?

She was about to set Minette aside from her lap and get up to leave when she heard a rustle in the doorway behind her.

A fresh-faced younger sister stood in the opening, bowing to Sister Mor before announcing, "Sister Mor, Father O'Brien sends his greetings. He's returned from the mountains and would like to meet with your visitor in the chancel."

Sister Mor could not hide the look of surprise, then disapproval, that passed fleetingly like rain clouds across her face before she set her expression to one of calculated composure.

"Well, Miss Castellanos, I'm surprised the Father has asked to see you, but I won't waste any of your time…"

She stood stiffly and led the way out like she was heading a choir procession into the chapel and down the central aisle. Father O'Brien sat in a chair at one side of the altar and rose to greet them warmly. He gestured for them to be seated in a front pew.

"Sister Mor, I won't detain you from your duties—I'm sure you'd prefer to be attending to other things. Perhaps we could catch up over lunch in a couple of hours? And I wonder if you could send in Sister Maria to help entertain this little miss here…"

He glanced towards Minette, seated close to Graysie in the pew. Rainbow colors streamed through the stained glass of the nave windows, haloing the priest in bright light.

The Sister masked her surprise as she rose to go, giving Graysie a perfunctory nod as she left. Quickly and quietly, Sister Maria, a young blonde postulant, arrived with a basket of musical instruments—triangles, Spanish maracas, Mexican pipes, and a small harp.

Within minutes, the music-making toys captivated Minette, and she and the new nun settled down a few feet away to experiment with the sounds of the mini orchestra.

Father O'Brien folded his hands into his lap and leaned forward to speak. "Miss Castellanos, I've been hearing disquieting whispers in my forays into the mountains, and I thought it might be wise for us to have a little chat."

His Irish brogue had a comforting lilt, but a bolt of fear shot through Graysie at his words.

Father O'Brien's eyes darted to where Sister Maria and Minette were making up a little song, the Sister on a wooden flute, Minette on triangles. Satisfied their game absorbed them, he turned back to Graysie.

"I was called to give last rites to an old fellow at Sixways earlier today. You appreciate I can't tell you anything that would break a death bed confidence, but neither do I want to remain silent if I have information that suggests a threat against the living." He paused and sighed.

"But before I get to that, perhaps you can explain to me, as no doubt you have to Sister Mor, why you are here today?"

Graysie wriggled uncomfortably in her

hard seat. "Since we arrived in Grass Valley a little over a week ago, we—Minette and I—have enjoyed very kind hospitality from Sir John Russell up at the Gold House.

"Sir John is an old business colleague of my Uncle Eustace. He describes himself as my godfather by proxy... He knew my uncle well, but we'd never met until last week."

Her face reddened, and she cursed inwardly. She was going on about their relationship too much.

"But..." She hesitated. "I've decided I can't prevail on his hospitality any longer, and I wondered if the Sisters might allow Minette and I to stay as paying guests for a time?

"I'd like to be close to Willie Watson, to help care for him." She paused, uncertain how to continue. "However,

Sister Mor has explained that doesn't fit the operating rules of the convent..."

Father O'Brien's hands lay still in his lap, and he nodded without speaking, the silence inviting her to continue.

Graysie clasped her hands together in a praying attitude. "I can't stay with Sir John any longer. I urgently need alternative secure accommodation."

Father O'Brien nodded again. "Secure? Have you any reason to feel unsafe, my dear?"

His quiet concern touched her somewhere deep inside, and she knew if she didn't hold herself tight, tears would spring to her eyes.

"There've been several disturbing events," she admitted. "I don't know what to make of them, or how worried I should be... But, yes, I have concerns."

Graysie fiddled with a rough edge on

one fingernail and suppressed the urge to nibble at it with her teeth.

"Explain what those are, young lady." Father O'Brien stared hard and waited.

"Well... You would have heard about the upset with Madam Ring. Minette went missing, and it seemed the Madam was to blame. Except the troubles didn't end with the Madam's unfortunate death... Mrs. Guilliame, Mr. Nathan Russell, me and now Willie Watson..."

A lump in her throat blocked off the rest of her sentence, and she swallowed hard. "We've all been attacked or threatened. Honestly, I don't know who I can trust," she rasped. "And I'm worried that people who've helped me are in danger." She sighed.

"Willie's beating is the final straw, honestly. I feel responsible. Perhaps it would be wise for me to go somewhere else and to relinquish my hopes of making something of the inheritance Uncle Eustace left for me, but I so want to give Minette a normal life."

Father O'Brien nodded. "And Minette? How do you come to have the care of the child? You're not her mother, I understand?"

Graysie shook her head. "No. Minette's mother died in a fire at the Golden Galleon Casino nearly six months ago. We've been dear friends for years, and long before the fire, I promised Francine if anything happened to her, I would treat Minette like my own daughter. Minette's father left them when she was tiny, and she has no other family here."

"And your family, child? Haven't you others you can call on?" Father O'Brien's worn face wrinkled in concern.

"My mother died and my brother and

sister went missing in a stage coach crash when I was young."

Her throat closed up, and her voice came out in a strangled croak. She hated talking about her siblings. She couldn't bear to think of how they might have suffered.

"The crash stranded us in the wild for hours in the dark before help arrived, you see—my mother dead, the coach driver unconscious."

She thought of the many times she'd pretended the twins had come home unharmed, that they were all together again. When she was little, they were the only ones she'd tell her secrets to.

"My father never got over the loss, even though he remarried. It wasn't a happy union, and he died a few years after that. I've been responsible for myself since I turned fourteen. I sang with the Carlton Family Singers until I was seventeen and then branched out in a solo singing career.

"I love music, and so does Minette. I know it's frowned upon in some circles, but singing as a professional career is finally gaining respectability. Look at the careers of Antoinette Sterling and Madam Adelina Patti. Or Pania Hayes."

A sudden thought struck her. "I could give singing lessons to the pupils in the convent school—if that would be a help." She knew she sounded desperate, but she couldn't help herself.

Father O'Brien tented his fingers in front of his nose and blew out a gentle breath.

"Strangely enough, the Sisters were saying the other day they need help with the children's choir and your experience could be invaluable, as long as you know some sacred songs as well as the more popular ones."

He tapped his fingers together in a light rhythm and smiled. She guessed the conversation was drawing to a close. And then he suddenly interjected, "Miss Castellanos, can you think of any reason someone would want to harm you or Minette?"

This was the question she'd been turning over and over in her head the last few days, and she wasn't any closer to an answer, but she was shocked to hear it from the priest's lips.

"I have asked myself that question endlessly, Father. All I know is that someone seems to want to stop me taking any interest in the mine..." Her voice trailed off.

Father O'Brien nodded. "The man I saw at Sixways today was knifed during a brawl. He was trying to break up a fight—it was a tragic case of being in the wrong place at the wrong time—or so I was told. I got the impression he knew more than he was letting on.

"He was close to Madam Ring, and I wonder what she told him. In his deathbed confession, he wanted to warn you. He says you should talk to Willie Watson, who knew more about it."

He consulted a pocket watch on a long chain in his cassock pocket and sighed. "Of course, you have already done that and we know how it turned out."

He reached out and rang a little silver hand bell that sat on the chair beside him. "I need to prepare for midday prayers, my dear, so I can't tarry any longer talking. I'm going to instruct Sister Mor that we will appoint you as singing teacher and assistant choir leader."

A sudden warmth, she recognised the feeling as elation, coursed through Graysie's body at the Father's words.

He continued. "Please sort out the details with the Sister. As part of your annuity, we'll provide you with quarters in the orphanage annex, if you require them—you and Minette."

A job and somewhere to stay. I can't believe my good fortune.

At the sound of the bell, Sister Maria had paused in her music-making. Fastening closed a small accordion, she turned to Minette and said, "Father must leave now, Minette, and I will go with him, so can you pack up your triangles and maracas in the basket for the other children?"

She rose and glided to Father O'Brien's side as the older priest stood slowly to his feet and gathered his priestly robes around him. He turned towards Graysie, clasped both her hands in his, and stood silently, his head bowed for a few minutes, as if saying a silent prayer.

"There is one other thing I would like you to do, my dear. This man you call Uncle Eustace, who left you this legacy. What more do you know about him or his other business affairs?"

Graysie hunched her shoulders in defeat. "Nothing much, Father. Why do you ask?"

"I recall a fellow called Eustace in one of my early parishes on the coast. Probably not the same fellow, of course—as I recall it, he came from an important family back East—but perhaps the answer you are looking for lies in your uncle's affairs."

He squeezed her hands lightly and walked out, leaving a faint aroma of incense stirring in the air behind him.

Thirty

"So where is it?" Hector de Vile's mouth set in a hard line. Willoughby Martens clenched his back teeth and willed himself to look bold. "I haven't got it—but neither has anyone else. It's not around to cause any further problems—for anyone. The fire at Watson's place destroyed it."

He glared at de Vile, challenging the man to contradict him. De Vile raised a skeptical eyebrow.

"Really? How do you know that?"

De Vile half turned away to lean against a chest high railing that enclosed a grassy enclosure where three thoroughbreds were going through their paces. His eyes keenly surveyed the action, but Martens knew he was listening for any hint of weakness or deceit in his voice.

One of De Vile's passions was horse racing, and he was preparing his stable for a five-day racing carnival at nearby La Porte in a few weeks' time. Martens followed his lead and stood alongside him at the trackside. He propped one leg on a lower railing, relaxed and in command for all the world to see. He cleared his throat.

"The Mexican kid took us up there. He'd been there with the uncle. But when the old guy realized what we were after, he set fire to the report before I could get to it.

"He killed Fat Jack as we were storming him. Silly bum destroyed the report rather than turn it over. I figured we may as well finish the job, so we torched the place. No way of them pinning it back to us. He got his, though."

"And the kid?"

"The kid's terrified. He won't be talking because he knows what's good for him. He ran off into the forest while the boys were busy with the old codger."

De Vile's attention snapped back to the track, where a dark gelding and a sable mare were thundering along shoulder-to-shoulder. The young jockeys were bent low in the saddle, whips flailing, intent on winning at all costs. Martens could see this was more than casual exercising for them.

Leaning back on his heels, de Vile rocked in evident satisfaction. A distant, unfocused smile flickered on his lips and was gone.

"Which one would you back to win?" He turned to Martens with a triumphant edge to his voice. There was no mistaking this was a test. With de Vile, everything was a test, he thought sourly.

"The dark horse." Martens replied before he'd even thought about it. "Always the dark horse," he said and laughed.

"You might be right. We'll have to see, won't we?" De Vile's eyebrows drew together, and his expression tightened.

"So why was the Castellanos woman up at Watson's place a couple of hours before you got there?"

Martens' mouth fell open before he could mask his shock. "The Castellanos woman?"

"That's right. The Castellanos woman." Hector de Vile's face creased in a nasty sneer. "You know her?" The tone was hard, sarcastic. Martens scrambled to recover lost ground.

"Of course I know her. I was with her last night. I gave her that report of Bill's to soften her up for the share sale." He stamped his feet on the ground, as if to underline his control. "She probably went up there to show it to him, is what I'd guess."

"And he wouldn't have pulled out Vance's little piece of work to compare notes?" de Vile said in a voice that could cut diamonds. "What if he was bluffing when he set fire to the report— presuming that touching scene actually happened? 'Cos it might have all been a fake show."

The acid burned in Martens' gut. How he hated this overbearing cockerel who thought he was better and smarter than anyone else.

Give me a chance and I'll show him who's top man.

He'd been unlucky to come up against Nathan Russell, that's all. If they hadn't thrown him out of the investment house, he'd be one of the richest men in Sydney by now. And now that little tart was causing him more grief.

"A fake show?" Martens echoed. "I doubt it. Highly unlikely." He eyeballed de Vile. "I've got an idea. Why don't I offer to show Miss Castellanos through the Ophir, say I can explain aspects of our report to her? Let her see why Lightning Bill came to the conclusions he did. Soften her up a bit?"

A low laugh bubbled up from deep within him. Suddenly, everything promised to be a lot more fun. The groin itch distracted him again and was hard to suppress the urge to scratch himself. He licked his lips in anticipation at the prospect of conducting the little princess down the dark tunnels.

De Vile gave him a hard look. "I'll leave you to work out the details. But don't you dare let me down…" Again, unsaid comments hung in the air.

There was a shout from the track, and both men turned to see what was happening. The horses came thundering around the circular arena. Stride for stride, there seemed nothing to separate them. As they passed de Vile in a shower of dust, he raised his hand exultantly in salute at their neck and neck charge.

Then, a few yards from the finish line, the black gelding shied as a hare broke cover from the long grass lining the track and sprang across their line of sight. The sable surged unchecked and won by a neck.

De Vile turned to Martens, lips pressed together in a slight grimace. "Hope you've got better judgment with woman than with horses," he said with a sniff as he turned to go.

Thirty One

Graysie was sitting with Minette on the veranda having scones and tea when she heard the squeak of coach wheels and she knew John Russell had returned. Her stomach cramped at the prospect of confronting him, but she also knew she could not turn tail and run, although she wanted to. She owed him an explanation and her thanks.

The servants had already loaded their two trunks and leather carry-alls onto the wagon, which was drawn up at the gate. She was certain he would not have missed that detail as he arrived. His scowl as he came up the front path proved it. He strolled up the steps and stood directly in front of her.

"Miss Castellanos." He gave a little mock grin, as if to show he was playing, but a muscle pulsed under his left eye, like a warning light flicking on and off. Funny. She'd never noticed the nervous tic before.

"We've seen very little of you recently. I was wondering if we'd offended you."

Graysie rose with a quick gasp. "Sir John. You've been wonderful. I'm sorry for my absence. It's been... unavoidable." She turned and paced a few steps. "Your hospitality really has been unrivalled."

She saw his face remained stony. "However, we can't continue to take advantage of your kindness..." Her voice trailed off, and she stood, hands hanging at her sides, for a few seconds before resuming her seat.

Nothing for it but to charge on, she thought. Delay would only make things worse.

"This morning I called on the Sisters of Mercy, and they have kindly offered me a position teaching singing at their school." Again, she was aware of her sentence trailing off, sounding like an apology.

John's eyes were flinty. "I see. So, you've made alternative arrangements." Graysie detected treacherous undercurrents:

You've rejected me.

Minette fidgeted in her chair. The child was picking up on the rising tension without understanding its cause once again.

She turned to Minette. "Sweetheart, why don't you help Mrs. Snively knead the dough while Sir John and I have a little talk?"

Minette rose, gave a dip of her head

towards Sir John and skipped off towards the kitchen. Graysie turned back to the magnate.

"Sir John, I've had a wonderful stay. You rescued us when we were in desperate need! But I cannot continue to accept help from you when I've nothing to offer in return."

As soon as the words were out, she knew she'd been clumsy. When she glanced up, she saw she'd lit a rage that John had, until now, concealed.

"Nothing to offer? You've forgotten that I suggested there could be a future for you here at Gold House?"

His jaw set in a hard line, and then, as suddenly as his rage bubbled up, it died, replaced by an icy detachment.

"Frankly, Miss Castellanos, I question your sanity. Why you would reject a comfortable future here for both you and that child to scratch away in poverty with the nuns? I can't fathom it."

She sensed he was beyond the reach of her logic and any answer might provoke him further.

"Sir John, I have to be certain Minette is safe. Those bizarre attacks unnerved me, and Willie's injury is the final straw. I blame myself. I want to be there to do anything I can to help him get well again. And I'm worried about people close to me being attacked. I couldn't stand it if anyone else got hurt."

He snorted. "And you think the nuns can protect you better than I can? That really is a joke." He strolled to the balustrade and stared out into the garden, silent for a minute or two, while she held her breath and willed herself not to jump in with nervous explanations.

Then he spun back to face her. "Has it ever occurred to you might be the problem?"

"Me?" A sharp griping sensation deep in her gut warned Graysie she might faint, but it passed, leaving her feeling merely queasy.

"I don't know what you mean. What are you hinting at?"

He skewered her with his icy stare. "You somehow persuaded Eustace to leave you that mine, God knows how. We'd been lifelong partners, yet he hardly ever mentioned it to me. And he left it to you—someone I understand he barely knew and hadn't seen since the night your mother died."

Graysie chilled to her soul. "The night mother died? Was Eustace there? I don't remember..."

The flicker in his eyes hinted that he'd

said more than he intended. He took a deep breath. "There is a very great deal you don't know or remember, Miss Castellanos. And I'll be the very last person you'll hear it from.

"Now, if you are determined to go to the nuns, you'd better do it. Off you go." He fluttered his hand dismissively, like he'd remembered far more important things that required his attention.

She shot him one last apologetic look, then fled for the kitchen. She could hear the peal of Minette's laughter in the hall. At least she was having fun.

She opened the kitchen door and skidded to a stop. Minette was at the kitchen table with a tea towel tied around her front, holding a knife dripping with vanilla cream over a tube-shaped pound cake. The cake was Minette's favorite, and Mrs. S knew it.

She had a dab of cream on her chin, and while Mrs. Snively was up to her elbows in hot water at the sink, Minette was applying the thick frosting under Nathan's watchful eye.

From the doorway, Graysie watched as he playfully dabbed her chin with his handkerchief while Minette giggled. Then he sensed Graysie's presence and his head jerked to where she stood watching them.

She gave him a brief nod and fixed her gaze on the child. "Come on, sweetie, finish up there now. We have to leave." Graysie paused and turned to the housekeeper. "I hope she hasn't been a nuisance, Mrs. Snively."

"She's been a total pet as always," Mrs. Snively said, wiping her wet hands on her apron. "The cake is pretty well finished, poppet. You'll have to come back and eat it later when the cream topping has set."

Minette stuck her bottom lip out as if to dispute her directions, but Nathan jumped in. "Come on, princess! Off to fresh adventures!" He untied the tea towel, gave her cheeks a cursory wipe with it, and turned to Graysie.

"Where are you off to, if I may be so bold to ask?"

Graysie steeled herself to reply. "Actually, we're moving to the Sisters of Mercy today. You always thought that would be more suitable for us, as I recall. I've come around to agreeing with you."

Mrs. Snively gave a yelp of protest. Nathan stared. Graysie took Minette by the hand.

"Come on, baby girl, we've got to get moving. We'll come and visit Mrs. Snively another time."

Thirty Two

Nathan Russell swung the big boar carcass onto Anna Santa Maria's kitchen table. It landed with a satisfying thump. "There you are. That will keep you going with pork and beans for a little while."

The sack of beans leaned against the table leg, full and round.

Anna had aged ten years since he'd last seen her. Had it really been only ten days since Vance had been killed? Her cheeks were dark hollows, and her collapsed shoulders signaled distress, but the kitchen smelt of welcoming food.

Red chilis dried overhead, and on the stove a bubbling stew filled the air with the fragrance of garlic and tomatoes. He pinched the bridge of his nose and took a deep breath.

"Anna, it's probably pointless to ask. It's self-evident that things will be difficult. But how are you making out?"

"How do you think?" Life was beating her down, but Nathan heard the steel in her voice.

Okay. Try again. This family deserves help, and I can sacrifice a little dignity to do it.

"Anna, I want to help. I know it must be hard…"

"Hard? You don't know how hard." She glared at him but didn't elaborate.

He stared back in a stalemate of silence. The twins were playing in the room next door, and little riffs of playful giggles penetrated the thick adobe walls. Freshly washed greens lay on the bench.

Maria's sense of loss was raw, but the

home had an emotional heart, a sense of warmth and provision, that reassured him. "I'm sorry I haven't visited sooner. How is Antonio doing?"

At the sound of Antonio's name, Anna flinched, as if he'd hit her across the shoulders with a lump of wood.

"Antonio?" she echoed. Her stiffness dissolved. "Antonio's in a dark place. He's having nightmares, but he won't say what they're about. He's pretending nothing's wrong."

Antonio isn't saying, and neither is she.

Nathan could tell by the way she evaded his gaze and crossed her arms in front of her chest she too was hiding things.

"Where is he?"

"I don't know. He spends a lot of time at the stables. When he's not there, he disappears. He's rarely here."

"Like he's frightened of something," he suggested. Nathan was certain of it, even before her confirmation. She nodded.

"Yes, like he's frightened. We're all frightened."

She paused, as if considering whether to say more, but thought better of it. "You don't know what it's like."

He sighed. "No, I don't, Anna. You're right. And the only way I can understand is if you explain it for me."

She shook her head vigorously and dashed a hand across the corner of her eye. It came away wet with tears.

"Look, I'm very grateful for the food," she said. "Don't think I'm not. Thank you for remembering us, from the bottom of my heart.

"But we're safest if we keep to ourselves. It's dangerous if we're seen talking to people."

"Seen? Who is there to see you?"

"It doesn't matter who. Take my word for it."

He shook his head in frustration. "You can't handle this—whatever it is—on your own. You're caring for six children alone! It's not reasonable to deal with more."

She stared, hands on hips, her face a dark scowl of raw indignation. "Reasonable? Life isn't reasonable. It's remorseless. Do you dispute that? Comprendes?" Her voice had a staccato ring.

A picture of Charlotte, curled up in a big chair, her knees tucked up under her skirt as she smiled contentedly, flashed before him. She'd so loved being a mother.

Remorseless? She's right.

"I understand, Anna. And No. I don't dispute that life isn't reasonable. But that doesn't mean you have to do it alone."

The conversation had reached another dead end, but the atmosphere was more mellow and accepting than when he'd first arrived. Anna's anger had dissipated, replaced by a sense of fatality.

They sat like that for several minutes. Then Anna roused herself to offer him a coffee. From his seat at the kitchen table, Nathan could see out to the front door. He glanced in that direction, hearing the trip of little bare feet across wooden floorboards.

The younger children were running for the front door. They'd divined a visitor arriving and lined up, looking fit to explode with excitement when the door opened.

"An-to-nio, An-to-nio," they chanted in sing-song unison. And again, savoring the delight of the chant. "An-to-nio."

Anna shot Nathan a quick look and put her index finger up to her lips. She didn't have to say a word. Her gesture conveyed all he needed to know. If Antonio sensed he was there, he'd disappear again.

The boy stepped into the room and immediately the little girls each took one of his hands, so delighted to have their cousin who was more-like-a-brother home they wouldn't allow him to escape their clutches.

They danced alongside him as he came into the kitchen, shoulders hunched, his face pale and drawn.

When he saw Nathan, he froze and attempted to whirl away, but the little sisters held on, blocking his exit. Nathan stepped forward quickly and gently took him by the shoulders.

"Take it easy, Antonio. I won't hurt you. I've brought food and something else, if you want it."

He flashed a half apologetic look at Anna. "That's if it's alright with your mother... I've brought you a dog. You can keep him for as long as you like."

A flicker of distrust flashed across Antonio's face, but his eyes lit up with an excitement he couldn't hide.

He stared at Nathan, and his boyish voice faltered. "A dog? A real dog?" He was having difficulty believing his luck. "What sort of dog?"

"A French hound called Vulcan. He's a splendid fellow. He belongs to my brother, but John gave him to me because Vulcan and I get on so well. I'm sure he'll be your friend, too."

A slow smile displaced the wariness. Antonio crossed to Anna and put his arms around her waist. He gazed up at her soulfully. "Mama, can we keep another dog? Can we?"

His arms dropped to his sides, and he bounced up and down on his toes as he waited for her reply.

Anna smiled at Nathan. "It looks like you've hit the jackpot here. When can we meet this dog? We can't decide until we see if he likes us and we like him."

Thirty minutes later they were all sitting around the table sharing the delicious stew while Vulcan lay snoring at Antonio's feet. Boy and dog had bonded at first sight, as Nathan had hoped they would, and already Antonio's careworn frown was fading.

"Can we get some food for him?" Antonio suddenly asked as they finished eating. "What does he like to eat?"

"Much the same as Neptune did, I'm sure," Nathan said. "Meat, bones, leftovers." Nathan looked from Antonio to Anna. "He's an excellent guard dog. It might help to have him here."

Antonio's eyes narrowed. "Would he attack someone if I wanted him to?"

"If he thought you were in danger, yes, he would. Is there someone you're afraid of?"

Antonio shrugged, and his gaze dropped to the floor. "Not really."

"Are you scared that whoever killed Neptune might come back?"

Antonio shook his head vigorously, but his face blanched and he restlessly flexed his fingers.

Nathan turned to Anna. "Do you need better locks? I'm happy to organize something for you. But if someone broke in, what would they be looking for?"

Anna shook her head a little too quickly and her words tumbled out in a rush. "No, no, there's nothing here for anyone to find. They've already searched…" She stopped mid-sentence. "I mean, if they searched, if they did…" she over-corrected, "they wouldn't find anything."

Her response was carefully measured, and Nathan didn't believe a word of it. Antonio was staring at a spot on the floor. Vulcan's sides rose and fell in rhythm with his soporific breathing. A couple of flies buzzed around his head, and he occasionally flicked an ear in his sleep to ward them off.

They were both lying. He knew it. But why?

"Anna, if someone has threatened you, the surest way to protect yourself is to tell me. We can't help if we don't know.

Vulcan will discourage them, but the very best safeguard is to be fully prepared if they try anything again. And to do that, we have to know what we're preparing for."

Antonio squinted up at his mother, as if trying to anticipate her response. Then he cleared his throat awkwardly and hesitated.

"Is Willie dead?" he asked in a tremulous voice.

The sudden change of topic startled Nathan. "Willie? Willie Watson? Did you know Willie?"

Anna stepped forward and slipped her arm around Antonio's shoulders, drawing him into shelter like a mother settling her chick. "Antonio gave him a helping hand sometimes, that's all. He liked Willie's dog."

Nathan suspected there was far more

to it. Antonio's hands trembled. He reminded Nathan of a bird poised to take flight. Something about the attack on Willie had deeply upset him.

And then, like a bolt from heaven, or a wild guess, a certainty in the pit of his stomach confirmed his hunch. Antonio had been there. He'd witnessed the attack.

The boy cringed into Anna's embrace, and as Nathan searched his face, he saw what he'd missed until now. Guilt. Antonio felt guilty. He turned the full force of his attention to the woman who shielded him.

"Anna, we have to put a stop to this right now. Don't you see? The boy feels responsible. And, goodness knows, whatever has gone on here, it's not Antonio's fault. They found a ruffian dead up there. Fire gutted the house.

Antonio didn't do that."

The boy gave a low wail. "Nooooo, you don't understand…"

The cry woke Vulcan, who stood and shook himself, then pushed forward so his nose pressed against Antonio's leg. The boy calmed instantly and stroked Vulcan's head. "You don't understand," he said, his voice cracking.

"Then tell me. I've got all day."

Anna caressed the back of Antonio's neck and he gazed at Nathan with imploring eyes. The rest of his face was blank with terror, and it struck Nathan like a lightning bolt; he'd been so traumatized by whatever he'd seen he'd tried to block it from the memory.

They stood locked in desolation, and then Anna gently propelled Antonio back to a chair by the table and sat down beside him.

"He's right, mi querido." *My dear.* Her voice was soft with love.

"We can't go on like this, living in fear. Be brave and tell the truth. Or as much as you can remember."

Thirty Three

Willie Watson was gray-faced and looked much older than the day before, when he'd stood smiling in the morning sun. He was still unconscious, but at least his breathing had a soft regularity.

That's something to be grateful for, isn't it?

Graysie watched as a serene young novitiate rinsed the cloth for Willie's early morning face wash. She flashed the nurse an apologetic smile.

"Is he going to recover?"

The young woman couldn't have been more than twenty years old, but she carried the serene calm of someone wiser than her years as she dabbed

Willie's forehead with a soft muslin cloth dampened from warm water in a china basin on the bedside cabinet.

Graysie inhaled the soap's lavender fragrance and the tightness across her should blades eased.

Sister Julia patted Willie's wrinkled face dry. "Too soon to know—and ye'd have to be asking the doctor that question, not me," she said in an Irish lilt. "Now I think ye need to be getting back to your babby and be leaving me to do my six o'clock rounds."

After lying in turmoil for most of the night, Graysie had finally fallen into an exhausted sleep as the faint bird twittering signaled dawn. Her first thought when her eyes flew open barely an hour later was, Is Willie still alive?

She'd been grateful to hear Minette's undisturbed breathing from the narrow bed in the corner. In the dim light, she could see her head peeping over the crisp white sheet and cream and aqua quilt bordered with angels.

She would normally have cherished the peaceful presence in this house of prayer, but the disturbance in her own soul had destroyed her rest.

She'd slipped out of bed and made her way to the hospital wing as soon as she heard the bell sound for Prime, the convent's early morning prayers, leaving Minette in her deep sleep, her little chest rising and falling rhythmically, her cheeks flushed a light pink.

Back in their room now, Minette hadn't stirred in the fifteen minutes she'd been gone. A sudden urge to pray overcame her.

She fell on her knees beside the bed and whispered to the Father God she'd ignored for much of her life.

"Holy Father, have mercy on us. Keep us from the hands of wicked men. Protect us from our enemies. Let your angels raise a hedge around us."

She rubbed her eyes with the palms of her hands and silently willed the heavens to give her a sign, but all she heard was Minette's feathery breathing.

Perhaps that's sign enough.

Her first choir practice sessions were scheduled for that morning. After a quick breakfast in the refectory, she settled Minette into her nursery class and, despite her sleepless night, the next few hours flew by in a blur of navy blue choir cassocks and sweet soprano voices.

She and Minette were sitting side by side in the communal dining room finishing a vegetable soup lunch when she caught a snatch of Pania's musical trans-Pacific accent and the opera star swept in.

She was wearing one of Cressida's new walking dresses, the skirt in a vibrant blue, slimmed down and shortened to ankle length, with a crisp white bodice and fitted sleeves braided in blue and a matching blue promenade hat.

"Graysie! So glad to have caught you. I need to see you."

At a second glance, Graysie saw from her awkward stiffness that her friend was on edge. She fiddled with the pretty little blue bag that swung on her forearm.

"Is something wrong?"

Pania shook her head. Not here, the gesture said. "Is there somewhere we can talk?"

"I'll settle Minette back in the nursery and we can take a walk in the garden. I've finished my work for the day."

When they'd seated themselves on a stone bench in the shaded cloister, Pania cleared her throat. "I haven't told you very much about my past friendship with John. It may come as a surprise to hear that I have known him for a very long time..." She hesitated, as if unsure of how to proceed.

Graysie waited, and when her friend didn't continue, she added; "Yes, it's obvious you're good friends."

Pania cleared her throat again. "I haven't explained how well I knew him—and Eustace as well—when we were all a lot younger and I was starting out.

"I saw and heard things then that have been popping up in my mind a lot these last few days. It's the strangest thing, but I can't help wondering if they're connected.

"You know, things like Minette

disappearing, and you and Nathan and now Willie being attacked."

Graysie's fingertips tingled with shock. Father O'Brien had vaguely hinted of something similar yesterday—what was it he'd said—"perhaps the answer you are looking for lies in your uncle's affairs."

Now Pania seemed to be on the same tangent. What was she hinting at? That she knew some secret about Eustace and John and the things that happened, what, over fifteen years ago? And why on earth would it have anything to do with today?

"What kinds of things?" Graysie asked, her voice almost a whisper, holding her breath for Pania's response.

"I heard them talking. Eustace couldn't accept Elanora married your father while he was away in the West Indies. He was still besotted with her when he came out to California.

"She was the reason he came. He fostered this fantasy that if he could get to talk to her alone, she would see sense and return to him. He said she was his first and only love…"

Pania's normally confident voice trailed off in uncertainty. "I can't shake the suspicion that John knows a lot more than he's ever let on. For a short time, those three were always together."

"Those three? You mean John, Eustace, and my mother?"

"Yes. While you father Rafael was away on a long trip to Sacramento. He won a big commission he couldn't afford to turn down, and he was away for a couple of months. Your mother was lonely with him away.

"None of her family were in San

Francisco. Eustace kept her company, and John tagged along as chaperone."

"Oh. So you knew my mother too? You hadn't mentioned it."

Pania gave her a faint smile. "We only met a few times. I was away singing a lot. She was exquisite, but out of her element. California in 1852 was a hard place for even strong women, and your mother was raised for a gentlewoman's life. She was headstrong but not emotionally strong."

Graysie felt the stab of a childish recollection; she'd been skipping in their San Francisco garden. She remembered the sun-warmed air on her skin, the smell of the orange blossom from the hedge, and the buzz of the bees as she jumped up and down.

The skipping rope her father had bought made a pleasing drumming sound on the paved path, until she noticed her mother standing before her, hands up to her cheeks in shocked disapproval.

"Graysie, you shouldn't be exerting yourself like that," she'd shrilled. "You'll get freckles and big legs. No decent man will want to marry you if you're too physical."

Pania was right. Nature and nurture had no fitted Elanora for the challenges of new settler life. Raised in a wealthy New York merchant's house, she'd lived a sheltered life until she ran away with Rafael Castellanos soon after her twentieth birthday.

But for reasons she didn't fully understand, she wanted to make excuses for Elanora.

"She'd have got used to California," Graysie said. "She wasn't here long enough to settle." Pania's dark eyes gazed back at her, faint disbelief etched in the fine lines around her narrowed eyes. Graysie felt compelled to continue.

"Things might have been different if she'd had longer to learn the ropes. It wasn't her fault she was killed in that stagecoach."

Pania hesitated and then said in a low quiet voice: "Not the crash, no."

They'd never mentioned the accident when she was growing up. It upset her father too much to talk about it and, after he remarried, her stepmother forbade anyone to acknowledge her mother's existence.

But she'd always understood she, her mother, and the twins were on the stage to Sacramento to rejoin her father when the accident occurred.

He'd dreamed of setting up a

daguerreotype studio in Sacramento, where he hoped to make a good living for his family. The stage coach crash had destroyed that dream.

The rescuers who'd arrived on the deserted mountain road hours after the collision had found Graysie in a dazed state, bruised and scratched some distance from the wreckage, but the twins had vanished.

Pania nodded in understanding. "I remember Eustace being extremely upset when Elanora decided she was going to join your father. I heard wild talk of Eustace trying to stop her. He suspected she was going out of fear of the social shame if she left her marriage. I've always wondered if he was involved."

"Why do you say that? I don't understand." Graysie's stomach roiled, and nausea jumped to her throat. She recalled John's comment. Maybe it was true. Perhaps Eustace had been there.

"Eustace was used to getting his own way," said Pania. "He was charismatic, and he didn't like being denied. I wondered if he carried through on his wild talk about intercepting her and persuading her to change her mind.

"Now I think back, things changed between John and him after the accident. John seemed to hold more of a sway over him. Their business collaborations increased, and Eustace gave John an entrée into money and status through his family connections that he couldn't have made himself."

Graysie's legs had been growing heavier as Pania talked. Suddenly, the shaded cloister felt claustrophobic. She jumped up. "Let's stroll awhile," she said and led the way out into the garden, opening her parasol as she went.

The afternoon was sultry, too hot for the birds to be singing, but butterflies danced over blossom bushes and Graysie caught a nostalgic whiff of orange blossom. The events all those years ago had happened in another universe.

"This is all more than my head can hold. Are you hinting that John had something over Eustace that he used to his advantage?" she asked. "Is that what you're suggesting?"

Pania stopped in her tracks, faced Graysie. "I feel awful saying it, but yes. Something like that is what I suspect. I don't know for sure. What if John considered Eustace 'owed' him for keeping quiet? It would also explain why Eustace kept details of the Ophir from him and bequeathed it to you."

Pania paused midstep and gazed at Graysie.

"I've always wondered because of something that happened about a week after the accident. I overheard Eustace say something to John that at the time meant little to me. It was only later I wondered about it."

Graysie walked on a few steps ahead, to the curve in the path which led them back up the way they had come, and then asked; "What was that?"

"Eustace said something like, 'I'm sure they were alive when we left them.' That's what I thought I heard him say, anyway."

"He what?" Graysie's mind was dizzy. Pania noticed her wobbling. She grasped her arm and supported her back to the bench. "Sit down and get your breath. I don't want to upset you."

Graysie slumped down. "I can't believe..." She couldn't think of how to finish the sentence.

Alejandro and Gabriela. Alejandro, dark-haired and thoughtful, Gabriela, with the same dark hair as her brother, but with a sparkling out-going personality.

Twins, yes, but the contrast in character couldn't have been more striking. She sometimes admitted to herself that not knowing what had happened to them was worse than knowing for sure they were dead.

Pania took her hand and gave it a consoling squeeze.

"I don't know what happened that night. But I have an unsettling sense we've never heard all the details... or at least the correct ones."

Thirty Four

"Ladies and gentlemen, I give you the next senator for California!" The rotund, red-faced eighty-eight-year-old governor raised Hector de Vile's arm in a boxer's victory salute.

And so he should. De Vile's meteoric rise from millionaire magnate and stock market king to the United States Senate was all about deal-making. Willoughby Martens knew enough about what went on in politics to know that much.

De Vile was replacing a senator who'd died from a stomach complaint after drinking the capitol's tainted water, and as was its right, the state legislature had appointed de Vile as his replacement for the eighteen months until the next election.

Technically, it was the legislature's decision. In fact, it was a cozy deal with the governor, who, in return for naming de Vile senator, received a handsome package of mining shares.

The only thing that puzzled Martens was why the tycoon hankered after a senator's seat when there was so much wealth ripe for the picking without leaving home. But de Vile would have his eye set on bigger opportunities. Martens recognized he didn't have the Belgian's foresight to know what those might be.

The cream of local society and key out-of-town supporters crowded the steamy reception room in Nevada City's National Exchange Hotel. The atmosphere was buoyant.

Beautiful women and free-flowing wine.

What more could a man want? The crowd gave de Vile uproarious applause. Some even cheered, and then the conversation rose again as they congratulated one another on being invited to the year's premier political party.

Martens hung on de Vile's elbow, ever aware of his need to make himself indispensable. He'd been relieved to escape dismissal for his failure to deliver the Vance Pedersen report, and he allowed himself a flicker of satisfaction at his lucky break.

Maybe de Vile remained unconvinced the report had gone up in smoke, but Martens had created enough doubt to give himself breathing space. And the bombshell de Vile was about to drop would take care of the other problem— getting hold of the Ruby and Ophir shares. He was confident of that.

The sweaty-faced governor stepped aside and, with a flourish, introduced Sir John Russell. The dark-haired tycoon stepped forward with the confidence of a man born to rule.

Curse his English blood.

The phony knight held up his hand for silence, and the room immediately quietened.

"Allow me, friends, a moment of your time, and then you can get back to celebrating Hector's success. I've known de Vile personally for a relatively short time, but of course I've respected his business acumen for a good many years.

"Hector is certainly a man you prefer on your side." John paused and raised a theatrical eyebrow. "As I'm sure many of you have found to your cost, he doesn't like to lose, and does so rarely."

The silence gave way to a waft of shuffling, light laughter, and some deep male coughing before John resumed. "He will be a great man to represent our interests, and I'm here to congratulate him on your behalf. I don't know anyone who could be as effective as he will be in opening the doors in Washington.

"I know you'll agree with me we want protection for business so that the investment we're making in mines and railway lines endures.

"Without guaranteed long-term benefits, what incentive is there for astute men to invest hard won dollars? The trend of amalgamation of mines into fewer and fewer hands is something we all recognize as inevitable if we're going to create jobs to keep men at work.

"You all understand, I'm sure, that there is no point in having a big capacity stamper if you haven't got the ore to keep it running around the clock. And if a few smaller players get burned in the meantime, well, that's life. To him who has much, more will be given. It's in the Bible."

A few women tittered, and men said, "Hear, hear."

De Vile was standing quietly at Sir John's side, surveying the room, occasionally nodding in agreement.

"Our friends at the Daily Bulletin might write about mine safety and shorter working hours, but most of us are more concerned with putting food on tables—ours and those of our workers. I'm confident that, in Hector de Vile, we have the man to help us prosper."

Sir John turned to a four-piece band and, on cue, they struck up the Star-Spangled Banner, a patriotic tune which was gaining wide popularity. As the music and applause faded for a second time, de Vile tipped his top hat and cleared his throat.

"Thank you all very much for coming here tonight. I plan to represent California's interests strongly in Washington, and I appreciate the opportunity to do so. And of course, tonight wouldn't be a true de Vile show without a stock tip to make you all rich."

The crowd snickered, as if they were enjoying the joke, but then, as one, leaned forward expectantly, craning to hear what he was going to say next.

"I know folks are saying Comstock silver is fading away, but they're not looking in the right places. I'm getting some very exciting news from the Lode, let me tell you. About finds that will leave the gold mines on the other side of the mountains in the shade. Keep a keen eye on the Lode, and you won't be sorry."

On cue, de Vile stepped down from the podium where he'd received the crowd's applause and joined a small group of men who stood waiting for him.

He paused outside the circle, examining the fingers of first his right and then his left hand, checking his manicure. He flicked a speck of dust from his sleeve, and, satisfied everything was in order, he stepped forward and began shaking hands.

"Ben, great to see you here," he said to Ben Shields, chairman of the state water and gas board. "Henry, you too." Henry Somerville, railways magnate, was about to negotiate the acquisition of another 60,000 acres of state land for railways use. And so it went.

Strong eye contact and firm handshakes all round. De Vile might be impervious to others' opinions, Martens observed, but he possessed that gift for making every one of these men want to be his most important ally and collaborator:

The Napa Valley vintner with a lucrative trade in the East thanks to his merchant brother in New York. The San Francisco sugar billionaire who'd bought Hawaii's entire sugar crop and was said to have the King of Hawaii in his pocket. They all wanted to be de Vile's best friend.

Martens realized de Vile selected each one to ensure he opened doors for them in Washington in return for a share of the gains, whatever they were likely to be. If there was one thing Hector knew better than most, it was where the money was to be made.

And where it wasn't. After his crafty tip earlier that night, word would spread to San Francisco by tomorrow and silver would be up and gold down. Sadly, he'd have to break that news to the two women tomorrow. Ophir and Ruby shares? They'd now barely be worth the paper they were printed on.

Thirty Five

Sunday, July 12

Graysie eyed Willoughby Martens in the opposite chair and tried to ignore Minette fidgeting on the seat beside her. Why on earth she'd agreed to talk to Martens in the convent's visitor room, she'd no idea.

Worse still, she'd dragged Minette along as some sort of safeguard against Martens in case he became over bearing—which he might do even in a convent—and the lack of action was boring the poor child to death.

Martens had arrived unannounced and requested a meeting to—as he explained it—help her understand more clearly the full ramifications of the mine report he'd handed her a couple of days before.

Of course, she hadn't admitted she no longer had it, that she'd handed it on to Willie Watson for appraisal. Presumably it, like everything else in Willie's house, had gone up in smoke.

"It's an enormous responsibility, deciding what to do," Willoughby Martens was saying, his voice low and soothing. His full fleshy face was too red, a clear sigh he relished his pleasures overmuch.

Graysie studied him as he spoke. He was a handsome man—with his black curls and rose-complexioned male energy—but give him five years… she could already sense he'd be over-blown and burnt out.

His eyes narrowed, and his eyebrows

drew together in sympathy. "I appreciate your difficult situation. I want to ensure you have all the information you need to make the best choice."

He cleared his throat. "For example, I thought you should know. There's been an exciting silver discovery near Nevada City. Shares in silver mines are likely to skyrocket over the next few weeks—and that can only have a negative effect on gold shares like yours. People obviously prefer to go for a 'sure thing.'"

He licked his full red lips. "Hector de Vile was saying last night that silver is where investors are looking to buy right now. Some of these Grass Valley properties—like the Ophir and the Ruby, unfortunately—are looking decidedly wobbly.

"It's likely their price on the stock

exchange will bottom out, but I'm happy to say our interested party is still willing to buy at the price we've discussed. But that offer will only hold for another two days. Mrs. Guilliame has already said she'll accept."

The knot in Graysie's stomach tightened with a sharp pang. "She did? When?"

"When I called on her this morning. Before I came to see you. I think she has realized that if she delays any longer, she may miss out altogether. Timing is everything."

Martens' eyes flashed with excitement, and then, as quickly, he suppressed any glint of triumph. He was trying very hard to maintain his air of calm logic, she could see.

As if reading her thoughts, he said, "I want to make sure we properly safeguard your interests."

"I'm sure. I'll consider your advice carefully, Mr Martens. And talk to Mrs Guilliame too, of course."

She saw the look of surprise flicker across his face.

If this isn't a blatant manipulation of share prices, I didn't know what is.

But it shouldn't surprise her. Everyone knew it happened. They were doing her a favor, really.

He was making it easier for her to say no. She might intend to lie low, but that didn't mean she was going to give in, and she'd urge Lisette to stand firm as well.

Fleetingly, she wondered what he'd say if he knew she'd got Vance's report. Would he maintain his smooth veneer or lose his cool and show his true colors? She'd find out soon enough, she thought, but that wasn't for today.

   Keep your cards close to your chest for now.

Thirty Six

Nathan waited in the convent's entry hall while a young nun went to find Graysie. His stomach was a black pit, and he suppressed the urge to pace up and down the small space as he waited. All the way over, he'd been rehearsing what to say, but now he was here, his mouth was dry, and his tongue stuck to the roof of his mouth like sandpaper.

Gold House was a tomb without Minette's sunny presence, but not seeing Graysie, not knowing how she was faring or what she was doing, was far worse. It ate away at his insides like acid.

He'd tried to counsel himself, reminding himself that it was best for both of them if he gave her the space she clearly needed, but Antonio's revelations of what had happened at Willie Watson's on the day of the fire compelled him to come.

He wanted more than anything to get back to the familiar, increasingly affectionate relationship that had been growing between them. But maybe that was too much to expect after he'd messed up so badly.

At the very least, though, he owed it to her to tell her about Antonio's trip to Willie's. Tell her how the poor kid was terrorized into taking his attackers up there. Antonio said he didn't recognize the men, but Nathan suspected the horror of what happened had paralysed the boy's ability to talk.

However, he'd recounted how events had unfolded. The kid was convinced that

Willie sacrificed himself to ensure his escape, and Nathan believed it, but that wasn't Antonio's fault.

Graysie had absolutely no reason to feel guilty for any of it. If he could reassure her that her visit to Willie had nothing to do with the attack, he'd have eased her stress. Not nearly enough, but something.

His hands were clammy as he brushed them down the sides of his moleskins. He silently cursed himself for not telling Graysie about his marriage, about his wife's and son's deaths.

He'd made pathetic excuses—they'd hardly had a chance, so much had been happening, they hadn't really had any private time together—but he knew these were pretexts

He hated talking about it, abhorred being reminded of the inevitability of it all, and he didn't want to admit to his kinship with Willoughby Martens. The man was an embezzler and worse. More's the pity that Charlotte hadn't wanted to believe he was a thief. He didn't want to drag all the family's dirty linen out for airing.

He pressed his hands against the sides of his trousers once more. Graysie still hadn't turned up, and he couldn't contain his nervous energy any longer.

He paced down the small flagstone hallway, clasping and unclasping his hands behind his back, berating himself for messing up. At the end of the hall, he's swung back toward the street when the sound of a child's quick footsteps stopped him in his tracks.

As he spun around, a flash of pink skirts and a tousled dark head flung herself headlong into his arms. "Uncle

Nat!" Her hot breath smelt of candy as she snuggled into his shoulder.

"Guess what, Uncle Nat? Sister Evangelina let me light the chapel candles. Lots of them—lots and lots."

He clasped Minette against his chest, inhaling the sugary fragrance of her curls against his cheek. How he'd missed her effervescence, her ability to unfailingly take joy from her surroundings. Then the light scuff of feet interrupted his exaltation, and Graysie stood stiffly in the doorway, her eyes narrowed in dismay.

She stepped forward and gently removed Minette from his arms. "Minette, darling, it's not a suitable time for you to be talking to Mr. Russell right now. Why don't you help Sister Evangelina polish the silver?"

The child's eyes widened in surprise

and she pouted her bottom lip, but as Graysie put her down and turned her to the door with a gentle pat on the back, she obeyed with a quick backward glance and a quiet, "Bye for now, Uncle Nat."

Graysie resumed her cool, withdrawn stance, her gaze neutral and level, maintaining her silence. She wore a simply cut pale lemon gown which highlighted her unadorned natural beauty.

Her loveliness took his breath away. He cleared his throat to speak, but before he'd uttered a word, she drew her shoulders up to her ears in a slow shrug.

"Nathan, you must go. This is a convent and the nuns don't like their guests having a lot of visitors, particularly male ones. I don't want to get on the wrong side of Sister Mor."

He shook his head and took a step

towards her. She immediately stepped back, maintaining her distance.

"Besides, as I told you, I don't want anyone else getting hurt because of me." Her voice cracked.

"That's just it, Graysie. You've got to listen. The attack on Willie wasn't your fault. I've been talking to Antonio and his mother this morning, and there are things you need to know."

He was pleading with her, but her stance didn't change. She frowned, and her green eyes narrowed in distrust. He pushed on, desperate to tell her the truth.

"Antonio was up at Willie's that day. Some men turned up at Anna Maria's. They forced him to take them up to Willy's, and he saw what happened. He'd no choice—they were threatening to kill his mother. They've terrorized him, the poor kid. But I wanted to assure you—it wasn't your fault. None of it."

Her ramrod posture sagged. Her hand flew to her mouth. "Oh, no! Poor Antonio. The troubled, darling boy." Her eyebrows contracted, and she smoothed her skirt with one hand, distracted. "How terrible for him. What happened?"

He braced his knees at the sudden giddiness that swirled through him, relief that she was listening to him.

"He says three men he didn't know showed up demanding Vance's papers. They threatened to kill Anna unless Antonio showed him where 'the papers' were.

"Neither of them had a clue what they were talking about, but Antonio grasped at straws. Somehow, I don't know how, he saved his mother by deflecting them up to Willie's.

"When they got there Willie wasn't home, and they turned the place over before he came back. But once he arrived, Willie gained the upper hand, even though there were three of them against one. He enabled Antonio to break free and yelled at him to run. Antonio says Willie saved his life."

Graysie shook her head in disbelief. "Poor Antonio. And Anna. Is there anything I can do?"

"It's okay. I'm keeping an eye on them. They're still frightened, but they're remarkably resilient. They'll come through. Perhaps if you had time to visit—woman to woman—that might help. But try to do it inconspicuously. She fears being seen with anyone who might cause them more problems."

There was an awkward pause. Sweet notes from a melodious harpsichord floated from the convent's heart. A cart rumbled by out front, the nose-tickling smell of newly cut hay drifting in through the open doorway as it passed.

This is me right now, thought Nathan. Immobilized in front of a woman who has reached into my heart like no other, and unable to say what I truly feel.

He fought to relax his face and jaw.

"How's Willie doing?"

"He's improved slightly, but he's still not conscious."

Another silence. He cleared his throat. "Graysie, I wanted to talk with you about that other matter... Martens and what happened back in Australia." He shuffled his feet, suddenly self-conscious in the open entryway. "Is there somewhere we could talk?"

She considered him with the same detached air she'd assumed from the beginning. "Anything that needs to be said we can say here."

She folded her arms in front of her. "I was silly in the way I reacted before—about your marriage. There's no reason for you to mention it. I don't know what got into me. Can I use the excuse of too much stress?" She gave a little shrug.

He jolted as if she'd poked him in the ribs with a hot knitting needle, but she stood watching from the doorway, an ironic smile playing across her lips.

"Can I ask…?" No, he saw he couldn't ask.

She gave a quick shake of her head. "Please, let's not." Again, her voice cracked almost imperceptibly, as if the detached composure she presented was as fragile as winter ice on a roadside puddle.

With an exhausted sigh, she continued.

"I accept what you say about him—he's a scoundrel and likely a murderer, too. And I'd rather not give him any more reasons to go after you.

"You say Willie's injuries aren't my fault, but if they hadn't suspected him of having that report, he wouldn't have been in the firing line. I don't want anyone else getting hurt."

As he stood staring at her, she dipped her head and drew her clasped hands down in front of her. "I have to go. Thank you for letting me know about Antonio. It's a terrible thing, but I'm grateful to know it's a lot more complicated than we thought."

She gave the hint of a mock bow, turned, and in a second had vanished back down the shadowy hallway into the convent's inner sanctum. Nathan could only stand dumbfounded and look after her.

Did that really happen? For a fleeting moment, I thought I'd found someone I can share my life with and then? Nothing? After Charlotte, don't I know better than to believe in second chances?

The dull ache in his chest mocked his protestations of indifference.

I came very close to believing she could be the one… But I don't deserve another chance, anyway.

He turned heavily towards the front door. Outside, the bright sunshine was blinding. On the doorstep, he squinted to get his bearings. Minette's cheeky laughter floated out to him. He braced his shoulders.

Time to call it quits, mate. To remember the reason you came to California. Your mother and sisters are counting on you.

Thirty Seven

Monday, July 13

Death softened the deep lines that gouged Willie's cheeks. In life they had made him look serious, even a little severe, but as he lay in his open coffin, he was a genial sun-tanned uncle, fresh from the fields, his mouth curved in a ghostly, satisfied smile.

The old codger almost appeared contented to be set free from this life, Nathan thought as he stood beside Willie's sister, Rose, in the convent chapel as the service ended.

He'd done nothing to invite his violent end, of that Nathan was sure. Beside him, Rose's matronly bosom heaved with quiet sobs, and she dabbed a soggy white handkerchief to her eyes, first one side, then the other.

"You were a good man, Willie. You didn't deserve this. God rest your soul." Her whisper barely reached Nathan, but he placed his arm consolingly around her shoulders.

"You are so right there, Rose. And we'll do our best to see whoever did this doesn't go unpunished," he murmured.

An image of Antonio's terrified eyes rose before him. Willie had sacrificed himself to ensure the boy had escaped. Of that, he was certain. As the last bell-like notes of the choir faded and he joined the other pallbearers carrying Willie's coffin out, Nathan vowed he was not giving up on tracking down his killers.

*****

A huddle of mourners stood blinking at the brightness of the day after the cool shade of the chapel, reluctant to leave the graveside but uncertain of where to go next.

Nathan watched as Graysie slipped a comforting arm around Rose, the busy and prosperous manager of a Grass Valley boarding house who often visited her brother in his forest hideaway.

Father O'Brien had insisted Willie's funeral be conducted in the convent chapel, even though Willie wasn't a regular communicant.

Lisette and Graysie now stood one either side of Rose at the graveside as the last mourner cast a handful of dusty soil onto his coffin, but the older woman seemed reluctant to move away.

"He's gone and deserted me," she croaked to no one in particular.

She lifted her gaze to the small group around her. "First my husband, Stan, and now Willie. I'm going to have to box on without either of them."

It struck Nathan again how Graysie imparted a sense of serenity and confidence to others, even when she was reeling from her own loss. Correction, he thought. She's steeling herself for battle. Tense cords stood out from her slender neck above the light ruffle of her light blue dress.

He wondered fleetingly how he'd ever thought she was only interested in herself. She never made a fuss about it, but she sought out the least fortunate around her to offer comfort wherever she went.

Nathan paused in front of Rose. He leaned in and gave her a light hug. "I recall you wanted to know how Argus is doing. I thought you'd be interested to hear he is recovering remarkably well after a slow start. He's walking under his own steam, and he should be back to normal within a week or two."

A brief smile chased across Rose's face and she lightly clapped her hands together. "Oh, Mr. Russell, I'm so pleased to hear that. You've done wonders in bringing that dog back from the brink. Willie so loved him."

"Yes, I believe he did," Nathan said. "And I was wondering if you would be interested in taking him when he is well enough—probably within the next few days. He's a good-tempered animal. He doesn't cause any problems that I can see. I could bring him to visit and see how you liked it?"

Rose's shoulders lifted, and she smiled again. "I'd like that very much." She clasped her hands together and let out a contented sigh.

"If I can't have Willie, then at least I can have Argus. He'll be a big comfort. Now I suppose I'd better be getting on."

She turned to make her way up the street, and Graysie shadowed her movement, intent, it seemed, on walking with her.

Nathan stamped forward. "Graysie, have you got a moment? I was hoping for a word."

Graysie stopped and turned slowly. "I'm not sure…"

Rose smiled and extended her hands forward in a freeing gesture. "I will be fine, dearie. I have plenty to do at the boarding house, don't you worry. And the thought of having Argus come and stay has made my day. Willie wouldn't want us brooding." She kissed Graysie on the cheek and walked on.

Graysie turned back and regarded Nathan, her head tilted to one side, a hesitant look in her eyes.

"I... I wanted to make sure you're alright." Nathan fiddled with his collar, searching for more air.

She squeezed her eyes shut, as if trying to block out something she didn't want to see. When she re-opened them, her jaw set in a determined line.

"I'm fine. Thanks for asking, Nathan. Of course, I'm very sad about Willie. Quietly devastated. It changes everything."

"Changes everything? How?"

"It's like the passing of the guard, isn't it? First Vance, and now Willie. Like the generation of the old style prospectors who knew every rock and gulch has now passed on. If I'd had any idea when I came here...

Well, I'm not sure I would have come at all if I'd foreseen the outcome."

She fiddled with her parasol, and after a moment's hesitation, put it up. "It's so hot already today." She paused as if she'd forgotten what she was about to say next and then cleared her throat.

"I know you've explained about Antonio and you've reassured me I'm not responsible for what's happened, but I'm still shocked. When school breaks for the holidays in a few days I'm going to Sacramento with Pania for a season at the Orleans.

"Harry has put together a package for us that's too good to turn down. It'll give me a chance to think. Maybe give time for things to quiet down here. I know you never thought it was a good idea for me to pursue the mine idea, anyway."

She gave him a wry, humorless smile.

Nathan wanted to protest that he'd

changed his view, that he admired her ability to remain calm and resolute under attack, that he didn't want her to leave, for goodness sakes. He opened his mouth to speak, but she jumped in ahead of him.

"I've enjoyed knowing you, Nathan, I truly have." Her voice trailed away. "And you know Minette adores you." She cast her eyes downward, as if reluctant to meet his gaze.

"But it seems life is taking us in different directions, and it's best she doesn't get any more attached to you than she already is." She gave him a quick smile.

"Now you don't have my affairs to worry about, I hope you can do what you came here for—look after your family concerns, and that it goes well for you."

Once again, he felt a strange certainty

that her words came from deep within, a place of pain.

She twirled the parasol playfully as she regarded the chapel garden, the cloudless sky.

"Reluctant as I am to return to performing, it seems right now it's my best option."

She gave him one last searching look, as if trying to read his mind. He resisted the urge to step forward and grab her arm to prevent her from leaving.

What have I got to offer her? She's right, isn't she?

We've set our lives on different courses, and he'd be wise to accept it and move on.

Her face softened as if she'd caught a yearning in his expression that pleased her, and then she tipped her parasol in a mock salute and walked away.

Thirty Eight

The pure notes of some old hymn that Willoughby Martens didn't recognize, but everyone else seemed to know, hung in the chapel air, the sweetness of the children's voices giving the chant a freshness that left him feeling grimy.

"All glory while the ages run, be to the Father and the Son, who rose from death; the same to thee, O Holy Ghost eternally..."

Seated in the back pew of the convent chapel for the town's annual service of celebration, Martens watched as choir leader Graysie Castellanos brought her conducting arm to a flowing conclusion. The singers, in simple white cassocks, visibly relaxed as the last notes died away.

Early evening light streamed through stone-arched windows as Father O'Brien, backlit by towers of altar candles, pronounced a final blessing on the townsfolk gathered for the diocese of St Mary's annual Praise and Redemption Concert. An exotic smell of incense hung like a comforting cloak over the crowded congregation.

The final hymn had been stately, but the occasion was anything but. It was a Grass Valley tradition to hold a concert to thank the town for its support of both the school and the orphanage every year before summer recess.

Local fiddlers and harmonica players added their merry tunes to the more serious choral music, and they now fiddled everyone out with a medley of folk melodies, a wave of gay sound filling the sacred space as everyone rose, chattering and laughing, and moved next door for refreshments.

It was one of Father O'Brien's greatest achievements to have built a church which nestled at the town's heart and was beloved by many who only came once a year for this celebration. Despite himself, the occasion's simple eloquence touched Martens.

But that wasn't why he was here, Martens reminded himself. Precious time was passing. He needed to fulfil his undertaking to de Vile to sort out the troublesome Castellanos woman or his patron would get restless. And ruthless.

Funny, he ruminated, how he'd been sick with rage to find Nathan Russell was here messing with his game in California, in the same way he'd spoiled things back in Sydney. Gradually, however, his anger was being channeled into something much more productive.

Having him here was providing the perfect opportunity to extract the revenge he'd long craved. He could kill two birds with one stone—get rich, get rid of Nathan Russell, and maybe even get his hands on the girl. A warmth at the base of his stomach spread up through his chest at that delightful thought.

Luring Graysie Castellanos down the mine might be the quickest way to do that. The dumb songbird wouldn't know what she was looking at. He was confident he could spin a convincing yarn to kick her interest. If not, he could frighten her so badly she'd sell for nothing to be rid of it and him.

His left foot twitched with a nervy

charge he often experienced at high-risk moments. The excitement gripped him deep in his belly, and he let out a low, slow breath. There was nothing like the exultant high he got chasing down a quarry.

He clasped his hands together to calm himself and rose from his seat. Graysie was slowly making her way down the aisle, stopping every few feet to greet someone or accept congratulations on the choir's performance from others.

He waited as she came towards him. He could sense her gradually realize his presence as she drew nearer. She stopped a few feet from him.

"Mr. Martens." She tilted her head to one side and raised her eyebrows. "I didn't take you for a man who'd be interested in church or children's choirs."

"Possibly not. But you gave us a

splendid show. Congratulations.”

“Thank you. Are you staying for the refreshments?”

“Let me escort you in. I thought it might be an excellent opportunity to follow up on my suggestion about showing you the Ophir at some stage.”

She pressed her lips together in a grimace. “I’m not sure where I am with that, to be honest. After Willie’s death, I’m at something of a loss. Unusual for me.” She gave a wavering smile. “His death has hit me hard.”

“Really?” Martens searched her face for any sign that she was concealing something, but could see nothing but sincere concern. “Why would it worry you? I mean, of course, it’s terrible when a man’s killed like that, but why is it of any note to you personally?”

Her eyes narrowed, and she lifted her

chin, suddenly wary. "Nothing in particular. He seemed a fine man. A knowledgeable one, too."

They had been making their way slowly towards the refreshments, but at this remark, Martens halted.

"Knowledgeable? Yes, he knew more than most about the mines around here. Is there anything in particular you wanted to ask? I could help…"

She drew back from him and flicked a glance towards the crowd gathered around the refreshment tables.

"I… I wanted to ask him about the geology. That's all."

She pursed her lips, and Martens sensed she was uncomfortable with the direction the conversation was taking.

"You talked to him? He mentioned nothing about a report by Vance Pedersen, by any chance?"

As soon as the words were out of his mouth, he saw he'd hit a bull's-eye. She flinched, and color slowly rose from up her neck to her face.

"Vance Pedersen. Why?" She turned towards the area where coffee was being dispensed. The crowd had eased as people ahead of them had been served, and she feasted her eyes on a steaming spout of hot tea being poured in cups nearby. Her gaze flicked back to meet his.

Martens let his shoulders fall into a relaxed droop, but inside his nerves were humming.

"Oh, someone mentioned that Vance had been working on a report on the Ophir," Martens said. "They even speculated it might have been why he died. I don't know—partners falling out or some such. No big deal."

She dropped her eyes over her shoulder, as if searching for a friend.

This woman is a terrible liar. She knows about that report.

It came to him like a sixth sense. Discernment. Foreknowledge. Call it what you will. Jumping Jehoshaphat, she had the accursed thing. Flaming fury flushed through him. This chit had made a fool of him. Worse yet, de Vile had been right. Watson had passed it on to her before they got to him.

The clatter of teacups and the spicy scent of home baking no longer penetrated his awareness. A consuming rage blinded him. He blinked to clear his vision. When he opened his eyes again, Graysie Castellanos was staring at him, her face taut with anxiety.

"He gave that report to you, didn't he?" He barked the query, his eyes fixed on her face, searching for minute changes in her stance and expression.

She shook her head and backed away from him towards the coffee. "No. I don't know what you're talking about." Her eyes flicked to the floor, and then she added with a hoarse rush, "And why is it so important to you, anyway?"

He regarded her coldly. She was lovely to look at, but she'd be hopeless at poker. She was too much of an open book. "It's my job to know things."

He planted his feet wide and braced his shoulders, as if he was gearing up for a fight. "That's what men like Hector de Vile pay for. How do you think they get rich? It's by learning things that will put them ahead of the market."

Her already wan face drained of further color. "And why would Vance's report—if there was such a report—be of interest?

I mean, couldn't anyone go in there and write a report?"

She widened her eyes, as if wanting to convince him and herself of her transparency. He smiled. She didn't fool him.

"I'm not saying it's of any special interest." He relaxed his stance and took her elbow. "Let me get you a coffee. I'm sure you're parched, and I've been keeping you talking."

As they glided the last few feet to the refreshments, he leaned down and said into her ear, "It may be of no interest at all. But Mr. de Vile always wants to know. Then he can be the judge. He likes to quote Benjamin Franklin: 'An investment in knowledge always pays the best interest.'"

She stopped in front of the coffee and turned towards him, regarding him with a steady, neutral expression. She might not be a good liar herself, but he suspected she picked up on the deceptions of others pretty swiftly, and he did not take her in either. He didn't care. He needed to rethink his entire approach to Miss Graysie Castellanos.

Now he was confident she possessed the Vance report, he must get his hands on it. Until he'd done that, he needed to keep her alive—and he'd have to back off on the rogue operations for a while.

If Vance gave her the report, then the Russells certainly now knew about the mine encroachment. Yes, he'd back off for now. But after he'd got hold of it? That was a very different story.

Thirty Nine

Tuesday, July 14

Nathan stood in the narrow, dark chamber and gazed in awe at the greenstone wall in front of him. It disappeared into the shaft beyond the reach of the flickering light from the candles he and Sebastian held in hooked holders, but he could see from the faint, reflected sheen of its mirrored surface that it stretched a long way back.

So, this was the greenstone dyke that Vance Pedersen's report had described as channelling one of the richest Ophir ore shoots. It shone like flowing water, the color variations like ripples over stone.

At its front edge, it spanned nearly thirty feet, a flying buttress heralding riches buried deep underground. For a moment, his heart was in his throat at its sheer beauty—and the certain knowledge that Vance's information had been accurate.

Nathan had been to see Lisette to confirm she knew nothing about any mining in the Ruby. They'd set a watch on the padlocked entries to both mines, but in the few days they'd been in place, all had been quiet, and no more gold stolen. He wondered if the perpetrators had got wind that they'd been exposed and were lying low.

What with Willie's funeral and Seb's normal law-making duties, today was the first opportunity they'd had to prise open the padlock and look underground.

Common mining wisdom had it that

one of the most valuable attributes of men like Willie and Vance was their ability to remember the detailed appearance of old working faces and to interpret the structural subtleties of diverging walls.

Muted rock face markings could show the continuation of a rich vein in a different direction or an ore shoot resurfacing some distance away after a barren section. An astute engineer could read the rocks and accurately assess the value of the gold likely to be extracted—saving the mine owners the expense and delay of doing a full survey.

Nathan had learned a lot about rock stratification at home, where the Victorian mines had many similarities to California, but you didn't need to be an expert to see what was right in front of your eyes.

Evidence of neglect lay around them in the rusted tools discarded at the end of a shift. In one section, a faint scent of decayed flesh lingered around the arched rib cage of a mule that had never made it back up to daylight.

The shaft floor was hard rock packed to a level surface to make it easy for the mule transports pulling ore, but after a year of disuse, the air tasted stale.

The farther in they ventured, the warmer the air became, until Nathan sweltered in his heavy canvas trousers. They'd been moving steadily for ten or fifteen minutes when they came to a widened junction where two chambers met at a cavernous crossroad; water seeped through the heavily braced pine log roof, and the ground was wet and boggy underfoot.

Nathan nodded towards the swampy

ground. "When the pumps are going, this would be a lot drier, but with nothing doing for a while…"

Seb held his light aloft and turned in a slow circle, his gaze searching the black void around them.

"Look over there." He gestured with his lamp. "Those timbers are new. It looks like they installed them in the last few months. And they're coming in from the north, where the Ruby workings are. I'd say we've located the rogue operation right here." He halted again and looked up. "Hear that?"

Nathan hesitated. Weird creaks that sounded like human moans sounded overhead.

"That talking noise?" Nathan knew miners got superstitious about the strange sounds. "That's the mine complaining. It usually only happens with new shafts. They shift a bit before they subside and settle down."

He moved towards the source of the noise and lifted his lamp to see if there was any evidence of rock shifts or cave-ins. "You've got the greatest risk of rock bursts happening a few days after that kind of subterranean noise."

"Rock bursts?" Seb said. "Great. We get rock bursts down here? Wouldn't want to miss out on that."

Nathan laughed at his brother's dry humor. "They're not common. It happens when the rock comes under extra pressures. It goes off with a boom and throws rock everywhere.

"Usually, the first explosion isn't the problem. There's more danger from the flow of rock debris that follows. Sometimes it buries miners standing up." The light jiggled as he swept his hand around the space.

"It's like Vance reported. This new drift runs at an angle to exit out into the Ruby. As he suggested, they've poached on the Ophir through the back door of the Ruby."

Seb bent down and picked up a lump of rock at his feet, fingering it speculatively.

"And apart from Lisette, do we know who owns the Ruby?" he asked. "Any idea?"

"It used to be a consortium of French men. Lisette's husband bought most of them out. They were hopeless organizers, and they moved on to fresh claims. But since they reduced ownership to Lisette and Weavers—well, who knows what Weavers did with his shares before Neptune ripped his throat out?"

As they were talking, the unsettling moaning noises continued. They were making Nathan jumpy, and he was about to suggest they should get out while they could when his ear caught a faint tread echoing off the main walls of the shaft.

Someone was descending the ladder at the entrance to the railhead where the ore wagons exited.

He put his hand to his lips. "Listen!" he whispered to Seb. His brother nodded. He'd also picked up the distinct sound of someone coming quickly down the iron ladder. It would be too dangerous to go back the way they'd come. They'd have to find another exit.

"We can't use the Ruby tunnel—we don't know where it ends. It might be right in their offices, and I don't fancy that," Seb said in a low voice, stepping closer to him. "We'd best try to make for Wolf Creek. You lead, and I'll follow to protect your back."

He turned to face down the main shaft and noticed their candles had burned down more than half their length. They started down the tunnel towards the creek at a steady pace.

Nathan gauged he was about ten feet ahead of Seb when a blast of hot air hit in the back with such force it brought him to his knees. His ears rang with a series of percussive booms. Grovelling in the dirt, his blinded eyes were gritty with suffocating dust.

Cup-sized rock fragments showered down, bouncing off his face and shoulders; his palms stung with abrasions from the debris, and blood trickled down over his left eye. Darn it. The dreaded rock burst had gone off right now.

The candle holder had fallen to the mine floor, and the light snuffed out. He scrambled to his feet and turned in a slow circle, hand over his mouth and nose, fighting to breathe, trying to orientate himself. Where should he look for Seb?

"Seb!" he yelled hoarsely, the taste of grit in his mouth. "Where are you? Are you okay?"

The only answering sound was a shushing from showering rock particles that kept falling, covering his feet, his ankles.

"Seb! Wake up, man."

In the gloom, it was impossible to see more than an inch or two in front of his eyes.

He turned back in the direction he thought he'd come from, but the dust was so dense he wasn't sure he'd got it right. Then another sound penetrated through the rattle of falling rocks: the sound of a man's tread on the hard rock surface and a hunting dog's baying echoing off the tunnel walls with an eerie reverberation.

The piercing howls sent shivers up his spine. From the reverberation, the creature was coming towards them down the tunnel at a fast clip. Nathan was in a dust cloud, hardly able to see his hand in front of his face, let alone an attacking mongrel.

He put his hands out in front of him like a child playing Blind Man's Bluff and shuffled in a direction he hoped would give him shelter. As he groped forward, the boom of a revolver shot reverberated close to him, and an animal screamed.

He stopped in his tracks and called again. "Seb. Are you there?"

This time, he heard a rusty-voiced response. "Over here."

He stumbled towards the sound of the voice. Seb maintained a low humming noise to guide Nathan to him. His foot struck warm flesh, and he stumbled back a step in relief.

"Found you," he said with a cackle, that instantly turned into a cough. He took another small step forward and leaned over his brother's prone form.

"Can you move? Is it safe for me to lift you up?"

Seb chortled like a deep drain. "Safer than not lifting me," he said, holding up an arm. "Big rock hit one leg. I'll hold the gun in the other hand and keep us covered."

Seb raised his upper body from the mine floor and Nathan locked both arms around him in a chest hold and dragged him carefully backwards.

As his eyes adjusted to the dim light,

Nathan saw that they'd chanced upon another junction point. The rail tracks ended, but tunnels led off in two different directions. A gust of fresh air stirred the dust particles—indicating that one of them exited at ground level.

Nathan's chest expanded, and his senses spiked to super alertness. Fresh hope surged through him, sending tingling into his arms and legs. Then the rocks farther up the tunnel rattled, and a bullet ricocheted into the wall behind him, flinging up another spray of stinging fragments.

A tunnel support. We must find a support for shelter.

Seb fired off an answering round, and Nathan kept dragging him, backing into what he prayed would be a safe haven.

He tripped over a sharp metal object and sprawled backwards, cushioning

Seb's fall with his body. Both men lay stunned for a couple of seconds and then his brother, flattened on top of him, shook with silent laughter.

"Looks like you've struck the equivalent of gold down here, old boy," he gasped. "I believe that's an old wagon we can get behind."

Nathan wriggled out from under and looked to one side. His brother was right. Lying close to them on his left was an old iron wagon, a perfect bulwark against further bullets. He scrambled up and dragged Seb into its cover before the next bullet hammered harmlessly into an upright above their heads.

"What's next?" Nathan breathed into Seb's ear.

"I didn't train as an engineer for nothing." Seb grinned, his teeth showing white through the grime that coated him.

"See those rolls?"

Lying on the ground amongst the discarded rubble of rusty tools and metal lunch boxes were rolls of old fuse cable. He stared at Seb, reading his mind as he gaped. Of course!

If they were rogue mining here, there were likely to be fresh explosives close at hand. What if they could set a charge to bring down this tunnel entryway?

As he surveyed the surroundings, he spotted a natural rock ledge on their side of the tunnel entrance which would provide an ideal resting place for a packet of explosive if they could lay their hands on one.

They could block their attacker's advance and then follow the fresh air flow to an exit. And hope that exit was big enough to allow two adult men to pass through. He gestured to Seb and quietly mouthed, "I'll search out some black powder. You stay here."

"Black powder's probably over there." Seb pointed down the new tunnel and added, "Where they've done the new work?"

"Cover me," Nathan mouthed, gesturing towards the new opening.

Seb nodded.

"One, two three!"

Nathan raced for the newest tunnel, flattening himself against the wall as Seb fired two more quick shots in their attacker's direction.

Around the corner from the tunnel opening, someone had cut a low shelf in the rock face. On it sat coils of new fuse lines and boxes of explosives, parked there in readiness for the next session. Grabbing an empty canvas bag, Nathan packed the dynamite and coils and waved a warning to Seb.

In response, Seb calmly fired his last round, and Nathan saw a shadowy figure make a wild dive for cover.

Back in position, he opened the canvas bag and showed Seb what he'd found.

"Perfect," the big man purred, for a moment all happy lion. Then he got to work with the fuse while Nathan stood guard, pulling out his gun and levelling more shots to deter their assailant from coming any closer.

When he was ready, Seb nodded and made a gesture like a baseball pitcher lobbing to the catcher for a runout.

He half rose on one leg and Nathan's confidence wavered. Did Seb have enough strength left to get the explosive where they needed it? He saw his brother flinch as he rose, nursing his injured leg, but with the natural advantage of his height, he could still fling a load with deadly accuracy.

With calculated intensity, he flung the armed bag in a curving arc; the fuse trailing behind it through the drawstring opening. It lodged with a gratifying thump on the ledge above the tunnel, far enough back that when lit, it would bring down the whole opening.

Seb held the other end of the fuse in his left hand. He gave Nathan a leonine grin of satisfaction and drew matches out of his pocket to light it.

Nathan grabbed his hand to restrain him and gestured to his knee. He mouthed, "Can you move?"

Seb nodded. "Slowly."

"We'll both wait." Seb shook his head in urgent disagreement, gesturing to Nathan to run as soon as he lit the fuse, but Nathan grabbed his arm again.

Shaking his head, he mouthed, "No. We stick together."

They were dangerously close to the opening. Not as close as their attacker, who was right next to it, but close enough for heavy debris to land on them. He gestured to Seb that they should try to take cover as best they could once the fuse was lit, and he nodded.

Seconds later, they watched as the worm of fire crept across the rock floor, lighting it up like a firework in the darkness, following the fuse line to the explosives on the overhead ledge.

Heads down, arms covering themselves, huddled under the shelter of the old wagon, they waited for the bang. When it came, Nathan's breath flowed out of his body in a great wave of relief.

The tunnel convulsed with the impact,

and mule-sized chunks of rock thundered down and filled the space which seconds before had been an open gateway.

A momentary hell on earth, but apart from a shower of pebbles and temporary deafness from the roar, Nathan and Seb were unhurt.

Whatever state their attacker was in, he wouldn't be able to follow them through the solid wall of rock that now separated the two chambers. All they needed to do now was get out.

Forty

"I thought you told me you had the girl under control? How hard is it to control one young singer for Beelzebub's sake? I doubt if she's seen her twenty-first birthday."

De Vile's usual suave composure had vanished, supplanted by a fury as hot as a Mexican chili. He was pacing the fine carpet in his spacious Nevada City sitting room, punching the air at intervals to emphasize a point.

Martens knew he needed to deliver the bad news himself, rather than wait for de Vile to hear it second-hand. He'd been expecting something to happen at the mines since he'd found out the

Castellanos woman had Vance's report, but he dared not tell de Vile.

He couldn't stand the man's smug conceit at being right again, so he'd pulled back on the night mining and kept watch. Sure enough, they'd discovered that deputy Seb Russell had men keeping a sharp eye on the place.

Martens had been sinking a quiet whiskey and planning to challenge de Vile to a game of poker when their guard had turned up, red-faced and indignant.

"They cut open the padlock and chain and damn near brought the whole caboodle down," he complained. "They killed my dog."

Martens didn't care about the man or the dog, but he needed to square things off with de Vile. Did that mean he'd also have to come clean about his suspicions that Graysie Castellanos had Vance's report?

No, he decided. It didn't. What he didn't know wouldn't hurt him. It angered him he was always dancing to de Vile's tune. It was time he exercised some initiative.

De Vile was shouting, spittle spraying from swollen purple lips. "I don't think you grasp how important this is to the de Vile legacy, Martens. I will not countenance any scandal right now when I'm about to go off to Washington."

The would-be senator stopped abruptly and pivoted to charge back down the room. He glared at Martens as he paused. "I'm playing a long-term game here, Martens, and I'm not having some chit come out of nowhere and blow the whole thing out of the water."

He strode the room, the corner of his jacket brushing a porcelain urn on a side table as he passed. The blue and white globe rocked perilously on its base, but de Vile didn't appear to notice.

"The de Vile empire is going to outlast me—it's going to be a force in its own right that my son, in his turn, will take over."

Martens could sense his patron was winding up, and de Vile continued paced, his face settled into a mask of fierce concentration, as if by willpower alone he could rule the world.

"I'm bargaining here for much more than cash flow from a gold mine—nice as that is to have. I'm talking about the power we will wield over future generations to go along with the money. I haven't orchestrated myself into public office to see it all leak away in a scandal."

He raised his gaze to Martens and, for a moment, he was in another place—one where he ruled the world. He blinked rapidly, as if bringing himself back from wherever his imagination had taken him, back to this room, this conversation.

"Nothing is worth risking that." He drew himself to a halt, as if the anger that had propelled his pacing had deflated, and turned once again to Martens.

In a more measured tone, he continued, "I'm withdrawing from this venture, Martens. I want nothing more to do with it. It's become more trouble to me than it's worth. I can do without the money. It's long stopped being an amusing sideline. It's time for a strategic retreat."

Willoughby Martens' mouth dropped open in ill-concealed horror. He snapped his crocodile jaws shut. Hector de Vile was backing down. Calling it quits. And all before he—Martens—had got rich.

He shrugged his shoulders to loosen the tension and smiled. "Always the tactician, Mr. de Vile. I guess that's why you always come out on top." He surveyed the room for a tray and decanter. "Another whiskey?"

He concentrated extra hard on keeping his hand steady as he poured de Vile his drink, while his insides trembled with rage.

How dare he decide he isn't playing anymore? It was all very well for de Vile to say he could do without the money, but what about him? And what about that sneaking snake, Nathan Russell?

He made a vow to himself there and then as he sipped his drink and nodded and smiled, ever the accommodating lackey. De Vile's opinions no longer mattered. He would not pack up his tent and steal away into the night. That wasn't his style.

He still had a few lives left, and he was going to make sure this time he didn't waste them.

Forty One

Wednesday, July 15

"Promise me you won't sell your Ruby shares. Promise!" Graysie placed her damp hands lightly on Lisette Guilliame's shoulders and gave her dark curls a teasing tweak. Lisette grinned.

While the girls played in the sitting room next door, their mothers stood at the kitchen bench together, elbow deep in apples, peeling knives in their juice-stained hands.

On the stove beside them, a big pot of apple pulp bubbled, scenting the house with fruity sugar and cinnamon. Pania watched from the kitchen table, joining in their chatter, but leaving the cooking to them.

They'd spent the last couple of hours stewing apple pulp for the winter. One pot was close to ready, a second was about to go on the stove. And Graysie had to admit, spending an afternoon doing 'women's business' with her friends was the best antidote she knew for the bleak heaviness she'd woken to that morning.

Nathan had called late in yesterday afternoon and explained he was speaking on behalf of Seb, who needed to rest a wrenched knee. He briefly outlined what had happened at the mine and confirmed to her that the property was indeed being rogue mined. She and Lisette would have the mind-bending task of deciding what to do about it. Sue the perpetrators, perhaps? Or seek other remedies. The challenge was daunting.

But it wasn't that news that had flattened her. It was the thought that once again, good men like Seb and Nathan might die acting on her behalf. She begged him to step away.

Yes, leaving Vance and Willie's deaths unresolved was a galling prospect, but she couldn't bear to think that anyone else being endangered.

The idea of re-opening the mine had always been a long shot, and things had become too dangerous, she'd told him. But that didn't mean she couldn't still hold out for a better price on her shares.

She'd struck out to visit Lisette as early as was decent, keen to go over it all again with the woman who was fast becoming an ally as well as a friend.

"Someone is robbing both of us blind," she told Lisette. "Problem is, we can't prove who, even if we've got a good idea. Nor do I have much idea how to stop it."

She told Lisette of the sinister warning Martens had delivered about the falling value of their shares. "It was straight-out bullying," she said indignantly. "Nothing less than talking down the stock and scare us into selling cheap. We must hold out, Lisette. We'd be falling right into their hands if we sell now."

She sniffed and wiped the back of her hand across her nose. "Let's agree. A pledge of solidarity. We either both sell or neither sell. We stand firm together."

Pania, a cup of half-drunk tea in front of her, clapped her hands. "Great idea, Graysie. Safety in numbers. And, in the meantime, we do our concerts in Sacramento for Harry, and Lisette can come along as a nanny. How's that for a cozy arrangement?"

The cooks stopped peeling and gazed at her, then at each other, in astonishment.

"What a great suggestion, Pania." Graysie did a little on-the-spot jig. "I need someone to be with Minette while we're on stage." She gazed at Lisette. "I can't bear to find another nanny after the trouble I've had keeping them. Will you do it, Lisette?

"You know Minette, and Minette would love to have Seraphine with her. It might help fill the gap Francine has left. And it's really not any more testing to have two children on tour than one—possibly easier because they amuse each other."

Lisette gazed at her, eyes wide open and disbelieving. Graysie's heart tightened with the familiar pang of loss. "I know it's been really hard without

Andre these past months. But don't you think it's time for you to come out of mourning and start afresh? If you are worried about the house, I'm sure Irish Pete would be happy to watch it for you."

Lisette nodded dumbly. "I... I guess," she mumbled, stroking her hands down her apron. "All this new information—it's been such a shock to find out what's been going on."

Pania gave her an understanding nod. "It's natural that it would be, Lisette. Anyone would feel the same." Pania's eyes narrowed in concentration.

"You mentioned not knowing what to do about the rogue drilling. I'm wondering if you should ask John's advice? He'd probably have some sound suggestions. Or even possibly his brother?"

The question hung in the air for a few moments, and then Graysie screwed up her mouth and winced. "Sir John? I'm not sure it's the right thing. I'm certain he would have good ideas, but I've made a total fool of myself with the way I broke the news I was leaving." She frowned and bit her lip.

"He's furious with me. I guess with all the stress, I wasn't thinking straight. I've offended him when it was the last thing I wanted. And as for Nathan? I think it's for the best if we keep our distance.

"I don't want Minette getting too attached and then being let down when he moves on..." Her sentence trailed off, laced with uncertainty. She gave Pania a tight smile. "Well, he will, won't he?"

"Is that what you want? For him to move on?" Pania patted the chair beside her. "Come and sit down for a moment. You've been standing at that bench for hours. You too, Lisette. Let me make us all a fresh pot of tea."

Pania put the kettle on the hob as they settled around the table, then came back to join them. "So, I ask again, Graysie. Is that what you want? For Nathan Russell to move on?"

Graysie considered the question. "It's not about what I want. It's about reality, Pania." She was embarrassed to hear a shrill edge to her voice, but she plowed on.

"He's a grieving widower. And he couldn't even bring himself to tell me he'd been married. I had to hear about it from that horrible Willoughby Martens, his brother-in-law, for goodness' sakes. It was humiliating."

Lisette nodded sympathetically. "Such a shame."

Pania shook her head, her dark eyes sparking shrewdly. "So, it's his fault that his wife died? Is that what you're saying?"

"Of course not. No, but... Well, if he'd any interest in me, surely he'd have mentioned it? I can only conclude he didn't have any especial interest— beyond being gentlemanly, which he always is."

She looked to Lisette for moral support. "And as I say, I don't want Minette getting attached to him and then being let down. She's already had enough setbacks in her brief life. She needs no more."

"Is it really Minette's obvious affection for him that worries you, Graysie? Aren't you conveniently letting yourself off the hook here?"

Graysie stared at the older woman,

aware of the heat rising up her neck and into her cheeks. "What do you mean? I don't understand what you're getting at…"

Pania laughed affectionately. "For a smart young woman, you can be dense, Graysie Castellanos. It's obvious to anyone with eyes in their head that you captivate Nathan Russell. You'd have to be deliberately obtuse not to see it."

Graysie was holding her breath, not daring to release it. What was Pania saying? That her fleeting glimpses of their rare fusion of closeness and heat, those flashes when the universe whispered she and Nathan were sharing something special, seeing into one another's depths, wasn't all a stupid woman's dreaming after all?

She cleared her throat. "I'm not sure… not sure what you mean," she said, gazing back at Pania. She felt she was on the brink of discovering amazing good fortune.

This must be what it feels like for a blind woman to see again, she thought crazily. Or to discover you've won the jackpot when you didn't know how you were going to feed your children.

As Pania continued to look at her with a quizzical smile on her lips, Graysie repeated, "What are you saying?"

"I'm saying, Graysie Castellanos, that anyone with half a brain can see there is a special chemistry between you and the younger Mr. Russell. Something that—if I say it myself—there definitely is not between you and old Sir John." She raised one eyebrow in theatrical irony.

"I know life's taught you to be staunchly independent. It's taught me many of the same lessons, so I understand how hard it is to trust someone with something as precious as your entire future—particularly now that you have responsibility for Minette as well.

"But I would be delinquent as a friend if I let you run away from this possibility without at least pointing out what seems plain to anyone with eyes. Perhaps Nathan Russell was slow in telling you about his wife for quite the opposite reasons you've imagined. He didn't care too little about what you'd think, but too much.

"Maybe the poor man considered himself unworthy, or was expecting rejection. Maybe he's dragging an albatross behind him. You know the poem?"

Lisette shook her head, and Pania smiled. "There's a famous English poem about an old sailor who brings down a curse on himself by shooting an albatross. As punishment, they hang the dead bird around his neck."

A great weight lifted off Graysie, as if she'd been carrying a load of bricks on her back without knowing it. Tears welled up, and lightness flooded through her. Perhaps Nathan cared about her after all. Perhaps there was a possibility they could make a future together.

She grinned broadly, guessing her face was glowing bright pink with a joy she couldn't hide. "Do you really think so?"

"I do really think so," Pania said, a soft expression in her deep brown eyes. "And it's imperative you give yourself a chance to find out for yourself."

Forty Two

Nathan Russell banged his head on his pillow with frustration. Another sleepless night punishing himself over Graysie Castellanos. How did he always end up saying the wrong thing where that woman was concerned? He chewed his lip in frustration.

It perplexed him at how he acted around her. One minute he was talking to her like a headmaster reprimanding a naughty pupil, the next he was fighting the urge to take her in his arms and kiss her. He shuddered with embarrassment.

Truth to tell, every time he thought of her getting hurt, his blood hardened in his veins. When he considered he might never see her again, his mouth went dry. He was a mass of contradictions where she was concerned.

She was right to mock him. He cringed for himself. She'd told him more than once that she didn't need his help, but he insisted on going back for more. He swung his legs over the bed and wandered to the window to look out over the garden.

It was going to be a scorcher of a day. The sun was already slanting through the windows, causing him to squint. He thought back to the previous day's crazy escape. After the rocks had stopped falling around them, they'd waited in silence for several minutes, hoping for some telltale sound betraying the whereabouts of their attacker.

Had the rock fall injured him? Was it possible there were more than one of them? Could someone still be buried under the rubble? Or was he a solo operator who had anticipated their movements and slipped silently out before the fuse lit the black powder?

They'd heard no cries, no footsteps. They'd moved as quietly as they could down the newly cut shaft, Nathan going ahead of his hobbling brother with his gun drawn in case their adversary had somehow circled around and was waiting for them up ahead.

But their ascent into daylight was uneventful. The shaft through which Nathan and Seb exited led upwards on a gentle incline and opened through a trapdoor into a tin shed on the Ruby claim, as they suspected. But the site was deserted.

Proving who had cut the shaft, proving that the Ruby's owners didn't know of its existence, would be well-nigh impossible, Nathan guessed. Sebastian was right when he'd said yesterday it didn't fall within a sheriff's responsibilities.

Complicated quarrels over mining licenses usually ended in gunfire at dawn or drawn-out legal proceedings. The culprits could always play dumb and deny they knew anything about it.

As he sprinkled honey and cinnamon on the breakfast pancake Mrs. Snively had left out for him, Nathan considered his options. He had to put Graysie Castellanos well and truly behind him.

She was going off in Sacramento with Pania, and he wanted to focus on the reason he'd come here, securing his family's fortunes back in Australia. Irish Pete had offered to show him how a new stamper at the Allison Ranch Mine was working. That might yield him with

answers for his own prospects back
home.

   On the way, he'd drop in and check on
Anna Santa Maria and family to make
sure they were getting on okay, as he'd
promised.

*****

Antonio was watering horses when
Nathan pulled up at the Excelsior. Shafts
of early morning light shone through
flecks of floating hayseeds and dust
motes as the boy stroked down a black
mare's rump and murmured quiet
reassurances. The smell of horses
somehow filled him with new hope that
there were some things he could rely on.

   Nathan had called on Anna on his way
into town, but there was no sign of either
her or the children, so he'd made his
way to the stables in search of Antonio.
At the Wells Fargo office next door, the

air was sharp with the sounds of departure.

Horses snuffled and snorted, harnesses clinked, drivers hollered. The passengers about to board the coach for Sacramento waited in a knot outside the ticket office, nervously checking their luggage and sharing stories.

"Hey, Antonio," Nathan called, his heart warmed by the sight of the boy, who stood with sturdy confidence attending to his task, his shoulders pulled-back, chest high, and chin up.

When he heard Nathan's call, he turned and grinned. "Mr. Nathan! Buenos dias."

"Buenos dias, Antonio. I called to see Anna, and she wasn't at home—is everything alright?"

"Yes, we're all fine. She's gone to spend the day with her sister. She'll be home later. We're getting by. We have enough food and the little ones are happy." His grin widened. "They love Vulcan."

"And you? How is it going here at the stables, Antonio?"

The boy glanced over his shoulder. Nathan suspected to check whether his boss was within earshot. "Yes, good. Old Hank treats me well. Gives me spare bread to take home, and he is teaching me a lot about horses."

"Good. That's all very good."

The black mare raised her head, water dripping from her muzzle, and shook it vigorously, splattering their trousers.

"Had enough, girl, have you?" Antonio asked, and patted her again. "Come on then, back to your stall for some feed."

He was leading her by the halter across the yard to the stalls on the other side when they heard shouting coming from the Wells Fargo yard next door.

"Stone the crows, woman. Shut yer mouth, will ya?" The voice was rough and threatening, and the accent took Nathan right back to Old Sydney Town. He could have been on The Rocks' cobbled streets, a haven for so many of the colony's freed convicts. It sounded like one of his countrymen was in strife or dishing it out.

He turned to Antonio. The boy clenched his arms at his sides, shrinking into himself, trying to make himself as small as possible. His hands were trembling. He'd clenched his lips, but a small whimper escaped as he stood, rooted in terror.

"Antonio…" Nathan was about to ask the boy what was wrong, but he stopped himself. Whatever was going on next door in the Wells Fargo yard had triggered a deep terror in the boy—and he understood with a sudden cramping in his gut what that meant.

He gently prised Antonio's fingers from the black mare's bridle and led her into a stall, then went back and guided the boy onto a pile of straw nearby, settling him gently and hiding him behind closed stall gates.

"Stay here until I come back," he instructed, and sprinted across the yard into the coach-loading bay next door. The harnessed up Sacramento coach looked ready to depart. The argument had momentarily distracted the driver from stowing the last items of baggage.

A bulky red-faced man stood over a sobbing, scrawny blond woman, a horse whip raised threateningly over her cowering back. "I told yer. Yer not coming. Now scarper! Vamoose! Git going!"

He wanted rid of her. That was plain. She raised her arm as if to ward off a blow and scrabbled sideways in the dust, dangerously close to the hooves of the coach team hooked up, ready to depart.

Unsettled by the disturbance, the horses stamped and snorted. The beast closest to the woman threw its head wildly, rattling the harness, and causing the coachman to round on the gesticulating man.

"Oi! Stand clear. Both of you! Stand clear."

The driver was a big fellow with a shock of white hair and side arms in plain view on his belt. He grabbed the woman by the back of her dress and, in one smooth move, effortlessly swung her clear of the horses and on her feet in front of him.

She gasped and rubbed her dirt-streaked face, her mouth opening and closing like a fish. Her crying quieted.

"Madam, unless you are boarding this coach, be on your way," he said in a voice which brooked no argument. "Right now." He let go, and she melted into the passing crowd.

The bruiser who'd been threatening her stepped away without a backward glance. Nathan moved into the shadow of the fence, reluctant to draw attention to himself. He was about to return next door when a sudden commotion warned of more horses pulling up in the yard. A late comer for the coach, he presumed.

And there, dismounting from a smart gentleman's hansom cab were Hector de Vile and Willoughby Martens. As they stepped down, the Sydney crim—

because Nathan was now certain that was what he was—rushed forward and took de Vile's suitcase.

He lugged it up to the coach and rearranged the load to fit it on top. A traveling party of De Vile, Martens, and a thuggish Sydney Duck? Interesting. Nathan slipped back through the stable fence before the coachman had time to mount his driving station.

Antonio was where he'd left him, hands jammed under his armpits, tiny beads of sweat glistening on his hairline.

"He's going," Nathan said. "You don't need to be frightened anymore. He's on his way to Sacramento, and I'll ensure he won't be back. Ever." He didn't know how he was going to keep that promise, but it was what Antonio needed to hear right now, and he'd do his darndest to fulfil it.

"Are you scared he was he one of the kidnappers?"

"I don't know." Antonio began shaking uncontrollably. "I didn't see his face. He wore a scarf over everything except his eyes. But he sounded the same. Talked the same funny way. Not like Americanos."

Not like Americanos. He thought of Graysie and Pania's plans to be in Sacramento in the coming days for their concerts. Was it a coincidence that de Vile and Martens were headed there with an enforcer—probably an ex-convict enforcer—in tow?

He doubted it. He could and would report all of this to his brother Sebastian, but even if he drew the same conclusions, Nathan had no proof and no way to stop them from going about their legitimate business.

But Graysie, exposed to danger, was

something he couldn't bear to think about. Getting a warning to her was essential. If she wouldn't listen, he'd ask Pania to talk sense to her.

He wrapped an arm around Antonio's shoulder. As he'd been reassuring the boy, they'd heard the grinding of the wheels as the coach pulled out of the stagecoach station.

"Come on, boyo, let's go see Old Hank. I think he'll be happy to let you finish up now—the coach has gone and there's not too much else happening today. Let's get you home."

He'd wait around with Antonio until Anna got back from her sister's and explain to her what had happened. Then he'd visit Sebastian and ask him to keep watch over the Pedersen family, and he'd be on the next stage to Sacramento himself.

What was it the Bible said? Go out like "sheep among wolves"? If he was going to ensure no further harm came to Graysie or anyone near her, he was going to have to follow the advice of the Good Book and be as shrewd as a snake and as innocent as a dove.

Forty Three

Wednesday, July 22

Challenge number one met and conquered. Graysie sank into a chair offstage at the Orleans Hotel and sighed. Her ears were ringing from the thunderous applause peppered with piercing whistles that had greeted the final curtain of their first night of their Golden Queens Show.

Pania was still out front, soaking up the acclaim, always happy to play the diva, receiving homage. Graysie had collapsed, relieved to have got through their first performance with no disasters. She and Pania had little time to rehearse together, but they shared a drive for perfection, and it had worked its magic that night.

It wasn't only their appearance that provided a charismatic contrast: Pania, majestic, dark, and exotic; Graysie, fair, slender, and, she hoped, winsome. Their voices blended and complemented each other in ways the audience apparently found spellbinding. Graysie shivered.

The convent school had taken summer break and so she was not required to teach. It was a relief to be out of school, but a few days around the theater had reminded her all over again why life as a stage performer wasn't ideal for a single woman with a small child. She thought ruefully about her dreams of an alternative life. Maybe it wasn't meant to be.

Minette loved having Seraphine with

them, but both children missed the fresh mountain air and the chance to run and ride. They got restless spending hours in their hotel room drawing pictures. And although Graysie toyed with asking Eustace's Sacramento lawyer whether he'd had any known enemies, she'd not pursued it.

Sacramento had changed from the wild gambling town it had been when she was growing up. Merchants, politicians, and businessmen with wives and families now outnumbered the throngs of gun-happy, heavy drinking miners of earlier days, and with their arrival came a swing in public opinion towards curbing the more reckless excesses of grog and gambling.

A ban on Sunday trading passed by enthusiastic temperance supporters was overturned within a month by the

California Supreme Court, but signs of the 'moderating' influence of family life were to be seen everywhere, most notably in the growing taste for entertainment from something other than a roomful of card tables. That worked well for the Golden Queens.

At the Orleans, women could comfortably meet and eat with friends without a male escort, and the hotel provided a separate entrance for women, so they did not have to enter through the noisy public bar.

The applause faded and Pania interrupted Graysie's reflections when she slipped into the room and gave her a light hug.

"You did wonderfully tonight," she said, eyes sparkling. "We can be thrilled with our reception."

Her hand was warm and reassuring on

Graysie's shoulder, and Graysie patted it in appreciation. "Thank you so much, Pania. You made it all so easy. But now I probably need to slip away and check on Minette."

Pania sank into a chair beside her and shook her head. "She'll be in dreamland by now. Why not take a little time to relax and unwind? Besides, there's someone I want you to meet."

She stood and led Graysie down the corridor to her suite. Pania's Orleans sitting room was like an opulent cave, furnished with deep gold velvet sofas lit by gilded lamps that set up a mellow intimacy. The room seemed to wrap itself around you and embrace you.

It took a few seconds for Graysie's eyes to adjust, and then she saw with a start they were not alone. An elegant woman in an emerald green and white striped silk dress reclined in a wing chair on one side of the room. She exuded the confidence of someone who expected to be obeyed.

Her white blonde hair sat elegantly knotted in a plaited chignon at the back of her neck. With a peculiar little leap in her heart, Graysie noticed a tiny gold-coated fir cone exactly like hers hanging from the fine gold chain that encircled the woman's neck.

The stranger leaned forward in her chair, fixing Graysie with a searching look for longer, surely, than was polite. Graysie didn't know how to respond. Should she keep holding her gaze or defer and look away?

Pania raised an eyebrow at her in a theatrical caution and gestured towards the occupied chair.

"Graysie, I'd like to introduce Mrs.

Alycia Mountfort Stockton. Mrs. Stockton, this is Graysie Castellanos, your brother Eustace's beneficiary."

In the shocked silence that followed, no one spoke. Graysie was aware of Mrs. Stockton making a cool appraisal of her. When she spoke, her voice was unusually deep for a woman.

"Miss Castellanos, I don't know what tricks you played to win my brother's high regard, but I will be a lot harder to beguile, I assure you."

She patted the ottoman beside her. "Come and sit here and tell me about yourself. As your benefactor's sister, I believe I have a right to know a lot more about you."

Graysie felt her heartbeat surge. Her head snapped back, and her shoulders tensed. Her hands curled into tight fists. She was taking on a fighting stance. She didn't want to be confrontational, but neither was she going to lie down and meekly accept this woman's unfair assumptions about her.

Tricks to beguile indeed.

As far as she knew, the last time she'd laid eyes on her 'Uncle' Eustace, she'd been nudging five. She couldn't bear to think what Mrs. Stockton was imagining, but that was all it was, vain imagining.

With a sharp uptake of breath, she settled on the ottoman, uncomfortably close to the imperious woman in the wing chair. But she felt a new rush of indignation; she could stare someone down with the best of them.

"Mrs. Stockton, I'm not at all sure what you mean to imply, but I'm as much in the dark about your brother's intentions as anyone. I do not remember the last time I saw him, but I can swear I would have been no more than five years old. And whatever encounter we might have had then left no lasting impression on me. None."

Alycia Stockton gazed at her, as if waiting to catch her out in a lie.

"You haven't seen him since you were a child?" She seemed genuinely surprised. "How very peculiar. I thought..." Her voice trailed off.

Up close, Alycia Stockton was mesmerizing. Her skin was flawless, with few signs of the aging you might expect in a woman reaching midlife. Her eyes were a deep hazel with amber flecks that made Graysie think of gold mines. But it was her steely poise which made the biggest impression.

Someone you'd definitely want on your side, Graysie thought.

She sensed Mrs. Stockton was a

woman who, despite her wealth, had endured a lot of challenge; she apparently had little time for frivolities. "Your mother and my brother were close once. Of course, you knew that."

Under her intense gaze, Graysie was like a baby rabbit scrabbling to escape a hawk circling high overhead on the lookout for prey.

"I really only know what I've been told. After my mother died and my father remarried, we barely mentioned my mother's name." She let a silence hang in the air. She didn't want to elaborate.

After an uncomfortably long pause, Alycia Stockton said softly, "I imagine that must have been a tough time for you."

The change of mood took her by surprise, and to her astonishment, tears welled up behind her eyelids. She was furious.

You're crying here? Things really must be getting on top of you. You never cry.

With fierce resolve, she stuffed the sadness back deep down inside her, clenching her jaw as she did so.

"Life in the West *is* tough and unpredictable." She felt her jaw setting in a tight line. "I've enjoyed more good fortune than many."

Alycia nodded. "And now I understand you have undertaken to raise someone else's child. Rather an unusual assignment for a single woman, wouldn't you agree?"

For the first time since this conversation began, Graysie felt the urge to explain herself. She shuffled her weight on the ottoman so she was facing Mrs. Stockton full on and shook her head.

"Unusual, I agree. But unacceptable?

No. Minette's mother, Francine, and I had a special understanding. Minette's father has been absent since her birth, and Francine had no other family here in California.

"Her widowed mother in France has little means to give Minette support. It's terrible that Francine died, but it's a labor of love to care for her daughter. After my own life without a mother… Well, let's say I know what it's like."

"You had a father and a stepmother?" Alycia's statement was a question.

"Technically speaking. My father never recovered from my mother's death, and my stepmother never forgave him—or her—for that. Their home was not a happy place to be."

Pania had been sitting quietly in the corner, but now she cleared her throat and said, "Graysie, it's been a big night and it's getting late. Maybe we should continue this conversation in the morning?"

Graysie felt her throat constrict. She might never see this woman again, and she'd so much she still wanted to ask her. "Of course," she said. "But do you mind—I have a lot of unanswered questions."

She turned back to Mrs. Stockton, who was gathering up a reticule which had sat on the floor by her side, as if getting ready to leave.

"Mrs. Stockton, I don't remember ever meeting Eustace, and I don't understand why he left me any part of his estate. But I have some questions of my own, not the least of which is, why do you have a gold fir cone identical to the one my mother gave me, hanging around your neck?"

Forty Four

Thursday, July 23

The chilled marble-floored gallery at Nobilo's Italian Ice Cream Parlour on 10th Street was overflowing with family groups eager to avoid the soaring temperatures outside. The Sierras had been experiencing a heat wave, and even though it had barely reached ten in the morning, Graysie guessed it was going to be another 100-degree day.

Nobby had been dispensing his icy confections from this store on 10th Street for more than a decade, but the place was barely recognizable now from the canvas-walled caboose she'd come to as a child.

Graysie marvelled at the changes since she'd last been here with her father. Marble tiles had replaced the packed earth floor. Chilled air from the basement ice cellar—stocked with Arctic ice imported by the California Ice Company—gave the parlor a delightful coolness.

As well as the family gallery, there were private rooms where ladies could sip on sodas or delicately nibble from dishes of ice cream undisturbed, but they had opted for the public seating. Minette was wriggling beside her with excitement; she'd never had ice cream before, and this outing was a special treat.

She was uncomfortably aware it might also be her way of assuaging her guilt for leaving Minette every night to go on stage, but she brushed the thought away. They were here, and they were going to have fun!

Alycia Mountfort Stockton sat at the head of the table, coolly assessing the menu. Graysie had surprised Alycia with her invitation to accompany them to Nobby's, and it secretly amazed her when Alycia had agreed.

She figured she had nothing to lose. Alycia had already decided she was a con artist, sight unseen, and she wasn't about to waste energy trying to change her opinion. She would get on with what she needed to do, and Alycia could fit in. Or not. Either way, it didn't bother her; she told herself.

But it seemed Alycia was more than willing to fit in. She was as supremely confident here as she'd been last night in

Pania's dressing room, resting a relaxed elbow on the mosaic-topped table, deaf to the rising tide of chatter from nearby tables.

"So, girls, what kind of ice cream would you like?" she asked in her slow, deep voice. "Do you like chocolate?"

Minette brightened at the query and wriggled some more. "Yes, I like chocolate a lot, Madam. Do you like chocolate too?" Her blue eyes twinkled, and dimples showed on her cheeks.

Alycia made a circular gesture with her finger and thumb—A-OK. Minette's dimples deepened, and she giggled.

"Shall we both have chocolate ice cream, then? What about you, Seraphine?"

"Strawberry for me, thank you very much," said Seraphine, licking her rosebud lips in anticipation.

Graysie felt as if her control of the social occasion was slipping away. How did this woman seem to assume charge so effortlessly? She chimed in, "I think I'm a strawberry girl too, thank you. But let me order and buy."

Alycia shook her head. "No. This is my treat." She beckoned the waiter who had been hovering nearby and, order completed, turned back to Graysie. "It will take them a little time to bring our order when they're so busy. Why doesn't Mrs. Guilliame take the girls to see the miniature railway until they arrive?"

The miniature railway was the other big attraction offered at Nobby's Parlour. Mounted on a big podium at the far end of the gallery, a scaled-down steam train wound its way over a mountain and through a gorge, down into a valley, offering a Lilliputian representation of the real thing under construction from Sacramento into the mountains.

People talked incessantly of the Central Pacific project; how far it had reached, what bridges and tunnels were being built, when it would reach Donner Pass, the Sierra summit where the railway crossed over into Nevada on its way to Reno. The romance was irresistible for any child who dreamed of one day riding on a train.

Minette got up and took Lisette's hand without hesitation. "Let's go see the train!"

As soon as they were out of earshot, Alycia turned back to Graysie. "I owe you an apology, Miss Castellanos. On reflection, I admit I made unwarranted assumptions about your behavior which don't hold up to scrutiny. My only excuse is that such an unexpected bequest seemed to require an extreme explanation."

Graysie felt her mouth momentarily drop open before she regained control and snapped it shut. Alycia Stockton was apologizing to her?

She hesitated before replying, "Please call me Graysie. And I understand, Mrs. Stockton. Believe me when I say it was a shock for me too, when I got the letter from your brother's lawyer."

Alycia leaned in closer. "Tell me, my dear, were you and your father close? Did he spend a lot of time with you?"

The sudden change of tack. startled Graysie. Why was Alycia interested in her father?

"Not especially. I suspect my mother was the one and only love of his life. No one else came close. I always felt as if he escaped into his work after she died.

He was away a lot with his mobile daguerreotype studio, and he left me at home with my stepmother.

"Having married her, it seems he found it hard to live with her, so he disappeared often. That wasn't good for me or my stepmother."

Alycia nodded and stared off into middle distance before rallying herself with a shrug of her shoulders. "I knew your mother when we were girls, you know. She was exquisite, and you look so like her it's unnerving."

She regarded Graysie and sighed. "She ruined my brother for any other woman."

"Um… sorry?" Graysie felt like a gauche teenager. "I don't understand."

"He was crazy about her. We all expected he would marry her. Then my mother died suddenly, and my father stepped in. Mother had always been indulgent of Eustace's wishes. She protected him from father.

"But with her gone, my father decided it was time Eustace hardened up and learned the business. He sent him to the West Indies for two years to run things there and, within a few months, Elanora married your father. It was a surprise for everybody."

"I see." Graysie realized she knew very little about her mother and Eustace, except for one embarrassing kiss she'd witnessed that she was certain she wasn't supposed to see.

"When he came out West, we were concerned he was going to make a fool of himself over her all over again. I still think that might have happened except for her untimely death. I don't think he ever got over her."

Graysie cleared her throat. "Do you

think…?" She hesitated, and her voice came out in a whisper. "Do you think he left me those mine shares as some kind of memorial to my mother?"

"It's highly likely," said Alycia. "And you're not to blame if he did." In the natural pause that followed, the waiter bustled up bearing a silver tray with an array of glass ice cream bowls and silver spoons.

"Your order is waiting, Madam," he said with a deferential nod to Alycia.

Over Alycia's shoulder, Graysie could see Lisette and the two excited children were heading back to their table. Minette was swinging the hand she clasped in Lisette's and was chattering nonstop, her face flushed with excitement. She slipped into her chair and clasped her hands together in a prayer-like gesture.

"Oh, the ice cream is here," she said.

"This is the most perfect day ever."

They were scraping their bowls clean when a shadow fell across the table. Graysie half expected to see the waiter back to check on progress, but with a shock, saw Hector de Vile standing over them.

"Mrs. Hayes suggested I might find Miss Castellanos here with you, Mrs. Stockton," he said to Alycia with a slight bow. "I have had a most agreeable morning with your husband." He nodded courteously.

"Miss Castellanos? Delighted, I'm sure. I've been suggesting to Mrs. Stockton's husband, Basil, that your mine could be an excellent investment for us to join in partnership together."

Graysie felt like someone had punched her in the stomach. "My mine?" she paused in confusion. Only a few days ago, he'd been peddling a fake prospector's report and talking down its prospects. Now he was talking them up again?

"I thought you considered it a poor prospect? From what your colleague Mr. Martens said... I thought he was operating under your guidance?"

De Vile returned her questioning gaze with a bland, surprised expression. "Martens? Oh, he has his own opinions on these things; they aren't necessarily mine."

Ten days ago, finding potential investors like Basil Stockton and Hector de Vile would have seemed like a dream come true. But now? De Vile's newfound bonhomie rang false.

She wondered desperately how she was going to fend him off. How dare he? He'd been perfectly despicable when

Minette went missing, and she'd vowed then that she'd never have another thing to do with him. She lowered her gaze and bit down on her lower lip.

When she glanced back up, Alycia was watching her keenly. The older woman's face registered brief surprise, and then she turned imperiously to de Vile, who was leaning over her chair like he was staking a claim on the space between them.

"I'm sure there will be a good time for you to discuss business, Mr. de Vile, but we're enjoying a little private outing at present. Now is not that time."

She flashed Graysie a look that said more than words could.

You've got someone watching your back now, girl. You've come home.

Forty Five

Saturday, July 25

Nathan sat at the Sitka Ice House windows, cooling off with an iced coffee when he caught sight of Martens' distinctive tall frame passing by. He gulped down the rest of his drink, slipped out and fell into step behind him, hanging back and dodging carts and other pedestrians, staying out of sight.

They were moving farther and farther away from the prosperous stores frequented by the middle class burghers, towards the scrappy docks.

Soon they were on a levee road on the Sacramento River bank, and the crowds, which had made it easy to keep himself hidden, were thinning. It was a futile exercise, he told himself. What did he hope to achieve with it? But while he was here...

He could hear faint sounds of Chinese music coming from a building that was part Chinese temple, part community hall. Attracted by the sound, he started down the alley and saw Martens ahead of him, slipping into the building through a side door.

From where Nathan stood, near the junction with I Street, he could see a large sign over the main entry in Chinese characters announcing the Canton Chinese Theater. Of course! Some girls at the Exchange had family who performed here, he recalled.

He was about to follow Martens in when an iron-hard forearm locked around his throat, cutting off his breath. The cold steel of a pistol muzzle pressed against the side of his neck.

"Turn around slowly, mate. Now. Yer coming with me." The Sydney Duck from the Wells Fargo yard hissed his instructions into Nathan's left ear, and he felt spittle on the side of his face.

The sounds of people going about their normal business on I Street filtered down the alley; shop owners bustling to get goods unloaded and on their shelves before the close of business, a newspaper boy's cry above the rumble of cartwheels on the hard-packed dirt road, "Sacramento Cour-ier... On sale now!"

He could smell dead fish and decaying water weed on the light breeze from the river. He turned cautiously under the pressure of his captor's arm to face the slow-moving water. The levee regularly flooded in heavy rains, but it offered a quick anonymous exit for anyone able to leave via the water.

It would be stupid to try anything smart here. He's got it all over me. How am I ever going to get out of this one alive?

Nathan took a deep breath and started walking towards the river.

✶✶✶✶✶

Graysie stepped onto the boardwalk outside lawyer John Piedmont Fisher's offices right next door to the courthouse and slowed to allow Alycia to catch her up. Eustace's sister had insisted on accompanying Graysie to this appointment with the lawyer. In fact, she'd arranged it.

There was no other way Fisher would have been likely to make himself available at short notice on a Saturday,

Graysie thought. But if Mrs. Stockton spoke, the world obeyed. Fisher's office was all dark wood and austerity, and the man's demeanor reflected the same restraint.

Tall and thin, with faded blonde hair and skin mottled by faint freckles, his appearance showed evidence of too many hours spent at his desk. A model of rectitude, he appeared to have forgotten how to relax and breathe easy.

Quite the opposite of Eustace, Graysie imagined. Alycia took the lead, as usual. She'd exchanged letters with Fisher and addressed him as if he was already a valued acquaintance.

"Mr. Fisher! So pleased to meet you at last. My brother's death was distressing to us all, but it is reassuring to know his wishes are being impeccably executed. You have already met Miss Castellanos, I understand, one of Eustace's beneficiaries?"

Fisher acknowledged Graysie with a nod. "Yes, we have met. How is it progressing, Miss Castellanos? Have you read the legacy documents in their entirety?"

"The legacy documents? No... Should I have? I didn't realize..." Graysie would have liked the floor to swallow her up, she felt such a fool.

"When I saw you last, you seemed overwhelmed by the death of your friend and the child's arrival. It didn't seem like an appropriate time to spell out certain conditions. And Eustace also left me with confidential instructions."

She sat still as a statue and concentrated on making sense of what the lawyer was saying. What is he getting at? Certain conditions?

Confidential instructions? Like what? But before she'd a chance to frame a sensible response, Alycia cut in.

"Mr. Fisher, I hope you can discuss everything that needs to be said at this meeting in front of both of us? Nothing is confidential to only Miss Castellanos or to myself—I mean, there's no detail one may hear but not the other?

"As you know, Miss Castellanos's share is a small part of my brother's overall estate, and there are still some loose ends I need to attend to as the executor appointed on behalf of the family."

Mr. Fisher steepled his fingers as he rested his elbows on his desk and considered. Right hand against his left—index against index, middle finger against middle finger… Graysie felt a strange calm descend as she watched his fingers play silent notes.

"The question of confidentiality?" Fisher furrowed his brow. "He's left sensitive material with me, I grant you. But it probably impacts both of you in different but equal ways, so it is doubtless best if you hear me out together."

At the word 'sensitive', Graysie sensed Alycia stiffening. The matriarch plunged in. "Sensitive material, Mr. Fisher? Can you explain further? I expect it may surprise us both to hear you use that term. I would have thought my brother's life was an open book."

Fisher cleared his throat. He was plainly getting uncomfortable. "Not as transparent as you might have assumed, Mrs. Stockton. We find in our profession it's not so unusual for our clients to take secrets to the grave..."

He looked from Graysie to Alycia and

then back to his hands, which he folded flat on the desk in front of him.

"Mr. Mountfort left two documents of a personal, confessional nature, with instructions they were only to be delivered to the named parties if those parties came forward and requested further information. If no one came forward within a year of his death, these documents were to be destroyed. If someone close asked, I was to make them available."

"Stop! Stop, please!" Graysie wrung her hands together. "This is all too much to take in. What are you talking about?"

Mr. Fisher regarded her gravely for a long minute and re-steepled his fingers. "What I have to tell you will be a shock, Miss Castellanos." He paused and nodded courteously in Alycia's direction. "Mrs. Stockton. I think it is best if I hand over Mr. Mountfort's documents for you both to read for yourselves."

Fisher began rustling through a folder on his desk and drew out two papers that appeared to have been written on the same expensive cream parchment. He placed them on the desk in front of him and protectively drew his hands along the sides of the paper, tracing the pages silently.

The rigid line of his shoulders fell forward a fraction.

"In effect, Miss Castellanos, he wanted to make a clean breast of a very turbulent period in his youth relating to his relationship with your mother, Elanora Grayson Castellanos.

"Events occurred which cast a cloud over the rest of his life, and I believe he wished to clear his conscience before he died."

Graysie and Alycia stared at each other; neither spoke. Alycia's normally acute gaze had a glassy sheen. Graysie swallowed hard against a wave of dizziness. The lawyer stood up and walked around his desk to place one of the sets of parchment in Alycia's hand.

The other he offered to Graysie. Her fingers were so stiff from clutching the solid arm of her chair, she fumbled to take hold of it.

Eustace had addressed it to Miss Grayson Mountfort Castellanos. Her cheeks were hot, and her fingers tingled. As she unfolded the page, she smelt a faint whiff of masculine cologne. How she wished Eustace was here to tell her in person whatever it was he thought she needed to know. She smoothed the paper and read.

My dear Miss Mountfort Castellanos,

As you are reading this letter prepared after many years of heart-searching, I can only assume my solicitor Mr. Fisher is satisfied my conditions for its release have been met—namely that you sought further information about me and the bequest I made to you within twelve months of my death.

I would never have been able to disclose the information following here if your mother, Elanora, had not died so prematurely and tragically, as I would have felt that it was not mine to make known.

However, with Elanora now long gone, I have convinced myself the needs of the living should take precedence over the vanished desires of the dead. What is it our dear Lord says in Luke? "Why do you look for the living amongst the dead?"

You, my dear Graysie, are our living legacy. Your mother and I are no longer here to love and to fear, and it is incumbent on me to make you aware of your remarkable birthright.

Your mother and I were very young, very foolish, very much in love, and certain we would be together forever when we celebrated our1848 New Year's Eve engagement in the most intimate way a man and woman can. We had no notion my mother's unexpected death on New Year's Day would change everything.

My father's insistence that, with her gone, I take over the family business in the West Indies ripped us apart. Within a few days of my mother's funeral, I was on a boat to Kingstown, shell-shocked and feeling like I was walking underwater.

He would not countenance the idea of us marrying. Apart from anything else, the family was in mourning.

I did not know I had left your mother in an appallingly exposed situation, with no one to appeal to. She married within a few months of my departure and you were born a very short time after that.

Her family shunned her, and it is one of the great griefs of my life that, because she died so young, she never had the chance to reconcile with them.

I have watched your life from afar these many years and have felt ashamed I could not step in and ease the hard times you have faced, the disruption of your life after your mother's death, and loss of a family life that was never restored in her absence.

I did not replace Elanora in my life, and I understand you could never replace her in yours, either.

I have been in awe of the resilience and courage you have displayed as you have grown. I wonder not only at your strength but also at your blossoming as a gifted artist.

I have had the pleasure of sitting in your audience on several occasions, basking not only in the beauty, so like your mother's, that

Graysie had to stop reading. Her eyes blurred with tears. Her heart swelled to such a size it blocked her throat, so she struggled to swallow.

This can't be happening. The man I thought was my father all these years was an imposter? A pretender? I have another father altogether?

She sat for several minutes staring at the page without reading a word. When her pulse had returned to a steady calm, she resumed.

I made my decision to leave you the Ophir as an inheritance after many years of reflection. I could not ease your path while I have lived, but perhaps I can help a little when I am no longer there.

I want you to know that, as the daughter of Eustace Mountfort and Elanora Grayson Travers, we would have planned the fullest of life and love that any loving parent wishes to bestow on their child. Your forbears on both sides are amongst the most noble and upright people you could hope to know.

It is the tragedy of all of our lives that our good intentions did not prevail and brought disaster for us both. I do not want your legacy to be tainted by our lack of wisdom.

I have good evidence that, with

Graysie hesitated from her reading and squeezed her eyes shut. When she opened them again, the room was exactly the same. The shelves of ancient leather-bound legal tomes, some dusty from disuse, hadn't moved. Alycia was sitting in an unnaturally still pose, reading. Graysie could only guess at what Eustace had told her.

The older woman seemed unaware of the tears trickling slowly down her face as she read on, deeply absorbed in the letter's contents. Then, perhaps realizing Graysie's was gaze on her, she glanced up quickly and shot her a wan smile.

"More bad news to come, I'm afraid. My brother was a lot more foolish than I ever realized."

Forty Six

With the gun barrel in his back, the Sydney gangster marched Nathan over bumpy sand to a ramshackle jetty on the water's edge. A tall man with blackened teeth slipped from the shadows under the jetty. He held a rope in one hand. Nathan saw they'd attached it to a bow ring on a battered dinghy that gently rocked on the shoreline.

They were on a deserted section of the river, where the levee, built up to protect against flooding, obscured any view of the water from the warehouses, granaries, and lumber yards which lined this commercial strip of Sacramento. The turpentine smell of cut logs and wheat dust tickled Nathan's nose.

He could see an old man in the distance fishing, but apart from that, the river moved with a slow oily sheen, undisturbed by man or wildfowl. The afternoon had that strange calm of a sharply falling barometer, of the eeriness before the storm. Hot, still, and ominous.

Clouds were rapidly closing in so that the line between water and sky was a vague, misty border. It was unclear where one ended and the other began. There was no one to call on for help, no one who had noticed his abduction.

The brown depths seemed to rise before his eyes, and icy terror clutched him in the pit of his stomach. The unwelcome memory of another fateful afternoon two years ago flooded back. A storm at sea, the waves hammering against a foundered ship.

Despite the steamy Sacramento day, his teeth chattered. The gun dug painfully into his back. The toothless man grabbed his shoulder and squeezed it hard; pain shot down his arm into his elbow.

The man motioned towards the dinghy. Nathan stumbled over the rotting side and collapsed onto a bench seat. The dinghy bottom slopped the water, and his panic rose.

His senses concentrated in one place, an instant in time back on the New South Wales coast two years ago. The same cold wetness soaking through his trousers. The sharp smell of salt. A whine of rising wind. Sand stinging his face.

With hundreds of staring spectators he'd watched from the beach as the *Cawarra's* funnel and then foremast broke away. A steamship on her maiden voyage, the pride of the line, reduced to a wallowing hulk battered against the Nobbys Head sand bar as they'd stood by and watched, helpless.

Next day the bodies began washing ashore, but he'd never found Charlotte and Joshua to give them the funeral they'd deserved, despite patrolling the beach and scratching through the wreckage for days afterwards.

Thunder rumbled an ominous warning over the Sacramento River and brought his memories to an abrupt halt as. Every sense came alive, as if searing this moment in his mind forever. The pearly grey draping of delicate chiffon where water and sky met. A rising odor of dead fish and jute rope in his nostrils. Light beams sparking off the glassy surface, as if sending darts to heaven.

And the clawing conviction he'd never see Graysie again. Every cell in his body was drinking in the scene, as if these were the last things he would ever see and smell.

Is this what it was like for Charlotte, before she went down with the *Cawarra*?

Except she'd borne the added agony of having Joshua with her.

He'd repeatedly tortured himself with this question in the night's stillness, and he was no nearer to any answer or acceptance.

I pray he was with her. That he didn't die alone.

And I'm going to drown, just like they did.

That's what you call true poetic justice.

The toothless crook gave a nervous glance skyward, then thrust the dinghy into deeper water and leapt aboard. The vessel tipped to one side dangerously with three of them on board, and more water slopped in.

The man with the rotten teeth also had a foul breath, Nathan discovered, as he lent in and wrenched Nathan's arms in front of him. The thick marine rope he used to tie Nathan's wrists together chafed his skin and sent pins and needles up his arms.

"Try anything smart and we'll dump you overboard and leave you to drown," the man with the gun hissed in his right ear.

Lightning sliced the grey horizon as Rotten Teeth settled in the middle seat and began rowing with smooth control. Halfway across, that changed. The heavens opened.

The wind whipped up in their faces, and the mirror surface danced. Waves slapped over the sides of the low-slung vessel, making hard work for the oarsman to pull his way across the main river channel to a small island at the confluence of a trickling tributary.

Nathan was facing the island, but through the gray, sheeting deluge, it was hard to make out any detail until they were close enough to go ashore. He saw there was no jetty, only a muddy sloping bank fringed with straggling swamp trees. Rotten Teeth angled the dinghy into the shallows and beached it.

When he leapt overboard to drag it up and tie it to an old stump, he sank halfway up his calves in the mud. Each foot made a plopping sound, which released a smell of rotting vegetation.

"Get out," the other sailor snarled, his teeth clenched.

Nathan pitched forward, half in and

half out of the boat, unbalanced by his tied hands, and Rotten Teeth clutched his elbow in a vise grip.

He swore and pulled some filthy rags from his pocket, gagging and blindfolding Nathan before shoving him forward.

"Move. We haven't got all day."

Walking blindly, half falling every few yards, Nathan fought to stay upright. If he got off course, Rotten Teeth cursed and pummelled him. The gag made it difficult to breathe, and he was panting raggedly when they finally called on him to stop.

The cloth was wet from his saliva, and his eyes hurt from the pressure of the blindfold. His throat was dry, and he had a raging thirst.

The river sound had faded as they had walked, and Nathan sensed that, although they had not gone very far, they had moved inland. Not above the waterline, however. He calculated they were slightly below the river level, in a dip which, from the unevenness of the ground under his feet, was sand pocked with boulders he'd stumbled against.

The rotting smell had also disappeared, replaced by an acrid bird dung odor. He could hear the cry of gulls wheeling in the sky overhead; he guessed they must be near some kind of nesting place.

He focused on what his nose and ears were telling him until someone shoved him in the back again, this time so hard he fell forward on his knees.

He raised his hands to protect his face as he collapsed. He rolled on his side and flipped over so he was sitting up, momentarily dizzy. Was he facing the river or inland, and where were his captors? He answered the question when one of them spoke.

"This is where your journey ends."

Even through the blindfold, Nathan sensed the shadow of the man leering over him, his voice laced with malice. He caught the slight onion fragrance of a popular hair tonic, said to repel insects.

"Big storm." He was almost certain it was Rotten Teeth who spoke. "It's exactly the right place for a man who doesn't mind his own business."

With his mouth stuffed with the soppy gag, it was impossible to reply, but Nathan knew it would be useless, anyway. The man was following orders. He needed no further confirmation that Martens was issuing them.

He sank onto his elbows. He smelt yellow gorse, heard the mourning keening of seabirds. And then a blow across the side of his face knocked him sideways. He curled up to protect himself from the next one. He heard a high-pitched, derisive laugh.

"You're done for, mate. At the rate this rain is falling, the water will swamp you in no time. I'd say you've got a couple of hours before the flood waters and river will meet and you'll be a dead fish."

A second cracking blow landed, and then he felt nothing more.

Forty Seven

Graysie and Alycia had less than half a block to walk from the lawyer's office to a café and ice cream parlor that advertised 'sedate and elegant' rooms for ladies. The boardwalk was busy with families on weekend errands or taking their children out for a treat, and the two women didn't talk until they reached one of the parlor's private rooms and sat down.

The news that Eustace was her father had numbed Graysie. So many wild thoughts clamored for her attention that she couldn't single out one, and she was anxious about what further revelations Alycia might have for her.

She could tell by the older woman's tense movements and tightly clamped jaw she was doing the best she could to suppress her anguish.

When the waiter had taken their orders and left, Alycia drew the lawyer's document from her reticule and offered it to Graysie across the table. She shook her head.

"Maybe later. I'm quite happy for you to tell me what it contains. I don't need to read it now."

Alycia creased her brow and took a deep breath. Graysie had the impression that, like her, she wasn't sure where to start.

"He's been very honest about his conviction you're his daughter, conceived on New Year's Eve 1848. I have no reason to doubt his account, and I acknowledge there is an uncanny resemblance to Eustace in some of your gestures: the way you hold your head in a certain erect manner, a particular little movement you make with your mouth when you want to speak but then decide to keep silent. Small unconscious body language that no one could fake.”

She leaned forward confidentially.

“Honestly, that disclosure was not a complete surprise, though I never discussed my suspicions with anyone. No, the details that upset me very much, and which I believe will also cause you more pain, relate to your mother’s death.”

Alycia paused, her face drawn and white. She fingered the gold cone at her throat, almost as if seeking reassurance from something familiar, and took a deep breath.

“From what he says, it’s clear Eustace

was involved in the events of that dreadful night when your mother died."

As if on cue, the waiter returned with their coffees, and Alycia paused while he set their cups down. After he left, they sat in silence for another long minute.

Alycia vacantly plucked a sugar cube in silver tongs from a bowl on the table and added it to her cup. Although it was not cold inside the parlor, Graysie felt comforted holding the warm vessel in her hands. She postponed taking the first sip.

Alycia resumed. "When Castellanos asked Elanora to join him with you children in Sacramento, it appears Eustace conceived this mad scheme of intercepting the stage coach and convincing her to run away with him.

"He was certain she was going to be miserable. It was a plot conceived in nothing but craziness, that's clear. I told you he was out of his mind where Elanora was concerned."

She sighed, took a sip of her coffee, and cleared her throat before continuing.

"He'd heard a month or two previously about some jape where a miner had kidnapped his beloved and eloped with her—and everyone thought it was a tremendous joke. It was like that in the early days. Actions with no consequences.

"Eustace was under the illusion he could pull the same stunt. They were wild boys who thought the rules didn't apply to them—and out here in the early days of the Gold Rush, they mainly didn't. You could get away with such pranks.

"From what he says, it all went tragically wrong when the stagecoach driver lost his head and tried to run him down. The horses took fright and bolted, the coach overturned, and the impact threw your mother out."

Graysie was aware of a painful tightening in her throat, and spots flashed before her eyes. Fierce pain skewered her heart; she could not have risen from her chair even if she'd wished to, the agony was crippling.

She heard again the terrible screech of wagon wheels, the terrifying rasping of the coach walls hitting looming trees, the twins crying in the darkness.

She wanted to pull her hair and wail loudly. Instead, she clutched her chest and concentrated on breathing in and out slowly. Involuntarily, she pinched her lips together; she wasn't sure if it was to stop herself from trembling or crying.

Had she never grieved for her mother

until that moment? All those years when she'd felt angry about being left alone, the loss of the twins gnawing away at her. She'd sometimes blamed herself for it, but more often, she blamed her mother.

Now with a rush she understood: her mother had only been a few years older than Graysie was now when she'd died, and it was so different for women then, especially women with children.

"Does he say anything about the twins? Anything at all?"

A crushing weight pressed down on her chest. As she waited for Alycia to speak, she wondered if she would ever breathe properly again. The squeeze on her windpipe was so tight.

"Only that they both survived the wreck. They were securely fastened into a traveling cot. They were crying, but seemed otherwise unharmed. He says he left them in their cot in the shelter of a cave near the crash."

"Left them in a cave?" Graysie thought of the white wolf in her dream. "In a cave?"

She felt dazed and sick at heart. Did this confirm the babes had fallen prey to the predators? She put her head in her hands and sobbed into them, wracking, soul-baring dry sobs.

Eustace hadn't left her a legacy. He'd passed her a poisoned cup. The Ophir—didn't they say the name meant 'rich in gold'?—no longer seemed like a magnanimous endowment from a loving father.

It felt like blood money, a paltry trade in guilt, contaminating her for being alive to receive it.

*****

Graysie slouched in her chair, as jumpy as a flea, but too exhausted to get out of her sparkly concert gown. The Saturday matinee crowd was going home happy, but at the sound of the rain drumming against the windows, her mood dipped, despite the positive reception they'd received.

She didn't normally give in to confusion, and she didn't know what was wrong with her. She was elated one minute, wracked with anxiety the next.

Sacramento loved the Golden Queens. The local paper lay discarded beside her, trumpeting a glowing review, 'The Golden Queens: Enthusiastic Reception of Talented Artistes in Sacramento Pleasure Palace.'

For the first time since Francine's death, she felt hopeful. She could provide herself and Minette with a good life. Harry the impresario was enthusiastic about putting together a wider tour and was pushing for a definite commitment.

"I can make you both bigger stars than you can imagine—but you have to decide by the end of the week. We need to get a fall season booked before winter storms disrupt everything."

Graysie's stomach fluttered like it did before every first night. Could she make life on the road work for them?

She sighed, poured herself a second cup of tea and turned to the soft-sided brown leather valise where she'd stored all of Eustace's papers. She'd snatched the chance to read through them earlier and wept for the gigantic loss of it all: hers for the father she never knew, and Eustace's and Elanora's for the love they never shared.

But saddest of all, she wept for the twins and their unknown fate. She still wasn't ready to talk about it with anyone but Alycia.

She finished her tea, folded up Eustace's letter, and turned her attention to the mine legacy documents. She admitted she really had not taken time to stop and take in the full picture before. Now, with the full bequest documents before her, she was shocked as she combed through the fine print.

Her continued ownership was conditional on her making progress by reopening the mine within twelve months of receiving the bequest. If she failed to do that, the mine would pass to Father O'Brien and the parish of St. Mary's.

Graysie twisted a dangling lock of hair around her finger as she considered the implications. She'd already owned the mine for four months. It had taken her that long to move to Grass Valley.

They were progressing into fall and then winter, when it would be difficult—maybe impossible—to get men working. A lot of miners drifted back to San Francisco or down south when the snow came in.

The clock was ticking, and not only for the mine's future. The heavy drum of rain outside on Second Street brought her back to the present. She needed to get some sleep if she was going to be sensible the next day.

She got up from her chair and tiptoed into the room Minette shared with Seraphine. Minette lay carelessly on her back, one arm thrown outside the covers. The child was totally at peace, undisturbed by the torrent that was rattling the windows.

Graysie shivered as she readied herself for bed, rain roaring down the gutters as she turned out the light. A scrappy idea was forming. If the Ophir paid a yield in years to come, maybe she could use it to lay to rest the mystery of her siblings' fate. Then it wouldn't be blood money anymore.

First thing tomorrow, she'd seek a meeting with Basil Stockton and see if he had any interest in the Ophir Mine. She didn't trust Hector de Vile, and she didn't want him as a business partner, even if he was to become a senator. She hoped her newly sealed place in the Mountfort family would be enough to claim Basil Stockton's attention.

I'd never have stood a chance of getting a meeting with him without that card to play, she thought. As she slipped into bed and pulled the sheet up around her shoulders, she felt a ton weight of anxiety descend. She'd made tenuous links to a new family, but she'd never felt so alone.

Forty Eight

Nathan Russell opened his eyes to wet blackness. He was lying in the sand, his body half submerged in water that was slowly creeping up his back. The rising floodwaters Rotten Teeth had forecast were here, leaving him soaked to the skin and shivering. His head throbbed. He struggled to recall what had happened.

Then he remembered the boat ride, the head blows. The threat of drowning. A surge of fear jolted through him and he tried to rise to his feet. He struggled briefly, then remembered they'd tied him at the knees. He toppled back, overcome with dizziness.

Joshua's piteous cries—Daddeee... Daddeee... hung in the wind. He knew his son's tiny voice could never have reached him, but how many times in the past two years had he been woken by that cry?

He'd lost one family then and any chance of building a second was again being swept away. Pain clawed at his insides. He would never see Graysie, ever again. Never secretly delight in the fleeting parade of emotions that skittered across her face when she was unaware anyone was watching her.

What a fool I've been, to discover what's most important to me when it's too late.

His stomach cramped, and he brought his bound wrists up to his face. Even tied tightly as he was, he could lean forward, half spread his fingers and bury his face in his hands. He did that now, awkwardly raking his aching forehead to relieve the crippling throb.

I can bury my face in his hands!

What an idiot he was. If he could touch his face, he could gnaw at his bindings with his teeth. Even if it took all night, he would dislodge this damned gag. And then he'd get his teeth started on his wrist bindings.

The fear that had paralyzed him evaporated, replaced with a passion so that warmed him from the inside.

He might have stupidly, blindly refused to see what was right before his eyes, but he knew with a certainty he'd never known before that if he survived, he'd choose love over fear. He'd do everything in his power to win over Graysie Castellanos.

How long did he have before the rising flood swamped the delta? Four hours?

Three? Or maybe even less. He wouldn't stay sitting around waiting to find out.

It was the work of a few minutes to get rid of the gag and his free his mouth. He maneuvered his hands up to his face and tugged the cloth down. He tasted blood as he dragged it free, but the gag was soon dangling around his neck.

He gulped into the rain-spattered wind, savoring the wet drops in his mouth as he turned his face to the sky and sucked in big drafts of the salty air. In another few minutes, he'd loosened his blindfold, desperately ripping it clear with his still bound hands.

He blinked as the deluge washed his eyes clear. It felt so cleansing, to have his eyes and mouth clear, that for a moment he stood and exalted in having come so far.

Thank God they had tied his hands in

front rather than behind. But as he looked around him, the joy died in his throat. The boundaries of river and island were merging. Already he could not see where one ended, and the other began.

There was no time to lose. He sank back down and pressed his wrists against his mouth. He was desperately gnawing at the rope bonds, ignoring the stream of drool that was washed away as he chewed, when he heard a noise more terrifying than a lightning strike—the howl of coyotes, and very close by.

He reared up on his knees and shuffled forward in a praying position for a few strides before falling face first into the water pooling around him.

The last thing he needed was to be taken for some wounded prey, a sitting target for a band of hungry coyotes. He pushed himself back up to a kneeling position and, using his hands as ballast, propelled himself to his feet.

With his knees tied, his balance was precarious. At full height, he could see two coyotes, a male and female pair, in a crouching prowl, advancing up the gully, two sets of yellow eyes fixed on him.

The larger male was in the lead, with the female tucked in behind him, sable gray fur standing on an excited end. Even through the rain, he could see their teeth gleaming as they advanced on him. And they'd be the scouting party. There'd be more to follow.

He focused on the male front runner and raised his arms over his head while he gave his best bull's roar.

Face them down. Don't let them think you're easy meat.

They kept coming, undeterred.

Nathan bent down and scooped the

water up in his tied hands, sweeping it in their direction with a deep growl. "Get outta here. Get out..." His throat felt raw and bloody, but he kept on.

He sprayed the water several times to get them to back off, but with the rain pelting down around them, he wasn't having much effect. They broke into a brief run as they pointed their noses down and came in for the attack.

He jumped backwards—the only way he could move with his knees still tied—and to his amazement, the sudden movement seemed to frighten them. They halted their forward rush.

On instinct, he took a risk and jumped towards them, bobbing up and down and growling like a grizzly, deep and imperious.

Go on the offensive. Don't appear weak.

As he jumped, a branch washed along in the current bumped against his legs. Without taking his eyes off the coyotes, he swooped on it as he landed in a jump and grabbed it with both hands, brandishing it as he rose, poised to jump forward again.

There was a mountain-splitting crack of lightning overhead, and a tree trunk near the coyotes split in two in a blazing charge. The heavens had coordinated a two-pronged assault.

The coyotes turned and fled.

The energy rush he'd felt under the threat of having his throat ripped out drained away as quickly as it had come, leaving him weak and light-headed. But the suck of cold water creeping up his legs brought him back to earth with a start. The faint-hearted would not survive.

Keeping focused on escape was imperative. He redoubled his efforts to chew through the rope that bound his wrists. Luckily, he'd had the presence of mind to bunch up his fists when they'd tied him and now, when he flexed his hands, he made wiggle room.

With an increasing sense of desperation, he gnawed at the ropes, at the same time opening and closing his hands. Getting his teeth in the right position was difficult, and progress was slow. The cold water was slowly creeping up his legs.

Another bolt of lightning cracked and fizzled overhead. Some bushes off to his right flared up in a shower of sparks, the fire instantly doused by the rain. He swung his gaze back to the tree truck struck by lightning earlier and saw it was still smoldering.

Half jumping, half stumbling the short distance to the stump, he began searching desperately through the rubble for a fire brand—a branch or piece of broken-off trunk that was still burning.

Impervious to the sting of hot coals, he raked through the smoking remnants. He could taste the salt of sweat mixed with rainwater in his mouth. And then he found something he could use.

At the base of the tree, a half-burned meadow grass fish trap lay smoking. Someone had probably tied it to the tree for future use. A salmon fisherman most likely—either a Miwok local who, though much reduced in numbers, still fished the river, or a settler using a traditional trap.

Only one side of the horn-shaped trap remained, the rest was black ash, but caught deep in the curved neck end was an antler handled knife with an obsidian tip. Perhaps in his haste to get back to firm land in the storm's face, the fisherman had overlooked it.

With a triumphant howl, Nathan bent down and picked it up with both hands. He shuffled to an elevated area where he could slump down with his back against a marshy mound of rushes and draw his knees up to his chest.

He made blundering attempts at angling the knife downwards, restricted by the awkward movement of his tied hands. He cut his through trousers several times, scoring his skin as he positioned the knife to cut the leg bonds, but he kept going feverishly.

After several attempts and losing precious minutes, he got the obsidian blade braced in the right position against the rope, and within half a minute, his legs were free.

Now for his hands. He transferred the knife to his teeth and clenched so hard he thought he'd shatter them. Once he'd gripped the knife, he brought his hands up to the blade and delicately started sawing at the rope binding.

He worked patiently, attacking the rope as close as he could manage to the section he'd gnawed. It seemed like a lifetime, but finally his hands were free.

His jaw ached from the exertion. He staggered around, stamping his feet, swinging his arms like windmills to loosen his shoulders and soothe the tight cramps that gripped him.

What now? In the sheeted rain he'd lost any sense of direction. Where had they come from, and where would it be best for him to head? He wondered for a crazy minute whether the fisherman who had left the trap and knife might have a boat somewhere nearby as well.

He dismissed the idea as soon as it came to him; if he did, he'd probably use it to get away himself.

But a fisherman's presence in the vicinity showed that the edge of the river ran pretty close, though it might be hard to pick out with the general flooding.

On that hunch, Nathan began following a muddy wandering thread leading away from the burnt-out tree, winding through banks of marshy reeds and around occasional larger bushes into the gray curtain of rain.

He must keep a sharp watch on where he was going. It was still dark, and he'd lost track of time. He shivered all over, his soaked shirt and trousers drawing off his body heat as fast as he generated it. He shook his frozen fingers and swallowed down on a ravenous hunger.

If I don't find shelter and food soon, I'm going to be in a bad way, whether or not I get off this damned island.

The track, such as it was, gradually became submerged in deeper and deeper water. With a lurch of his heart, he accepted he could no longer see whether he was on a path. The water level had risen from his calves to his thighs as he walked on.

I can't keep walking. I'll end up walking into the river in a flood. Not a good idea.

As if to confirm his thoughts, he felt the tug of the current around his legs. Scanning the dimmed-out gray horizon, he thought he could make out little white caps of river water roiling in a left-to-right direction in front of him.

He was at the river's edge. A large dead pine log went floating by, ten yards from where he was standing, its skeletal branches outlined like eerie arms.

And then out of the mist he saw a vague shape. A salmon dinghy loomed up out of the haze. He could make out two men on board. One was rowing while the other stood at the bow on lookout.

He began yelling and waving and they turned his way.

*****

The next day, he could remember little of that boat ride back to the city and a dry hotel. The fishermen had been transporting an injured child struck by a tree in the storm. It was his good luck that a medical emergency had driven them to make the hazardous journey.

More than once he was convinced they were going to capsize in the fierce torrent, or rogue logs were going to hole and sink them, but the amazing skills of the boatmen had seen them through. He dragged off his wet clothes, fell into a dry bed, and slept.

Forty Nine

He was standing on a beach, desperately searching the line of breaking waves, but for what? The sun was warm on his face; melodic birdsong echoed from nearby scrub, and a reassuring smell of fresh eucalyptus wafted on a light offshore breeze. All was right with the world except... a leaden sense of doom swamped him as he scanned the breaker line repeatedly... watching... watching... but what for?

A hand gripped his shoulder. A man's hand. Broad and firm. It squeezed in a friendly fashion along the ridge of his collarbone. He jerked upright, arms rigid, his mind disoriented.

Seb's handsome, tanned face bent over him, and the hand went from his shoulder to the top of his head. He ruffled his hair with brotherly affection.

"You're usually up with the birds, brother! Don't tell me you've had a hard night?"

Nathan's mind was still racing. Where was he? What was he doing? He screwed his eyes tight shut. He was in bed in a cheap Sacramento boarding house. And after the nightmare of the day before, he was still alive. He opened his eyes again, taking in the room.

Seb hastily withdrew his hand and hesitated, rocking on the balls of his feet, before taking a slow step back.

"Sorry. Didn't mean to give you a fright. Are you okay?" His keen hazel eyes searched Nathan's face.

Nathan rubbed his eyes and neck, took a deep breath. "Yes, yes. All good."

He drew the sheet up around his armpits and swung his legs over the side of the bed. "Except for the minor matter of nearly getting wiped out yesterday, I'm fine." He hugged the sheet to his chest and scratched his eyes to wake up.

"Martens' goons just about did for me down on the river."

"What the heck? What are you talking about?"

Nathan stood and stretched, surprised to find that apart from a few bruises and scratches, he felt pretty good.

"Man, I'm glad to see you. Let me have a quick wash and get some clothes on and I'll tell you all about it over coffee. How on earth did you find me?"

*****

An hour later, they hunched over the remains of a lumberjack's breakfast, sipping their second cups of coffee. Seb's jaunty manner had leaked away, replaced by a dark detachment, as Nathan told his story.

Nathan sensed the turmoil in his brother's inner thoughts. Seb hesitated before speaking, as if weighing his words.

"I'm kicking myself. It didn't click earlier. It was staring me in the face and I didn't see it."

"Now *I* don't get it. What are you talking about?" Nathan fiddled with his cup. "*What* was staring you in the face?"

"I chased you down here because of things I've discovered in the last few days that I should have cottoned on to long before this."

Nathan frowned. "You're talking in

riddles, Seb. Cottoned on to what?"

"Cottoned on to what Vance Pedersen was telling us in that report. You recall in the last pages there were tables and diagrams with a lot of figures, but no explanation of what they all meant? We skimmed over them. The revelation of the rogue mining had us fixated."

Seb drummed tense fingers on the table edge. "The night you left I went to look in on Anna Santa Maria and the family as you'd asked, to make sure they were alright."

He paused. "They're doing pretty well, by the way. Vulcan has settled in as another member of the family. I don't think you'll be getting him back." He grinned.

"But seriously, when I told Anna that Martens had left town, it was like a dark cloud lifted. They both—her and Antonio opened up. I got the impression when Antonio saw her talking, he found the confidence to follow suit. They said they'd suspected it was Martens who'd killed their dog and killed Willie. But they were terrified he'd come back and kill them if they identified him.

"Thing was"—he leaned across the table, and lowered his voice—"I challenged Antonio to a chess game. When he brought the board out, I noticed the stitching was coming undone along the edges of the board.

"I was fiddling with it while Antonio was contemplating his next move. There was a bit of paper slipped into the space, tucked right into the base of the board." He paused and leaned back.

Nathan felt his breath suck in involuntarily. "Yes... And?"

"I'm certain it relates to that last page

in his report. It's a key to what the figures mean. I'm sure of it. But the only way we'll know is if we check with Graysie and look at the report. I presume she's got it with her?"

"What sort of key?" Nathan's mind whirled. "What have you got in mind?"

Seb paused again and took a deep breath. "Looking at it as an engineer, I'd hazard a guess it's a record of the readings from a series of well-calculated mining assays. That's about as much as I can tell without having all the paper in front of me."

Seb glanced away. His distracted air was so unlike his normally intense focus.

"That's not all, is it? There's something else."

Avoiding getting cold egg yolk stains on his sleeve, Nathan leaned over and grasped his brother's wrist. "What is it? Tell me."

Seb laughed a short, low laugh. "You don't miss much, do you, Nat? Yes, there is more." Nathan let go of his wrist as Seb grinned.

"Antonio nearly beat me at chess, I might add! But after I left them, I reflected on the entire case from when Vance died. I went back home and made a list of everything, everyone, who'd been attacked, threatened, extorted.

"The next day I started retracing all the steps. I went back up to Sixways and talked to the barman. Funny how people are a lot easier to talk to once they know Martens has left town.

"Martens and de Vile were both hanging around the Exchange visiting Madam M at the time Minette went missing. The Sixways guy told me Martens had been up there too. There were rumors circulating that Vance was onto something big. It all fit together like it hadn't before.

"I talked to John about it yesterday and he agreed I needed to get to you as soon as I could. I'm not sure we've got enough evidence to convict Martens in a court of law, but we have enough to run him out of town and make sure he never comes back."

"Then we'd better get onto it," Nathan said. "Graysie and Lisette and the girls are staying at the Orleans."

Fifty

Before Graysie decided on the best way to approach Basil Stockton, a note arrived with her breakfast tray addressed in a bold, flowing script: Private: Miss Castellanos. The tissue-thin writing paper rustled expensively between her fingers. Stockton was inviting her to attend a business meeting later that day at his Lake Diablo mountain resort.

Confidence oozed from the masculine curves of black ink. 'My man will come to your hotel and accompany you to the 10am Folsom train and then coach transfer to the lake. Please prepare for an overnight stay and bring a warm wrap. The mountains can get cool in the evenings.'

She felt a pang of uncertainty at the thought of leaving Minette behind with Lisette. But a wave of excitement engulfed her at the prospect of a breakthrough with the mine at last. Could what she'd been hoping for ever since she'd first met with Fisher nearly four months ago be about to happen? Would Mr. Stockton help her meet the critical deadline?

The Golden Queens had the night off, being Sunday, so Graysie had the perfect opportunity to talk with Stockton in a private setting.

Without bothering to taste the toast on the breakfast tray, she bounced out of bed to warn Lisette of what was afoot and started packing.

A short while later, she was on the train for Folsom.

*****

As he and Seb waited at the reception desk at the Orleans for Graysie to come downstairs, Nathan vowed he wasn't taking any more chances with their lives—his or hers. They'd had too many close shaves, and he didn't want to tempt fate any further.

"Nathan! You want to see Graysie?" Lisette bit her lower lip. "I'm sorry, but she's not here. She's away on a business trip."

"A business trip? Where?" Nathan felt rocks in his stomach.

"Somewhere in the mountains. At Mr. Stockton's resort. She didn't know exactly where. One of his men is with her."

"Stockton? How does she even know Basil Stockton?"

Seb braced his shoulders and addressed Lisette. "How long ago did she leave?"

"Three—maybe four hours ago. They went on the train this morning. Perhaps you could check with Mrs. Stockton. She's staying here too. Although she might have gone as well. I really don't know what the plans were."

Lisette frowned and shrugged. "Look, sorry, but I have to get back to the girls. That storm last night frightened Seraphine. We're having a quiet day."

She turned to go back upstairs. Nathan quickly stepped in front of her, his hand up to halt her departure.

"Lisette. Promise me you will be extra cautious until Graysie returns. Don't answer the door to strangers. Stay in the hotel. A quiet day is a good day. I don't know what's going on but I've got bad juju about it. Promise me?"

Lisette's eyes widened in surprise, but

she assented with the dip of her head. "Certainly, Mr. Russell. I'll be extra careful."

Sebastian had wasted no time in presenting his deputy credentials to the hotel desk, requesting an urgent meeting with Mrs. Stockton. Within a few minutes Alycia Stockton descended the stairs, a picture of calm elegance. Seb once again flashed his deputy badge.

"Mrs. Stockton, we're told Miss Castellanos is meeting your husband today, for some kind of business meeting?" Seb raised his eyebrows in inquiry.

"I wondered if you could tell us where that meeting is taking place? It's a matter of urgency."

Alycia Stockton frowned and shook her head. "Not to my knowledge. And I'm certain I would know of it."

Nathan stepped forward. "Nathan

Russell, Mrs. Stockton. Sir John's brother and a friend of Miss Castellanos. So, you don't believe they were meeting at your husband's resort?"

Alycia gave him a stern look. "Definitely not. My husband has business in quite the other direction today, in Placerville I believe. What makes you think otherwise?"

Seb and Nathan exchanged a charged look, and Sebastian stepped forward. "I'm afraid we believe Miss Castellanos may be in grave danger. Can you give us clear details of how to find your mountain property?

"And please—can I ask you to concern yourself with the safety of Miss Castellanos's family here in Sacramento? Have you got a man you could detail to provide extra security in the meantime?"

"Certainly." Alycia's strong and

resolute voice cut through. She gave them a curt nod. "If Graysie's in danger, I won't hold you up any longer. But please," she paused and her expression softened. "Please. Bring her back safely." Amen to that, Nathan thought.

As Nathan dodged around Orleans guests, heading for the street, he shot an arrow of prayer heavenwards. Please God, don't let her die. He thought he heard a distant rumble of thunder in answer, but he couldn't be sure.

*****

The man who came to meet her had a ruddy complexion and rough hands. Surprising, she thought, for someone who presumably worked as a businessman's factotum, but he'd said little and she'd been happy to be left with her thoughts. They departed the rail depot, at the corner of K Street and

Levee, and trundled along the eastern bank of the Sacramento River to R Street.

The heavy deluge of the night before had left flooding on all the lower-lying areas, and river channels that were usually separate now merged into one far-reaching inland sea.Luckily for Graysie and her traveling companion, with train tracks high on an embankment above the water, the steam engine's progress was unhindered. The skies were still cloudy, but the rain had stopped.

Soon they were turning eastward away from the water, and an hour and a half later, after crossing an oak-studded plain dotted with prosperous farm houses, fat cattle, and rain-drenched orchards heavy with fruit, they pulled into Folsom, for the transfer to the mountain stage coach.

The coach threaded its way across a river on a long suspension bridge. The countryside changed from gently rolling foothills to steeper slopes covered in blue oaks and then, higher up, scrubby, thorny chaparral bushes.

As they neared their destination, she became increasingly nervous about her first meeting with her newfound uncle. She hoped Alycia had filled him in on Eustace's revelations or she'd look a bit of a fool. She tapped a nervous rhythm under the seat—heel and toe, heel and toe—as the stage labored up the steep hill to the hotel.

The Lake Diablo Resort stood on a flattened promontory reaching out from a prominent ridge, offering panoramic views. The purple line of the southern Sierras stretched in one direction, the watery expanse from last night's flooding like an internal silver sea in another.

The hotel perched on the lake shore, set amongst the glossy dark canopies of blue oaks and the russet and gray foliage of the rugged mountain grasses.

Artful plantings of wild lilac complemented craggy natural boulders positioned to set off the resort's stone-fronted arcade. As they pulled up outside, the man accompanying her seemed oddly diffident in his manner. He stammered slightly as he took her bag and ushered her into the hotel foyer.

"T-t-t-take a seat. Him will be along shortly."

What an odd thing to say.

Graysie rubbed her hands down the sides of her skirts to get rid of a clammy dampness that hadn't been there a few minutes ago. Why was she getting the jitters? Was something wrong? And where was Basil Stockton?

Her hand bumped against the Derringer muff pistol she'd tucked away in her side skirt pocket, and relief rushed through her. Thank goodness she'd remembered to bring it. Years in the West had taught her the need for a gun might be rare, but sometimes a lady had best arm herself.

She'd been sitting quietly for several minutes when the servant returned.

"Um, miss." The mousy assistant was back. "Mr. Stockton is delayed. He's arranged for you to meet him up at the Summer House. The coach is waiting to take you there now. I'm sure he will have arranged for you to have your lunch there."

Things were getting stranger by the minute.

Graysie searched the hotel lobby.

There was no one there she could call on for help. Her throat choked with alarm. "The Summer House? What is that exactly?"

"It's Mr Stockton's private retreat. He frequently entertains there."

As he spoke, the man took up her overnight bag and moved towards the courtyard, where a gray mare hitched to a mountain buggy stood waiting.

She'd paused uncertainly in front of the small enclosed vehicle, wondering what to do next, when she heard a familiar sneering voice behind her.

"Well, well, if it isn't the beautiful Miss Castellanos. Fancy meeting you here."

Graysie swung around to face Willoughby Martens, who was standing leering at her. In front of Martens stood a chalk-faced Hector de Vile, Martens' gun pressed into the back of his neck.

She gagged, unable to believe her eyes. "What? What's going on?" The sound was strangled, and she was gasping for breath.

Martens laughed. His eyes sparked arousal in his flushed red face. She gazed wildly around her, heart leaping with a mad hope that someone near might help, but the courtyard was empty.

Stockton's man—or the one she'd thought to be Stockton's man—sat with his back to them in the buggy driver's seat, ignoring the unfolding events.

"Mr. de Vile… Why are you here?"

"He's playing some idiotic game he'll live to regret." Hector de Vile's nostrils flared and his lips tightened into a thin, hard line. He twisted his head to look behind him, but Graysie could see he was careful not to move too suddenly.

"Tell me that thing's not loaded, you fool." He spat on the ground.

"Playing? I'm well past playing, Mister de Vile." Martens heavily emphasized the honorific. "Yes, I'm weary of being pushed around, treated like dirt. I turned myself inside out for you, and then I discover you're planning to do the dirty on me."

He waved de Vile towards the carriage with the hand holding the gun. "And to answer your question, yes, it's loaded. And now we'll all go for a ride—and this time I'm the one in charge."

Graysie watched in stunned silence as de Vile held up his hand in a gesture of submission. "Martens, don't be stupid. I don't know what you're talking about, but I'm sure we can come to an understanding..."

"No more understandings, de Vile,"

said Martens. "I've done your bidding for long enough. I got rid of the Aussie for you, but that was a personal pleasure." He curled his lip. "And don't go imagining Basil Stockton will be along to rescue you. He has no idea you're here."

He waved the gun toward the open carriage door, this time including Graysie in the sweep of his arm. "Hurry up and get in, both of you." He jerked his head towards the vehicle. "I'm planning to take what's mine, and you are going to help me do it."

He lurched at Graysie with a menacing leer. "Get in the carriage, woman. You, me and the man, we're taking a ride. How many of us return depends on how nicely you cooperate."

Fifty One

Graysie sat opposite Martens and de Vile, their knees bumping in the cramped space, and knew she was staring death in the face. But that wasn't what consumed her.

Martens killed Nathan.

It buzzed there, like a poisonous wasp, silencing every other thought. He'd dripped with contempt as he'd said it.

"I got rid of the Aussie for you, but that was a personal pleasure."

A numbness started in her toes and crept up her body. She no longer registered the comforting weight of the Derringer. She'd no opportunity to use it—yet. Martens had his gun pressed hard against de Vile's side, directly at his heart, and any sharp movement might set it off.

She should think ahead and prepare herself to jump Martens when the opportunity came. She willed herself to stay on high alert and shook her head to dislodge the incessant buzz: Nathan's dead.

No matter how many times her brain insisted, her heart refused to accept it. He couldn't be dead! A world without Nathan was as unthinkable as one in which the sun wouldn't rise tomorrow. She clutched her hand to her mouth as she tried to suppress a sudden queasiness.

She'd never see Nathan again. She'd probably never see Minette again.

She'd made no will. She wasn't expecting to die. How stupid could she be? And would that mean if she died, Minette was left destitute?

Her stomach churned, and she was about to beg Martens to stop the coach when she heard the horse's hooves slowing and they came to a halt.

Martens pulled open the door and turned back to face them, his gun aimed directly at de Vile. One false move and he'd shoot, Graysie knew. He eyed them like he'd enjoy destroying both of them.

"Congratulations, both of you. You can leave here alive if you play your cards right. Play them wrong…" He raised a sarcastic eyebrow. "Play them wrong and the outcome won't be so happy."

"Cut the crap." De Vile's face twisted in an ugly grimace. "You're already on notice of at least three counts of criminal behavior. This is utter foolishness."

Martens chuckled. "Only three? You

had no objections when I took part in criminal behavior at your behest." He spread his arms wide in a gesture of mock surprise, the gun waving wildly as he did.

"But I s'pose that's life. However, that brings me to agenda item number one of this unconventional business meeting—Hector de Vile's invoice and confession."

Martens swung the gun back onto them, his eyes glittering and fixed. He reached down with his free hand to a satchel on the seat beside him and drew out a fistful of documents he thrust at de Vile.

"You'll find these contain an invoice for the payment of a quarter of a million in gold to me for services rendered. Specified services, if you care to check, though you might prefer they weren't so clearly enumerated. You don't need to worry about delivery—I've already taken receipt of payment."

Shock replaced De Vile's earlier impatient disdain. His mouth dropped open, exposing his perfect white teeth. "You what?" His eyes bulged in disbelief.

"I helped myself, from a ready source known to us both. And seeing as how you're stealing from the same source, you can't object, surely? But just in case..." He waved the gun airily in a circle, gesturing to the papers in de Vile's hand.

"Apart from the invoice, there's your confession. It details the commissions I carried out at your request. It makes clear I did all work under your orders, as part of your accepted business strategy: extortion, threats, violence, blackmail, fraudulent boosting of mining shares... The late unlamented Madam Moustache even makes an appearance. That's my passport to freedom, signed by the about-to be-inducted senator for California."

Martens thrust out his chest and sneered. "Yes. A neat quarter of a million plus a confession and we can call it quits, Senator de Vile."

De Vile had gone very white. His Adam's apple bobbed feverishly. Graysie watched as he raked his pocket for a handkerchief and then mopped his sweaty cheeks.

Martens regarded Graysie over the gun barrel. "And I have a special destiny planned for you. I figure one Aussie bloke is as good as another." He paused. Tilted his head.

"But of course, you may not agree. Seeing as she's missed out on Nathan Russell, I thought to myself, she can marry me instead. We'll tie the knot today.

"Your wedding present to me will be the Ophir mine and the Vance Pedersen report." He drew his mouth into a frozen, fake smile, and his eyes were gimlet hard.

"I don't like to be beaten by a woman. And as my good little wifey, I'm sure you will be more than delighted to turn those over to me, your adoring husband."

A malevolent glitter did not hide his serious intent. Her stomach roiled.

Martens stepped off the carriage onto the rocky ground and gestured for them to follow. Her knee gave way as her foot hit the ground, but she grasped the doorjamb and righted herself before she crumpled in the dirt.

The road ended here, in front of an arresting rock formation, a spacious cavern like a natural cathedral, with striated pink ripples in the stone rising to a domed rock ceiling.

As her eyes adjusted to the bright glare, she saw half a dozen heavily armed men loitering in the shade. They completely outnumbered her. Pulling a gun on Martens would be equivalent to committing suicide.

Martens pointed to the path that led to an opening in a rock face and waved her ahead of him. "Now come and meet Billy, our marriage officiant. We've got a lot to accomplish before sundown."

Graysie gazed around her. They were standing under the outer edge of an expansive rock cupola that stretched up to a pink- and gray-streaked stone canopy high overhead. It was an extraordinary geological formation, a natural dome with wide open sides.

There was something timeless about it, and in different circumstances, her surroundings would have entranced her. Today, the scale of it overwhelmed her.

She stumbled along in front of Martens, dazed and unseeing, like a sleepwalker in a bizarre nightmare, fighting to convince herself this was all really happening.

They'd separated De Vile from her and immediately taken him away once they'd left the buggy. She'd no idea where he was, or what his fate they had planned for him.

As for Martens, he was all blustering confidence. But she didn't think he was bluffing when he boasted his men would kill de Vile if anything happened to him, Martens, so she complied with his demands like a mechanical doll.

She signed the fake share documents ceding him ownership of the Ophir. She denied flat-out that she held onto the Pedersen report, but she was under no illusion that if she survived, Martens would seize it.

She agreed to the wedding arrangements, nodding wordlessly at Martens' instructions. But when it came to getting dressed in the gown he produced, she risked fighting back, insisting she needed somewhere private to change.

Even in her bewilderment, a deep survival instinct drove her, and some part of her continuously scanned her surroundings, watching for a chance to escape.

She donned the wedding dress, a full skirted white chiffon creation, in a small cave to one side of the main cavern, pulling it on over top of the beige riding skirt she'd worn as suitable for a mountain outing.

Martens wouldn't notice the extra volume, she was certain, and she'd go to the altar with a pearl-handled pistol bumping in the pocket on her thigh.

A fierce certainty burned in her gut; she would unload her pistol into her prospective husband's chest without flinching if she could do it without endangering anyone else.

They stood facing Billy in front of the small table set up like an altar with a candle burning on it. Martens was creepily suave in a quarter-length black evening coat and starchy white shirt, the hip-bulge of his gun belt under his jacket strangely at odds with the elegant attire.

Sour-smelling Billy B wore a bizarre brocade cape which he might have imagined made him look like a bishop, Graysie thought. The cheap mockery was like a knife in her ribs. The difficulty he was having reading the order of service led her to suspect he was barely literate.

Whenever an image of Minette or Nathan came to mind, she tamped down the bubbles of hysteria that rose from deep within her. Each time, she deflected her attention by searching out tiny details to avoid pitching into desperation.

The striated colors of the rock walls, the twittering swallows that darted and swooped from nests on high up ledges, the light clink of the tiny shells fastened at the neck and wrists of her 'wedding' dress as she moved, the fly that buzzed around Billy B's noxious smelling hair. She watched anything to hold off her total collapse. Most critical of all, she shut her mind to what would follow the 'wedding'.

She'd been adrift, barely aware of

Billy's mumblings, when she realized she couldn't hear what he was saying. His words were being drowned out by the drumming of noise.

From a barely audible distant tapping, it grew to a thundering tattoo of horses' hooves that demanded attention. She glanced at Martens. He was slack-jawed, staring behind her with bug-eyed incredulity.

She wheeled around riveted, as the posse—she saw at once, that's what it was—rode up, headed by a familiar tall, lean figure wearing a deputy's badge who dismounted in one swooping stride.

Sebastian! Sebastian was here. And at his shoulder, grim-faced and galvanized for action, rode Nathan. Nathan, who slipped from his mount and, in half a dozen strides, was standing before her.

Nathan is here. Nathan is alive?

She'd found it impossible to accept he was dead. Now she could hardly comprehend that he was standing in front of her. Her tongue filled her mouth, leaving no room for air. She choked to speak, but no words would come.

She gazed at his tousled head, swallowing hard to free her vocal chords.

"I…" she croaked. "I thought you were dead."

He took her face in his hands gently and it surprised her to see his fingers were immediately shiny and wet from the tears that streamed down her face. "I nearly was. I kept going for you."

He leaned forward and kissed her gently on the forehead. "Thank God you're alive. Now don't move. Stay here while we finish this."

She turned back towards the cave and saw that Martens and his noxious offsider had vanished. Pages of the marriage order of service fluttered on the ground, and the sacrament table lay overturned. A smoky wisp rose from the snuffed-out candle that lay at her feet.

Sebastian came up alongside her. "What's going on here?" He cocked his head to one side. "It's all too blasted weird."

"They've got de Vile." Graysie gasped out the words in a rush. "Hidden out back somewhere. You've got to stop them." Nathan was watching her intensely.

"Where? Where do they have him?" he rasped.

"I don't know. Somewhere out there." She waved wildly to the back of the cavern. "They held him at gunpoint too. They separated us when we got here."

Sebastian turned urgently to the men

who backed him. "Jeb, Sam, spread to the right, take any right pathways into the underground system. Russ and Lightning, take the left. Nathan and I will take the center."

As one, the brothers set off at a run. Their companions fanned out on either side of them. Graysie stood for a moment, unsure of what to do next. She couldn't do nothing. The shells on her filmy white wedding gown tinkled as she hoisted up her hem and ran, following Nathan into the center path.

Fifty Two

The tunnel leading out of the back of the dome was sandy floored, wide and level. Graysie could see well enough in the dim daylight to half run, half walk, the Russell men's backs sometimes bobbing into view, at others disappearing out of sight.

Shards of daylight slanted through narrow ground-level fissures high above. The air tasted fresh on her tongue. They were in a twilight zone, moving into deeper shadow as they ventured on.

She loped on for fifteen or twenty minutes. Then her soft leather ankle boot struck something hard, and she crashed forward onto her hands and knees, unprotected skin on rock. Her grazed palms stung, moist with bloody abrasions. She limped a few steps, trying to ignore her bruised, cut knees, and knew she must slow down.

The twilight dimness was slipping into darkness, and it was a lot harder to see. Something light and hairy landed on her shoulder. She forgot her burning knees, slapping her bleeding hands up and down the white chiffon to stamp out whatever had landed on her.

She was panting. Spider, cockroach. She knew not what; it had to go. Her nostrils caught the stale mustiness of bat dung. She'd lost sight of the men, the darkness forcing her to move more cautiously. As she rounded a corner, she heard the sibilant hiss of a waterfall.

Another spacious cavern opened before her, the water falling from a high overhead cliff face to form a sluggish, dark lake at the bottom. Spray filled the air with a damp mist, and as she peered through it, her heart caught.

One of Martens' men stood at the lakeside, his rifle trained in the darkness, straining to hear any sign of human intrusion. She slowly sank to the ground and froze until she saw he was slowly rotating, his back now facing her.

She shrank onto her belly and wormed her way over to the cover of a rocky outcrop on her left. The hated wedding dress snagged and ripped as she slithered over the rough ground. As soon as a rock pillar concealed her, she rose and shredded the skirt, smiling to herself as the water's roar masked the rasp of tearing fabric.

She was left standing in her durable riding skirt and the fraying wedding dress bodice. Dirty and bedraggled, she undeniably was, but she felt like a butterfly freed from its chrysalis. Her be Martens' wife? She'd rather die. She felt in her pocket and pulled out the Derringer.

Pebbles rattled behind her and she went on high alert, cringing into the darkest crevice of her monolith, hardly daring to breathe as she waited for the source of the noise to show.

She didn't have long to wait. Coming down the trail were four heavily armed men, rifles held at the ready in front of them. From their Mexican garb, she could tell immediately they were not from Sebastian's party, regrouping from one of the other arms in the cave network. That meant they must be in Martens' pay. She shivered and froze in her hiding place.

They passed so close that the foul-smelling bear fat men smeared themselves with for keeping lice and fleas at bay snatched at her throat. Her chest heaved as she fought to keep silent.

They'd barely gone past before their guns boomed in a kettle drum volley on her near right. Her knees sagged. The calamitous barrage told her they'd armed themselves with the latest weaponry, the sixteen shooter repeating rifle used by Civil War raiding parties that was rapidly gaining popularity in the West.

Against them, her Derringer and the revolvers Nathan and Seb carried would be powerless.

Her stomach rolled in nauseous turmoil as she waited, collapsed in a heap at the base of the rock pile, for what would happen next? After half a minute, a second series of shots shattered the background noise of falling water.

They sounded like they had come from revolvers—probably the Russell men returning fire. Against the rifle noise they sounded puny, like a Fourth of July firecracker. She hugged her ribcage in icy terror and prayed as earnestly as she ever had in her life.

Dear God, please get us all out of here alive!

*****

Nathan stood with his back pressed hard against a cleft in the cave wall. The noise of tramping feet had alerted him and Sebastian to someone coming and they'd had time to get under cover before the intruders arrived.

They'd barely got in position before the guns opened fire uncomfortably close to them, but they weren't the target.

As he'd had made his way underground in Seb's dauntless, steady wake, Nathan was awestruck at the evidence human occupation in the network of grottoes, caverns, and tunnels they were passing through, going back no doubt to ancient hunters.

The charcoal remains of long extinguished fires, scattered animal bones from past meals, discarded leather boots and rotting fabric, mankind left the detritus of human occupation scattered all around them as they walked on in silence.

But the past was never more strikingly brought home than in the grotto they'd entered minutes before the shooters turned up. They'd paused as their eyes adjusted to the cavernous space, with water cascading from overhead, an errant shaft of daylight from a ground level crevice highlighting white foam edges as it fell.

A wide shallow pool had formed at the base, the light reflecting off gentle ripples rolling onto a dark sandy shore. The remnants of a blackened fire circle provided evidence of the men - and possibly women - who'd once gathered here to rest.

One of them remained. As Nathan took in the scene, he saw a man sitting, his back propped up against a loaded canvas pack, feet turned towards the ash circle, frozen in time. The ambient light from above caught the sepulchral slash of white cheekbone, his face partly obscured by a broad-brimmed hat.

A steel cooking pot lay on the sand beside him, any meal he may have thought to prepare superfluous now.

Nathan did not need to step any closer to satisfy himself that this fellow had been at his ease in this grotto for a long time.

He was reaching out to catch Seb's arm to draw his attention to the tableau when the thumping of heavy feet warned them they were not alone.

They couldn't see the men who had barged in on them, but their skittish reaction to the campfire scene told them they shot first and asked questions later. They peppered the cadaver with long, raking bursts of gunfire before realizing their mistake and breaking into hysterical laughter.

"It can't be bad luck if he's already dead!" hooted one. The light from the lamp they carried swung in wild, jittery arcs.

Sebastian leaned into Nathan's ear and hissed, "Give me time to circle behind them and then create a diversion." He gestured down the trail with his revolver. "I'll immobilize as many of them as I can, and we'll scare the rest off."

Seb vanished into the darkness. Nathan concentrated on listening hard to interpret what the intruders were doing while they still clustered at the campsite.

The clang of iron on rock gave him a clue they might be taking a drink from the fresh waterfall, catching the flow in the pot he'd seen lying on the sand. He caught snatches of conversation, enough to confirm they were expecting to join Martens farther up this trail.

From the high-pitched giggles of the two men, he wondered if water was all they were drinking. A man the others referred to as Bruno seemed to be the leader, and after more drinking and chatter he guessed it was Bruno who spoke: "We'd better get moving or he'll slat our brains out. We can get drunk when the biz is done."

More nervous laughter, followed by concurring mutters. "The sooner we get out of this hellhole, the better."

Nathan edged furtively out of his hiding place.

It must be about time for Sebastian to make his appearance.

Hugging the dark side of the rock, he worked his way into a position where he could see the men. They were standing in a group around the cold fire pit. The tip of a cigarette glowed in the dark, filling the air with an exotic spicy smoke that hinted at cinnamon and pepper.

The lantern was sitting on top of the dead man's pack, spreading a circle of light at thigh level. The miner was no longer propped up and, in the dark,

Nathan could only guess he lay sprawled somewhere outside the circle of light.

Then an uncanny keening shriek, like an angry owl contesting for territory, pierced the cavern. Its source appeared to be from the far side from where the men were standing, between the fire circle and the trail leading farther in, and the group swung to face it.

The hairs on the back of Nathan's neck stood on end even as he congratulated his brother silently at the scouting skills he'd gained, tutored by the war. Then, with a deep breath, he prepared to play his part.

He braced himself against the rocks at his back and, in one long infinitesimally fluid movement, he aimed his revolver at the lamp. With a marksman's direct hit, he shattered the lantern glass and snuffed out the light.

As the bullet struck, the men screamed in terror, and Nathan fell belly-down on the cavern floor. A wild volley of retaliatory fire zipped harmlessly over his head.

The frightened mutterings died. He could hear the men's feet crunching on the shore debris, sticks cracking underfoot, and then more wild chattering broke out. "What the devil... Bruno. Where's Bruno?"

Nathan could hear them stumbling around in the dark, falling over one another, calling for their leader by name. Silence answered. They paused as a group, and then a wail rose from one of them, and the others joined in. "Aiee.... The black witch... Lechuza. Lechuza, the black witch, is here."

Strike three. Nathan felt warmed by a sense of jubilation. Lechuza was the malevolent being of Mexican belief who whistles to men in the night to tempt them into disaster.

The curse of the owl had found its mark, and Bruno was gone, spirited away. It had been Sebastian's specialty in the war that ended three years ago, this secret, subtle extraction of men and information, leaving no trace that he'd ever been there.

The men left behind wasted no time in beating their retreat down the dark trail, farther underground, to their rendezvous with Martens. He and Sebastian would have to follow.

Sebastian emerged from the shadows as their adversaries disappeared, dragging a big man who was knocked out cold and securely trussed, while his other hand clutched his rifle.

"We'll leave him here for later,"

Sebastian said, as if that explained everything.

Nathan nodded. "Well played!"

Sebastian shrugged. "Surprising what you can achieve with a rifle butt if you get the jump. Your diversion was all it took." He glanced around him. "He'll be okay here for a couple of hours. Let's keep moving. The sooner we get this thing sorted, the better."

"No argument there," Nathan said and fell in behind as Sebastian moved ahead, his long limbs relaxed and fluid, a stealthy cat out on territorial patrol. A shaft of overhead light caught a momentary flash of his red-gold hair and then he seemed to fade back into his dim surroundings.

They moved on in silent single file, cautiously double-checking new terrain to avoid ambush at every divergence, so progress was slow. Once or twice Nathan thought he heard men's voices echoing off distant walls, but then wondered almost instantly whether he'd imagined the sound.

The further in they went, the more difficult the path was to see, and the colder and damper the air became. He was breathing in a stale, swampy aroma that he could taste in his mouth, and he rolled his tongue around his teeth to clear it.

Sebastian suddenly slowed to a halt and put his hand up behind him in warning. Nathan thought his hearing was pretty keen, but his brother had picked up something he'd missed. Seb leaned down and spoke right into his ear, "Action ahead. Wait here while I look."

Before Nathan had time to respond, Sebastian melted into the blackness.

Nathan took cover off the path. Who knew when one of Martens' free-wheeling henchmen might show up, he thought irritably.

Sebastian was back within minutes. "Bad news up ahead, bro. They're expecting us and they've got the reception ready."

Nathan stared, searching out his eyes in the dark. "Yeah? What kind of reception?"

"One we can't avoid. They've got de Vile trussed up like bait. You can bet they've got him wired and fit to explode like a Roman candle, but we can't ignore him. We'll have to go in."

They squatted on the ground and examined their options in hushed voices. Regroup with the men they'd brought and come back? "Too much of a risk they'll kill him in the meantime and then simply disappear," said Seb.

Hide in the darkness and pick them off one by one like a sniper? "They're in there for sure, but it's impossible to see anyone in this light. Not sure that's workable as a full strategy. I mean, how long can we wait them out? But it might be useful as one tactic in a bigger scenario," Seb responded.

After a while longer spent talking and drawing maps on the sandy cave floor with a stick, they'd decided on their strategy, a variation on what had worked last time.

They planned another surprise diversion, more help from the black witch and her blood-freezing whistle, and they'd have to find a way to call Martens out and put him in such a lather of dread he'd be willing to trade his own skin for de Vile's.

"Is that all?" Nathan said. "We'll be out of here and back at the resort in time for lunch. No problem."

"You reckon?" said Seb with a sickly grin. "I hope you're right."

Fifty Three

De Vile lay slumped like a sack of flour against a rock in the middle of a stone circle that might have once had some ancient religious purpose, but there was nothing supernatural about the detonator-loaded bandolier wrapped across his chest in diagonal stripes from his shoulders to his hips.

The twine fuse from the monstrosity trailed between his legs and disappeared into the darkness. Sebastian hadn't exaggerated when he'd surmised they'd trussed him up like a Fourth of July firecracker waiting to be torched.

Nathan didn't want to consider the destruction he'd set off if their wildly conceived plan went awry and he accidentally lit that fuse.

Sebastian had done his usual trick of melting into the black velvet of the cave. How a big man could insinuate himself into such complete invisibility was beyond Nathan's understanding, but he'd never felt more grateful for a dark art.

While Sebastian reconnoitered the space and determined where Martens was to be found, he loitered behind, slipping in minute, barely discernible movements into the chamber, growing ever closer to his target, the ten-foot circle in which de Vile sat.

Stuffed under Nathan's armpits were the wads of balled up rags soaked in saltpetre they'd cobbled together from the dead miner's discarded kit. Clothes that had gone mildewy beside their entombed owner might finally serve life.

As Nathan inched forward, he hugged the rags close, savoring the dampness against his skin because of what it promised to provide—one helluva of a smokescreen to obscure their movements.

The space he was working his way into was much smaller than the earlier cavern, hemmed in by smooth walls rising perpendicular to the circular floor. There was no obvious escape route out. As far as he could tell, the chamber finished in a dead end, and they'd need to all come out the same way they had come in.

He listened for any unusual sounds, but heard nothing. No sign of where Martens and his men were hiding. They'd either found a cleft in the walls that was veiled in the low light, or crouched concealed by the piles of stone rubble that backed onto the walls in several places. If they were smart, they'd be in several places, so they could jump them from several directions at once.

He was edging into the zone he and Sebastian had discussed—the ten-foot circumference of the prisoner—when he sensed de Vile was alert and vigilant. He caught the softest whisper. "Confound those who would destroy me… Drive back those who wish me evil…"

De Vile's rasp fell silent for several seconds, and then Nathan heard him draw a long, ragged breath and begin again, "Confound those who would destroy me…" De Vile was appealing to a higher authority, in words very similar to those King David had used in the Psalms.

Nathan paused in the murk, his armpits freezing from their wet cargo, his abdomen stinging from grazing from the rocks he'd slithered over, but he could shake those things off.

At least de Vile is conscious and capable of moving.

De Vile's voice suddenly rang out again. "Martens! Willoughby Martens! Get me out of here! Get me out of here now!" It wasn't a plea, but a command, one that was compelling and not to be denied. "Get me out of here now!"

Nathan thought he heard a rattle of rock against rock, of a man stumbling in the darkness over to his right, but there was no other response. And then Sebastian gave his pre-arranged signal, the eerie owl whistle which had jinxed Martens' men earlier.

They'd agreed Nathan was to count as soon as the whistle began and launch his offensive after waiting for exactly the same time as the whistle had taken.

That way, Sebastian could set the timetable for his own offensive. Five, seven, nine, eleven, fifteen seconds. Nathan focused all his attention on the spine-tingling call. Then Sebastian fell silent.

De Vile began again, chanting as if he was a monk at evensong. "Confound those who would destroy me... Drive back those who wish me evil." Pause. "Confound..."

In the dark, a man screamed. "Shut him up! He's bad luck. Mala suerte! Mala suerte!"

A shot rang out simultaneously with another scream.

Twelve, thirteen, fourteen, fifteen. Nathan had huddled against a small rock mound to obscure his moments as he covertly settled into a sitting position while he'd been counting. He'd lined his rag ball wads up along his thighs. He drew out the Lucifers he kept in his watertight tinder box on his belt and lit each wad in turn.

He waited with his heart in his mouth for the saltpetre to catch in the wadding and then he lobbed them, one after another, encircling Hector de Vile's position a few feet clear of him.

When the last one was airborne, he dropped to the cavern floor on his belly again, narrowly missing being hit by another volley of shots.

He counted to ten and raised his head to survey his handiwork. Out of the five smoke bombs he'd created, three appeared to have taken full ignition and were burning strongly, filling the cavern with a blinding gray vapor which reduced visibility to a few inches.

His eyes were already stinging at the

acrid burnt-charcoal fumes. When they hit the back of his throat, he tasted metal. No time to waste. With a knife thrust through his belt and revolver in hand, he sprinted fast and low towards de Vile.

As Nathan reached the man's sprawled form, he heard an eruption of gunfire ahead of him, behind the smoke curtain. Sebastian would get to work, he knew, and Nathan silently prayed he wasn't on the receiving end of that last shot.

He came up fast and close on de Vile's shoulder. The businessman raised a hand to rub his eyes and Nathan saw his grazed and bleeding hands; his nails were broken and dirt encrusted. His eyes had the ferocious red-eyed glare of a man bent on revenge.

Nathan lent down to speak. "We're doing this as quietly as possible. Keep still. I'm cutting this explosive vest off and then we're out of here."

He felt for the fuse that ran into the darkness. Almost simultaneously, with the sharp thrust that severed the fiber, he saw a small fountain of sparks erupt over in the corner.

Someone had tried to light the fuse, but they were too late. He slashed the vest free and brought an arm around de Vile's shoulder and under his armpit. "Can you stand? Walk? Run? The faster we're out of here, the better."

The magnate momentarily crumpled as he rose to support his own weight, but he was vigorous and determined. He scuttled crabwise, keeping low but moving fast, ushered from behind by Nathan.

After what seemed an eternity, they were clear of the worst of the smoke and were back at the waterfall beach where they'd left the earlier captive.

"Here, take this." Nathan thrust a revolver into de Vile's hand. "Keep watch on him. Anyone unfriendly, don't hesitate. Shoot. I've got to help Sebastian."

*****

An hour later, Sebastian and Nathan were back with de Vile, three of Martens' men disarmed and in handcuffs on the ground before them. The Sydney Duck, Rotten Teeth, and a third sinewy Mexican Nathan had never seen before who appeared to speak no English were in custody. But Willoughby Martens was still at large, nowhere to be found.

Sebastian shook his sooty, sweat-streaked face. "Where in the heck did he go?" He grimaced as he observed the motley crew in front of them. "Let's face it. These guys will go down on a count or two, but we're here to get Martens."

By the time Nathan had returned to the smoky chamber, Sebastian had located the hoodlums from their convulsive coughs. With their mouths and noses protected by their heavy cotton jackets, the brothers had little trouble in rounding the bandits up.

Nathan suspected that once they understood no one was going to be shoot them, they were happy to surrender and escape the suffocating cloud. But when questioned about Martens' whereabouts, they shook their heads. The big man, it appeared, had deserted them.

Nathan turned his back on their prisoners and regarded Sebastian. "Now what?" he asked in a low voice.

Seb shrugged. "Get these guys out of here, then meet up with the rest of our fellows and regroup. About all we can do."

They were fifteen minutes into the single file trek to the surface, the Sydney Duck in front, then Nathan with Rotten Teeth between him and de Vile, the Mexican and Seb coming up in the rear, when they a piercing cry brought them to an abrupt halt.

"Nooooo... Run, Nathan... Run..." A woman's voice. High-pitched and anguished. Graysie's voice. Nathan stopped so instantly the man behind him pushed into his back.

Everything was happening in slow motion. His heart felt as if it had stopped beating altogether, and then it started up again at a frenetic double-speed hammering.

He gazed wildly around. The closer they got to the surface, the more the dark eased to a twilight zone where blurry shapes loomed out of the dim dusk.

They were entering a narrow gravelly path rising uphill to mountains of rocky rubble on either side. Near the top, the rubble came down to within touching distance of the path. Where they stood now offered a perfect line of sight from the crest. A perfect ambush site.

He caught a flash of white to his left, a good twenty feet above where they stood.

"Down!" Nathan screamed. "Down now!" He pushed the Sydney Duck forward as gunfire erupted. The man collapsed like a bag of flour, blood spraying across Nathan's arm and face as he fell.

Every man for himself, they hit the ground and scrambled for the paltry cover available—low shelves of gravel banks left by underground flooding in previous aeons.

Nathan was gasping for breath, his sides heaving in and out as he struggled to grasp their situation. Alongside him, the stamina de Vile had showed looked dangerously close to finally running out.

His face was white and shining with sweat even though the cave temperature was still close to freezing. His body was shaking. Nathan squeezed his shoulder. "Don't faint on us now."

De Vile hesitated. "Bastard killed one of his own men," he said. His dazed eyes and his tentative voice showed he couldn't believe what he'd seen.

"That he did. And if Graysie hadn't warned us, it would likely have been you and me."

Fifty Four

His arm across her voice box like an iron bar, Martens held Graysie in a stranglehold that left her hovering on the edge of consciousness. Brilliant little white dots flashed in front of her eyes, and a wave of dizziness almost swamped her. The skin on her throat burned, but her hands and feet were icy cold.

"Bitch!" he hissed in her ear. "You'll regret you did that."

He increased the pressure on her throat and she felt herself sagging, sinking into oblivion. A last consoling thought came to her. At least she'd warned Nathan. Then, when she was sure she could hold on no longer,

Martens abruptly released his hold. She felt the barrel of a gun pressed hard against her spine instead.

"You're not dying on me. Not yet, anyway." He snickered as if his jest was irresistible. "I need you as a lure for a while longer."

She searched down the slope and could make out the body of the man who had been in front, lying face down in the dirt, a dark stain seeping out from under his prone form. She didn't recognize him, guessed he must be one of Martens' men, and she cursed herself again for getting herself into this situation.

They'd freed her once from Martens' vainglorious fantasy, his Willoughby rules the world delusion. How could she have been so stupid as to fall into his clutches a second time?

She deserved everything she got this

time. Regardless of her dire situation, a giddy, exultant tide flooded through her. At least she's used her one last chance to alert Nathan. She went over it all again in her mind.

She'd waited in hiding for what seemed like an eternity after the first burst of gunfire, hoping to see Nathan and Sebastian return safely up the track they had disappeared down, but no one came.

When she heard more gunfire much farther away, she resolved to steal out of her hiding place and get closer to see what was happening. And it was there, exposed on the track with nowhere to escape, that Martens had found her.

She'd no idea why he'd become separated from his men, and why he was so far away from the major action, but it took him only a couple of seconds to jump her and overpower her. He'd then half-walked, half-dragged her to the position above the exit track where they'd sat and waited for the Russell men to return.

She shivered in the dark. She'd warmed up being frogmarched here, but now she felt cold again. The wedding dress bodice chafed under her arms. She stood as rigidly still as she could, fearful she might inadvertently prompt Martens to fire if she moved unexpectedly.

She rubbed her hands down the outside of her legs to get warm and felt the bump of the Derringer against her thigh. The pistol! She'd thrust it back into her pocket before Martens grabbed her and he'd overlooked searching her. She still had a chance, she promised herself, but she must time her moment perfectly or it would surely end in disaster.

She squeezed her eyes tightly to clear her head and when she opened them again, the blinding white needle points danced in front of them again. She scrabbled with her hands in front of her like a blind woman.

"Can't see," she rasped.

Martens slightly loosened the lock on her throat with one arm while thrusting the gun against her temple with the other. He thrust his pelvis against her back and leaned his mouth to her ear, intimately close.

"You're mine," he whispered. Her body shuddered in reply. Then he abruptly changed his demeanor.

"Russell, you listen up," he yelled into the dimness. "The lady is my free ticket out of here. I'm walking, and she goes with me. Anyone tries to stop me, and she's dead."

There was a long silence, with no sign of movement below them. Then, to Graysie's horror, she saw Nathan slowly rise from behind a gravel bank and put his hands in the air in a gesture of surrender.

"Let her go, Martens. She's done nothing to harm you. Take me instead." His voice rang around the underground space, a confident, steady bass note. "I'm coming in now. Let her go, I say."

Graysie felt Martens' body go rigid at the sound of Nathan's voice; she could sense the hostility vibrating up her back where they touched.

Nathan began a slow, deliberate walk towards them, his eyes fixed on Martens, his hands raised. No one else moved, no one showed themselves. Graysie felt her chest clench. She hardly dared breathe. He was taking such a gamble. What if

Martens gunned him down and used her as a hostage to escape, anyway?

She sensed Martens' animosity towards Nathan was so rampant he wanted his revenge to be close and personal. A random gunning down at forty feet wouldn't satisfy him.

As Nathan drew closer, he switched his attention from Martens and fixed it on her. His expression was intense, mournful, and she didn't want to read what he was telling her.

Sorry it has to end this way. I wish it could have been different.

No! She would not accept that their situation was hopeless. She wrenched herself forward a few inches, putting space between herself and the hateful, intimate pressure on her back.

Martens seemed momentarily shocked at her audacity and then pulled her tight again, pressing the gun even harder against her temple. He hissed in her ear, "Stand still or he dies."

Nathan was five or six feet away now, still advancing at the same slow drumbeat pace, daring Martens to pull the gun away from her temple and shoot him. Graysie braced herself for the confrontation.

"I feel sick," she gasped. "I'm going to vomit." She made a retching noise in her throat.

Martens froze and involuntarily pulled infinitesimally away from her. The moment was here. She plunged her hand into her skirt and pulled out the Derringer, ducking under Martens' arm as she did. In a flash, she pressed the little pistol hard and close under his ribs.

Nathan had anticipated her move, and as she spun and ducked, he sprang forward and brought a stiff upper cut to Martens' gun arm, jolting it upwards. The gun exploded with a roar, and fragments of rock rained down on them.

The gun rattled uselessly on the gravel at their feet. She shoved her pistol harder into Martens' gut.

He reared up, his lips stuck in part sneer and part shock. A ghostly disbelief filled his entire face, and in the strange twilight, his eyes lit in a strange, hateful yellow gleam.

"Go on then. Do it. Kill me." The words rang with contempt. "Bet you can't do it."

They stood like that, suspended in time. And then, purposefully, he placed his meaty hand over her much smaller one and squeezed the trigger.

Fifty Five

Monday, July 27

After she'd had time to luxuriate in hot baths, to sleep as long as she wished, and to eat and recover her equilibrium—although Graysie was unsure how long that last item was truly going to take—they gathered together around the table in a private dining room at the Orleans.

Basil and Alycia, mortified to discover their names had been used to lure Graysie into jeopardy, joined them, but they did not invite Hector de Vile. As the investigating deputy, Sebastian took the lead role, and over a long, lazy beef and pork pie lunch, he gave them a full account of how the saga of the Ophir and Ruby mines had played out.

Graysie sat between Alycia and Nathan, overcome with a numbness that reached right to her fingertips, strangely disconnected from everything going on around her. Despite the warmth of the day, she was shivering.

She'd only slept in brief snatches. Every time she'd drifted into a deeper rest, she'd jerked awake with one memory playing repeatedly in her head.

The pistol exploding under Martens' crushing fist, the warm blood flooding over her hand as Martens crumpled over it. She snuck an anxious, sidelong look at Nathan, but he was fully engaged in what his brother was saying.

"De Vile originally heard about Vance Pedersen's assay reports because he sent his samples through Burnadetti and

Co," Seb was saying.

"Vance was doing the report for Andre Guilliame, though Andre hadn't mentioned that to Lisette. They may have even been considering working the property together, but then Andre broke his leg. After Andre died, Vance didn't have the money to buy her out, so he shelved the report."

He shot a look around the table and caught Graysie's eye. "That's where Octavius Weavers came in. He was in charge of their assay program," said Sebastian.

"That information should have remained confidential, but somehow, Weavers found out. That isn't so surprising. We all know it happens. But when Weavers suggested to de Vile that he could take advantage of the situation, that's when they crossed over to the dark side."

He paused and took a sip of water from his glass.

"With the mines owned by a grieving widow on the one hand and an absent and then more recently deceased owner on the other, I suppose they saw it as a perfect opportunity for might to triumph over right.

"De Vile has a reputation for being ruthless for grabbing lucrative properties. They basically went in and helped themselves, based on what they'd been able to glean from Vance's assays."

The dining room door opened. Sebastian waited for the hotel staff to collect their empty lunch plates and then bring in the dessert—a holiday trifle with candied cranberries. For a few minutes, the talk ceased as they loaded their dessert dishes with the delicious concoction, but gradually, their attention returned to Sebastian.

"Thing was, although they got a sniff of the value, they had no grasp of its true depths. Even if they'd got their hands on the report, Vance was wily.

"He obscured the most detailed information by separating it into two parts; one section contained records of dozens of samples he'd taken along the line of the ore outcrops in different parts of the mine.

"The other part showed their exact location, and that was the part he concealed in the chessboard.

"To fully understand what you were looking at, you needed both documents, so you could cross-reference them. Only with the two together did you have a complete assay plan, noting the ore values and calculating the reserves.

"With both documents together, Vance could reach a highly scientific assessment of the total value of the blocks."

Sebastian viewed Basil and Alycia further down the table. "I'm sure as an experienced mine owner you'll appreciate how valuable those details are when they are married up."

Basil gave him an appreciative smile. "Most certainly. I suppose when Graysie turned up asking questions, they had to silence Vance to stop her from understanding the value of her inheritance. It's such a shame Eustace died before he grasped the Ophir's full significance."

Basil gently squeezed Alycia's hand, which rested on the table beside him, as he spoke of her brother.

Sebastian nodded. "As for the mayhem

that erupted after Graysie arrived and made it known she intended to try to re-open the mine? I've concluded that was mostly Willoughby Martens' doing.

"But De Vile was in on the plan to abduct Minette. Amazingly, he saw it as a justifiable way to exert pressure on a commercial rival. But after that, Martens ran amok and de Vile wasn't able to control him."

He looked around the table. "It's a sad thing to say about another human being, but Martens did us all a favor by pulling that trigger on himself."

Graysie felt her heart lurch and her eyes filled with unshed tears. She took a deep breath and willed herself to keep a tight rein on herself. What was wrong with her? Martens was a monster who certainly would have faced the hangman if he'd not shot himself, so why was she so upset?

Nathan was watching her, but she couldn't look at him. She was frightened that if she glimpsed his sympathetic eyes, she'd burst out crying. She stared at her empty dessert dish as the room fell silent.

She'd wanted to save Nathan, and in a roundabout way she'd achieved that, but Nathan had also saved her. He'd slammed the gun out of Martens' hand at the exact right moment, or she would have been the one bleeding out on the cave floor.

As they rose to go, Alycia gently restrained Graysie's arm. "Can I come by and pop in to see Minette? It will only take a minute or two."

A curling sense of surprise licked up her spine. Alycia's eyes searched hers, and Graysie saw that the woman she'd judged as cold and judgmental on their first meeting was regarding her with gentle appreciation.

"I want to get to know my new nieces as well as I can—and that's very well indeed," she said with a fleeting smile. "We've practically lost a lifetime already. I don't want to lose another day."

*****

Lisette had Minette and Seraphine sitting on floor cushions beside an occasional table in fits of giggles around a deck of cards while she hovered, supervising their moves. She gestured to the girls with a smile as they came into the room.

"They're learning to play 'Old Boy—Vieux Garcon'—the French version of Old Maid," she explained with a Gallic shrug. "Confirmed Bachelor—so much more fun than Old Maid."

Alycia chuckled and slid into an armchair beside Minette. "This I must see." She opened the reticule that hung from her arm. "And look what I've found to help your thinking." She pulled out two twists of brown paper. "Here we are. This is what you need!"

Alycia untwirled the paper necks and handed them on to Minette as the girls danced around her.

"Diablotins—little devils!" squeaked Seraphine. She clapped her hands in excitement. The chocolate-covered candied fruit was a favorite with children and adults alike, and for a few minutes they spared the cards from mauling by chocolate-covered fingers as the children consumed their treat.

Much later, when the children had finished their game and retired to play with their dolls and the women relaxed over coffee, Alycia's face grew serious. "Graysie, it's been such a turbulent time for you."

Her eyes flickered to Lisette, who nodded sympathetically. "You may not really have taken in the full implications of what Sebastian was saying in there today." She looked from Lisette to Graysie and then back again.

"He's confirmed you're sitting on valuable property. Both of you. And I know Basil will be more than happy to back you as an investor if you are interested. My brother made some grave mistakes in life, but he's gone a long way to making good on them in death."

A peal of joyful, girlish laughter rang out from next door, the excited chatter of childish voices barely audible from where the women sat. Graysie swallowed hard to push down the lump in her throat that was threatening to find release in tears and felt herself shuddering.

Imagine if she'd been the one to die in

the cave yesterday. Her heart froze at the thought. She'd never felt as vulnerable and fragile as in the past twenty-four hours, and she seemed to have difficulty shaking it off. If she'd died, what would have happened to Minette?

Alycia reached out and placed her hand on top of Graysie's. She squeezed it reassuringly. "We're all safe. You have nothing more to fear, my dear girl." Eustace's gold coated cone—a twin for the one Graysie wore, shone at her throat, keepsakes from a quixotic dreamer perhaps more cherished now, in death, than he'd been in life.

Alycia's amber-flecked eyes searched her face. She suspected Alycia had somehow been reading her thoughts.

"Eustace never could take care of you the way he wanted, but he's made a way for you to do what he couldn't for Minette. He would be so pleased if he knew."

Graysie swallowed hard again. The lump was still stuck hard in her throat, but the familiar numbness was melting. "I know. I know." She laughed a shaky laugh and dashed her hand across her eyes.

"He's given me the chance to do what I dreamed of doing, and I'm not wasting a minute getting started."

Graysie smiled at Alycia and felt the cloak of death she'd been bearing since the day before lift from her shoulders. She was alive, and she'd barely got started.

Fifty Six

Friday, July 31

Graysie gazed around the table shimmering with silverware and candles in one of the Orleans' luxurious private rooms and gave a satisfied sigh. Seated with her were all the people who, in a few short weeks, had become precious to her. She tried to think back to her life before Grass Valley, before Sacramento, before the Ophir, and it seemed like a distant dream.

Basil and Alycia, Pania, Lisette and Seraphine, and of course, Nathan and Minette. All here with her. All safe. And tonight all wonderfully replete after a magnificent celebratory dinner hosted by the Stocktons.

They'd supped on Sacramento salmon, roast pork and apple sauce, wild duck, and venison with redcurrant jelly, with half a dozen side dishes, followed by dessert. Fruit pastries and custard, wild raspberries and vanilla ice cream, lemon cake and ladyfingers, and the final flourish—nougat and candies.

Graysie noted with a smile that Minette had been determined to hold out for the candy. The Orleans chef was renowned, but tonight he'd really outdone himself.

Five days after the calamitous showdown with Willoughby Martens, life was settling back into normal rhythms. The Golden Queens had finished their Sacramento season showered with superlatives. More stage dates were in the offing if they wished. And when she wasn't on stage or spending pleasurable hours with Lisette and the girls, Graysie and Lisette had been talking with Basil Stockton about the future of the Ophir and the Ruby.

The only gaping hole was Nathan. Apart from whispering her thanks to him as they'd stretchered her out of the cavern where Martens had perished, they hadn't talked.

He'd returned with Seb to Grass Valley immediately after the rescue on urgent family business, so Alycia had said. No one seemed to know any more than that, and she admitted it. His absence haunted her thoughts.

When they'd met up this evening, she'd felt uncharacteristically shy. She swallowed a last spoonful of raspberries as Basil clinked his glass to get everyone's attention and took a deep breath.

The familiar butterflies in her stomach feeling she experienced when she thought of Nathan made it hard to focus on anything except him. A conviction of coming destiny froze her ability to speak.

The next few minutes would decide her future. Either Nathan would be part of it. Or he wouldn't.

"Ladies and gentlemen," Basil began with a wide smile. "We aren't very formal, I know, but this is a very special night that calls for solemn and ecstatic thanks. As the head of the household, I think a celebratory speech is called for—and you all know how much I hate speeches." They acknowledged him with scattered laughs.

"First, Alycia and I want to welcome Graysie and Minette into our family. It's come as an enormous surprise to discover Eustace had a hidden life, but it's brought us new joy we weren't expecting."

Led by Pania, everyone beamed and clapped loudly.

"Second, I'm formally announcing we will set up a consortium amalgamating the Ophir and Ruby mines and recommence mining there in the next month."

More spontaneous applause.

"Third, and this may come as a surprise to some here, we're hoping that Nathan will join us in a management role in the new venture. Details to be agreed upon to allow for his responsibilities to his mother and sisters in Australia."

Graysie allowed her eyes to rest on Nathan as Basil spoke and saw him give a start when his name was called. His face reddened, and he took a gulp of wine from the glass at his elbow.

"Nathan, we'll be eternally grateful to you and Seb for assembling Graysie's rescue team so quickly. If there'd been any delay, the outcome could have been very different."

Nathan ducked his head and stared at his plate. "Mr. Stockton… Everyone."

He slowly rose to his feet as Basil sank back into his seat.

He glanced down at Graysie, and his eyes burned with admiration. Graysie's heart felt like it had momentarily stopped beating. She couldn't breathe, nor look away. After what seemed like an age, he continued speaking.

"Graysie…" The yearning in his voice was plain to hear. "I don't deserve any special thanks, for, truth is, I don't know how my life could continue without Graysie and Minette in it."

He paused and stared directly at Basil.

"I'm touched by your invitation to join the Ophir venture, Basil. it's a wonderful opportunity, and I would very much like to talk with you further to see how it might work for us all. We can do that later, I'm sure.

"Meantime, I want to apologize to everyone, but especially Graysie, for my absence these last few days. Seb and I had some critical business to attend to in closing up the Martens file and dealing with Senator Hector de Vile."

Lisette drew in a sharp breath and Graysie saw she wasn't the only one who tensed at the two names. Basil and Alycia were the exception. They sat holding hands, the picture of marital contentment.

Nathan smiled around the table. "Unexpected, perhaps, but very necessary, and I'm thrilled to tell you we reached the desired outcome."

He picked up a couple of envelopes Graysie hadn't noticed previously, which were lying beside his plate, and waved them in the air.

"You'll recall Willoughby Martens claimed to have siphoned off funds from the Ruby and Ophir operations as his fee for services provided—paying himself something like a quarter of a million dollars' worth of gold.

"It didn't take too much effort to locate that bullion as part of Seb's clean up. And as Martens' brother-in-law, I stepped in to arrange his funeral and finalise his affairs. De Vile's involvement with Martens will always remain murky, but I'm delighted to tell you he was positively insistent that the gold Martens helped himself to should be distributed to the mine owners."

Nathan paused and looked around the table with a beaming smile. "Lisette, Graysie, it's my pleasure to deliver to you the proceeds from your investment—one hundred and twenty-five thousand dollars' worth of bullion each, safely deposited in your names.

"These documents simply advise you of the details of where it is secured." He stepped around the table and gave each of them an envelope.

No one spoke for a moment. Then Lisette let out a spine-tingling wail that echoed around the room. Whether from joy, or a release of long-held grief, it was hard to say, but it was soul deep. The table broke into uproarious applause, and everyone was talking at once.

When the excitement faded away, Nathan still held the floor.

"There is one more thing. I've

arranged a little after-dinner entertainment, which I hope will delight you all."

As he crossed to the door and called for the waiter who'd been serving their meal, Graysie's heart was beating so hard it could have leapt out of her chest. She watched, enthralled at Nathan's every move, no longer caring if her affection for him was plain for all to see.

The doubts, the thinly veiled disappointment of the last few days, evaporated. Far from forgetting her, he'd been devotedly working behind the scenes on her behalf.

The servant appeared. "Can you tell Mr. Herrmann we're ready for him?"

Herrmann! Not Maximilian Herrmann? The French magician she'd done a stage show with in San Francisco? That had been only a month ago, but it felt like a lifetime.

A familiar curly-headed young magician with a thick goatee and imposing twist-ended moustache entered with a twirl of his black velvet coat and a flexing of his white-gloved hands. It was the very same Max.

His eyes were intense beneath his black top hat, and when he spoke, his voice was mesmerizing. "I can do some wonderful tricks." He paused and his dark eyes darted around his audience.

"Disappearing cards, appearing rabbits—yes." He made a smiling bow in Graysie's direction.

"But I cannot bring people back from the dead, so I'm thrilled to see you alive and well amongst us."

Nathan slipped into the empty chair on Graysie's right and took her hand. "All for you, my love," he whispered as he raised her fingers to his lips and kissed them, gazing reverently into her eyes.

The room erupted into exuberant applause that faded into mirth and merriment as, over the next half hour, Max displayed his unrivaled dexterity with a succession of sleight of hand tricks.

He filled his top hat with silver dollars, poured them into a box, then turned them into candy. He produced a pack of cards from behind his knee, put them in a goblet, and then mysteriously made selected cards rise one by one.

He took the pack out of the goblet, tossed them upwards, and they appeared to melt into thin air. Graysie could see it wasn't only the children who were captivated as the show continued.

"And now, ladies, gentlemen, and little girls... Our finale."

He produced a toy drum from nowhere

and beat a jovial roll. He took the top hat off and tipped it upside down to prove it was empty. Then he spun it twice on his index finger and—Voila!—drew out a white rabbit.

Max stroked the rabbit before it disappeared up his sleeve, leaving no discernible bump. He spun the hat again, and the rabbit reappeared in the crown. This time, he gently carried it to Minette and deposited it in her lap.

"He wants a cuddle," he said. He gazed about, milking the suspense, and then spun the hat again. This time it wasn't a rabbit he withdrew, but a prettily wrapped gilt parcel topped with a white bow. "For the heroine of the story," he said with a bow to Graysie. "And I'm not making that one disappear again. Open it."

Graysie's eyes flicked to Nathan. He was watching her with a strange expression, at once intense and whimsical. What was he playing at? She pulled the gilt paper aside and saw there were two smaller parcels within.

The first was tiny and wrapped in tissue paper. She unwrapped it delicately and found a beautifully crafted gold brooch, decorated with a miner's pick and a miniature gold pan engraved Ophir Mine, 1868. Tears jumped to her eyes.

"You were right all along," Nathan whispered.

The second parcel was much larger. It was soft, probably some kind of fabric, she guessed. Aware of the eyes on her, she ripped the paper away to reveal a flowing white and gold gown, modeled on the lines of her favourite stage costume.

Her mouth dropped open. "How did you...?" She couldn't complete the sentence.

She took some deep breaths and turned to Max. "Dear friend, thank you for a most wonderful performance."

The table went wild as Max bowed again and retrieved the rabbit from Minette.

Graysie turned to Nathan. "Nathan, what can I say? First, you saved my life. And now you arrange these wonderful surprises—the mine pay-out, and marvel upon marvel." She choked up. "Words fail me. Except, thank you a million times over."

Later, when she'd tucked Minette up in bed, they talked. Nathan explained the gold miner's brooches depicting the tools of trade were a popular item in Victoria, where his mine was located.

Like nowhere else in the world, diggers celebrated their success and expressed their pride at overcoming the hard knocks with designs depicting the tools of their trade.

"It seemed appropriate. Graysie. You're beautiful. You're fiercely loyal. And you sing like a nightingale. But the thing I most value about you is your resilience and integrity. You absorb the hard stuff and keep on rolling.

"You're not afraid to be yourself. Under your vision, the Ophir deserves to prosper. You let nothing deter you from doing what you believed in. I want that quality—I want you—by my side for the rest of my life, no matter what course you choose."

He took her hands in his and gazed into her eyes. The charge she'd felt from the first day they'd met lit up again within her. She guessed what he was going to say next, and she jumped in ahead of him.

"Nathan. One thing I want you to know, with no doubt. You are the right man to work with Basil in the mines, no matter what. You are the one we both want. Whatever else happens, don't doubt that."

Nathan gazed deep into her eyes and brushed his lips across hers.

"Will you marry me, Graysie Castellanos? Mine owner or the star of the stage, or indeed, anything in between. As my gifts have tried to symbolize, the important thing is that you're there and we're together. We'll work on the rest."

Fifty Seven

Saturday, August 15

Starlight nuzzled Minette's hand gently, scooping up the apple pieces that lay there, while Minette giggled. It always tickled when her pony ate apples, she knew that now, but it was a nice sort of tickling.

She turned to Uncle Nat, who was standing watching her, smiling down at her in a way which made her heart warm and squishy.

"Starlight's mine now," she said, speaking to herself as much as Uncle Nat. Aunt Pania had told Sir John that Starlight liked Minette more than anyone else in the whole world and he'd agreed it was only right he should go with her.

She did a little dance on the grass in her excitement. Since they had come back to Grass Valley, she'd never been happier. Uncle Basil and Aunt Alycia had bought this house, which they said she and Sissy could live in as long as they wanted.

She'd started at Father O'Brien's school with Seraphine, and she was in the choir and making lots of new friends.

Best of all, Uncle Nat had been visiting nearly every day, mostly for long talks with Uncle Basil about business things, but he still had time to take her to the duck pond and tell her and Sissy stories that made them laugh. They'd both been having so much fun it was hard to remember when the scary things happened.

There was a field next door to the house where Starlight stayed, with fresh green grass Starlight loved to eat and a stable where he could sleep. She gave an enormous sigh of contentment and turned to Uncle Nat.

"I think it's time we went back to the house to see Sissy and the others for lunch, little angel," he said and took her hand. "Come on. We can come and see Starlight again later."

They walked across the grass to the side gate, which let them into the Stockton House garden. As they came up the path, Sissy appeared on the side veranda overlooking the garden. She waved.

"Come on, you two. We're all waiting!"

They'd only slept in this new house for two—or was it three—nights, but the Major and Mrs. Cook, the housekeeper, had made everything look like they'd been here for ages.

The beds were soft and snuggly, and the windows were big enough to let in lots of cool air and allow you to hear the birds singing outside. The noise from the mining stampers was far away. Minette hoped they would never have to leave.

Sissy led them into the dining room where Uncle Basil, Aunt Alycia, and Auntie Pania were already sitting around a table big enough for them all, piled with food. Seraphine and her mum and Mr. Pete were waiting for her.

"Seraphine, you sit here, next to Minette," said Sissy, showing them both their chairs. "And Lisette and Pete, sit here next to Nathan and me."

Uncle Nat said grace and then they helped themselves to cold meat, potatoes and salad. Everyone was talking and laughing, and soon it was time for dessert. Mrs. Cook cleared away the dishes and brought in some peach ice cream she'd made, especially for the occasion.

Before Sissy served everyone, Uncle Nat banged a glass with a teaspoon, and everyone was quiet. He stood by his chair. When he was around, Minette felt fizzy inside. She felt safe.

"Graysie and I have something we want to share with you all, and this first celebratory lunch at Stockton House seems exactly the right time and place," he said, looking around the table at everyone and especially at her.

"Graysie has made me the happiest man in the world by agreeing to become my wife. We plan to marry before the end of the year."

Everyone clapped and Mr. Pete cheered

and then they laughed and drank something they called a toast, where they clinked their glasses together before they drank. And Minette was sure this was the most perfect day she'd ever known.

THE END

FREE PREVIEW

Brother Betrayed, Book Two, Of Gold & Blood

The oldest brother, John Russell's
and Pania Hayes' story.
A mysterious death. A missing
partner. Can an opera singer and
businessman catch the culprit before
he strikes again?

'No matter how big your hands may
be, they can't cover the whole sky.'
Chinese proverb

Prologue

August 1868, Grass Valley, California

Comprador Chung Ting Hon sprawled facedown across the capacious bed, patrician profile smooth and unlined against the white linen of the down pillow, his right arm flung protectively across his young wife, Beautiful Jade, who snuggled against him.

The only sound the man in the doorway heard as he paused, a dark shadow backlit momentarily in the ambient light from the Gold House hallway, was his own breathing, rhythmic and deep.

The rising New Moon tipped the Sierra Nevada's mountain ridge, magnifying the

Milky Way's white light dazzle through the upstairs windows, outlining the honeymooners' naked bodies in a dim lunar gloom.

They had thrown off their bedclothes, love and the heat of the night all the warmth they needed, legs entwined like the new lovers they were.

The smell of orange-blossom oil lingered, reminding the man who loitered on the threshold of the earliest memories of his father's house. He stepped lightly in and closed the door with a barely audible click.

He leaned back against it as he steadied his breathing, stroking his leather-gloved fingers from tip to base as he savoured the peaceful scene. He'd become hardened to the idea of necessary death. Kill a chicken to frighten the monkeys. Or, as the gweilo say, the end justifies the means.

He'd told himself that many times in the past months, never more so than on this night. But this one would differ from all the others.

He moved with purpose, balanced and light on the balls of his feet, going to the man's side of the bed first. Macau's onetime merchant prince doesn't know he is going to end here, in the home of a man he regards as a son. With calm deliberation, he drew a long thin blade from the sleeve of his tunic and leaned over the sleeping form.

One hand tightly clasping the knife's leather handle, he placed the other on the top of the man's head and pushed the lethal tip down hard into the slight depression at the base of his neck. With a wrenching slash upwards, he severed the lower brain stem and cut off all involuntary functioning, like breathing and heartbeat.

His face thrust with suffocating pressure into the pillow, the compradore died before he could draw one last breath. Slippery as lightning, the attacker moved to the other side of the bed, the sharpened blade he held red with his father's blood.

His hand closed over the woman's mouth, and in one smooth movement, he wrenched her head sideways and slid the ten-inch stiletto across her throat.

A few seconds more and he was back at the door. He paused and took in the room with a sweeping glance. Blood from the woman's ugly neck wound spilled onto the hand that had caressed her lovingly minutes before.

Her killer stood in the doorway, his head tipped back, exultant, face washed

in an affirming starlight. Then he struck
a match, cupping the flickering flame in
his hands until it caught hold. It was the
work of seconds to set alight the
discarded sheet that lay on the floor. He
allowed himself a final triumphant glance
and turned and left the smouldering
room.

One

Business magnate and mine owner Sir John Russell had slept only fitfully when he had retired after saying goodnight to Chung Ting Hon and Beautiful Jade, his exquisite young wife.

He'd woken several times and drifted back to sleep, but this time round he knew it was hopeless to wait to fall into torpor — he had too much on his mind to slumber.

He lay curled under a single sheet in the muted midnight light and listened to the usual night noises: the whispering scuttle of ceiling mice, the creaking of the pine rafters as they cooled from the heat of the day. Otherwise, a comforting silence mantled Gold House, filled as the spacious villa was with out-of-town guests, his revered Chung Ting Hon among them.

He smiled ruefully. The old man who founded Russell & Chung Trading with his father Sir Robert Russell over thirty years ago was now eighty, but at thirty-eight he was trailing the comprador in vitality. He had been very successful at diversifying and expanding the business his father had founded, but at what cost?

He had no wife, no family, and the kinship ties he'd taken for granted were disintegrating around him.

The one bright spot was his recent reunion with his half-brothers Sebastian and Nathan: they'd been separated by the Pacific Ocean since their father's death over fifteen years ago. Nathan and Seb were just boys when Sir Robert had died; Nathan had gone with his Australian mother to Sydney, Seb to his Boston uncle, and the three brothers had not seen each other again until a few months ago.

He sighed and gave up on the idea of sleep. Instead, he rolled onto his back and laced his fingers behind his head, thinking back over the evening's discussions.

He'd invited the comprador to stay so they could settle the dangerous rivalry boiling up between Ting Hon's two sons, the first-born Chung Ji Ming, known to him as Ollie or Oliver, the name his English mother, Amelia Russell, Sir Robert's sister, had given him, and his half-brother Chung Ji Zeng.

The Chung sons ran not just the China side of the family trading company but also headed the Black Dragon

Benevolent Society — one of the six powerful organisations that effectively governed California's Chinese settlers, recruiting labor for railroad building, policing their movements and completing the essential ritual task of sending their bones back home to China if they died.

Part social agency and part business, Black Dragon had grown exponentially in the two decades that men from the Pearl River delta had flooded into Gold Mountain — or Gum Saan, Cantonese for San Francisco — seeking their fortunes in gold and other commodities.

Ji Zeng had always resented his brother, the first son of comprador Chung Ting Hon. After John's own mother's death when he was four years old, his Aunt Amelia had been a mother to him as well as to Ollie. They had grown up together, more like brothers than cousins.

But until yesterday he had not grasped the younger Chung's escalating ambition, nor his new obsession with returning to opium trading — the commodity that had got Russell & Chung started, but had long ago been discarded.

John knew Ollie vehemently opposed Ji Zeng's desire to get into the vice trade, but the discussion had never taken place because Oliver hadn't turned up for the meeting — and that just wasn't like him. Ollie put his heart and soul into his role as his father's successor and he would never stand his father or him up.

Even more mysteriously, no one — including Ollie's English wife, Selina — had a clue where he was. Ji Zeng had floated a fanciful story that he was in Hong Kong on urgent business, but John knew that was pure fantasy.

Ollie would never have left without telling Selina about his plans. Something just wasn't right.

He yawned, suddenly feeling weary. In a few hours, he would put Ting Hon and Jade on the San Francisco stage coach.

He still had faint hopes the patriarch could talk some sense into Ji Zeng, who was adamant that Black Dragon would be left behind unless it followed some of the other Six Societies into opium and prostitution.

He rolled onto his side and hugged a pillow close. Despite his restlessness, he was on the verge of dropping off when he smelt the faintest whiff of smoke.

He sat bolt upright, his senses on high alert, his eyes stinging. Then he heard a sharp crack, like the snap of wood burning. Galvanized, he was off the bed and to the door in two strides, the sheets trailing behind him.

His eyes were streaming before he got his hand to the door handle. He opened the door slowly, unsure if of what lay in store. Dense black smoke was curling up from the hall.

He peered down the hallway to where his guests slept, his ears singing with the unmistakable roar of fire, cheeks smarting from a wave of heat that rolled towards him. The guest room door was closed, but an eerie flickering of light from under it confirmed his worst fears.

Grabbing the sheet at his ankles as a mask for his nose and mouth, he sprinted down the passage, wrenched it open, and stopped dead. Flames were already creeping into the ceiling from the wall on the far side of the room.

Through the smoke he could see two figures sprawled on the bed, the man on his front, the woman on her back, her face an other-worldly white except for the bloody gash at her throat.

He sprang to the bed, although instinct told him they were already dead. He had just taken hold of Ting Hon's wrist when a heart-stopping boom sounded overhead.

He dropped Ting Hon's limp hand and dodged back to the shelter of the hallway as burning ceiling fragments rained down on the bed, showering him with hot embers.

He was standing gawping in disbelief at the burning bed when more debris rained down, striking him heavily on his left side. Pain shot from his knee to his groin and he staggered to remain upright.

Where was everyone? The house was full of family and friends, among them soon-to-be-married Nathan, and the celebrated Maori opera singer Pania Te Awa Hayes, a friend from New Zealand who had lived in California for some years.

Where were Mrs Snively the housekeeper, and his Chinese house servants, Mr and Mrs Lee?

"Wake up! Fire!" Oblivious to the pain in his leg, he staggered back down the hall, banging on walls and doors, shouting warnings. His voice, which had started as a raw croak, grew louder and more urgent with every step. "Fire!"

Want to read more of Brother Betrayed?
The first four chapters are available for FREE
Download at
www.jennywheeler.biz/brother-betrayed-free-chapters/

Enjoy this book?
You can make a big difference.

Reviews are the most powerful tools in my kit when it comes to getting my books noticed. Much as I'd love it, I don't have the budget of a big publisher to buy bill board ads and other national advertising.

But I have the promise of something more powerful–something publishers envy.

And that's a committed and loyal bunch of readers.

Honest reviews of my books help them gain the attention of others who might appreciate them, too.

If you've enjoyed this book, I would be grateful if you could spend a few minutes leaving a review (it can be as short as you like) on the book's page. You can jump right to the page by visting the links on the next page

.

Thank you very much
Jenny Wheeler

ACKNOWLEDGMENTS

Second Edition: This revised MS has tidied up minor errors in wording and expression that bothered me as I gained more experience as a writer. Like many first-time authors, I looked back and shuddered at things I could have done better. I didn't want these to become sticking points preventing readers from continuing with the Of Gold & Blood series, which I'm unreasonably proud of completing! I changed nothing in the plotlines and story development, so Poisoned Legacy is essentially the same book, but hopefully a little easier to read. JSW.

First Edition:

To my developmental editor Faith Black Ross, who gave me the confidence to believe I could do it, huge thanks. To my proofing editor Nikki Crutchley for identifying overlooked grammar and continuity snafus—so grateful for your discerning eye. And to my family and many friends who never seemed to doubt I could write fiction—don't know why that was—but a big thank you for your confidence!

(And, of course, as they say, any remaining gaffes—hopefully very few— are entirely my responsibility and no one else's!)

To the Birkenhead (Auckland) Library staffers who are unfailingly polite and helpful in sourcing Interloan books and pushing the limits on my borrowings.

To the resourceful Romance Writers of

New Zealand organisation for more than a decade of timely conferences—and amongst those wonderful writers, special thanks to pioneer romance writers Daphne Clair and Robyn Donald and to former president Abby Gaines for encouragement and inspiration in my early days of exploring fiction.

Treasured life partner Tim Bickerstaff and fellow director Sam Kamani were essential co-workers in the supplements business which, when sold, gave me the breathing space to launch myself on this next adventure.

So many others who should be here, including my publishing support crew—sorry I can't name you all—but know I deeply appreciate your feedback and support.

And last but not least, Senior Pastors Paul and Maree de Jong at LIFE Auckland

who always bring the right word in season
and never fail to inspire me to "enlarge
the place of your tent"–Isaiah 54:2.

ABOUT THE AUTHOR

Jenny Wheeler is the author of the Of Gold & Blood Old California mystery series:

Poisoned Legacy #1.
Brother Betrayed #2.
Double Jeopardy #3.
Tangled Destiny #4 (Christmas novella and Prequel.)
Unbridled Vengeance #5
Hope Redeemed #6 (A Spanish Novella)
Tainted Fortune #7
Unfinished Business #8
Captive Heart #9
Dangerous Desires #10
Boxed Set/Book Bundle Series #1 Of

Gold & Blood Books 1-3
Boxed Set/Book Bundle Series #2 Of
Gold & Blood, Books 1 & 4
Boxed Set/Book Bundle Series #3 Of
Gold and Blood Books 5 –6
Boxed Set/Book Bundle Series #4 Of
Gold and Blood Books 7 –8
Sadie's Vow #1 in the Home At Last
series

Jenny's online home is at
jennywheeler.biz or email
Jenny@jennywheeler.biz

You can connect with Jenny on:
Facebook: @JennyWheeler.Biz
Twitter: @Jenny_Biz
Instagram: @jennysbingereading
Pinterest
www.pinterest.nz/Jennywheelerbooks